Narratives of Memory

Also by Victoria Stewart

WOMEN'S AUTOBIOGRAPHY: War and Trauma
(*Palgrave Macmillan, 2003*)

Narratives of Memory

British Writing of the 1940s

Victoria Stewart

© Victoria Stewart 2006

All rights reserved. No reproduction, copy or transmission of this publication may be made without written permission.

No paragraph of this publication may be reproduced, copied or transmitted save with written permission or in accordance with the provisions of the Copyright, Designs and Patents Act 1988, or under the terms of any licence permitting limited copying issued by the Copyright Licensing Agency, 90 Tottenham Court Road, London W1T 4LP.

Any person who does any unauthorised act in relation to this publication may be liable to criminal prosecution and civil claims for damages.

The author has asserted her right to be identified as the author of this work in accordance with the Copyright, Designs and Patents Act 1988.

First published 2006 by
PALGRAVE MACMILLAN
Houndmills, Basingstoke, Hampshire RG21 6XS and
175 Fifth Avenue, New York, N.Y. 10010
Companies and representatives throughout the world.

PALGRAVE MACMILLAN is the global academic imprint of the Palgrave Macmillan division of St. Martin's Press, LLC and of Palgrave Macmillan Ltd. Macmillan® is a registered trademark in the United States, United Kingdom and other countries. Palgrave is a registered trademark in the European Union and other countries.

ISBN-13: 978–1–4039–9703–6 hardback
ISBN-10: 1–4039–9703–9 hardback

This book is printed on paper suitable for recycling and made from fully managed and sustained forest sources.

A catalogue record for this book is available from the British Library.

Library of Congress Cataloging-in-Publication Data

Stewart, Victoria.
    Narratives of memory : British writing of the 1940s / Victoria Stewart.
      p. cm.
    Includes bibliographical references and index.
    ISBN 1–4039–9703–9 (cloth : alk. paper)
      1. English fiction – 20th century – History and criticism. 2. Memory in literature. 3. Amnesia in literature. 4. Experience in literature. 5. Memory – Psychological aspects. 6. Psychoanalysis in literature. 7. World War, 1939–1945 – Literature and the war. 8. History in literature. I. Title.

PR888.M44S74 2007
823′.91209353—dc22   2006044610

10 9 8 7 6 5 4 3 2 1
15 14 13 12 11 10 09 08 07 06

Printed and bound in Great Britain by
Antony Rowe Ltd, Chippenham and Eastbourne

Contents

Acknowledgements	vi
Introduction	1
1 Remembering the Last War	20
2 Damaged Minds: Crime and Detection	58
3 Remembering the Country	94
4 In Time of War	132
Conclusion	168
Notes	175
Bibliography	191
Index	213

Acknowledgements

I would like to acknowledge the financial support for this project given by the Arts and Humanities Research Council Research Leave Scheme, and by the Research Committee of the Faculty of Humanities, Languages and Social Sciences, University of the West of England, Bristol. Librarians at the British Library, St Pancras, the British Library, Colindale, St Matthias Library, UWE Bristol, Bristol University Library and Bristol Central Library also provided valuable assistance.

Thanks also to all those in the School of English and Drama, UWE Bristol, and beyond, who gave help, advice and support during the research and writing of this book.

Introduction

This book considers the ways in which memory was represented in novels during the 1940s. Memory could feature as a structural device, with, for example, the loss of a protagonist's memory causing narrative complications. Its workings were also, on occasion, discussed and analysed within the narrative. In fact, these two aspects of memory – its structural and thematic functions – are not cleanly separable from each other, and their interaction can assist us in understanding how memory was conceptualized during this period. In this introduction, I will describe some of the ideas about memory, and about the condition of the novel, which were current in the interwar years. I will also consider debates about what the role of the novel ought to be that appeared once the conflict had begun. Such debates, which mainly took place in the pages of literary journals, are important and interesting, but I will not be confining my discussion to the 'highbrow' or 'literary' end of the fiction spectrum. Critics including Nicola Humble have recently acknowledged that the divisions we now perceive between literary fiction, usually of a modernist kind, and popular fiction, usually closer to realism, were not as absolute in the interwar years as they might now appear. During the 1920s, for example, 'middlebrow novelists were quick to adopt many of the themes and stylistic developments of the avant-garde, making meaningful distinctions very hard to draw' (Humble 19). John Baxendale and Chris Pawling have similarly argued that, '[c]ategories such as highbrow/middlebrow/lowbrow are not embedded in the texts to which they refer [...]: rather, they function as elements in a socially constructed system of taste' (52). The consideration of memory is one area in which supposedly 'middlebrow' writing, and genre fiction, can be seen to touch on concerns to do with the representation of subjectivity that might more usually be associated with modernism. Modernist conceptions and

2 *Narratives of Memory*

depictions of memory are important but by the 1940s these ideas were no longer the sole preserve of writers who would usually be described as modernist. Another narrative form in which an interest in memory can be discerned at this period is film. A number of the novels that I will be considering here were made into films and differences between novel and adaptation as regards the incorporation of flashbacks or the use of point of view, for example, can prove illuminating. The novel does not necessarily provide a more complex or sophisticated narrative of memory than film, and film has its own range of techniques for evoking the subjective experience of, for example, memory loss or recovery. But cinema is itself used as a reference point in a number of the novels I will be examining. As Keith Williams has argued, discussing the period 1930–45, new media 'irrevocably altered the consciousness of writers at the most fundamental levels', and, in particular, '[c]inema seemed to rupture the very fabric of the space-time continuum' (112). Both film and photography are often cited as metaphors for how memory works, comparisons that can shed light on attitudes towards memory itself, the medium with which it is being compared, and the interaction between the two. In some instances, film and photography are depicted as objective, unchanging and straightforwardly interpretable images of a past event; the apparent materiality of these images appears to act as a guarantee of their reliability.[1] This attitude can also be reflected in the way in which film itself depicts memory, but I will also identify examples that appear to challenge this notion of memory as fixed and easily recoverable.

Some critics have downplayed the significance of the literature of the 1940s, suggesting that historical circumstances necessarily circumscribed the viable types of literary production and experiment. Surveying the scene in 1951, P. H. Newby suggested: 'It is debatable [...] whether so overwhelming and universal a catastrophe as the late war can be reckoned the sort of experience out of which an artist can create' (13). For Bernard Bergonzi, in 1993, 'Although reading was so popular in wartime it was not a good period for the novel' (27), with no significant new novelists emerging. More recently, Maggie Clune, Gary Day and Chris Macguire have claimed that '[t]he nature of the experience was such that it proved difficult for authors to write about it. Elizabeth Bowen, indeed, failed to produce anything at all' (62). Whilst the first part of this statement may be accurate, citing Elizabeth Bowen as an example of a writer who produced 'nothing at all' is not, as it ignores both the fact that Bowen was engaged from 1943 onwards in writing *The Heat of the Day* (1949), and that two volumes of her short stories were published during the war years.[2] This is not to minimize the impact of wartime conditions on literary production and attitudes towards writing. Joseph McAleer notes that, at least in part because of paper rationing, the number of new works of fiction fell from 2046 in 1936 to 1095 in 1944 (52).[3] But new writing was being produced, even if is not necessarily easy to categorize in literary-historical terms. Since the mid–1990s, critics including Jenny Hartley, Adam Piette, Gill Plain and Mark Rawlinson have done much to challenge the idea that the war years were a literary hiatus; here I will consider the origins of this resilient attitude.

Debates about literature that were underway during the 1930s, as well as the pressure of immediate exigencies, necessarily influenced literary culture in the following decade. In some of the novels I will be examining, the 1930s were themselves remembered and the progress of literary history can itself be seen as a sequence of remembering, mis-remembering and forgetting. As Renate Lachmann suggests, 'there is no erasure in cultural memory; what is forgotten can be culturally reactivated and can take on its own (or a different) semiotic value' (23). I will not be principally concerned with instances of direct influence between one text and another, but it is important to recognize that both genre fiction and more traditionally 'reputable' literary products rely, to some extent, on the reader's ability to remember (or indeed forget) other examples of a similar kind. This process, while it might have been affected by the conditions of wartime, was not completely halted. The new conditions might be seen by some as demanding new methods, but there were still writers who attempted, often with success, to refigure existing methods for the current situation.

Narrative and memory between the wars

Like the 1940s, the 1930s has often been considered 'a fallow decade so far as the novel in England is concerned. The rich harvest of modernism had been gathered in, and had […] left the ground impoverished.' (Widdowson, 'Between' 133) Writing in the 1970s, Widdowson attempted to correct this view by stressing the variety of types of experiment perceptible in 1930s writing, including not only 'the structural and textural discoveries of modernism' but also 'documentary reportage, fable, allegory, satire and dystopia' (134). Andy Croft has shown how a variety of popular literary forms, including the thriller, were mobilized in the belief that 'literature was no longer just another way of interpreting the world, but a way of changing it too.' (*Red Letter Days* 187) More recently, though, critics such as Keith Williams and Steven Matthews have found it necessary to counter 'the persistent aftermyth of the thirties as a homogeneous anti-modernist decade' (1), calling for a renewed acknowledgement of the extent to which modernism persisted, and indeed developed and changed, in response to a new political situation. However, the interchanges that could occur between these different types of literary representation are also important. Valentine Cunningham identifies James Hilton's *Lost Horizon* (1933) as the novel that 'incited a great deal in Auden and Isherwood's *The Ascent of F6* [1936] (mountains, a lama, a frontier drama) and presented a myth of attractive longevity for Huxley's *After Many a Summer* [1939] to undo' (*British Writers* 98). For Cunningham, Hilton's work is evidence that it is 'often the minor writers who express most fully the meanings of a time' (124). The reputations of particular writers, or indeed particular types of writing, can also shift over time. This process is reflected in the anxiety Virginia Woolf expressed about how her work would be received in comparison not only with a writer such as Katherine Mansfield, but with others, including Rose Macaulay, who, as Nicola Humble points out, would not usually figure alongside Woolf or Mansfield in considerations of modernism (26–7).[4]

Inevitably, perceptions of what the key literary ideas or influences might be at a particular point in time will shift according to what kind of narrative of the period one wishes to create, and the temporal perspective from which one is writing. To give a further example, in *Lions and Shadows* (1938), Christopher Isherwood describes how, in planning his novel *The Memorial* (1932), he intended to adopt modernism as a structural device whilst retaining the subject matter of a family saga:

> I would tell the story of a family; its births and deaths, ups and downs, marriages, feuds and love affairs [...] The worst of all epics, except the very greatest, is that their beginnings are so dull [...] epics, I reasoned, should start in the middle and go backwards, then forwards again [...] which sounds Einstein-ish and brilliantly modern. (182)

This self-deprecatory analysis of his own narrative technique implies that Isherwood perceives an amount of opportunism, or at least naïveté, in his own early attempts at experiment. However, it is notable that it is the 'Einstein-ish' presentation of time that is considered here as marking the text as 'modern', rather than, for example, the consideration of social problems. What seems striking now about *The Memorial* is not so much the disruption of chronology in its narrative structure – it is divided into four sections that deal with the events of 1928, 1920, 1925 and 1929 in turn – but its use of a quasi-modernist narrative technique in the depiction of the protagonists' perceptions of the legacy of war. Widdowson suggests that 'the influence of Virginia Woolf's fiction is appreciable in *The Memorial*' ('Between' 156) and characterizes this novel as a work in which, both formally and in terms of its content, Isherwood attempted to confront the legacy of the previous generation. From the perspective of 1938, however, what was 'Einstein-ish and brilliantly modern' at the start of the decade seems, to judge from Isherwood's tone, shopworn. According to Janet Montefiore, this tone is characteristic of memoirs produced by men of Isherwood's generation in the late 1930s: 'The writer's autobiographical gaze moves [...] between the years of his growth and the ominous moment of writing [...] [H]is awareness of writing at a "present moment" of political crisis retrospectively illuminates his youthful illusions' (47). The narratives that I am concerned with here also show a concern not with the past in isolation from what has happened since, but with the process by which the past is revisited or recovered.

However, neither an explicit engagement with psychological ideas and terminology, nor a commitment to the detailed representation of consciousness, are prerequisites for a narrative concerning itself with memory. An important source of evidence for identifying the prevalent understandings of memory in the interwar years are novels themselves, but the types of discourse about memory in extra-literary fields that over time fed into and became naturalized by literary representations should also be considered. Stephen Rose has shown how descriptions of memory processes in the emergent science of psychology can be mapped onto contemporary developments in communications technology; comparisons with existing technologies would be used as a way of positing how memory might function. Thus, where Plato records Socrates' comparison between the action of memory and the impress of a signet ring on a wax block (99–100 [191d]), late nineteenth and early twentieth-century experimenters drew on more advanced technologies.[5] Rose suggests, for example, that the discovery that the nervous system functioned through electrical impulses, led the brain to be considered as 'first a telegraphic signalling system and later, at the start of the [twentieth] century, a telephone exchange' (77). Importantly, however, these and succeeding technologies do not only provide metaphors through which the functioning of memory can be described: 'photography, film, video and audiotape, and above all the computer [...] restructure consciousness and memory [...] imposing new orders upon our understanding of and actions upon the world' (Rose 95).

What Rose points to here is a complicating factor in the drawing of comparisons between memory and, for example photography. The referent of a photograph can be used as a means of representing linguistically, through metaphor, the manner in which we might perceive events from the past; we might believe that, when reflecting on past events, we conjure up images that are in some way like photographic images. This seems to be the implication of the statement at the start of Isherwood's *Goodbye to Berlin* (1939): 'I am a camera with its shutter open, quite passive, recording, not thinking. [...] Some day, all this will have to be developed, carefully printed, fixed' (13). But an actual photograph represents these past events in an apparently similar fashion and, in acting as a supplement to memory can cause a blurring between the remembered and the perceived. Memory can be said to be like a photograph, but the comparison can also be reversed as it is at the start of Aldous Huxley's *Eyeless in Gaza* (1936) when the narrator observes: 'The snapshots had become almost as dim as memories' (5).[6] This reversibility allows us, as Michael H. Whitworth has argued

> to understand how metaphors can circulate between science, literature, and other areas of culture. Not only can scientists understand new phenomena in terms of familiar material objects and social institutions, but non-scientists can defamiliarize the familiar, reconceiving it in metaphors provided by new scientific theories. (*Einstein's Wake* 12)

However, as Laura Otis warns, 'Metaphor, an assertion of similarity that can be so fruitful in opening up new possibilities of inquiry and expression, can easily evolve into an assertion of identity' (33). Otis is concerned with the slippage between descriptions of social and organic processes in late nineteenth-century scientific writing; in relation to twentieth-century writing, one important (and misleading) identification that can occur is between memory and either photographs or the cinema, because, as I have indicated, this can imply that memory is fixed and easily retrievable.[7] In terms of Rose's description of the development of analogies alongside the development of technology, cinema is one of the most important points of comparison in the period I am discussing, with implicit and explicit references being made to it in a number of texts under consideration. The relationship here works in both directions, as Maureen Turim explains in her study of the flashback:

> The etymology of the term 'flashback' includes a fascinating migration into our language beyond its original reference to narrative technique. It has now been adopted by psychology to refer to the spontaneous recall of a memory image [...] The phrase even has a more general colloquial use to describe an individual's personal memories [...] This colloquial use of the term indicates how movies as popular culture begin to affect the way people think about their own experience. Cinematic renderings of storytelling and memory processes may have borrowed from literature and sought to reproduce human memory mimetically, but ironically, the cinematic presentation of the flashback affects not only how modern literature is organized [...] but perhaps also how audiences remember and how we describe those memories. (5)

Both Turim and the narratologist Gerard Genette recognize that interchanges have also occurred at the level of film and literary theory. Turim notes Genette's use of the term 'analepsis' to describe, broadly speaking, the narrative equivalent to the flashback and Genette himself looks to the structuralist film theorist Christian Metz in his discussion of the double temporality of narrative (Turim 8–10, Genette 33). Part of my intention is to defamiliarize the kinds of comparison that Turim, Rose and Otis identify and to suggest why particular conceptions of memory might have seemed to be especially suitable at the historical period that is my focus here.[8]

Discourses of memory

This type of cultural tendency towards a particular way of describing memory can be placed alongside the more self-conscious attempts of some writers, like Isherwood by his own account, to engage with current thinking about time and memory. The influence of the ideas of theorists including William James and Henri Bergson on modernist writing has often been noted. In particular, James' use of the image of the *'the stream of thought, of consciousness, or of subjective life'* (239) was taken up as a means of expressing a resistance to the exigencies of clocktime, albeit one still expressed in linear terms. Bergson, meanwhile, rejected the spatial aspect of this image, as Stephen Kern explains: 'James saw a sharp distinction between recent memories that are part of the present and distant memories that are recollected as something separate; Bergson emphasized the constant interconnection of all past experiences with the present regardless of how far back they may have occurred.' (*Culture* 44) There are similarities here with Virginia Woolf's description of experience as being not 'a series of gig lamps symmetrically arranged' but 'a luminous halo, a semi-transparent envelope' ('Modern Fiction' 8). As Whitworth notes, 'Leonard Woolf doubted that [Virginia Woolf] had ever read Bergson [but] [o]ne may reply that Bergsonism was part of the intellectual atmosphere of the years from 1910 to 1912' ('Virginia Woolf' 147). Woolf could therefore have had indirect contact with these ideas, which William Troy, writing in 1932, considers 'the most popular ideology of her generation'(85). Woolf's *Mrs Dalloway* (1925) shows, in its depiction of Clarissa Dalloway, how past and present experiences can become entwined in complex ways, although this does not mean that the distinction between memory and present experiences is ever completely effaced. Nor does Woolf ignore the potential impact of historical events on the subjective life. The inclusion in the narrative of the psychologically damaged war veteran Septimus Smith allows Woolf to explore a different type of memory, one which intrudes with a violence that is counter to the free-flowing associations experienced by Clarissa (although this is not to say that these are without their unpleasant aspects). Smith's experiences illustrate the paradox identified by John Talbott, that ' "flashback", a vehicle employed in cinematic and literary time travel, to evoke a past distinct and different from the present, also applies to an experience that obliterates such distinctions' (440). This type of traumatic memory – traumatic both in that it is uncomfortable to experience and brings back an event that was itself uncomfortable – is relevant to the discussion of many Second World War texts, especially those I discuss in Chapter 1 which attempt to forge a connection between the aftermath of the previous war and the present conflict.

Woolf's modernist style simultaneously depicts and enacts a particular understanding of memory and subjectivity. Woolf is known to have read Proust, and his exploration of 'involuntary memory', when an external sensory stimulus provokes the vivid reawakening of past sentiments and feelings, also contributes to the manner in which the past re-emerges into the present in modernist works such as *Mrs Dalloway*. At the end of the 1930s, George Orwell uses involuntary memory in a realist context, when, in *Coming up for Air* (1939), George Bowling reflects: 'The past is a curious thing […] it's just a set of facts that you've learned […] [t]hen some chance sight or sound or smell, especially smell, sets you going, and the past doesn't merely come back to you, you're actually *in* the past' (30). Samuel Beckett explains that: 'involuntary memory is an unruly magician and will not be importuned. It chooses its own time and place for the performance of its miracle'(33–34). George's own reverie about his youth is provoked by seeing the name of King Zog of Albania on a newspaper hoarding, and by the smell of horse manure. Attempting to encompass new understandings of consciousness within a realist framework, as do many of the novelists under discussion here, may produce less startling results stylistically than modernist experiment, but it can nevertheless attest to the widespread currency of these ideas.

Remembering is an important means by which the protagonists of a number of novels, like both Septimus Smith and George Bowling, attempt to understand the effect on their lives of their involvement in historical events. An understanding of the damage that might be wrought on memory by involvement in war did not necessarily imply an acquaintance with psychoanalytic ideas on this topic. Certainly, many psychoanalytic ideas did filter into public consciousness during the interwar years, but it was Freud's ideas about sexuality and family relations that appear to have been most prevalent rather than his work specifically on memory, although the former ideas do frequently invoke the processes of memory at some level.[9] Heather Ingman suggests that 'repression, sublimation, dreams, the Oedipus complex [and] childhood trauma' (28) were the key ideas that became widely known and were evident in 'middlebrow' fiction during the late 1920s.[10] Looking back to the interwar years in a lecture delivered in 1944, E. M. Forster identifies the ideas 'connected with the awful name of Freud' especially 'the subconscious, [...] the persistence of the irrational, [...] the importance of dreams and the prevalence of day-dreaming', as having given 'great enrichment to the art of fiction' (268). When authors make explicit references to psychoanalysis, their tone can help to elicit whether they are presuming a familiarity, on the reader's part, with the concepts being cited. Aldous Huxley makes such a presumption in his 1925 novel *Those Barren Leaves*, when Mr Cardan laments the fact that, 'Too much light conversation about the Oedipus complex and anal erotism [sic] is taking the edge off love' (39). However, the appeal to a knowing reader can also be found in texts aimed at a popular audience. In *And Now All This* (1932), their follow-up to the debunking history book *1066 and All That* (1930), W. C. Sellar and R. J. Yeatman include a chapter on 'Psycho-Babycraft' which plays with the notion of polymorphous perversity (redesignated 'polyversive permorphosis' [21]), as well as dream analysis. These sketches were first published in *Punch* and the *Daily Mail*, and therefore support Ingman's claim of a broad familiarity with psychoanalysis in the 'middlebrow' reader. The work of Freud's rivals also gained currency: Dr Bickleigh, the village general practitioner who is the protagonist of Francis Iles' crime novel *Malice Aforethought* (1931), is able to diagnose himself with an inferiority complex, a term associated with the work of Alfred Adler. Indeed, in his survey of the 1930s, Malcolm Muggeridge contended that during that decade 'Inferiority, Oedipus and other complexes, were made available for all, and even typists knew that they were not fond of apples for nothing' (286). In the case of memory, particularly damaged memory, many authors appear to have felt free to devise aetiologies to suit the circumstances of their characters, as George Orwell does in *A Clergyman's Daughter* (1935), but a lack of detailed knowledge of Freud or other theorists does not mean that their conceptions of memory are lacking in complexity.

Whilst psychoanalysis could be seen as focusing on autobiographical memory, and the manner in which earlier life events might persist or reimpose themselves in the present, in interwar psychology and popularisations of it, positivist models were dominant. The desire to establish psychology as a science with an experimental basis led to a focus on types of memory that could be measured easily in an experimental context. As Janice Haaken suggests, a positivist approach to memory tends to minimize the 'interdependence of the observer and observed' (43), and positivist experiments might be based around the remembering and recall of decontextualized lists of words or abstract symbols. Frederic Bartlett's *Remembering* (1932), which used narratives and recognizable images rather than abstract signs or forms as its experimental material, and is still often cited in the literature on memory, was important in challenging this 'storehouse' model of memory. However, the disciplines of educational and industrial psychology, which had become established during the 1920s, were more concerned with memory as an aspect of training, an exploitable and improvable tool rather than a speculative faculty. (Cyril Burt, writing in 1942, notes that these and other branches of psychology had their roots in work undertaken during the 1914–18 war with the intention of improving the efficiency of both combatants and civilians.) Popular memory systems such as Pelmanism, which Robert Graves and Alan Hodge describe as the 'first form in which psychology reached the wider public' (54), promoted self-improvement based on the training of memory. The Pelman technique was based on condensing the information to be remembered through the use of alphabetical and numerical codes, and concentration and observation were considered essential prerequisites for successful registering and recall of material. Over the first half of the twentieth century, the

Pelman Institute's courses placed increasing emphasis on the potential for improving one's financial and social status that these techniques could provide; their course books also show that by the mid-century, mastering willpower has been supplemented by overcoming complexes as a central element of self-improvement. This type of approach conceptualizes memory as an instrument, ignoring involuntary or associative memory, which might arise unbidden in disturbing ways, and the tension between these two aspects of memory is apparent in a number of the texts I will be considering here.[11]

Psychoanalysis and psychology were not the only available discourses for the understanding of memory at this time. Isherwood's reference to Einstein is one example of how literary writers attempted to absorb the impact of new discoveries across the sciences, but there are other thinkers whose influence has not been so widely acknowledged. Graves and Hodge, writing in 1940, note the prominence in the late 1920s and early 1930s of the ideas, now largely forgotten, of J. W. Dunne. His book *An Experiment with Time* (1927) posited a means of explaining the phenomena of the predictive dream through a rethinking of the process of time that also had an impact on subjectivity. This dual focus on time and subjectivity means that Dunne situates his work in relation to both physics and psychology. Explaining dreams that foretell the future, Dunne suggests that the consciousness, within the dream, that perceives these events, is a kind of sub-personality, an observer of one's experience existing in another temporal dimension, able to encompass both 'past' and 'future'. Dunne's conclusion was that individuals each have a soul 'whose immortality, being in other dimensions of Time, does not clash with the obvious ending of the individual in the physiologist's Time dimension' (*Experiment* 207). Thus Dunne suggests that 'the old distinctions between past, present and future are meaningless, and that their coexistence is a powerful and valid reality' (Evans 55) as well as implying 'an immortality without the necessity of a deity' (Evans 57). One writer who found Dunne's ideas suggestive was H. G. Wells, who initially got to know Dunne through Dunne's work as an aeronautical engineer, and in Wells' 'The Queer Story of Brownlow's Newspaper' (1932) Dunne's theories are a possible explanation for Brownlow's receipt of a newspaper from the future. *The Shape of Things to Come* (1933) develops this conceit further as well as introducing some playful intertextuality. The body of the novel consists of a history book from the year 2106, which, in the prefatory chapter, Raven claims to have transcribed after dreaming about reading it. Wells' earlier story is constructed as a pre-echo Raven's 'actual' experience: 'If I'd known this before, I wouldn't have written *Brownlow's*

Newspaper' (Wells, *Shape* 17), the narrator, 'Wells', comments when his friend reveals what has happened.[12]

Dunne's ideas, and particularly his ideas about memory, were taken up by other writers, including James Hilton, whose novel *Random Harvest* (1941) I will discuss in the next chapter. In the interwar years, however, the most thoroughgoing (and not uncritical) engagement with Dunne's theories came from J. B. Priestley. In particular, *Time and the Conways* (1937) dramatises Dunne's theory that it is sometimes possible for an individual to 'observe' the present from a point in the future.[13] Whilst such ideas, like those of Bergson, are concerned with perceptions of time rather than memory as such, they do have an impact on how memory is conceived. Disturbing the unidirectional relation between past and present leads to an uncertainty as to what is recall of the past and what projection from the future. However, like P. D. Ouspensky's idea of 'eternal recurrence', which Priestley explored in *I Have Been Here Before* (1937), Dunne's conception of time does not disallow the possibility of change. The individual is not seen as being irrevocably trapped in an ever-repeating cycle, and indeed the possibility of instituting change in one's own life or another's is seen as a motive for self-improvement. Dunne's mathematically expressed explanation for his ideas in the second half of *An Experiment with Time* may well have defeated many of his readers, but their general import did filter through, not least because of their exposition in works such as Priestley's. Agatha Christie also attests to the impact of Dunne's work, claiming that reading *An Experiment with Time* helped her to see things 'more in proportion; myself as less large; as only one facet of a whole, in a vast world with hundreds of interconnections' (qtd. in Morgan 194). Graham Greene refers to the potential for Dunne's work to explain apparent 'previsions' when trying to account for incidents in some of his novels that seem to anticipate things that actually happened later: 'Dunne has written [...] of dreams which draw their symbols from the future as well as the past. Is it possible that a novelist may do the same, since so much of his work comes from the same source as dreams?' (73).[14] The narrator of Frank Baker's *Miss Hargreaves: A Fantasy* (1940), in which a character invented by two friends for a joke takes on all-too-real physical form, comments: 'I'd read Dunne's books on the past, present and future; and though I couldn't follow half of what he said, it did seem to me there was a quality about time which had nothing whatever to do with clocks and calendars' (100).[15] Beginning his study with an examination of experiences with which the reader is likely to be familiar – dreams that appear to predict the future, the experience of *déjà vu* – gives

Dunne's theories roots in the everyday that can provide a semblance of accessibility.[16]

Some of the novels I will discuss in this study are concerned not with damaged memory, or with the kinds of new ideas I have outlined, but with 'normal' memory processes. On the one hand, it is when memory does not function properly that an understanding of what constitutes proper functioning can be ascertained; on the other, a lack of apparent problematization, or the naturalization, of memory can also be revealing about a writer's attitude to the past and its relation to the present. A desire for continuity between past and present, or a longing for the return of the values or way of life that appear to be lost can be interpreted as nostalgic and, often, reactionary. It can seem to demand a neutralizing of historical processes through a focus on individual actions and desires and, as Alison Landsberg has suggested in a different context, 'threatens to prevent individuals from acting in the present, from being productive, politically engaged members of society' (144). However, as Alison Light has argued in a discussion of the interwar works of Ivy Compton–Burnett, the family group, often the focal point for apparently nostalgic or escapist narratives, can be seen 'not as the opposite of, or different to, the public stream of history but as the place where its meanings are both learnt and shaped' (44). The relationship between individual memory and public or collective expressions of memory also comes under scrutiny by George Orwell in *Nineteen Eighty-Four* (1949), where the latter is seen as crucial in underpinning the former: 'When there were no external records that you could refer to, even the outline of your own life lost its sharpness' (34). Winston Smith experiences disappointment when the old man he meets in the prole quarter remembers only a 'rubbish-heap of details' (96) rather than anything that might either correct the 'official' record or ratify his own recollections. Attempts to forge a shared memory can result in nostalgia; particularly in my third chapter, I will consider why nostalgia, a positive valuation of the past, has come to have almost solely retrogressive and negative connotations. Its escapist aspect might seem irresponsible or disloyal in a time of national crisis but a longing for security could be seen as a not unreasonable reaction to the uncertainties of wartime.

Literature in wartime

The question of what place literature should have in wartime was a manifold one. Not only were there discussions as to how a writer, particularly a novelist, might, at the purely practical level, be able to continue working amidst the disruptions of war; there was also a debate about whether writers should have a role in the war effort, and what this might comprise. Inevitably, the terms of such debates shifted as the war progressed. For example, in 'The Ivory Shelter', published in October 1939, Cyril Connolly suggests that as writers had failed to prevent the war through their interventions in politics, they should look to the example of the last war when, according to Connolly, 'the escapists carried on a literary renaissance. Joyce wrote *Ulysses* in Trieste and Zurich [...] Moore, Yeats, Gide, Eliot, Forster, and Virginia Woolf are other writers in whom it is vain to search for [...] any reference to the last war whatever' (482). Connolly's disaffection in the face of the apparent impotence of art is transformed into a call to liberate art from having to attempt to serve political ends: 'War is a tin-can tied to the tail of civilisation, it is also an opportunity for the artist to give us nothing but the best, and to stop his ears' (483). However, two years later, Connolly put his signature to 'Why Not War Writers? A Manifesto', which appeared in his journal *Horizon*. This explained why and how many writers on the left had repositioned themselves in view of recent events:

> When war broke out, many writers were hesitant. They did not see the issues as clearly as they had seen the Spanish Civil War, for example, or the last European war. [...] With the invasion of Russia [in June 1941], feeling has crystallized. It is no longer possible for anyone to stand back and call the war an imperialist war. For every writer, the war is a war for survival. Without victory our art is doomed. (Calder-Marshall et al. 236)[17]

The war, which had been labelled as imperialist by the Soviet Union after the signing of the Nazi–Soviet Non-Aggression Pact could now be refigured as antifascist, and in the manifesto literature was seen as an important means of promoting '*cultural unity*' (238).[18] Writing prior to the invasion, Lord David Cecil also noted that the ideological issues were more complex than in 1914–18, and that younger writers in particular, 'have not, most of them, a stable point of view from which to envisage [the conflict]' (18). Cecil, like Connolly in 'The Ivory Shelter', defended the right of the artist not to engage with the war directly in his or her work, but also suggested that complete detachment was rendered impossible by the nature of the present war: '[Writers] cannot forget about the war, it seeps into every cranny of their consciousness. They must write about it, if they are going to write at all' (18).[19] The signatories of 'Why Not War Writers?' could thus be attempting to make a virtue out of necessity. Such a determination to contribute had to be balanced against the practical difficulties that any such effort might face, not just in terms of lack of recognition or support (official war writers never became established in the way the manifesto hoped), but also in view of the physical damage to the country's infrastructure that the war wrought. However, in a response to 'Why Not War Writers?' Goronwy Rees, who signed his letter 'A Combatant', was scathing: 'It has been too easy to write in recent years. Genius overcomes privation and inferiority. If these young men *must* write, they will do it the better for suffering some inconveniences. [...] I am afraid that I do not believe for a moment that these young men want to write; they want to be writers' (438). Whilst apparently hard-nosed, this argument does fall back on the notion of genuine creativity or genius, as somehow transcendent of physical circumstances. The accusation that the signatories to 'Why Not War Writers?' want to 'be writers' rather than 'to write' implicitly condemns writing to being a hole-and-corner activity rather than a profession, and it is some form of professional status that the signatories wished for.

John Lehmann's series of articles, 'The Armoured Writer', published in *New Writing and Daylight* between the summer of 1942 and the winter of 1943–44 is an attempt to assess how the war has affected writers, and what kind of literary legacy will be left after the end of the conflict. In his first article, Lehmann laments that while there have been 'interesting fragments' of different kinds, there has as yet been no literary representation of the war that has 'depth and power' ('Armoured Writer – I' 153). He lays the blame for this, in part, on the circumstances in which many writers are working: 'one should restrain one's impatience, remembering how difficult it is to write against the bombs, and the rasping of radio-sets in barracks, and the ever-ringing telephones and never-concluded conferences in innumerable offices' (153–4). However, he also acknowledges the difficulty of writing a prose narrative about an experience, or series of experiences, that is ongoing, an argument that is echoed by Alan Munton:

> Fiction written during the war was end-stopped by history. [...] Some writers felt this constraint very heavily and abandoned the attempt to develop an unfolding narrative in favour of fragmentary structures that proceed without direction [...] 'Wartime' was a special kind of time; begun at a specific moment, it had – as everyone knew – to end, but the moment of its ending moved ahead of all anticipation, requiring a constant adjustment to the psychological space that still lay ahead. (Munton 21)

Robert Hewison similarly comments that, 'There was an inhibiting awareness that this was a "period" with a beginning and expected end, cut off from past and future alike' (*Under Siege* 87). I will be suggesting that this inhibition was not as widespread as Hewison might imply, and that the foregrounding of memory within a narrative is one way in which the 'adjustment' identified by Munton could be managed. Whilst Lehmann might suggest, as Munton and Hewison do, that only with historical perspective will a complete vision of the war be realized, memory can be a way of providing a new perspective on events that are still ongoing. In Chapter 1, I will suggest that this could be one reason why writers turned to comparisons with earlier conflicts, particularly in the first years of the war. A reconsideration of existing genres is another way of providing such perspective; Lehmann notes that detective and spy stories have taken on a new importance, suggesting that this is because the paranoid and violent world of the modern thriller presents 'the truest picture of our home, our inescapable environment' (159). It is also appropriate, as I will show in Chapter 2, to the exploration of damaged memory, especially amnesia.

Lehmann's discussion of the thriller is also a reminder that Munton's and Hewison's comments apply more to the literary than the popular end of the market. Tom Harrisson's article 'War Books', published in *Horizon* in December 1941, shows that many popular writers simply attempted to adapt their habitual technique and style to wartime conditions, although the results of this adaptation were rarely to Harrisson's liking. He implies that, if anything, there needed to be a slowing down of literary production: 'Not nearly enough thinking is being done in this war. You don't have to stop firing to think' (436). Although I will chiefly be concerned here with novels that do attempt to address the events of the war, it should also be noted that beyond the pages of journals like *New Writing and Daylight* or *Horizon*, sentiments that might appear to be less honourable were being expressed. Many readers, and indeed cinemagoers, wanted an escape from the exigencies of war rather than to have to engage, at the end of the day, with representations of the kinds of problems that they had themselves been confronting. One reader told Mass-Observation in 1943: 'There's enough tragedy in real life not to want to read about it, and that's one of the reasons I *never* read a war book' (qtd. in Chibnall 135). In 1947, a librarian explained the continuing popularity of romances by commenting that 'it's the times – they don't want anything deep' (qtd. in McAleer 80). James Chapman acknowledges that 'the majority of the cinema-going audience [...] preferred the escapist fantasies offered to them by both American and British feature films'

(33–4) to more realistic offerings, citing *Gone With the Wind* (1940) and the Gainsborough costume drama *The Man in Grey* (1943) as two of the most popular films of the war years (61). As one female wartime cinemagoer, quoted by Antonia Lant, remarked: 'Carry me into the past with Laurence Olivier, Nelson Eddy, Greta Garbo and the others and I'm happy' (23). Even escapism or apparent escapism does of course express a particular attitude towards the war, even if this is a negative one. In relation to my argument here, a memory plot can provide an element of escape tempered by a return to the present; indeed, although *The Man in Grey* does not use memory as a structuring device, its Regency plot is bookended by a wartime romance.

The fourth article in Lehmann's 'Armoured Writer' series, which appeared in late 1943, sees Lehmann echoing his earlier views on the difficulty of producing a substantial piece of writing about the war whilst the conflict is still ongoing: 'It is by now becoming increasingly clear that, with rare exceptions, the real novels about this war are not going to be written until the war is over' ('Armoured Writer – IV' 162). Lehmann expresses particular concern about the apparent lack of new young novelists: 'the under-thirties [...] have temporarily at least abandoned the novel, as too heavy luggage for active service, in favour of the poem and sketch' (162).[20] Lehmann therefore focuses on how novelists who were already active during the 1930s appeared to be developing new approaches to deal with the new situation. Like Harrisson, Lehmann found much to praise in Rex Warner's *The Aerodrome* (1941); in 'The Armoured Writer – I' Lehmann discusses it alongside Virginia Woolf's *Between the Acts* (1941), citing both as examples of novels which, 'though not directly concerned with the war, have been written or finished under its influence' (158).[21] In his later article, Lehmann again mentions *The Aerodrome*, and in particular the 'search for new technical methods' it appears to exemplify ('Armoured Writer – IV' 163). What Lehmann identifies, and what appears to unite novels as apparently diverse as *The Aerodrome*, Henry Green's *Caught* (1943) and Graham Greene's *The Ministry of Fear* (1943) is that they 'supplement their basic realism with other techniques [including] dreams, symbolism, poetic asides [and] internal monologues' (163–164). The action of Warner's novel takes place in a twisted or even surreal version of the English countryside, and in this respect is a step further away from Green and Greene's novels which do maintain a surface realism in their settings. It is also striking that Lehmann does not try to align *Caught* and *The Ministry of Fear* with earlier, modernist works. All these novels, including *Between the Acts*, are seen to be reacting, stylistically, to the current situation, rather than positioning themselves in relation to an earlier school or movement. Notably, Lehmann also allows himself to blur the boundary between the pre-war and wartime when he considers Woolf's and Warner's novels, a manoeuvre that is relevant in the context of Hewison and Munton's assertion that the war should be considered as a self-contained period. Works begun, or even completed, before the war can be considered as war books, as Sebastian Knowles indicates when he includes in his taxonomy of Second World War writing the category 'Literature of Anticipation', encompassing works written between May 1937 and May 1940 (1). Similarly, many works written while the war was ongoing did not appear until after it had ended, and were therefore received by an audience with a different perspective on the events being described.[22] I will be arguing that writers' perceptions of 'wartime' inevitably shifted as the war itself progressed; as Johanna Alberti suggests, in a discussion of women writers, 'War's impact was not constant, it could suffocate, but it could also liberate' (162).

In the *Times Literary Supplement* Leader for 4 August 1945, R. D. Charques expressed sentiments that chime with Lehmann's: 'The literature of this war [...] is still to come. Is it not possible that its quality as literature will depend in some degree, even in large degree, on when it comes?' (Anon [R. D. Charques], 'The Urge' 367) Charques, whose reflections are prompted in part by a collection of writings by servicemen and women, continues that for those in the services, writing has often been 'an escape or respite from the extinguishing anonymity of his conditions of existence' (367). A comparison with writing of the previous war suggests that it might be necessary to wait for the best books about the conflict; Edmund Blunden's *Undertones of War* (1928) and Frederick Manning's *Her Privates We* (1930) are cited as examples here.[23] By the 'literature of this war', Charques evidently implies the *combatant* literature; underpinning his discussion is a belief that it is servicemen and women who will provide the most authentic accounts of war experience. However, I will argue that the division between 'combatant' and 'non-combatant' writing is not necessarily clear-cut, not least because of the many different kinds of war service that the existence of the so-called 'Home Front' produced. Thus for example, Henry Green and William Sansom both drew on their experiences as members of the Auxilliary Fire Service; they were not, strictly speaking, 'combatants' but certainly had an experience of the war that in some respects was closer to that of the combatant than to that of the civilian. Even Vera Brittain, whose pacifist views are well known, saw her writing as a kind of active service, as I will show. Therefore, whilst it is necessary and important to acknowledge the varieties of war work that different individuals undertook, I will be considering 'combatant' and 'non-combatant' writers alongside each other, and exposing both the consonances and the divergences between their representations of the war. As I have shown, P. H. Newby was still waiting for 'the literature of this war' to appear in 1951. I will suggest that, taken in historical perspective, it becomes clear that such a literature did exist but that because it did not take the form that Newby, Lehmann, or Charques expected, they did not recognize it as such.

1
Remembering the Last War

Looking back to earlier conflicts as a means of understanding the current one is a strategy that functioned in different ways at different stages of the Second World War. Writers could draw on their own personal experiences of combat as a means of endorsing their predictions about the future, or they could appeal to cultural memory, reference points that the reader might be presumed to share. Both individual and collective remembrance could be used to ratify a particular vision of the present and immediate future. Prior to the outbreak of war, predictions about the methods by which a new conflict would be prosecuted were based on the analysis of earlier developments. The pacifist Bertrand Russell, writing in 1936, attempted to raise awareness of the potential horrors on the horizon by reminding readers that during the 1917 air raids on London, 'there were times [...] when large parts of the population [...] were terror-stricken. A bombardment from the air will be a far more appalling experience in the next war' (Russell 44). Although, as Tom Harrisson argues, the potential impact of an air war was often overestimated in the interwar period (*Living Through* 19–30), the effects of aerial bombardment during the Spanish Civil War provided an illustration of what could be to come. The grounds for comparisons with other wars shifted once the conflict against Nazi Germany was in train. J. B. Priestley, writing in June 1940, saw a parallel with the threatened Napoleonic invasion of 1805 (*Postscripts* 12),[1] whilst invasion fears led other writers to look to the guerrilla fighting of the Spanish war as a potential model.

Whether influenced by personal experiences or not, such analogies as these have particular ideological sources and effects, which can be compounded by the manner in which the processes of recalling are depicted. In many cases, I will argue, an unresolved personal conflict comes to stand for the damage wrought on the nation by war; what is more difficult for these writers is how such conflicts might be resolved. Beginning with an examination of texts that use memories of the war in Spain as a means of establishing the particular political beliefs or aspirations of their protagonists, I will move on to examine novels including James Hilton's *Random Harvest* (1941) and Vera Brittain's *Account Rendered* (1945), in which memories damaged in the Great War feature as both subject matter and structural device. Both broadly speaking pacifist in intent, Hilton and Brittain attempt to illustrate the negative impact of war on their protagonists and to show that a positive outcome can result from the working-through of these experiences. This balancing act between personal and political, and between condemning war, whilst not condemning, as such, the war effort, is one that is both fascinating and precarious. Attempting to encompass the memory of one war and the experience of another also has an impact on narrative form, with the protagonists' memory loss producing disjunctions in the narrative that prove difficult to smooth over.

Remembering the Great War, remembering Spain

In his essay 'Looking Back on the Spanish War', written in 1942 and first published in 1943, George Orwell not only reminisces about his own experiences in Spain, but also identifies a series of striking continuities between the kinds of rhetoric used to describe both the Spanish conflict and the 1914–18 war. Whilst the ideological stakes were very different, the same 'romantic warmongering muck' (Orwell, 'Looking Back' 250) is found in each case.

> [H]ere [during the Spanish Civil War] were the very people who for twenty years had hooted and jeered at the 'glory' of war, at atrocity stories, at patriotism, even at physical courage, coming out with stuff that with the alteration of a few names would have fitted into the *Daily Mail* of 1918. (251)

The war in Spain was the point at which many who had previously espoused a pacifist position moved to one of pacificism, which, according to Martin Ceadel, 'sees the prevention of war as its main duty and accepts that [...] the controlled use of armed force may be necessary to achieve this' (*Pacifism* 5); but not all were as cynically motivated as Orwell might imply. Sardonically, Orwell ascribes the lack of recognition of the type of *volte face* he identifies to the fact that '[o]ur memories are short nowadays' (250);[2] evidence from other Second World War writing shows that memories of the Spanish war were on occasion either overlaid with a gloss of nostalgia or used highly selectively. Orwell attempts to avert such accusations in relation to his own recollections of the war by focusing on the base physical hardships of soldiering, which persist, he argues, no matter how idealistic the combatant's motivations. He also acknowledges that his own experiences may not have much significance to the reader; personal encounters, or the power struggles he witnessed, perhaps have no real bearing on the wider causes or implications of the conflict. Wars, Orwell implies, may be motivated by 'causes' but being part of a fighting force is about interacting with individuals.

Writing during the 1930s, Virginia Woolf used reactions to the 1914–18 war, and specifically the works of Wilfred Owen, as a means of showing that not all men see war as 'a profession; a source of happiness and excitement; and [...] an outlet for manly qualities' ('Three Guineas' 122). However, Woolf also knew, from the example of her nephew Julian Bell, killed while driving an ambulance in Spain in July 1937, during the time when she was writing *Three Guineas*, that the experiences of those such as Owen did not always imprint themselves on short memories.[3] Considering Bell's generation, which had no direct experience of the First World War but laid a claim to its legacy, Tom Buchanan notes a particular prevalence of the switch from pacifism to support for the war in Spain. He quotes the Duchess of Atholl, a campaigner for the Republican cause, who observed that 'meetings in support of the Spanish Republic were largely attended by "young men who, a year or two ago, might have supported the notorious [1933] Oxford peace resolution"' (Buchanan 68). Refusing to fight for king and country but agreeing to fight for the 'cause' of Spain flies in the face of Woolf's argument that all wars foster aggression and are therefore equally to be condemned. What is exposed here is the complexity and ambivalence of attitudes towards the 1914–18 war among those who were too young to have any personal memories of it but who nevertheless felt the weight of its legacy. Describing his friend Esmond Romilly's return, disillusioned and battle-hardened, from fighting in Spain, Philip Toynbee points out that even the apparently anti-belligerent writings of Owen, cited by Woolf, could have unpredictable effects:

> I suppose that what Esmond had experienced should have been no surprise to either of us. We should have known it all already from those bitter books about the first world war which we had read with such envious avidity. But Siegfried Sassoon and Wilfred Owen,

Remarque and Barbusse, had not convinced us that war is dull and dispiriting: still less could they have persuaded us that our own war might disillusion us. In fact it seems to me now that our picture of war was as falsely romantic, in its different way, as anything which had stirred the minds of Edwardian boys, brought up on Henty and the heroics of minor imperial campaigns. [...] [W]e felt less pity than envy of a generation that had experienced so much. Even in our Anti-War campaigns of the early thirties we were half in love with the horrors which we cried out against, and, as a boy, I can remember murmuring the name *'Passchendaele'* in an ecstasy of excitement and regret. (*Friends* 91)

Even disillusionment is 'half-expected from the beginning; it had become an element of the romantic experience' (92).[4]

Clearly, as G. D. Sheffield has argued, 'The First World War exercised a terrible fascination for men who had not been old enough to serve in [it].' (30) Toynbee was born in 1916, Romilly in 1919; similar sentiments differently nuanced can be found in works by those who were old enough to have some personal memory of the war. Cecil Day Lewis, aged ten on the outbreak of war, recalls how, as a teenager, he read 'a bound set of an illustrated magazine extending over the war years [...] with an extraordinary feeling of recognition', and sees this as evidence of how he was 'unwittingly steeped' in the war's 'sluggish, desperate course' (84). Christopher Isherwood's feelings about the war during his school and university days appear to have been less explicitly nostalgic than Toynbee's; the war, or rather its symbolic force, is the nexus for a struggle expressed in psycho-sexual terms:

> Like most of my generation, I was obsessed by a complex of terrors and longings connected with the idea 'War.' 'War,' in this purely neurotic sense, meant The Test. The Test of your courage, of your maturity, of your sexual prowess: 'Are you really a Man?' Subconsciously, I believe, I longed to be subjected to this test; but I also dreaded failure. (Isherwood, *Lions* 46)

Isherwood's self-regarding attitudes are later challenged by an encounter with Lester, a shell-shocked veteran not many years his senior, whose 'horribly matter-of-fact anecdotes' (157) bring home to Isherwood what 'The Test' might actually mean – not 'the idea of "War" ' but its actuality. Writing in the late 1930s about an encounter that took place in the late 1920s, Isherwood describes Lester as an anomaly: 'He had no business to be here, alive, in post-war England. His place was elsewhere, was with the dead' (158). A man like Lester does not fit into Isherwood's preferred narrative of the war, but even before meeting him, Isherwood refigures 'The Test' in personal and aesthetic terms: 'Isherwood refused the Test – not out of weakness, not out of cowardice, but because he was subjected, daily, hourly, to a "Test" of his own: the self-imposed Test of his integrity as a writer' (60).

George Orwell explained his decision to take part in the war in Spain as, in part at least, a result of the place the Great War had in his own consciousness when he was growing up. His comments in 'My Country Right or Left' (1940) also provide a further context for the anger he expresses in 'Looking Back on the Spanish War' about the romanticizing of war. Orwell admits the difficulty of attempting to 'disentangle your real memories from their later accretions' ('My Country' 536), but maintains that what impinged on his consciousness most strongly during the 1914–18 war were the small details rather than what later came to be the historical landmarks. Having to eat margarine made more of an impression than advances on the Western Front. This focus on the personal, even visceral, impact on the war on a civilian child serves to emphasize why a young man such as Orwell might have reacted the way he did to the reminiscences of an older generation. Events that existed only on the fringes of his consciousness were central for them:

> As the war fell back into the past, my particular generation, those who had been 'just too young', became conscious of the vastness of the experience they had missed. You felt yourself a little less than a man, because you had missed it. [...] I am convinced that part of the reason for the fascination that the Spanish civil war had for people of about my age was that it was so like the Great War. (537–8)

As Kevin Foster suggests, Orwell, like Isherwood, felt the need to undergo an experience comparable to the one that had apparently been missed: 'Orwell visualised the Test that he both dreaded and desired as a symbolic and physical rite of passage across an archetypal First World War battlefield' (13). Whilst admitting that the use of airpower did 'raise the [Spanish] war to a modern level', Orwell contends that for the most part 'it was a bad copy of 1914–18' ('My Country' 590). He thus exposes his own category error in thinking that Spain could be for him the rite of passage that the Great War was for others. This rite was itself constructed retrospectively by Great War veterans in an atmosphere of 'steadily growing nostalgia' ('My Country 589). Such a nostalgic version of war experience is at odds with what Isherwood hears from Lester, not least because it is more easily assimilated, socially.[5] As I will show, it is the disjunctive, shell-shocked and anti-nostalgic version of the Great War that is the preferred focal point for a number of novelists. This choice facilitates the reconfiguration of the accepted mythologies of the Great War that are alluded to here by Orwell, and also shows authors trying, with varying degrees of success, to challenge pre-emptively the nascent mythologies of the new war.

As well as drawing connections between the Great War and the war in Spain, in 'My Country Right or Left', Orwell explains his support for the current war, which he sees as akin to the Republican struggle in Spain, and as a positive, non-conservative expression of patriotism. For others on the left, the question of what relationship there might be between the war against fascism in Spain and the war against Nazi Germany was complicated by the position taken by the Soviet Union. Valentine Cunningham suggests that the Molotov–Ribbentrop Non–Aggression Pact of August 1939 was 'for many Party members as well as fellow travellers a traumatic extension of the already devastating trauma of Spain' (*British Writers* 462). Whilst the pact could be construed as an attempt to avert war, Andy Croft argues that for many, 'it seemed that the Soviet Union had unforgivably betrayed the cause of anti-fascist unity and abandoned Britain to an unwinnable war with Germany' (*Comrade Heart* 97). Croft discusses the case of Randall Swingler, writer, composer, and, on the outbreak of war, book reviewer for the *Daily Worker*. Swingler initially saw the war as an opportunity to challenge both Hitler and Chamberlain, and a chance to make good the defeat in Spain. Drawing a comparison with the 1914–18 war, Swingler suggested that then 'there was no cause [...] in which the people believed and for which they could be roused to fight. Now there is a cause. We intend to make this a war to end Fascism' (qtd. in Croft, *Comrade Heart* 98–99). However, these comments were made before the official Communist Party line was announced, and Swingler found felt himself obliged to defend, in public at least, the view that the war was inter imperialist and should therefore be opposed by communists. This meant that until the Nazi invasion of the Soviet Union in 1941, Communist Party attention was largely focused on popular campaigns around issues such as deep shelters and the treatment of evacuees.[6]

The New Zealand writer Dan Davin depicts the kind of manoeuvring that Swingler found himself obliged to undertake in his novel *For the Rest of Our Lives* (1947), set in the Middle East between late 1941 and 1942. Tom O'Dwyer, an Irishman who has fought in Spain, decides to join up at the start of the war despite the party line: 'It's the same fight [as Spain], and it's not finished. [...] [The Party] think that while Chamberlain handles it it's an imperialist war. And they're probably right. But I'm going all the same.' (Davin, *For the Rest* 28) Later, Tom attempts to explain to his fellow soldiers how the war could change from being imperialist to being antifascist:

> You have a number of powers in one stage of capitalism at war with another power-group in another stage of capitalism. Men can fight on the same side for many reasons. [...] [I]n a war run under the capitalist system, it's Churchill's democracy that's going to win. Imperialism, that is [...] And then what happens? The USSR, the socialist sixth of the world, comes in. Its entry guarantees that democracy will have a rallying point at the end. (180)

In Jack Lindsay's *Beyond Terror* (1943), a novel set during and after the battle for Crete, one protagonist, Ray, presents a more simplistic analysis of events with less sophistry: 'I joined up the first week of the war, a bit drunk and still thinking of the Spanish Civil War. But [...] [t]hose Greek lads opened my eyes. This is a people's war now, they've done that to it' (49). Later, however, he realises the difficulty of attempting to impose his version of the war on the people of Crete, who have their own understanding of events and their own goals: 'How then hold them in union by telling them that the tradition was outworn, the sense of kin antagonistic to the needs of antifascist union?' (219) In Davin's novel, Tony, another veteran of the war in Spain also seems alert to the difficulties of squaring war aims with more domestic political concerns. Asked why he decided to join up, he replies, 'Apart from anticipating conscription I'm still an antifascist. So I'm all for fighting the Nazis and the wretched Ities. It's the question of whether anti-fascism shouldn't include fighting the Tories as well that bothers me.' (152) Thus Tony prioritises the defeat of fascism over the reformation of British government and society, but does not deny that both may be necessary.

In the depiction of Tony, Davin also gives a brief insight into how Spanish veterans were treated by the British military. Tony recalls, '[W]hen the war started, I joined the British Army. They sent me to an OCTU [Officer Cadet Training Unit], and I got a commission before they found out I'd been in Spain.' (29) The implication seems to be that he might not have got the commission if the army had known about his time in Spain. Evidence from elsewhere supports Tom Buchanan's suggestion that treatment of Spanish veterans varied from regiment to regiment: 'although some [former International Brigade volunteers] suffered petty discrimination in being given lowly ranks and unrewarding postings, others did not' (Buchanan 191). In Alun Lewis's short story 'Private Jones' (1942), 'Dan Evans Spain' appears, in the eyes of the naïve focalising character, to make life difficult for himself by 'refusing a stripe and [being] barely civil to the captain and the sergeant-major' although it is not clear whether this is a cause or effect of the fact that 'both of them [have] their knives in him' (34). Similarly, in Edith Pargeter's *She Goes to War* (1942) Catherine Saxon believes that Tom Lyddon has been given menial jobs by the army as a means of commenting on the perceived value of his time in Spain, when in her view his experiences should make him a valuable asset (121).

This novel sees Pargeter making an interesting attempt to incorporate the figure of a Spanish Civil War veteran who joins the British army in 1939 into a narrative of a young woman's experience in wartime. A close examination reveals that beneath the wartime romance plot lie traces of the debates about the legacy of recent wars that I have been discussing here, attesting to their widespread cultural currency. The novel charts the relationship between Catherine Saxon, a journalist who joins the Women's Royal Naval Service, and Tom Lyddon, the soldier she meets, falls in love with, and then loses. However, it is also haunted by the presence of the First World War, in the form of Nick Crane, to whom Catherine's letters, of which the narrative is comprised, are addressed. Nick's letters to her are not included, but Catherine also forwards Tom's letters to Nick, and in this way the reader becomes party to Tom's thoughts and sentiments. Margaret Lewis suggests that this form was 'appropriate for a time when letters were a crucial, and often the only, form of communication' (25). It also means that, as Elizabeth Maslen notes, 'we seem to have access to three very different perspectives on the War, without the interference of an overall narrator' (45). Despite the evident confidence and attachment between Catherine and Nick, the exact nature of their relationship is never clarified. It is fair to presume that he is a family friend of Catherine's; he is older than her, there is evidently no romance between them, and, crucially, he has been badly disabled, indeed paralysed, during the First World War. He is Catherine's point of contact with the earlier conflict, an interlocutor who is unable to answer her letters of his own volition. Notably, though, his condition undergoes an improvement during the course of the narrative, the legacy of the 1914–18 war reviving and reasserting itself just as Tom is sent to Crete for the battle that will lead to his death.

I will return to the possible significance of the choice of Nick as a correspondent for Catherine; the chief focus of the novel, however, once Catherine has got used to life at Devonport and then gone through the upheaval of a move to Liverpool, is her romance with, and education by, Tom. On the occasion of their first meeting, she notices a scar on his face:

'Home-made mine. The man who sprung it was killed.'
I said: 'Flanders?'
He said: 'Spain. Outside Barcelona.' (Pargeter, *She Goes*120)

This misapprehension of Catherine's is partly prompted by the fact that Tom has the appearance of a veteran, prematurely grey and 'weather-beaten' (119). It is also implied, however, that until she meets Tom, the First World War is her main point of reference so far as combat goes, even though her understanding of this is channelled through her contact with Nick, she herself being too young to remember it. The name 'Flanders' seems to have an emblematic significance for her similar to that which the name 'Passchendaele' has for Toynbee. From the outset, then, the Spanish war is established both as a comparison with the current conflict, and as a means of romanticizing Tom. Effectively, for Catherine, and by extension, for the reader, these two aspects become blurred. Tom's politics mark him as an outsider and, as I have noted, appear to Catherine to be a cause of his victimisation, when his war record should be an asset: 'You've had experience of war as it's fought now. Of this war, because it's all one' (121). He initially questions whether this is the case: 'It was the dirty Reds then; it's the dirty Nazis now', but then qualifies this and agrees with her: '[P]erhaps you're right. It's all one war. England's changed sides, that's all' (121). Tom, as befits a free spirit, asserts that he does not subscribe to any party, and endorses instead a species of humanist egalitarianism: '[O]pportunity and happiness [are] meant to be shared by all humanity instead of a comparatively small part, yes' (122). Thus both Tom and Catherine eventually share a desire for a social, if not socialist revolution, and the war can be seen as a means of facilitating this and making good the disappointments of the inter-war years.

A number of direct comparisons are drawn, by both Tom and Catherine, between the conduct of and ideals fuelling the two conflicts in which Tom has been involved. Catherine laments the fact that Tom feels little emotional engagement with the current war, and connects this to the nature of British patriotism:

> I think Spain was a fiery inspiration to him, horrible in effect but unslackening in fervour; but Spain was a defeat. And Britain touched that pinnacle only once [...]; at Dunkirk we believed utterly in ourselves and our cause. [But] [o]ur war, which could have been a crusade, has become so commercialised and soiled and hung with bits of dirty jingoism [...] that only here and there has some unveiling of glory shown us the things at stake. (171, 181)

Catherine believes that the British have no strong sense of what they are fighting for and therefore have no impetus other than to make the best of things. '[D]irty jingoism' has been substituted for the kind of national pride that she sees to be epitomised by the Poles and the Greeks, comparisons that imply that only in defeat can this spirit be awoken. The letters from Tom that are received by Catherine after his death show him struggling against disillusionment: 'In Spain I fought my way, with a handful of companions [...] Now I do what I'm told, when I'm told, no matter how idiotic it is' (207–8). His final letter, written when he realizes it will be impossible for him to join the evacuation of Crete, contains bitter criticism of the army hierarchy for their lack of foresight on the issue of air attacks. He believes that they should have learned not only from the Spanish experience, but from the successful German invasions of Holland and Norway.[7] This disillusionment serves as an echo of the disappointment engendered by Spain:

> If I die here, as I believe, I die an angry man [...] I don't complain of death. I didn't go to Spain in 1936 to keep my body safe, I didn't join up in London in 1939 to ensure that I should live to enjoy peace again. Only that there should be a peace for someone to enjoy. (302)

Tom therefore predicts that the death which he is confronting will be in vain so long as the military hierarchy fail to use their resources appropriately.

The note of self-sacrifice underpinning Tom's assertion that he has been guyed by the army is foregrounded in the comparisons made between Tom and Johnny, the fighter-pilot boyfriend of Catherine's friend Gwyn. Johnny's death, 'in a blaze of glory' is set alongside Tom's less visibly heroic end, '[t]he legend, and the reality' (252). Throughout the novel Johnny has epitomised the manner in which '[a]viation reinvented the glamour of war' (Rawlinson 58), and although Catherine does wryly critique Johnny's elevation to the status of 'adolescent demigod' (198) she has to admit the force of the mythology in which he is entwined. But although comparing Johnny and Tom is implicitly a call for the recognition of the contribution of the ordinary soldier, Catherine seems instead to wish that Tom could also have had the opportunity to display his heroism. Her language also indicates the extent to which the masculinity of each has been honed by the war machine: 'Johnny [...] died effective and formidable, a polished tool. But Tom was a good weapon shamefully mishandled' (308). Tom's qualities as a soldier, formed by his Spanish experience, should have fitted him for a more important role in the war; instead he is doomed to a repetition of his earlier disillusionment and, ultimately death. Catherine is left attempting to reconfigure the war as an opportunity for 'cut[ting] away from our own national body all the inequalities and exploitations [...] that enfeeble it now' (312).

Although this rhetoric has a forward-looking, revolutionary tone, what is desired here are changes that, according to Catherine, ought to have happened at the end of the First World War. The bereaved Gwyn suggests that perhaps death was preferable to Johnny being seriously injured and having 'twenty-five years of a life not worth living' (227) like Catherine's correspondent Nick. Ironically, however, it is just at this point that there is an improvement in Nick's health, and Catherine expresses a hope that he might one day walk again. This unexpected, if minor, recovery of powers is open to a number of interpretations. It reinforces the suggestion that it is never too late to revive the ideals that somehow went astray during, and in the aftermath of, the First World War. It also implies, however, that recovery from war is a lengthy process, both for individuals, and, by extension, for society. More generally, Pargeter's choice of a First World War veteran as Catherine's correspondent means that even when Catherine is looking forward and expressing hopes for the future she is also having to negotiate with the past, no matter how partial her understanding of Nick's experiences might be. Catherine acknowledges receiving letters from Nick, and thanks him for sending a comforting letter to Gwyn, but, as I have noted, the reader does not have access to his half of the correspondence. Despite the absence of his voice, he is a controlling presence in the narrative, paternalistic but, for the reader, silent, his sudden reanimation coming as a rather sinister reminder of the uncontainable legacy of the last war.

Pargeter's novel illustrates, and fails to resolve, some of the difficulties of attempting to draw parallels between the Spanish Civil War and the wider European conflict (or indeed seeing them as more or less continuous, as Tom does). The apparent ideological certainties of the Spanish conflict are now not so clearly defined and whilst support for the Spanish cause could transcend nationalism, the current war mires Tom and Catherine in some of the less attractive aspects of patriotism. Even in novels where the comparison with Spain is less central, such issues are also recognised. The factory workers in Inez Holden's *Night Shift* (1941) show a degree of cynicism, or at least bemusement, over the issue of the war effort and their part in it. Sonny, one of the employees, recalls seeing his friend off on his way to join the International Brigade: 'We thought everything was going to be different. John thought him and his friends fighting would change things' (Holden, *Night Shift* 88). John returns after becoming ill, but Sonny nevertheless asserts: 'I wish I'd gone with John and the other fellows. Must have been a good experience being out there and knowing what it was all for' (89). Notably, Sonny here seems to stress the camaraderie as much as the cause. He is as vague about the detail of 'what it was all for' as he is about the nature of his friend's illness; he is nostalgic for an experience he did not share.

In Holden's novel, the enclosed world of the night shift becomes, despite the cynicism and petty infighting, a community. At the climax, it appears that the preceding narrative, slipping between first-person narration and the use of free indirect speech to present the states of mind of individual characters, is presented by the narrator as an elegy for her fellow factory workers, most of whom are killed in an air raid. From later in the war, Ralph L. Finn's *Return to Earth* (1945) uses another enclosed community, that formed in an air-raid shelter, as the means of bringing together individuals with divergent attitudes to the war. Frank Manning, the narrator, is a journalist whose desire for social change has been fuelled by his experiences in Spain, and who has not been in the armed services in the present war. His position as a dissonant voice on the fringes of the conflict means that certain of the paradoxes confronted by Tom Lyddon in Pargeter's novel are sidestepped. Frank is a champion of the working classes, and claims to have predicted that, in the event of a Nazi invasion, the East End of London would be the seat of resistance; later, when an Eastern European Jewish refugee strikes up a song in Yiddish, Frank replies with an English version 'as we had chorused it in Barcelona' (Finn 56). In essence, Frank's identification of himself with the displaced is another, less palatable, version of Sonny's nostalgia for something he never did; Frank closes the gap not just between two disparate historical events, but also between his own experience and that of the refugee, a rather questionable means of asserting the solidarity of the oppressed.

Saluting the flag

Paul Fussell has argued that: 'Everyone fighting a modern war tends to think of it in terms of the last one he [sic] knows anything about. [...] The act of fighting a war becomes something like an unwitting act of conservative memory' (*Great War* 314). Many of those who had participated in the Spanish war, and who saw the war against Nazi Germany as a continuation of the antifascist struggle, were keen that the military lessons of Spain should not be ignored in favour of a return to the paradigms of the 1914–18 conflict. George Orwell was not alone in seeing potential parallels between the Local Defence Volunteers (later renamed the Home Guard), established in the spring of 1940 in the wake of the use of parachute forces in the invasion of Holland and Belgium, and the Spanish militias. Tom Wintringham, who had served as commander of the British Battalion of the International Brigade, set up a Home Guard training school with the backing of Edward Hulton, the owner of *Picture Post*. Instructors at Osterley Park, which opened its doors in July 1940, included 'three Spanish refugee miners teaching the use of explosives against tanks' (Fernback 74). (British veterans of the Spanish War and an instructor from the Boy Scouts were also involved). In articles for *Picture Post*, Wintringham explained the aims of the school, and also gave practical advice, drawing on the Spanish experience, of what action individuals could take against the expected invasion forces. However, these were the early days of the Home Guard; in August 1941, Orwell wrote that although in the beginning 'the Home Guard was a heterogeneous force and structurally rather similar to the early Spanish militias [...] it has been gradually brigaded on the lines of the regular army' ('London Letter' 150). Wintringham was edged out of Osterley Park and resigned from his post as an advisor in May 1941, 'correctly suspecting that his views were being quietly ignored' (Mackenzie 76). For many Home Guard volunteers, then, the 1914–18 war remained the most compelling model of military experience and organization, although some would have been able, like Clive Candy in Powell and Pressburger's *The Life and Death of Colonel Blimp* (1943), to make comparisons with earlier, imperial conflicts.[8]

J. B. Priestley, himself, as I have noted, a member of the Home Guard, makes frequent references to his experiences in the 1914–18 war in his Postscripts, but often acknowledges the differences, as well as the continuities, between the two conflicts. In a Postscript from July 1940, Priestley asks his listener: 'Have you ever noticed how all the attempts – and there have been many – to see this war in terms of the last, have failed? You just can't give this war a "Tipperary", "Keep the Home Fires

Burning" flavour' (*Postscripts* 46). He suggests that this is partly because of a recognition among the public that more is at stake than national interests: 'this is a war between despair and hope' (47). Priestley identifies a further difference when in September 1940, he reflects that 'we're not really civilians any longer but a mixed lot of soldiers – machine-minding soldiers, milkmen and postmen soldiers, house-wife and mother soldiers […] and even broadcasting soldiers' (68). For other commentators, however, the similarities at particular points in the conflict were pronounced. Mollie Panter–Downes, an English writer who wrote regular letters for the *New Yorker* throughout the war, reflected on the fall of the Low Countries: 'Atrocity stories that everyone over thirty remembers from the last war have turned up again, as good as new but with different details. They produce, together with the photographs of refugees pushing heaped perambulators along Belgian roads, a horrifying sense of living the same old nightmare all over again' (*London War Notes* 62). Panter–Downes compares two representations rather than things she saw; in the fictions to be examined here, the difference between remembering one's own experience and remembering particular types of representation, as well as whether, in Fussell's terms, the previous war is remembered in a conservative way, are important for how the present conflict is understood.

As I will show, James Hilton and Vera Brittain both use the device of the generation gap as a means of dramatizing the contested legacy of the war, as well as focusing on the damage wrought on protagonists' memories by the conflict. Similarly, in Frank Tilsley's 'Reassurance', a short story published in *The Spectator* in January 1940, the well-meaning narrator attempts to calm a nervous-looking woman he encounters in an air-raid shelter, evidently by parroting what he has read in the papers. Reassuring her that this is probably a false alarm, he 'heartily' continues: 'Most of the effect of air raids on the nerves of civilians is the way in which it break up their old habits […] if you become used to it before the bombs begin to fall, the battle is half won' (41). His borrowed authority is countered by her harrowing description of being trapped under rubble for nineteen hours during a First World War Zeppelin raid, and by the end of the story, she, in a neat reversal, is reassuring him. Clearly, however, her earlier experience does not necessarily make the current situation any easier to confront, and initially at least increases her anxiety. In Edith Pargeter's *Ordinary People* (1941), a family saga encompassing both wars, Jason, who in the mid-1930s has won a scholarship to Oxford and become a pacifist, tries to persuade his working-class father George, who fought in the 1914–18 war, that the examples of 'heroism, and unselfishness, and comradeship' that he saw then 'existed in spite of the war, not because of it' (249). Jason challenges his father by asking him whether he is 'justifying war on the ground that it brings out the best in a few people?' (250) George, largely silent in the novel hitherto, is angry at his son's well-meaning attempt at consciousness-raising: 'you can't make a lively imagination do the work of memory, and that's what you're after. Nor you can't make a wrong out of resisting a wrong, however you try' (250). In presenting this clash between the generations, Pargeter, like Tilsley, pits experience against intellectual engagement and the latter is found wanting; in Pargeter's case, though, this does mean that the question of whether the last war was justifiable remains in suspense. Jason gives up pacifism after getting into a fight after a public meeting and, with the persuasion of his Jewish wife, joins up when hostilities again break out.

Even in fictions where the memory of the last war does not feature as a central theme, then, authors are often alert to the problems of such comparisons. In *Put out More Flags* (1942), Evelyn Waugh shows that, like Orwell, he was all too aware of the mythologies of the last war, and puts these to ironic effect. Reflecting, on the eve of war, on her brother Basil's potential involvement in the conflict, Barbara's only points of reference are

> the war books she had read. She saw him as Siegfried Sassoon, an infantry subaltern in a mud-bogged trench, standing to at dawn, his eyes on his wrist watch, waiting for zero hour; she saw him as Compton Mackenzie, spider in a web of Balkan intrigue [...]; she saw him as T. E. Lawrence and Rupert Brooke. (19)

The mismatch between these role models and Basil's own personal capacities is a source of grotesque humor, but Waugh also implies a more fundamental gap between the supposed heroics of the First World War and the tawdry bureaucracy and disorganization in which his protagonists, including Barbara, become entangled. A more dangerous aspect of a continued belief in the images Barbara conjures is revealed when, late on in the novel, Alistair Digby-Vane-Trumpington decides to join the Commandoes:

> '[...] They're getting up special parties for raiding. They go across to France and creep up behind Germans and cut their throats in the dark.' He was excited, turning a page in his life, as, more than twenty years ago, lying on his stomach before the fire, with a bound

volume of *Chums*, he used to turn over to the next instalment of the serial. (229)

Waugh here implies both the vapidity of Alistair's life prior to the war and also the effects of an early immersion in the heroic ethos fostered by interwar boys' publications: Joseph McAleer has characterized *Chums* as promulgating 'blazing patriotism' (227 n.47).[9] Barbara falls back on some of the more romantic images of heroism, whilst Alistair, it seems, is attracted by a sanitized brutality. To 'creep up behind Germans and cut their throats in the dark' sounds like a children's game rather than war.[10]

Later, in Waugh's *Brideshead Revisited* (1945), the memorial book that Mr Samgrass assists Lady Marchmain in compiling is critiqued, but not completely condemned, by Charles Ryder. The volume is to commemorate Lady Marchmain's brother Ned, 'the eldest of three legendary heroes all killed between Mons and Passchendaele' (97):

> Mr Samgrass's deft editorship had assembled and arranged a curiously homogeneous little body of writing – poetry, letters, scraps of a journal, an unpublished essay or two, which all exhaled the same high-spirited, serious, chivalrous, other-wordly air and the letters from their contemporaries, written after their deaths, all in varying degrees of articulateness, told the same tale of men who were, in all the full flood of academic and athletic success, of popularity and the promise of great rewards ahead, seen somehow as set apart from their fellows, garlanded victims, devoted to the sacrifice. (123)

This description has a mildly debunking, or at least disbelieving tone to it, although this is apparently undercut when Charles goes on to reflect that these sacrificial victims have been removed only to 'make a world for Hooper' (123), representative throughout the novel of the lack of grace evident in the next generation. At the end of the train journey during which he has been reading the memorial volume, Charles meets up with Sebastian and vows to unite with him against Lady Marchmain, having reflected that perhaps her world, like that of her brothers, must pass. What therefore seems to emerge is a critique not of Ned and his brothers, but of the manner in which their 'sacrifice' has been presented, or indeed co-opted, by Lady Marchmain. An interesting contrast here is the death of Charles's mother, which also occurs during the First World War, when she is driving an ambulance in Serbia. This version of First World War experience, existing only on the fringes of Charles' memory and self-identity, serves as a reminder of the dangers of oversimplifying the conflict by focusing solely on the memorialisation of men like Lady Marchmain's brothers.[11]

Waugh thus intertwines personal experiences and memories of the previous conflict with the ways in which it has been woven into cultural memory; indeed it is often difficult to separate these strands. This relationship is dramatized (literally) in James Hilton's *Random Harvest* (1941), a novel set largely, like *Put out More Flags*, in the months immediately preceding the outbreak of war. The 1942 film of *Random Harvest* replaces the analepses of the novel with a chronological structure and shifts the focus from Charles Rainier's struggle to recover his past to his wife Paula's attempts to remind him of their previous life together; social commentary is muted and the narrative is reframed as melodrama. In the novel, however, intrusions from the First World War into the present are central. The first-person narrator, a Cambridge student called Harrison, meets Rainier on a train journey in November 1937, taking notice of his fellow passenger when the dining car is observing the traditional Armistice Day minute's silence. They fall into conversation and Rainier, a businessman and Member of Parliament, offers to help Harrison find a job; a year later, Harrison becomes Rainier's assistant. During a weekend visit to Rainier's country seat, Stourton, Rainier decides to tell Harrison his story, having already confided that he has a gap in his memory stretching from his being injured at the front in 1917 until he recovered consciousness after a road accident in Liverpool in late 1919.

What Rainier tells Harrison about his life between 1919 and 1938, is retold by Harrison in the third person. This is the first break with forward-moving chronology, but the continued use of indirect rather than direct narration means that the largely anonymous Harrison smoothes over any potential dissonance between Rainier's 'normal' memories and those he later recovers. The first retrospective section takes Rainier from his return to the family home, to the bewilderment of his siblings who had presumed he was dead, and through the 1920s. Having resumed his studies at Cambridge, Rainier leaves to steer the family business through a difficult period. He becomes romantically involved with his step-niece, Kitty, but, at the climax of this instalment of his life story, she breaks off their relationship. What happens then is already known to both Harrison and the reader: Rainier's business flourishes, he is elected as an MP, and he marries his secretary, Paula. In the next section of the narrative, the chronologically forward-moving action resumes, and Rainier recovers his memory and is able to tell Harrison what happened in the missing years, before the accident in Liverpool brought him back to his former identity. In a final chapter, Rainier is reunited with the wife he married during his 'forgotten' years, and in a climax that one reviewer compared unfavourably with Mrs Henry Wood's *East Lynne* (1861),[12] Rainier's first wife and his present wife Paula prove to be one and the same, she having kept their earlier acquaintance from him for fear of traumatizing him. This revelation at the end of the novel comes about half-way through the film version when Paula appears as Rainier's secretary; the fact that film is visual medium makes it much more difficult for her identity to remain concealed. From this point in the film, suspense is created as Rainier repeatedly fails to recognise his former lover, who decides not to reveal her true identity to him after taking the advice of the doctor who treated Rainier during his time in an asylum towards the end of the war. In the novel, Harrison encounters a psychologist who knew Rainier when he was a student, and who explains that Rainier's memory of the missing years is likely to return gradually, 'a little bit here, a little bit there – till finally, like a key turning in a lock, or like the last few pieces of a jigsaw puzzle, the whole thing would slip into position' (29).

Rainier's resistance to remembering has its roots not just in the emotional conflict caused by his apparently new – and apparently loveless – marriage, but in the contradictions between his social attitudes then and now. The events leading to the recovery of his memory illustrate this. After a chance encounter with a Hungarian pianist, Navoida, and his wife, Rainier decides that it would be amusing for him and Harrison to treat the pair to some traditional English entertainment. They make the journey out to the 'Banford Hippodrome' to watch 'Berty Lowe in *Salute the Flag*' (138). Through Harrison's description of the probable evolution of the show, Hilton presents a critique of prevailing attitudes to past and future conflicts:

> [*Salute the Flag*] had been (I guessed) an originally serious melodrama on a wartime theme, dating probably from 1914 or 1915; its villains had then been Germans of impossible villainy and its heroes English soldiers of equally impossible saintliness. A quarter of a century of lucrative adaptation, however, had merged both the villainy and the saintliness into a common mood of broad comedy burlesque; such patriotic speeches as remained were spoken now only to be laughed at. (139)

This description of the transformations the show has undergone indicates both the implausibility of its original stereotyped representations of the nations, and the disquieting fact that, although such extremes of patriotism are now laughable, there seems to be little or nothing to stand in their place. What complicates this is that Rainier himself was the catalyst for these changes to *Salute the Flag*. Rainier's memory begins to return when he sees the minor character of the stuttering soldier, but his sudden announcement to Harrison, after the show, that he can remember, for the first time in many years, where he was on Armistice Day, comes not as a particularly dramatic or violent outburst, but rather in a meditative fashion. It reminds Harrison of their first encounter on the train, when Rainier believed he recognised the landscape through which they were passing:

> '*Armistice Day*,' he repeated. Then he added, quietly, almost casually: 'I was in hospital ... I mean on that first Armistice Day – the first one of all. The *real* one.' He suddenly clutched my sleeve. 'Yes, I remember – I was at Melbury!'
> I said nothing, anxious not to break any thread of recollection he was about to unravel. (142)

The image of a thread unravelling presents the recovery of memory as smooth, delicate and linear, rather than painful, uneven and complicated. Any difficulties, uncertainties or psychic pain that Rainier might be subject to are projected outward, into the performance they have witnessed. The retelling in the third person of Rainier's account of his life during 1917 to 1919, when he went under the name of John Smith, or Smithy, serves to ensure a sense of continuity between then and now, a continuity guaranteed by a uniformity of narrative voice and a safe foothold for Rainier and the narrator in the present.

Rainier's account of his involvement, as Smithy, in the show appears to contain a pointed message about the legacy of the war and the treatment of veterans. Sent home from the front in an amnesiac condition, Smithy is kept in Melbury Asylum until, amid the confusion of the armistice celebrations, he takes the opportunity to abscond. In the town, he encounters Paula, an actress, who realizes he is in difficulty and takes him under her wing. Rainier's description of the version of *Salute the Flag* in which Paula performed indicates that its transformation from serious play to music-hall farce began even sooner than Harrison suspects:

> *Salute the Flag* [...] was a hangover from wartime, having begun in 1914 as a straight melodrama with no comedy at all, but with many

rousing speeches that audiences in those days had liked to cheer. Then, as the war progressed and the popular mood changed from that of Rupert Brooke to that of Horatio Bottomley, the patriotic harangues were shortened to make room for the writing in of a comic part, which speedily became such a success that by 1918 the show had developed into a series of clowning episodes. (171)[13]

When one of the actors is too hungover to appear, Smithy is asked to stand in and deliver a few lines intended to rouse a cheer from the audience. His nervousness and temporary disorientation when he steps on stage, however, lead to a recurrence of the nervous stammer that he suffered from in the asylum: 'It was the old, the tragic stammer [...] all he could do was wrestle with the words until they came, one after the other, each one fighting to the last' (185–6). The audience, believing that his stammering is part of the act, greet it with laughter. Smithy's shell-shocked condition ruptures the show; although his 'turn' seems to have been incorporated, persisting in the later version of the show seen by Rainier and Harrison, the audience's reaction implies that his condition, and by extension, his experience, cannot be understood by society. The audience laughs at Smithy's 'performance', rather than recognising it as a symptom of his illness. Smithy's reaction to what he perceives as barracking is to flee from the town. Paula eventually finds him in the depths of the countryside; they decide to move to London and start a new life. Smithy makes tentative steps towards a career in journalism, focusing on creating a 'vision of a new England rooted far back in the old, drawing its strength from a thousand years instead of its weaknesses from a hundred' (217). This change of direction is brought to an abrupt halt by the accident during a trip to discuss his work with an editor, which restores him to knowledge of his true identity.

Smithy's foray into journalism is underpinned by his catastrophic war experience, and by his implicit desire to prevent a further conflict, a desire expressed in terms of the hope for a 'new England'. Rainier's impulse, on his return, is to seclude himself from the world, at Cambridge. Although studying history, he is disengaged from current events, only learning about the varying fortunes of the family firm by chance, and spending his time instead punting on the Cam and discovering hidden tributaries haunted by the spirit of Rupert Brooke (81). Indeed, until he is called in to rescue Rainier's, Charles is considering an academic career; fortunately, he proves able to make the switch from the contemplative life at Cambridge to the cut and thrust of big business and the firm weathers the storm of the depression. The dissatisfaction that Harrison, from the outset, identifies beneath the surface of the highly successful Rainier thus appears to stem from a double origin. Rainier has been forced to relinquish his academic aspirations but he has also relinquished, unbeknownst to him initially, another path, the campaigning, peace-making path of Smithy, but the loss of a potential career in journalism is displaced in the narrative by the loss of Paula. Having fallen in love with her as Smithy, Rainier can only love her again when he fully regains the lost portion of his memory. On one level, then, and it is this reading that dominates the film version, *Random Harvest* is about the restoration of a lost love through the recovery of missing memory, but Hilton is also attempting to address fundamental issues about the legacy of one war and the onset of another. Reunited with her husband at the end of the novel, Paula addresses him as 'Smithy'. This is partly because it is as Smithy that she first falls in love with him. However, this climactic encounter takes place in the countryside, at the place they escaped to after leaving the theatre company, implying that Smithy's post-war hopes of reconnecting to a more essential England are not completely dashed. Harrison's assertion at the end of the novel that he 'knew in a flash that […] the random years were at an end, that the past and the future would join' (248) implies a return to those earlier ideals, smoothing over the difficult matter of Rainier's relative complacency towards social issues in the intervening period.

Paradoxically then, it appears to be Smithy who is right-minded and Rainier who is not. Smithy's are the more authentic virtues, a notion reinforced by the fact that, when married to Rainier, Paula is not loved, and has merely to perform the role of society hostess, whilst, when married to Smithy, poverty and lack of opportunity do not prevent love from flourishing. Rainier and Paula have no children; Paula was pregnant when Smithy left her but the child died.[14] Hilton may appear to be advocating a return to the simple life and more basic human virtues, but it is unclear whether Rainier will have to renounce his fortune and his political position to achieve this. Moreover, because Smithy is unable to remember his life before the war, he is completely a product of the conflict; his partially remembered traumatic war experiences are the sum total of his past life. Whilst he inveighs against the double-crossing that led to him being injured, in other respects Rainier emerges from the war unscathed. It could even be implied that he forgets the war too easily, and is therefore unable to forestall the drift towards a further conflict. Rainier's time as Smithy is bookended by two shocks – the shock of injury in war and the shock of the road accident, events that recall Freud's aetiology of trauma (Freud, *Beyond* 6). The memory of the intersticial time re-emerges in a manner that is reminiscent of *déjà vu*, with Rainier as a spectator who is later able to relate Smithy's story to Harrison calmly, during the course of a car journey. Channelling Rainier's story through Harrison in this manner means that Hilton can focus on the completion of the narrative rather than the process of its recovery. Indeed, recovery and narrative completion become synonymous. The net result of this, as I have suggested, is to stress the continuities between Smithy's story and Rainier's rather than the dissonances.

The influence on Hilton of J. W. Dunne's *An Experiment with Time* (1927), mentioned in passing by Harrison near the start of the novel, is also evident here. Harrison uses a simplified version of Dunne's theories to explain the feeling Rainier experiences of 'a sort of wisp of memory that can't be trapped before it fades away' (5). Harrison suggests that this could be proof of Dunne's idea that 'dreams *do* foretell the future, only by the time they come true, we've forgotten them – all except your elusive wisp of memory' (5). Whilst Hilton does not engage so completely with Dunne's ideas as, for instance, J. B. Priestley does in his 'Time' plays, Rainier's 'other life' as Smithy is an attempt to explore Dunne's notion that life is neither straightforwardly chronological nor finite, and even the repeated performances, with accretions, of *Salute the Flag*, show that repetition does not exclude evolution. In Hilton's earlier novel *Lost Horizon* (1933), the 'lost' kingdom of Shangri–La serves a similar purpose to Rainier's memory loss, offering a way to explore an alternative reality beyond the exigencies of immediate historical events and the tyranny of chronology. Here Hilton also presents a situation in which personal happiness and 'the greater good' collide in problematic way. Rainier's may appear to be the 'real' world, with Smithy his damaged double, but Hilton asks the reader to consider the possibility that it is Smithy who has the more expansive, humane and truly pacifist values. Looking ahead to the next Armistice, the end of a war that in the narrative has yet to begin, Paula suggests that maybe 'the future will take us [...] back to the past. A simpler England. Old England' (246). Only the end of the next war will provide the opportunity to resume the project begun by Smithy at the end of the last one.

Old familiar war stories

Hilton, then, appears to wish that the experiences of men like Smithy had not been subsumed into popular cultural representations like *Salute the Flag*, although, like Waugh, he has to acknowledge the potency of such representations. In Harrison, Rainier finds a sympathetic listener from the next generation and their conversations stress the importance of passing on the lessons of the past. Intergenerational communication works in a different way in Vera Brittain's wartime novel, as I will show; it is also the topic of Josephine Bell's *Martin Croft* (1941). Martin Croft is not himself the central protagonist of this novel, despite the fact that it opens with a Prologue set in 1917 in which he awaits rescue from No Man's Land, contemplating the possibility that he might already have been reported dead. The main action begins in 1935, when Mary Hillman goes to work for Croft's medical practice as a receptionist and from this position she observes the Crofts' troubled marriage. She and Croft become closer; shortly before he goes in for an operation to remove some remaining shrapnel, he tells her that he had to wait in No Man's Land for two days before being rescued: 'Mary tried not to show the cold horror that struck at her heart. She had heard war stories from her childhood onwards, but never told quite like this, quietly, colourlessly, as though it had happened to someone else' (Bell, *Martin Croft* 91). This lack of affect in Croft's account of his experiences is a sign that he has failed to overcome their traumatic impact, but equally notable here is Mary's reaction. Like Catherine in *She Goes to War*, Mary has no personal memory of the events of the 1914–18 conflict; unlike Catherine, she does not have any ongoing personal attachment to a war veteran, until her involvement with Croft:

> As she grew up she ceased to listen to the old familiar war stories her elders were so fond of quoting to one another. Her own contemporaries never spoke of it at all. It was something you learned about vaguely in a history lesson and was also a part of your parents' incredibly distant past. (92)

Croft's story has a deep impact on Mary and she conjures vivid images of him 'lying in muddy shell-hole'(95–6); part of what attracts her, however, is the apparent fatalism with which Croft both went to war and accepted his probable death in battle. His death encounter takes on a sexual allure and shortly after his operation, they go on a secret night out together and kiss, but he shies away from any further involvement with her.

The bond between Mary and Croft is therefore cemented when he confides in her about both his experiences in and his attitude towards the first war. There are shades here of Paula's sympathy for the shell-shocked Smithy, when she essentially rescues him from being returned to the asylum. Although Mary's love for Croft is doomed, Bell conveys the sense that it is by no means incidental to their relationship that Croft has been psychologically damaged in the war, and indeed Mary seems even more keen than Croft himself to get to the bottom of his difficult relationship to the past. When the action moves to 1939, she regrets that their former intimacy has apparently evaporated: 'Her still treasured memories of all her early contacts with Martin had no counter-part in his mind. [...] While she has drawn strength from remembrance, had he wiped memory out and his love with it? How could you wipe memory out by an act of will?' (273) The implication is that this is precisely how Croft has attempted to deal with his First World War experience, by evading emotional engagement with it, hence his stilted and detached delivery of his story. Later though, in an exchange that serves as a reminder that Josephine Bell was herself a doctor, one of Croft's colleagues tells Mary that inherent disposition, as well as environment, has an effect on an individual's personality. By this analysis, which echoes Freud's arguments, Croft 'can't blame all his trouble on the last war' (282). Such a view seems also to be shared by Vera Brittain, as I will show; perhaps more surprisingly, Brittain also seems to endorse Bell's view that confronting the legacy of the last war is necessary, even if this means becoming involved in the current conflict.

In an epilogue set on the beach at Dunkirk during the evacuation in May 1940, Croft finally manages to come to terms with his earlier war experience. He decides to end his troubled marriage and reconcile himself with his estranged daughter, although he has missed his chance with Mary, who leaves for America at the start of the war with her new husband, a psychotherapist. Croft's death wish has been overcome after a return to the scene of his war trauma: 'It had seemed to him [...] that his long postponed end would come to him in Flanders at the scene of his earlier survival. But that neat finish, that obvious logical solution has not happened' (312). That he managed to survive a return visit to Flanders, the site of his death encounter and a principle cause of the predominance, in his life since, of a negative outlook, encourages Croft to reassess the legacy of the last war, even while in the midst of the current one:

> [H]e knew [...] with a quiet, growing conviction, that the river of his own life had changed direction, passing out of the stagnant flats where it had moved despairingly and slow for over twenty years, into a deep gorge where it could press forward [...] He had entered upon the new war in the firm hope that he would achieve the end that had been denied him in his youth. [...] He did not now try to discover

when the change had begun. It was enough that it had happened, and that he was a living man, desiring to live. (316)

Paradoxically then, in the midst of further death and destruction (although the losses accrued at Dunkirk are here less prominent than the victory snatched from the jaws of defeat), Croft is freed from his enslavement to a guilt-induced predominance of the death drive. What is also encoded here is the notion that the current conflict can offer political completion where the earlier one did not. War is seen, paradoxically, as life-giving, a means of moving out of a condition of stagnation.

Like Hilton, Bell concludes her narrative by welding together an individual's experience of the two wars, but in both cases, these conclusions are tinged with ambivalence. Hilton seems unsure how Smithy's pacifist project, and indeed Rainier's desire to turn the clock back and refashion the post-1918 world can be reconciled with the unavoidable fact of the current conflict. Meanwhile Bell leaves the reader with a sense that the second war was inevitable, given the incompletely worked-through conflicts (of all kinds) that the first left unresolved. The part played by the next generation in each case is also notable. Harrison in *Random Harvest* serves as a sounding board for Rainier but gives little sense of his own attitude towards the wider political situation; in *Martin Croft*, Mary's removal to America is portrayed not as escapism but as a sign that it is up to Croft's generation to solve the problems it has had a part in causing. In both cases, the war veteran, although certainly a victim of circumstances in that he did not show special enthusiasm for the 1914–18 conflict, and suffered deeply during it, is shown to bear some responsibility for the failures of the interwar period. What is at stake here is remembering in the correct fashion. Rainier's inability to remember the woman who loves him implies that he is not simply a victim of trauma but that he, like Croft, uses the superficial concerns of working life to mask the essential issues of responsibility to others. This message is communicated even more strongly in *Martin Croft* because Croft's memory disorder is not to do with loss, as Rainier's is, but to do with how he frames and interprets the events of the past. What complicates this, as Hilton's descriptions of *Salute the Flag* imply, is that memory is not simply about freezing an image of past events which can then be recalled at will, but about the accretion of details over time. Rainier might not have consciously chosen what to forget, but Croft certainly has a choice about what, and how, he remembers.

Combatants and others: Brittain at war

Attempting to think about both world wars together through the trope of the damaged veteran evidently involves a difficult balancing act, especially if an author wishes to avoid the conclusion that the current conflict is simply a repetition of the previous one (and therefore doomed to the same unsatisfactory conclusion). Reframing the goals of the war, as Pargeter does, is one way round this; implying that this is a repetition with differences, and that some lessons have been learned in the interim, as Bell seems to, is another. Matters were complicated further for Vera Brittain by her pacifist stance. Her conversion to pacifism began with an involvement in the League of Nations Union during the 1920s, and was cemented in the early 1930s when she found herself unable to support the League's policy of rearmament and signed up with the Peace Pledge Union. Brittain's anti-war sentiments were underpinned by a desire to believe that the loved ones she had lost in 1914–18 had not died in vain; in many of her writings she attempts to preserve an image of the heroism of her brother and his friends whilst simultaneously condemning the patriotic militarism underpinning and necessitating their heroic actions.

In a diary entry from late 1942, following a visit to the cinema to see the American film version of *Mrs Miniver*, Jan Struther's popular chronicle of upper-middle-class daily life (parts of which, she reluctantly admits, moved her to tears), she appears to acknowledge the difficulty of the path she has taken since 1918:

> I found myself envying those whose simple patriotic reactions & desire to serve the war machine (like mine at the beginning of the last war) give them the inspiration of feeling that they are fighting the powers of evil, & save them from the complexities of us who are critical of ourselves & our country, recognising the evil of war. (Brittain, *Wartime Chronicle* 175–6)

It is notable that Brittain here writes 'critical of *ourselves* & our country': this could be an acknowledgement of the difficulty of sustaining an anti-war stance whilst refusing to descend into cynicism as regards the war effort. Indeed despite the fact that she could have stayed in the relative safety of her cottage in the New Forest for the duration, Brittain took it upon herself to live in London for most of the war, including the worst of the Blitz, and to visit other bombed cities in order to create a record of the damage and suffering she saw there. Brittain implies, when for instance she compares bombed streets to 'Western Front ruin' (91), that her earlier experiences have prepared her for this task. Phyllis Lassner has noted, however, that Brittain was criticised for making this comparison, as it tends to downplay the experiences of bombed civilians, who had been 'victimized not by the misguided militarism of their leaders, but by the Nazis' design for world conquest' (*British Women* 35). Positioning herself as a veteran of the 1914–18 war, Brittain uses a reference point that she believes can help her to make sense of the destruction around her, but this does tend to pull the focus back to her *own* experience.[15]

If a cynic might argue that in seeking out these horrors, Brittain is simply perpetuating a self-serving project initiated with *Testament of Youth*, her own analysis of her attitudes should also be considered. Whilst researching *Account Rendered*, Brittain read *The Neuroses in War* (1940), a collection of essays edited by the Freudian analyst Emanuel Miller of the Tavistock Clinic.[16] Including contributions by a number of doctors who had treated cases of war neurosis arising from the first war, this volume introduced Brittain to psychoanalytic conceptions of human behaviour in wartime. In a diary entry she attempts to analyse her own behaviour in terms of the ideas introduced and discussed in Miller's book:

> How well I know the 'anxiety' conflict between standards of decent conduct & the instinct of self-preservation. It is because I know fear & despise myself for it that I get a 'guilt' complex when out of dangers that others have to endure – and therefore tend (as in the Blitz) to go into them deliberately for no purpose but the maintenance of my self-respect! (Brittain, *Wartime Chronicle* 181)

Brittain here echoes the essay on 'The Differential Diagnosis of the Psychoneuroses of War':

> [I]n the last war it was said that soldiers broke down because they could not stand the strain of the war, but it was really the strain of the conflict between their self-preservation instinct and the demands of the ideal they had set themselves in respect of duty and self-respect. Such a conflict, whatever it be, will induce a severe sense of insecurity with its attendant emotion of anxiety. ('R.G.G' and Hargreaves 86)

Using a model developed to describe combatant behaviour, Brittain attempts to provide a rationale for her compulsion to experience dangerous situations. Because she 'knows fear', she should be better equipped to endure it than others who do not know it. She would rather avoid putting herself through it but believes that avoiding the dangers afflicting others would lead to the erosion of her self-worth. Brittain's biographers have argued that her willingness to become involved with relief organisations reflected the fact that the 'central tenet of her pacifism was the maintenance of civilized values in wartime' (Berry and Bostridge 389). To give in to her own fear – to put self-preservation first – would, in Brittain's analysis be counter to these civilized values. In 1939, David Spreckley, a PPU official, identified two types of pacifist. Some argued that 'one cannot escape the war machine' (qtd. in Ceadel, *Semi-Detached* 398), and would therefore compromise with it to a greater or lesser extent, and others refused any such compromises. As Martin Ceadel argues, Brittain identified with the former group (*Semi-Detached* 398). Viewed in this light, Brittain's work during the Second World War has complex personal and social ramifications, and her position was a deeply ambivalent one. She was not blind to this ambivalence, and writing did not always provide a means of resolving it.

The tension between 'decent conduct' and 'self-preservation' that Brittain identifies in herself is also apparent in the protagonist of *Account Rendered*.[17] Brittain goes further, however, in showing Francis Halkin to be split not only between his sense of duty and his fear of combat, but also between his desire, under the influence of his mother, to have a career in music, and his sense of responsibility towards the family paper-making firm. With his mother dead, Halkin hopes that his musical ambitions will be a way of memorializing her, and, indeed, when he does attempt to become a composer and concert pianist he does so under her maiden name, Keynsham. But a memorial act also informs the pressure Halkin feels to take over running the paper factory: his brother, who died in infancy, would have been able to take on this role had he survived. As in many of her novels, then, Brittain sets up a complex series of relationships by proxy or substitution: it is not surprising, in the context of Brittain's earlier work, that Halkin marries a woman whose twin brother has been killed in action in the First World War. Unusually, however, Brittain focuses on a male protagonist, and it is Halkin, rather than his wife Sally, who is at the centre of the action in the novel, and is its chief focalizing character, although paradoxically key points of the narrative are occluded because of his attacks of amnesia. This device has a pragmatic function in that it prevents Brittain from having to recreate in detail the experience of battle; more importantly, however, Halkin's amnesia provides the means for First and Second World War experience to be collapsed into each other.

Francis Halkin goes to fight in 1918. He is caught in a bombardment and when he recovers consciousness, a number of days later, he is unable to remember the combat. The last thing that he can remember is a song he listened to before going into action: 'gradually, as the stretcher-bearers tramped evenly along, their steps seemed to beat out the rhythm of a familiar musical theme' (Brittain, *Account Rendered* 35). This song, the Anglo–German composer George Henschel's 'Morning Hymn', was his mother's favourite. Halkin already associates it with her death, which occurs just before he first goes into action, and he now comes to associate it with his own near-death experience. After the war, as he anxiously waits to give his first professional piano recital, this same music begins 'beating through his brain' (83) and he collapses, unable to perform. This failure means he has to keep an implicit agreement with his father to go back to take charge of the family firm, although he continues to compose in his own time. By this stage he is married to Sally, who was a nurse during the First World War, and who, as the Second World War approaches, becomes increasingly fearful about what will become of them. The fall of France proves a climactic point for the couple; after hearing the news reports, Sally becomes drunk and an argument ensues. The 'Morning Hymn' comes on the radio, and the next day Sally's dead body is found in the river. Halkin, lying unconscious near by, is unable to remember what has happened.

The contrast between Sally's and Halkin's behaviour as the war approaches is marked. Sally is portrayed throughout as a melancholy figure, unable to come to terms with the loss of her brother. With the approach of the Second World War, she becomes obsessed with the possibility of both her own and her husband's death. Significantly, political events cement the couple's decision not to have children: '[I]t was 1933 which […] seemed […] to mark the final, irrevocable stage of their decision to remain childless. For in that spring Hitler had come to power in Germany, and the shadow of war, […] had begun once again to creep over Europe' (103). Not having children becomes both a means of expressing anxieties about the future and a signal of the couple's inability to successfully share their concerns about the past with each other. Whilst Halkin begins to dream about the slaughter he witnessed on the Western Front, Sally follows the progress of the war compulsively in the newspapers. Both are shown to be suffering from anxiety, with Halkin fearful of an intensification of what he saw before, and Sally subject to more amorphous fears, expressed through unanswerable questions about the future. Halkin's apparent drowning of Sally can be read as a means of finally coming to terms with his mother's death, a repetition that allows him control over that event and breaks his negative attachment to both women. Simultaneously, the problem of how to overcome the loss of a loved one in war, a concern in much of Brittain's writing, is here solved in a brutal fashion. Taking Sally's life not only ends her suffering but also ensures that Halkin will not have to witness her being killed in another way. It also means that, implicitly, war neurosis and sexual neurosis are collapsed into each other. A relationship begun during the First World War cannot escape its shadow, and is dealt its death-blow when the new conflict seems about to impinge on the domestic sphere.

Through the expert witnesses at Halkin's trial for the murder of his wife, Brittain presents an analysis of his behaviour that relies on anxiety. So, the explanation for Halkin's collapse at the concert, not apparently a life-threatening situation, is that his nervousness about his performance is 'related in his mind to the tension preceding a military attack' (208). In fact, if not life-*threatening*, his performance is potentially life-*changing* because of Halkin's determination to give up music if his concert is unsuccessful. Including this incident as well as Halkin's collapse on the battlefield means that Brittain can introduce the idea that Halkin (like Martin Croft) has a predisposition to such reactions. His friend and supporter Ruth Alleyndene reflects that Halkin should never have had to go and fight in the first place: '[C]ivilisation [...] evolves these highly sensitive, creative types, and then sets them to do the work of barbarism' (191). Yet the logic of Halkin's recovery would appear to undercut this analysis of civilisation as ultimately to blame. Expert testimony attests that he killed his wife while in a dissociated state of mind, and he is eventually found guilty but insane, and committed to an asylum. Here, during an air raid, he performs an act of spontaneous bravery and is apparently cured of his blackouts. After keeping a clear head during the raid, Halkin reflects:

> This time, at last, his peril had been real. It was specific, and therefore limited; it had nothing in common with the vague, huge terrors that had possessed him before the fall of France. The acute external danger that he had just faced had released him, once and for all, from the twenty-year-old conflict arising from another acute external danger the memory of which he had tried to suppress. (289)

Mastery of his anxiety comes through facing the reality of an event; paradoxically, it is facing the life-threatening air raid that provides a cure for Halkin. Notably, however, Halkin never recovers his memory of the other anxious episodes; at the trial David Flint suggests that it is too long after the events in question for hypnosis to be used to reverse Halkin's amnesia (215). By retaining these lacunae in the narrative, Brittain can create the sense that what has happened to Halkin are death encounters. Lyndsey Stonebridge suggests that, '[a]nticipating death [...] is not what traumatises the subject; rather, it is the unmitigated repetition of an experience that feels *like* death that overwhelms the ego' ('Bombs and Roses' 58). This experience proves, to Brittain, to be unrepresentable. Halkin's lapses into unconsciousness are perhaps a cover for states of mind that are difficult or even dangerous to describe; notably, Josephine Bell also avoids such direct description of the events that have traumatised Martin Croft.

The solution for Halkin seems to reside in a form of ad hoc behavioural therapy under the guidance of David Flint, who appears early in the narrative advising Halkin on the use of the techniques of industrial psychology at his factory. Martin Stone has pointed out that: 'The study of the occupational neuroses and the "clinical" approach to personnel selection and problems of industrial productivity pioneered in Britain during the 1920s drew heavily from the wartime work on shellshock' (247). Flint focuses on identifying factors in a worker's home life that may make him or her unsuitable for particular kinds of work, and Brittain implicitly raises questions about whether suitability for conflict can be measured in a similar way. Halkin becomes involved in civil defence activities as the new war approaches, and Brittain may well have read Wilfred Bion's essay in Miller's book, which advocates such activities as a means of 'engendering [...] a corporate feeling' (Bion 189) and potentially preventing traumatic reactions. Bion, who undertook pioneering work in group analysis during the war, argues that if individuals have a sense of playing a role in the conflict, and can grasp the reasons for it, they are more likely to be in some measure prepared for the shocks to come. This leads him to advocate a blurring of the distinction between combatants and non-combatants, recommending the establishment, for civilians, of 'some modification of the disciplinary framework that exists in a fighting service' (Bion 186). He therefore provides a psychological justification for the mobilisation of civilians that characterised the Second World War and can be summed up in the concept of the 'Home Front'. Brittain appears to acknowledge the difficulty, in this context, of making a clear separation between combatant and non-combatant. Halkin's civil defence work in fact proves to be another source of anxiety, exacerbating the effects of the existing split between his composing and his factory work.

In describing Halkin's attempts to come to terms with what war means to him, Brittain attempts a more complex psychological portrait than, for example, Hilton does, even if the emblematic weight of Halkin, conveyed through the trial testimony in particular, is ultimately too great for the novel to bear. One reviewer saw in *Account Rendered* 'the final collapse of the artist and the emergence from the novelist's ashes of the unapologetic propagandist' (qtd. in Berry and Bostridge 457). But although Brittain's pacifist beliefs do infuse the text, she does not, for example, make Halkin's music his contribution to the war effort, nor does she have him campaign for the ending of the war. As novel's title suggests, in overcoming his anxiety Halkin apparently achieves psychological equilibrium, with the lessons of the First World War being put to positive, humanitarian use in the Second when he decides, at the end of the novel, to go to Europe to assist David Flint in treating victims of war trauma. His involvement with the relief organisation, which will be learning from and improving on the treatment received by soldiers in the last war, is shown to be a way for him to, quite literally, work through his disturbances.

Halkin's musical ambitions, apparently abandoned at the end of the novel, are more than simply a way of contrasting the influences of his mother and his father on his temperament. Throughout *Account Rendered*, music transcends both national and temporal boundaries and is a means of communication that bypasses the ambiguities of the textual or verbal. Halkin hopes to use his musical talents to promote unity between the nations; the choice of the 'Morning Hymn' by Henschel, who was born in Germany but later took British citizenship, as an emblematic composition in the narrative symbolises this hope. In this respect *Account Rendered* bears similarities to the 1941 film *Dangerous Moonlight*, in which Anton Walbrook plays Stefan Radetsky, a Polish pianist and composer who is torn between raising awareness of the plight of Poland through his music and taking a more direct role in the war by becoming a fighter pilot. At the start of *Dangerous Moonlight*, Radetsky has lost his memory following a plane crash. His doctors hope that giving him a piano may lead him to remember who he is but he can produce nothing other than tuneless tinkering, until the hospital is subject to an air raid. The doctors, in the next room, realize that Radetsky has started to play his Warsaw Concerto, and the process by which his memory has returned is signalled aurally and visually as a close-up on Radetsky's face is superimposed on an image of a war-torn city. The music and the sound of planes continue as the ruined city comes into focus; a flashback to the fall of Warsaw, when Radetsky first composed his concerto, is thus introduced. Music is also used as a cue for an extended flashback in *Account Rendered*, when Sally sings to Halkin and, 'her voice [carries] him back into the past' (65). This device emphasises continuity between then and now; music is shown to have a soothing, almost therapeutic quality, and in this case, the song reminds him initially of the day he proposed to his wife. A signal of his cure is that Halkin can eventually listen to the 'Morning Hymn', which had taken on negative connotations after his mother's death, with no adverse results. Rather than rupturing his ability to experience, and therefore to remember, the song eventually serves to suture the gaps in his memory. Ultimately Halkin recognizes the naïve romanticism of the song, again allowing Brittain to avoid any detailed examination of the traumatic incidents with which it has been associated.

Brittain also points to the difficulty, even for those who are not amnesiac or damaged in some other way, of binding together past and present. So, for example, the flashback in which we learn of Halkin's interwar career is punctuated by intrusions from the present: 'A lump of coal crashed into the hearth, startling Francis for a moment from his reverie' (78). Later, we are party to Enid's reflections on her past; towards the end of this narrative, we are told: 'As she turned down the hill which marked the last lap of her journey, Enid jerked herself back into 1942' (274). What these violent re-emergences seem to acknowledge is the persistent irreconcilability of past and present. Brittain could almost be implying that we are all to some extent dissociated, with memories not so much buried as existing in tandem with our present lives. The relationship between then and now is not, even ordinarily, a harmonious one, but is always liable to cause disruption and pain. However, Enid's optimism at the end of the novel, signified by her pregnancy, overpowers the fears she has for her husband, who, after all, may not survive the war. It is also predicated on the belief that the inter-generational conflicts which have evidenced themselves in Halkin's life will not recur in the life of his child. Halkin embodies a type of recovery that remains beyond the reach of the majority of Brittain's protagonists. In her next and final novel, *Born 1925* (1948), the death of the Sylvia Salveson's second husband during the Blitz serves as a trigger for the release of her feelings about her first husband, killed on the Somme: '[S]he was weeping [...] for the death of love, and its obstinate refusal to rise again' (335). Like Sally, Sylvia is by no means an ideal wife: the fact that she continues to work as an actress after her second marriage is just one indicator of her proclivity for dissembling; like Sally, she is unable to find release from the cycle of anxiety, loss and mourning. There remains the sense in Brittain's writing that, whilst knowledge of past (and present) conflicts can be a source of understanding or even of hope, it can also, simultaneously, be a burden.

The spectral past

In both *Account Rendered* and *Born 1925*, Brittain expresses a belief that true recovery from both wars can only be achieved by the next generation; although Halkin might appear to have recovered, he will never be able to relive the years that were shadowed by shellshock. Knowing what to remember and indeed how to configure one's memories proves difficult, as it does for the combatants in all the novels I have examined here. Creating a narrative of past events that minimises the traumatising impact of those events is hard work for both protagonists and narrators. One text which powerfully foregrounds these issues from a civilian perspective is Elizabeth Bowen's 1941 short story, 'The Demon Lover', an uncompromising exposure of the ambivalent relationship between past and present conflicts. The novelists I have considered so far focus on damaged memory as a symptom of wartime, treating this from medical and psychological perspectives, but Bowen conceives of memory as haunting. Whilst for Hilton and Brittain, external stimuli of different kinds can serve as the key to a recovery of the past, for Bowen, such stimuli intrude on the present in unexpectedly sinister ways. Rainier, Halkin and Bell's Martin Croft are ultimately able to neutralize, or naturalize, a past which at first seems threatening, but in Bowen's story, this is not achieved.

Arriving to collect some of her belongings, Kathleen Drover finds that her London home, now shut up against the Blitz, has been rendered unhomely by its abandonment. The marks of her 'former habit of life – the yellow smokestain up the white marble mantelpiece, the ring left by a vase on the top of the escritoire', serve only to leave her feeling 'perplexed' (Bowen, 'Demon Lover' 661). The implication is that the former life lived in the house will never be resumed; the house is already haunted by its past. Kathleen finds a note, signed only with the initial 'K', on the hall table, reminding her of a meeting to take place on this very day 'at the hour arranged' (662). Her confusion and fear are then partly explained to the reader when the narrative switches abruptly to describe the young Kathleen parting from her soldier fiancé in August 1916. At this climatic moment, she is unable to see his face, and therefore feels as though 'she had never seen him at all' (663); he reminds her that although she is concerned about him going away, he will keep to their agreement and will be with her 'sooner or later' (663). Kathleen eventually receives news that he is missing presumed dead. She marries, and after a time can dismiss 'any idea that they were still watched' (664), a comment indicating that she has at one time anticipated the possibility of the meeting that now appears to be imminent.

The new war is what has made the lover's return and this meeting possible: 'her married London home's whole air of being a cracked cup from which memory, with its reassuring power, had either evaporated or leaked away, made a crisis – and at just this crisis the letter-writer had, knowledgeably, struck' (664). The removal from the house of objects which normally carry associations reveals the fragility of memory; without these things Kathleen's immediate past seems less pressing than the more distant past conjured by the letter. However, what is at stake here is not simply a resurgence of Kathleen's youthful love affair, but the fact that the retrieval of a once comforting present seems impossible; the description of the empty house at the opening of the story is already an elegy for the life that was lived there. Bowen could be implying a compounding of the losses of the first war by those of the second, but Kathleen is not simply experiencing a renewal of old grief, as Sylvia does in *Born 1925*. The descriptions of Kathleen's feelings towards her lover both on their parting and afterwards are tinged with ambivalence, signalled most powerfully by her inability (or unwillingness) to see his face; and she, albeit unwittingly, delivers herself to her former lover when she enters a taxi at the end of the story, only to find herself being driven off into 'the hinterland of deserted streets' (666) by a driver whose face strikes her with horror.

Jenny Hartley has suggested that this conclusion shows Kathleen 'possessed by the faceless demon of war' (148). Just as, in 1916, she felt that her lover was 'set' on her, so again in 1941, is she 'powerless to resist' (Hartley 148) the exigencies of wartime. That a relationship initiated during and brutally curtailed by the first war can reach its conclusion because of fortuitous circumstances arising in the second, would certainly imply a continuity of the kind that Hartley implies. But although Bowen does draw a parallel between the loss of a partner in 1916 and displacement from the domestic sphere in 1941, there are also crucial differences. If anything, the story shows that parallels between the two wars are factitious; the re-emergence of the First World War veteran is grotesque and inappropriate. This is not to imply that the earlier conflict should simply be forgotten; once again, what is at stake is the difficulty of remembering in the appropriate manner. Kathleen's inability to perceive her lover's face stands for her inability to understand fully the impact the war has had on him, but even looking at him from a distance of six inches, 'an eternity eye to eye' (666), cannot bridge the gap between them. The lover's return is belated but even belated understanding of the past is foiled by the disruptions of the present. 'The Demon Lover' stages a confrontation between civilian and combatant that serves to emphasise that the meanings of these terms do not remain stable across the two conflicts. Kathleen's home has come under attack; she has had to 'retreat' to the country; or at least, she is a position to be able to chose such a retreat. This blurring of the categories of combatant and non-combatant is also recognised in other texts I have discussed here, and it is one of the aspects of Second World War experience that makes comparisons back to the First World War less and less tenable.

A similar sense of the tension between continuity and change is evoked in E. H. Young's *Chatterton Square*, a novel published in 1946 but set in the months preceding the outbreak of the war, which plays on the relationship between the protagonists' fears, and the reader's knowledge, of what is to come. Piers Lindsay, who suffered facial and leg injuries in the first war, hears that Rosamund Fraser's sons James and Felix are going on a climbing holiday and reflects that his own holiday in the same place in 1914 was interrupted by the start of hostilities in Europe:

> 'I was having my first climbing holiday when the war started. [...] I can't imagine anything better,' he said, remembering the dusty smell of heather on an August morning, the gritty warmth of the rocks, the blue arch of the sky and the sheep calling, the perfect peace [...] But that peace had suddenly become ironical when, at the top of the little mountain, the climb over, some inferior being who had walked up and was scattering orange peel, gave them the news and, chiefly because of the orange peel, they had made no comment beyond a grunt. What unfriendly snobs they had been! (Young 109)

Young then anticipates the parallel that the reader is likely to draw between the two holidays when Paul, the youngest son, remarks, 'And it'll be funny if the same thing happens when Felix and James go climbing in September' (110). Lindsay is sensitive to the fact that talking about the previous war can seem like boasting, unaware that the visible nature of his injuries mean that his past is in any case never far from his interlocutors' minds, and 'now there was this new danger of uttering omens' (110). Towards the end of the novel, the potential of the past collapsing into the future, also implicit in Bowen's story, is given material form when Rosamund Fraser's husband Fergus, from whom she has been living apart, makes a nocturnal visit to her house. Fergus, another Great War veteran, seems to have suffered greater psychological damage than Lindsay, and Rosamund expresses guilt about her treatment of him: 'My own memory was too short. I didn't make allowances enough' (40). Fergus's visit is described retrospectively after he has left, adding to the reader's sense of him as a spectral figure, and it becomes clear that Rosamund will not be able to leave him for Lindsay as she had thought she would: 'she knew it was impossible to cast [Fergus] out altogether, to tell him she wanted to be free, now, [...] when the future was so uncertain [...] And once again, as she done so often years ago, she pictured him lying dead or wounded, with no one, this time, to call his own' (366). Where Kathleen Drover appears to have been punished for forgetting her lover too quickly, Rosamund chooses to remain loyal to her husband, despite the fact that she believes any reconciliation between him and their children will be impossible. Young implies that Rosamund's sons will only truly understand their father when they have experienced war themselves but underpinning this is an implicit acknowledgement that this war will not be – by the time of writing, has not been – simply a repetition of the previous one. Arguing with her son about his dismissive attitude to Fergus's psychological condition, Rosamund remarks:

> "I've never actually seen a really nasty sight in my life [...] legs blown off and faces pulped and bits of a friend scraped together in a shovel. And neither have you. Who are you to judge?"
> "Well, perhaps my time's coming," said Felix sullenly. (195)

Indeed, Rosamund herself, like other civilians, may not be exempt from such sights this time.

Conclusion

Evidently, there were ways in which it was possible to learn from earlier conflicts, both militarily and socially, but as many of these writers acknowledge, it was also necessary to recognise that such a learning process demanded that the particularities of the present situation be recognised. Both Vera Brittain and Josephine Bell, for example, show an awareness of how those working in the fields of psychology and psychiatry were attempting to build on discoveries of their predecessors, whilst acknowledging that the process of coming to terms with the events of the Great War had itself to continue. For many of the protagonists in the texts I have been considering here, the residual anxieties associated with earlier conflicts have to be faced before any positive engagement with current events can be undertaken; one war has to be finished before another can be begun. 'Finishing' is not here coterminous with forgetting, of course, and as I will show in a later chapter, the ceasing of hostilities in 1945 provoked further anxieties as servicemen reflected on the social and psychological difficulties that had faced their coevals in 1918.

Two aspects of the memory of the 1914–18 war are dominant in the texts I have been examining. Many writers show a sensitivity to the complex relationship between their personal understanding or experience of that war and its dominant cultural inscriptions: Isherwood, Orwell and Toynbee attempt to distance themselves, often through the use of irony, from narratives of the war that they now consider to be egregious but they nevertheless acknowledge the allure of such narratives. A second powerful cultural paradigm of the first war is figured by the shell-shocked veteran, who would seem to provide a counterweight to more nostalgic or sentimental representations of the war. However, in these narratives, the new war can itself paradoxically provide the opportunity for a cure, implying that only war, not peace, can solve the problems produced by war. Writing before the ending of hostilities in 1945, Brittain, Bell and Hilton perhaps intend to show that the creation of a satisfactory narrative of the last war will be proof against a repetition of a similarly traumatic experience in the current conflict. This is a message that has resonance on a political as well as a personal level. However, the fact that each of these narratives end with the protagonist set to face new and difficult challenges in the future points, implicitly, to the fragility of such a message during wartime. Individual memories can be damaged, culturally inscribed means of remembering can be tainted by ideological concerns, and, most importantly, memory can manifest itself unexpectedly and with unpredictable consequences. This often results in narratives that are uncertain in their presentation of the relationship between the past and the present, with disjunctions more prominent than continuities. Any attempt to fix past events and particularly past conflicts as a point of reference is problematized, and, as I will show in the next chapter, the issue of the damage that the current conflict might itself inflict on memory was also a pressing one for authors during the Second World War.

2
Damaged Minds
Crime and Detection

Writing in late 1941, the American historian of detective fiction Howard Haycraft noted that a ban on works by Agatha Christie and Edgar Wallace imposed by fascist Italy in 1939 was followed two years later by a Nazi party order for the 'withdrawal of *all* imported detective fiction from German bookshops' (312).[1] Haycraft elaborates a connection between detective fiction and democracy, suggesting that it is precisely the existence, in democracies, of the 'credo that no man shall be convicted of crime in the absence of reasonable *proof'*(313), as well as strict rules of evidence, that provides the underpinning of the detective genre. Detective fiction therefore depends on and reinforces those regulatory systems that are absent under dictatorship. The corollary of this is an increase in the popularity of detective fiction, within democracies, at times of 'doubt and distress' (321);[2] Haycraft believes in the power of these fictions to serve as a reminder of the civilized values that may appear to be under threat. Implicitly, then, the uncertainties of daily life in wartime can be subsumed by the temporary anxieties of the 'whodunit'.

However, the championing of democratic ideals is liable to be complicated when the detective plot is combined with elements from the thriller, a genre that usually has an explicit concern with national security and is often overt in its representation of violence. The 'amnesia thriller', a subgenre identified by Martin Priestman, will be an important focal point here. Whilst Priestman identifies Wilkie Collins's *The Moonstone* (1868) as one of the 'major early examples' (49) of the collision of detection and amnesia, he suggests that it was in the 1940s that the use of amnesia as a plot device became prevalent.[3] Loss of memory on the part of the main protagonist can lead him or her to be uncertain as to whether or not s/he is guilty of a crime, thus complicating both the manner of the narration and the presentation of subjectivity. Helen Small's comments on *The Moonstone* seem equally applicable to many of the novels I will be discussing: 'in spite of the plot's direction towards elucidation and recollection [the text] speaks more persuasively of the elusiveness of memory and the difficulty and hazardousness of recollection' (73).

Perhaps to a greater extent than other types of narrative, detective fiction also relies on the reader's own powers of memory and on their ability to sift through detailed information and retrieve that which is relevant. It is dependent as well on the memory of generic conventions.[4] In fact, a foregrounding of such conventions is prevalent in texts including John Mair's *Never Come Back* (1941) and Graham Greene's *The Ministry of Fear* (1943), and this tactic further complicates Haycraft's characterisation of the detective story as an essentially reassuring form of writing. Although a reader may be gratified at recognizing an author's intertextual references, these can also serve to disturb the illusion that the narrative is self-contained and controlled. In other novels I will be discussing, including Patrick Hamilton's *Hangover Square* (1941) and Dorothy Cowlin's *Winter Solstice* (1942), the act of detection takes an inward turn, with the psychology of a criminal or potential criminal, rather than the solution of crime, in the foreground. These narratives are not usually considered by critics to be genre fiction, but they show that the detective novel's concern with the ratification of subjectivity, especially as expressed through memory and memory loss, has implications beyond the confines of the genre.

Detective fiction and the thriller in wartime

Elaborating the relationship between the changing characteristics of detective fiction and the historical circumstances that such fiction might be seen to reflect, Julian Symons identifies the Second World War as a

> watershed [...], separating not only the world of housemaids and nurses from that of daily helps and *au pair* girls, but also the world of reason from that of force. The conscious assumption of the classical detective story was that human affairs are ruled by reason. Crimes were committed by individuals, small holes torn in the fabrics of society [...] The War forced upon [authors] the acknowledgement that quite a different world existed, one in which force was supreme and in which irrational doctrines ruled more than one nation. (148)

The war is characterized by Symons as dividing the world of the 'golden age' country house murder from the world of the thriller;[5] the works he considers from the Second World War are seen as examples of either the tail end of one tradition or the beginnings of the other. For Symons, the pre-war detective novel, based on the reconstruction of events leading up to the commission of a crime and the exposure of the criminal, gives way to the crime novel, which is often concerned with psychology and motivations rather than puzzle solving (173–4). Agatha Christie's Poirot concurs: 'the eternal *why?* of human behaviour [...] is what interests the world in crime today' (*Five Little Pigs* 64). Or, to use Stephen Kern's terminology, the 'whodunit' is displaced by the 'whydunit' (*Cultural History* 3). However, as Alison Light points out, even in Christie's novels from the 1930s, 'psychological explanation of crime and motivation is taken for granted and direct references to psychoanalysis are not unusual' (102). Gill Plain has also argued that the distinction between pre-war and post-war crime writing was not as absolute as Symons and other critics have implied; indeed 'the concept of detection as a narrative *raison d'être* was augmented rather than undermined by the parallel growth of the American hard-boiled tradition' (*Twentieth-Century* 21).[6] A model which acknowledges the hybrid nature of novels dealing with crime and detection in the war years is certainly best suited for shedding light on the texts I have grouped together here.

Graham Greene self-consciously deployed aspects of both the thriller and the detective story in *The Ministry of Fear* and his comments on the genesis of this novel illustrate how these two kinds of writing could interact. Greene explained that he began to plan *The Ministry of Fear* after reading a novel by Michael Innes whilst en route for West Africa:

> I had never cared much for English detective stories. With all their carefully documented references to Bradshaw's railway timetables or to the technique of campanology or to the geography – complete with plan – or a country house, I found them lacking in realism. [...] Michael Innes's book provided a surprising and welcome change. It was both fantastic and funny. [...] I developed the ambition to write a thriller myself which would be both fantastic and funny. If Innes could do it, why not I? (*Ministry* vii–viii)[7]

It is notable that Greene does not draw a clear distinction between the thriller and the detective story, apparently seeing one as a more intense, fast-moving and exciting form of the other. There are explicit references throughout *The Ministry of Fear* to detective and thriller writers, as well as implicit references to the conventions of these forms. Brian Diemert has suggested that the novel presents 'Greene's own movement from the classical detective story to the modern thriller'(177), with the Orthotex investigation bureau representing an outmoded style of detection that cannot tackle the international conspiracy in which Arthur Rowe becomes entwined. However, in using conventions from both forms, rather than displacing one form by another, *The Ministry of Fear* is similar to earlier 'entertainments' by Greene, such as *A Gun for Sale* (1936), in which the hunt for the assassin of a European statesman is initially overshadowed by, and then entangled with, a domestic crime involving counterfeit money. Like John Lehmann, Greene saw this type of writing as a particularly appropriate way of exploring the new, paranoid reality of wartime and indeed its aftermath.[8] Marc Silverstein notes that in the mid–1950s Greene explained his use of the conventions of the thriller by remarking that, 'It sometimes seems as though our whole planet had swung into the fog belt of melodrama' (qtd. in Silverstein 27).

Priestman also acknowledges that elements of both the detective story and the thriller can appear in a single narrative, when 'our interest [is divided] between solving a past mystery and following a present action in which the protagonists may confront a dangerous conspiracy alone, or step outside the law, or both' (2). Recovering lost memory, an important plot device in the texts I will be examining, often necessitates such a split between reconstructing past events and attempting to evade dangers in the present. However, the difference between the detective novel and the thriller is not only a structural one. The two forms have different genealogies, with the thriller having its roots in spy fictions such as the works of John Buchan and Erskine Childers, and a concern with issues of national security, rather than with a crime whose impact is relatively circumscribed, is also typical. As Allan Hepburn puts it: 'Detective fiction assumes guilt within the context of a home or family; espionage fiction assumes guilt within the context of statecraft and diplomacy' (25–6). However, particularly in wartime, the distinction between what W. H. Auden called the 'closed society' of the detective story, which presents a limited group of suspects, and the 'open society' of the thriller, introducing the possibility that 'any stranger may be a friend or enemy in disguise' (Auden 149), seems to be difficult to maintain.

Whilst Haycraft asserts the power of detective fiction to act as a symbol of the strength of values and social structures currently under violent assault, other critics have produced a more complex picture of the often problematic relationship between violence and death within these narratives, and the contexts in which they are produced and consumed. In comments which are intended partly to explain the post–1918 rise to popularity of writers including Agatha Christie and Dorothy L. Sayers, Plain attributes to detective fiction an explanatory and restorative power which also seems relevant to the 1939–45 conflict:

> In the excesses of death that characterise a world at war, the individual corpse is obliterated; it becomes impossible to mourn for each and every loss. But in detective fiction the reader enters a fantastical world in which the meticulous investigation of a single death is not only possible, but central to the narrative [...] Thus the fragmented, inexplicable and even unattributable corpses of war are replaced by the whole, over-explained, completely known bodies of detection. (*Twentieth-Century* 34)[9]

Susan Rowland also notes that, in the interwar years in particular, death in detective fiction is 'disposed of as unnatural, solvable', and, in an echo of Symons, 'a mendable tear in the social fabric' (26). A similar kind of logic seems to underpin Nicholas Blake's suggestion that the appeal of detective fiction 'derives from a conflict between the humanitarian ideal of the sanctity of the individual human life on the one hand, and the instinct of the blood-feud [...] on the other' ('School' 69). In this psychoanalytically informed analysis, detective fiction is a means of sublimating otherwise threatening instinctual urges; but the conflict Blake describes, in this essay from 1950, could also be an analysis of warfare, which similarly tries to hold two contrary drives – towards destruction and towards preservation – in balance.

Whilst both Rowland and Plain acknowledge that smoothing over the disruptive potential of crime is essentially conservative, George Orwell, in his 1944 essay 'Raffles and Miss Blandish', sees the prevalence of death and violence in the post–1918 detective novel as a symptom of much more dangerous attitudes. Noting that '[s]ince 1918 [...] a detective story not containing a murder has been a great rarity', Orwell focuses his discussion on the extremes of violence and brutality to be found in a novel more often considered as a thriller than as detective fiction, James Hadley Chase's *No Orchids for Miss Blandish*, which, although 'published in 1939, [...] seems to have enjoyed its greatest popularity in 1940, during the Battle of Britain and the blitz' (216).[10] Orwell identifies the irony underpinning a situation in which the violent world of such, often American, novels seems more 'real' than the violent events the reader experiences day-to-day. (As Orwell notes, contrary to popular belief, James Hadley Chase was a British writer.) What is being missed by such readers, according to Orwell, is precisely the correspondence between the 'world of gangsters' in the novel and 'the modern political scene, in which such things as mass bombing of civilians [...] are normal and morally neutral, even admirable when they are done in a large and bold way' (Orwell, 'Raffles' 223).[11] In fulfilling the function, identified by Gill Plain, of assisting in the process of mourning, detective fiction can mask the question of why that mourning is necessary in the first place.

Certainly not all wartime crime fiction evidences an explicit engagement with the kinds of issues I have been discussing here. Ngaio Marsh's Inspector Alleyn has an attack of conscience towards the end of *Death and the Dancing Footman* (1942), an example of the 'snowed-in country house' subgenre: 'Does it seem odd to you, Fox, that we should be here so solemnly tracking down one squalid little murderer [...] while over our heads are stretched legions of guns?' Detective Inspector Fox replies simply, 'It's our job' (267–8). Perhaps more problematic than Marsh's gesture towards political events here is the use of the war as a picturesque background in, for example, Jean Marsh's *Death Stalks the Bride* (1943), in which a dramatic escape from occupied Europe is little more than a prelude to a murder plot set in an English village. The overall effect is of two quite different novels being stitched together. In Ruth Adam's *Murder in the Home Guard* (1942), however, the murder plot is used as a means of facilitating the exploration, through extended flashbacks, of the wartime fate of a nurse, a young man rejected by the RAF, and an unhappy evacuee. Whilst in plot terms these flashbacks help explain the protagonists motivations, they also mean that the novel can be read as an analysis of the impact of war on a cross-section of society. Ultimately, the whole village, a 'closed society' in Auden's terms, is indicted, largely for its reluctance to acknowledge that it is in fact part of an 'open society' and particularly for its behaviour towards evacuees: Adam dedicates the novel to 'Those who sat tight in safe areas' (v).

An attempt such as Adam's to adapt the detective genre to new circumstances raises a debate which Orwell also touches on, and which has continued around detective fiction, and indeed popular fiction more generally: is the propensity of such fiction towards the preservation of the status quo or can it be resistant to conservative ideologies? In a comparison of the approaches taken by Franco Moretti and Ernst Bloch, Scott McCracken suggests that this is partly a matter of perspective. Classic detective fiction could be seen as serving to 'contain and subdue creative or speculative reflection' (McCracken 67) on the part of the reader; thus, Franco Moretti identifies a 'totalitarian aspiration' (Moretti 136) underpinning the Sherlock Holmes stories. However, Bloch suggests that detective fiction can be seen as 'prompting [the reader's] active participation' (McCracken 67). To some degree, different types of detection are being considered here. Moretti, in focusing on Holmes, draws on the 'rational-scientific model' in which 'the clues leave a trail of abnormality in the midst of a normal world' (McCracken 67). Bloch, however, draws on the 'intuitive-artistic model' often associated with Agatha Christie, in which 'the clues provide an opportunity to [...] reflect on that which goes beyond the rational-scientific model' (McCracken 67).[12] Like Plain, however, McCracken does not see these two models as necessarily succeeding and displacing each other; rather they can both be present in a single text, and can interact in complex ways. In a similar way, the overlaying of detection onto the more explicitly political scenarios of the thriller or spy plot can expose the ideological bases of detection itself.

Challenging identity in the amnesia thriller

As I have suggested, both the detective story and the thriller rely on the memory of key pieces of factual information as the means by which a series of events can be established or re-established, and in both cases, the central investigating protagonist acts as a filter, assisting the reader in distinguishing between relevant and irrelevant material. Whilst in the classic detective plot the reader may not be party to the reasoning that has led the detective to the identification of the perpetrator until the denouement, there is a kind of reassurance to be had from the knowledge that the cause and effect sequence of events and actions, and the significance of clues, will ultimately be revealed. The thriller typically depends more on the protagonist's ability to interpret events as they happen, rather than retrospectively, but here too the recall of the significant detail can prove crucial to the satisfactory resolution of the plot. Introducing an amnesiac protagonist necessarily disturbs this reliance on memory, but in the texts I am considering here it also has other effects, because it is not only semantic memory (the memory of factual information such as the name of the Prime Minister) and episodic memory (the memory of specific events or incidents) but also autobiographical memory (the memory for information about family relationships and life-history) that are lost. Whilst some authors might seem to follow Nicholas Blake in aspiring to create a detective protagonist who is 'like a piece of blotting paper [...] with no personality' ('School' 62–3), the loss of autobiographical memory in particular can lead to a profound disturbance of the role of the investigating protagonist. This disturbance has added point given the novels' wartime context.

The positioning of the reader in relation to the amnesiac protagonist is also important. In Greene's *The Ministry of Fear*, for example, Rowe loses his memory part way through the novel and wakes up in Dr Forester's asylum having been given the name Digby. The reader understands before Digby does that he is in fact Rowe, not least because the reader has the advantage of being able to interpret events in the light of the preceding action; Dr Forester is recognised from Mrs Bellairs's séance, for example. In other instances, however, the protagonist is amnesiac from the outset and the reader may not necessarily have an advantage over him or her. Margery Allingham's *Traitor's Purse* (1941) begins with her detective Albert Campion unable to remember who he is. Readers familiar with Allingham's protagonist and his girlfriend Amanda from earlier adventures will see that events in the novel reflect existing tensions in their relationship, and therefore have an advantage over both Campion and those readers unfamiliar with the prehistory to the novel. Even with such prior knowledge, however, the reader is liable to share in Campion's disorientation as he gradually pieces together a plot to flood Britain with counterfeit currency. As Susan Rowland has suggested, it is difficult for either Campion or the reader to establish 'whether he is a murderer or a saviour' (23), or indeed whether he is forming allegiances with the powers of good or evil. This is certainly an unsettling book, even for the reader not familiar with Campion from Allingham's earlier works, largely because the manner of the narration does not allow the reader fuller understanding of the protagonist's situation than he has himself. Julian Symons suggests that in *Traitor's Purse*, Allingham 'grafted the spy theme on to [her] usual detective story pattern' (231), but it is more accurate to suggest that Allingham complicates the 'detective story pattern', in which Campion would usually explore a crime which has already been committed, by replacing it with a plot more akin to the thriller, in which Campion is attempting to prevent a crime. He not only has to anticipate what might be going to happen, but, simultaneously, has to re-establish his sense of who might be on which side, by attempting to reconstruct what has already occurred.

As Rowland suggests, Allingham disturbs the notion that the detective will always be a force for good, because Campion, for much of the novel, does not know what to do for the best. Campion's amnesia is compounded by what Julia Thorogood has described as 'an extraordinary sense of oppression; a nightmare feeling of urgency coupled with complete vagueness about what it is that must be done' (229). She also notes that the cause of Campion's memory loss is eventually revealed to have been a blow to the head, and quotes Allingham's *The Oaken Heart* (1941), where the violent image of 'a blow on a numbed head' (Allingham, *Oaken* 289) is used to describe the impact of the fall of France in June 1940. Thorogood thus connects Campion's anxiety with the author's own disquiet during the period of the novel's composition. The notion of destabilizing Britain economically through the creation of hyperinflation, whilst it could have been introduced into a peace-time narrative, would have had particular piquancy for readers being warned to exercise economic prudence.[13] Similarly, the anxiety resulting from Campion's memory loss is shown to have a specific connection with the wartime setting of the novel. Unlike the protagonists of *The Ministry of Fear* or *Hangover Square*, whose existing memory problems are intensified by the war, Campion suffers a memory disturbance that has as its absolute cause in wartime events, but which brings to the surface anxieties that have a deeper history, such as those surrounding his relationship with Amanda.

For much of the novel, Campion is in fearful anticipation of some unknown future event, and this is compounded by his attempts to continue interacting with those around him without revealing his true state of mind. This concealment of his condition is necessary because he interprets an overheard conversation as meaning that he has killed a policeman, although he has no memory of this event: 'Slugging a policeman. He knew what that meant, whatever condition his mind was in. That was pretty serious. [...] Now he came to consider the matter it seemed to him that he had known policemen very well and had liked them' (Allingham, *Traitor's Purse* 9). Campion therefore knows what is morally right and wrong, even while worrying that he might have transgressed. He also has periodic glimpses of past events and associations, but he finds these a cause of further anxiety rather than reassuring. The repetition, especially early in the novel, of the figure 'fifteen' has a particular importance; Campion knows this is significant, but cannot remember why and eventually decides that it must refer to the fifteenth of the month. As he regains consciousness in his amnesiac state on the thirteenth, this adds a temporal urgency to his actions, even though he eventually discovers, while amnesiac, what was perfectly clear to him before: that 'Minute Fifteen' is the codename for the plot he is trying to foil.

An even more audacious use of an amnesiac protagonist, one which, like Campion's amnesia, is liable to provoke anxiety on the part of the reader, is found in Manning Coles's *Pray Silence* (1940). Manning Coles (a pseudonym for Cyril Coles and Adele Manning) had a success with *Drink to Yesterday* (1940), a novel focusing on the First World War adventures of the spy Tommy Hambledon and his protégé Michael Kingston. Hambledon was killed off in this novel, but such was its popularity that Coles decided to 'resurrect' him for a sequel, and his adventures continued to appear into the 1960s. *Drink to Yesterday* uses memory as an overarching structural device, as the body of the narration is an extended flashback from 1926 to Kingston's First World War experiences, prompted by the arrival at his house of an intruder who intends to kill him. Part of the reader's incentive is to discover why Kingston's life is to be taken, and by whom. This (detective) framework encloses a plot which has affinities with the thriller, detailing as it does Kingston's and Hambledon's exploits while working as undercover agents in Germany. In *Pray Silence*, memory is used to melodramatic effect, chiefly as a means of bringing Tommy Hambledon back to life but also to probe the questions of national identity and loyalty that are also important in the earlier novel. Following a present-day prologue, *Pray Silence* begins in 1918, when an unknown man is taken to a German naval hospital after being 'picked up on the beach, having evidently swum or floated ashore […] [H]e was wounded in the head' (Coles, *Pray Silence* 23). Unable to remember who he is, the man is taken for a German when he begins to speak in that language, and is given the name Klaus Lehmann by his doctor. He begins to map out the extent of his memory loss, in the process providing further clues for a reader familiar with *Drink to Yesterday*:

> [O]n one of these occasions Klaus heard a Naval officer call a seaman 'you insubordinate dog.' At that the little door in his mind opened for an instant, and he heard himself saying, 'Look at that, you insubordinate hound,' something to do with petrol, a dump somewhere, and men in field grey. The door closed again at once and he could remember no more. (Coles, *Pray Silence* 30)

Lehmann has a glimpse here of a minor altercation which occurs in the earlier novel, when he pulls rank in order to obtain enough petrol to get him to a rendez-vous (Coles, *Drink* 165–6). But of course, what he actually remembers is Hambledon masquerading as an officer. Lehmann is tricked by his partial memories into believing that he is actually German; a reader who is aware by this point that he is really a British spy therefore reads on with a double sense of anxiety. Not only is there the suspense of what might happen when his true identity is revealed; there is also the fact that Lehmann soon begins to work his way up the Nazi hierarchy and seems, however unwittingly, to be contributing to the renewed German war effort. Like Campion, Hambledon seems to forget which side he is supposed to be on, and could even be in danger of direct collaboration with the enemy. However, a careful balance is maintained in these novels between what is forgotten and what is remembered. Like Arthur Rowe, neither of these protagonists is left a blank slate, and, importantly, it is what they do remember that provides both the key to their recovery and a guarantee that they will remain on the side of right. In *Pray Silence*, Lehmann finds that it is not just memories of discrete incidents that occasionally return to him. During a discussion of the turbulent political situation in Germany in the immediate aftermath of the Great War, he also uncovers deeply embedded memories of democracy:

> Klaus drifted off, for something had just occurred to him as strange. A democracy based on universal suffrage was something Germany had never had before, yet to him it had seemed so natural as to go without saying. Where, then, had he been brought up? Was it possible that he was not a German after all? (42)

These sentiments are important, as they signal an inbuilt resistance to any non-democratic regime. They also present, implicitly, a diagnosis of Germany's descent into Nazism. Encountering Hitler in the early 1920s, Lehmann is 'unimpressed by the little man's mental capacity,' but believes that he 'could be useful' (54). Lehmann regains his memory on the night of the Reichstag fire in 1933, a timely point at which to begin subverting the Nazi regime from within. Similarly, in a key moment of revelation, before Campion has received the blow to the head that will restore his memory to him, he expresses an understanding of his social and historical situation that also encompasses his feelings towards Amanda, who has (temporarily) broken off their engagement:

> [A] fact came to him without recollection. He knew something suddenly as surely and clearly as if he had arrived at it by a long process of thought.
> He belonged to a post-war generation, that particular generation which was too young for one war and most prematurely too old for the next. It was the generation which had picked up the pieces after the holocaust indulged in by its elders, only to see its brave new world wearily smashed again by younger brothers. [...] Yet, now,

recently, [...] something new had appeared on his emotional horizon [...] a deep and lovely passion for his home, his soil, his blessed England, his principles, his breed, his Amanda and Amanda's future children. That was the force which was driving him. (115–16)

These reflections, which echo Lehmann's deep memory of democracy, mark a turning point for Campion, as he has hitherto been unable to assess just how important his investigation is. In both these examples, a recognition of the individual's defining values is shown to somehow transcend the action of memory. Lehmann's knowledge is 'natural' and goes 'without saying', whilst Campion does not even have to use his powers of recollection.

This type of understanding, which seems to exceed cognition, could cynically be branded as an unquestioning adherence to an ideology, the kind of unthinking behaviour that these protagonists are implicitly striving against. Notably, whilst Campion and Lehmann retain a strong sense of the values and beliefs they are fighting for, in *The Ministry of Fear*, Digby is initially confused when he starts to learn about the war:

[T]he fact that Paris was in German hands appeared to him quite natural – he remembered how nearly it had been so before [...] but the fact that we were at war with Italy shook him like an inexplicable catastrophe of nature. [...] Why, Italy was where two of his maiden aunts went every year to paint. [...] Then Johns patiently explained about Mussolini. (126)

Whilst Damon DeCoste offers a reading of *The Ministry of Fear* which stresses the continuity between the two world wars, with the second a repetition of the first, a distinction is drawn here between the continuing, and to Digby, explicable, predominance of Germany and the much more shocking involvement of Italy: Digby has forgotten totalitarianism. The current war is not simply a repetition or even intensification of the earlier conflict; there are crucial differences that Digby must relearn, not least because of how they involve him personally. 'A bad war, this', his fellow patient Major Stone remarks. 'Civilians with shell-shock' (140). Peter Leese has suggested that this comment indicates the extent to which, 'by the mid–1940s [...] in popular imagination shell shock was acknowledged and tolerated as a part of modern conflict' (160). The Major's remarks, however, compound the sense that, since the last war, the distinctions between combatant and non-combatant have been disturbed, that the rules of war have been recast.[14] This complicates further the kinds of assertions made by Campion and Lehmann.

The use of violence as a means of attempting to protect one's deep-seated values is another problematic consequence of the upsetting of apparently well-established binaries (such as that between detective and criminal) that the use of amnesia brings in its train. In *Drink to Yesterday*, Hambledon kills a scientist, Professor Amtenbrink, who is believed to be furthering the German war effort, only to discover later that the man had been approached by the German government but had refused to collaborate. This mistake is downplayed by Hambledon's and Kingston's superiors, who claim that Hambledon has probably saved the scientist from a worse fate, but it is an incident which serves to pave the way for Hambledon's, and indeed Kingston's, own death. It also proves to be important in *Pray Silence*. Although it was not the event that led to Hambledon's memory loss, which was caused by a blow to the head, Amtenbrink's murder is portrayed as a trauma, which the Reichstag fire, the precipitating event for Lehmann's recovery, then revives. The impact of the retrieval of these memories is compounded by the fact that Lehmann does not immediately remember his true identity as Hambledon, but instead first recalls his alias:

> He could feel the heat [of the Reichstag fire] upon his face. He turned suddenly faint, staggered, and clutched at the arm of the man standing next to him. [...]
> 'I – this is a frightful sight,' gasped [Lehmann], but in his mind he was seeing another fearful blaze, a country house burning among trees, and a dead man on the floor of a laboratory reeking with paraffin.
> 'Then I am a murderer,' he thought [...]. 'I remember now, I am Hendrik Brandt [...].' His mind raced on.
> 'I am not really Hendrik Brandt either, I am Hambledon, an agent of British Intelligence [...] and now I am a member of the Reichstag.'
> (58–9)

Thus the dubious nature of Amtenbrink's death is passed over, when Hambledon recalls it, because he attributes the murder to his alias Hendrik Brandt. Similarly, because Hambledon eventually understands the Reichstag fire to be a terrorist action of which he should approve, this effectively cancels any questions about the earlier fire at Amtenbrink's house. The reader who is familiar with the previous book is guided in how they should remember its action.

Following these revelations, Hambledon has immediately to reconceal his identity, and adopt what is now a pose as a member of the Reichstag. His earlier comments about democracy are perhaps intended to show that his allegiance to Nazism has always been uneasy, but now the true undercover work can begin. Hambledon decides to remain in position and work for the British cause and the remainder of the novel (the recovery of his memory occurs about a fifth of the way in) is an episodic account of his undercover work. Hambledon is able to convince in the role of Lehmann precisely because he has been living as Lehmann for the past fourteen years. He also has attachments to German civilians which serve to undercut his political intrigues by emphasizing the humanitarian aspects of his work: 'The [German] people were all right, they were fine, it was only their rulers who were so impossible to live with internationally, first the Kaiser and now this fellow Hitler' (63). Killing Lehmann off through the use of a substitute body as Hambledon makes his escape to England at the end of the novel, however, functions as a means of reaffirming Hambledon's true allegiances on the brink of the renewal of hostilities.

Whilst Coles thus attempts to retain a division between good and bad violence, as well as between good and bad Germans, in *Traitor's Purse*, the moral framework is established in a different way. After Campion has his moment of insight about the values he is fighting for, his anxiety lessens, partly because he has also been reunited with his faithful servant Lugg, who is able to flesh out the events surrounding his memory loss. Campion is implicitly framed as the 'superman' detective, capable of averting national ruin, a figure who can be seen as having reactionary overtones. However, as Susan Rowland notes, just as the dangerous 'internal otherness' Campion experiences when amnesiac is 'reconfigured into his double, the true villain and mad traitor' (Rowland 78), Aubrey Lee, who temporarily turned Amanda's head, so Lee also subsumes the negative aspects of powerful masculinity. Campion is positioned in the correct relationship to death, even if his final foiling of the counterfeit plot involves a violent action, the consequences of which are described in an unpleasantly off-hand manner. He throws a hand-grenade into the cave where lorries are preparing to leave to distribute the fake money: 'Injured men swore and died under their lorries, while others fought each other in their attempt to clamber on to the ledge.' (197) These men are to be understood not as victims of Campion's desperate action, but as victims of Lee, the scheme's mastermind, and any moral dubiety is therefore transferred from Campion to Lee.

Similarly, at the climax of John Mair's often parodic thriller *Never Come Back* (1942), the narrator, Desmond Thane, having escaped the clutches of the mysterious Committee, is relieved of his fears when he decides to enlist and feels safe in the anonymity of the army, '[k]nown only by a number, embedded amongst ten thousand others in a [...] distant country' (247). Thane finally feels removed from his old life, preferring to look forward to the future rather than back to the past; the two murders he commits in the course of the novel are seen as insignificant in the context of the war. However, there is a seed of doubt in Mair's comparison between these instances of killing: in the novel's final sentence, the narrator asks, 'what [...] were two small murders in the midst of so much slaughter?' (248) This rhetorical question throws the onus back on the reader to decide; it also closes the gap that Mair has attempted to establish between Thane as the good-for-nothing anti-hero of the thriller and Thane as an upstanding soldier. Thus, in attempting to distinguish between deliberate murder and the licensed killing of wartime, Mair in fact superimposes them on each other.

If Campion's amnesia initially brings to the surface anxieties and worries that had previously been kept under check, in *The Ministry of Fear*, Rowe's amnesia allows him to discover and then incorporate into consciousness a braver or even idealised version of himself: 'He was Arthur Rowe with a difference. [...] It wasn't all fear that he felt; he felt also the untired courage and the chivalry of adolescence' (169). Digby is attracted to particular values and types of behaviour that are not necessarily portrayed in a positive light, even though, in this section of the novel, he is, as the title of Book Two describes him, a 'Happy Man'. Digby appears willing to act in emulation of books including Charlotte M. Yonge's historical children's story *The Little Duke* (1845), a frequent reference point throughout the novel and the source of its epigraphs. Rather than feeling cowed at the thought of being involved in a conspiracy, Digby is prepared to best his enemy. His suspicions about Dr Forester's hospital having been raised, he undertakes a 'raid' on Forester's private rooms while the doctor is absent: 'the words "Pathfinder" and "Indian" came to his mind' (155). Whilst Brian Diemert suggests that Greene 'discredits the ethos of the romantic-adventure tale by contrasting it with the thriller world of war-ravaged London', (158) DeCoste sees the relationship between the adventure and the thriller rather differently. He suggests that Rowe's 'need to be the extraordinary man [...] allies him with those very fifth columnists who drive the novel's thriller plot' ('Modernism's shell-shocked History' 439), and identifies a continuity between the violence underpinning the apparently innocent derring-do of the adventure story and the brutality of the war. It is in recovering his belief in heroic values that Rowe becomes better equipped to deal with the conspirators on their own terms, but his attempts at bravery serve only to reveal that such a belief is misplaced.

Asserting that there are some things – such as faith in democracy – that surpass memory and therefore survive the depredations of amnesia is one of the ways in which the potential challenge to identity that amnesia poses is fought off in these novels. A fundamental allegiance to what is right can serve as a thread of continuity, as it also can in texts where a protagonist has chosen to adopt a different identity. Manning Coles acknowledges the impact that going undercover might have on one's personal attachments when, in *Drink to Yesterday*, Michael Kingston returns to London after the dangerous escape by sea that apparently causes Hambledon's death, reports to Headquarters, and is told to take some leave. He is initially at a loss as to where to go:

> Dinner somewhere, presumably, and later on a train to Weatherley Parva – he stopped in the middle of Whitehall so suddenly that a taxi missed him by inches [...] Diane, of course. Incredible, impossible, idiotic but true, he had completely forgotten Diane. He stood outside the Admiralty and tried to remember when he had last thought of Diane, somewhere ages ago, yes, at Ahlhorn, he had noticed the moon one night [...] Diane the moon-goddess, so far away [...] He had never told Hambledon about her and now he never would. (179)

Thinking of the village where he grew up reminds him of his Diane, his wife; his shock at his own forgetfulness indicates the tension between his identity as a husband and his identity as a spy. This is a more extreme version of the kind of psychic splitting in the face of trauma that can be found in other literature of the period. In H. E. Bates's *Fair Stood the Wind for France* (1944), it is only some days after the air crash which has left him stranded in occupied France with a badly injured arm, and after the tentative beginnings of an involvement with a young French girl, that John Franklin remembers his girlfriend at home: 'She seemed, as he looked back, an unreal person, as all experience before [the crash] seemed also unreal' (118). As in Coles's novel, the extreme and often violent events occurring on active service are the more real because the more pressing and this inevitably causes problems of reintegration into home life. Kingston's dissociation from civilian life serves as evidence of the difficulty of simply slipping from one alias to another, and his murder, whilst he is living as Kingston, in revenge for deeds carried out when he was living as Hendrik Brandt, also seems to imply the lack of control that Kingston has over these different personae. The choice between them is not simply his choice, and actions that appear to be consigned to his past, wartime life, have consequences that spill beyond the boundaries of the war.

Michael Kingston is unfaithful to his wife while living undercover, and Coles therefore seems pessimistic about the possibility of retaining such attachments in the face of a life of duplicity. It is perhaps not surprising that it is the less psychologically complex and certainly less personally troubled Hambledon who survives into next volume. Even where authors do appear to assert the continuity of emotional bonds across the gulf of amnesia, this assertion is often tinged with ambivalence. In *The Ministry of Fear*, Digby constructs a love affair that never actually happened with Anna Hilfe from hints she lets slip while visiting him in the hospital and when he comes to himself, Rowe determines that he will not lose her. His desire to protect her leads him to omit her brother from the account that he gives the police once he has escaped from Forester's hospital. He claims not to be able to remember who helped him, exploiting his loss of memory to keep the police away from the Hilfes. Yet this protective gesture is itself misplaced. During the climactic confrontation with Willi Hilfe, Hilfe reveals to Rowe the key event that Rowe has thus far failed to remember: Rowe's killing of his wife. Rowe ends the novel having had his memory restored to him, but instead of directing violence against himself when he discovers what he did in the past, he hands Hilfe back his gun. Allowing Hilfe to take his own life might indicate that Rowe is once again indulging in pity; Hilfe's death functions as a repetition of Rowe's wife's, which was a mercy killing. But Rowe also facilitates Hilfe's death in order that he can preserve, with Anna, the charade of being unable to remember his first wife. Rather than reconciling himself to what he did in the past, Rowe seems to condemn himself to return to the world of the criminal, nursing a guilty secret, even if he will be feigning happiness with Anna. This is perhaps further evidence of the lack of distance between the 'good' violence in which Rowe indulges and the 'bad' violence of the conspirators, and, indeed, the war. Rowe's supposed heroism does not exculpate him from what he continues to regard as his original transgression.

Conceptualising memory in the amnesia thriller

As I have shown, even before memory is fully recovered, authors will often allow the protagonist, and therefore the reader, to glimpse what has been forgotten. Coles and Allingham use similar kinds of language to describe this experience and their choice of imagery can help to elucidate how they conceive of memory as a process. Whilst democratic or patriotic sentiments may be known without cognition, memories of particular salient episodes from the past tend to be described in visual or spatial terms. When Klaus Lehmann recalls his argument with the naval officer, the image of a 'little door' opening in his mind and then closing again implies that that particular incident has been shut away and remains unchanged and straightforwardly recoverable, if only Lehmann could keep the door open. In some respects this is the case, in as much as both this incident and the description of Amtenbrink's death are directly quoted from the earlier volume, but what is downplayed here the fact that these events have effectively been remoulded by being placed in a different context. The imagery Allingham uses in connection with Campion's recollections also implies an understanding of memory as an essentially static and fixed repertoire of images and facts. When Campion finally remembers what part of the country he is in, this knowledge comes:

> not as a raising of the curtain of darkness which hung between the front and the back of his mind, but as a sudden rent in it which flashed a whole scene from the brightness within, only to close again a moment later as the folds resettled. It was all very confusing and alarming. (28)

This theatrical image is fitting in view of the fact that Campion is placed in the position of an actor having to improvise without knowing the plot of the play he is in. Like the image of Lehmann glimpsing the past through a partially opened door, it also implies that events are stored away in memory in a more or less pristine form. The problem is simply how to retrieve them from behind the door or curtain.

This simplified topographical model of the mind, in which the temporal aspect of memory is, through metaphor, displaced by the spatial, does away with the complications of a split between conscious and subconscious; all information will be visible and recoverable once the impediment of amnesia is overcome. Later, when Campion is able to tell at a glance how a man has died, he feels more sure of himself, 'as if the dark curtain across his brain were already practically transparent' (48). When not a stage on which he can watch his past being performed, Campion's mind is a cinema screen. Waking up after a packed evening, the events of the previous day, currently his only stock of autobiographical memories, return to him in a rush: '[E]verything he had discovered or experienced since he had awakened in the hospital bed sped past his conscious mind like a film raced through a projector at treble speed' (80). This reliance on the storehouse model of memory – a model which views memory as simply a place for holding past events or knowledge until they are needed, rather than as an activity which can transform and even betray – is perhaps a prerequisite for a detective plot, even one which posits memory's unreliability. Christie's *Five Little Pigs* (1943), in which Poirot reinvestigates a murder for which a woman was hanged sixteen years previously is a further example of this. Despite Poirot's acknowledgement that his witnesses will not remember 'bare *facts*' (73) but will subjectively embellish them, the solution of the case nevertheless rests on the reinterpretation of words and actions that can be remembered accurately even at sixteen years distance. Eventually, a complete picture, with no gaps, is revealed.[15]

Campion's recovery of his memory occurs about three-quarters of the way through the novel. It is only at this point that the reader is provided with the type of exposition that would more usually come at the start of a detective novel. His amnesia means that he has to start from scratch in piecing events together, and therefore functions as both a delaying tactic and a means of defamiliarisation. Information that the amnesiac Campion has been scrabbling to recover proves to be already known to him when he regains his memory, at which point the generalised anxiety that he has been experiencing is displaced by dread, which has a definite object. Initially he is unable to remember the events of his amnesiac period, but when he does, and his 'two minds and personalities' (180) merge, the details of the case are laid before him, 'a mad, uncomic strip' (180). To see Campion restored to his full powers and capable of smashing the plot is a relief for the reader, but his amnesia, and particularly the theatre and cinema related imagery used to describe his experience of it, is a reminder of the extent to which he is always having to dissemble. This is underlined by a number of incidents throughout the novel when behaviour that is in fact a consequence of his amnesia is interpreted by others as being part of his investigation. Early on, Campion's reticence when confronted by Anscombe's corpse is understood by the police officer, Hutch, to reflect his unwillingness to discuss a possible murder in the presence of one of Lee's dinner guests. Campion is thus interpellated as the detective even when he is unsure what exactly it is he is investigating.

Both Coles and Allingham eschew the use of medical discourse in relation to their protagonists' disorders. Memory loss is essentially a narrative rather than psychological problem. Introducing a medical or diagnostic aspect may not always lead to a convincingly realistic depiction of amnesia but it can serve both to complicate its narrative function and to provide some indication of the regard in which sciences of the mind were held at this time. In *The Ministry of Fear* and *Never Come Back*, suspicion seems to be the principle sentiment expressed towards the medical profession. Apart from when he is amnesiac, Rowe is haunted by the knowledge of his mercy killing of his wife. From the outset, he has expressed a wish for the effacement of the immediate past. Whilst the fête he visits at the start of the narrative has nostalgic associations for him, it also exposes the impossibility of retaining a memory of childhood which is not sullied by later events: 'it wasn't a girl he wanted or a magic ring, but something far less likely – to mislay the events of twenty years' (6). Once he has forgotten his own crime, Rowe can focus his energies on exposing wrong-doing at Dr Forester's sanatorium. The reader knows that this is, essentially, a means of continuing the plot that began before Rowe's memory loss; for Rowe, it is only when disburdened of the weight of his own crime, equated with his past, that he can take action. Unlike Campion, he is more certain of his own rightness when he is amnesiac. It is significant in this respect that Rowe, or rather Digby as he is known in the hospital, has in fact lost only the portion of his memory beginning when he was twenty years old. His memory has returned him to a point at his life before things started to go wrong.

Rowe loses his memory after being tricked into carrying what he believes to be a suitcase full of books into a hotel room, which lies at the centre of a maze of corridors. Shut away here, he and Anna Hilfe are deprived of light and contact with the outside world; this seems to be a locked room from which there can be no escape. A bomb in the suitcase resolves the situation, if only to deliver Rowe into the hands of Dr Forester and his assistant Johns. Johns explains the method by which it is hoped Digby's memory will be restored: 'When the time's ripe, I expect the doctor will give you a course of psycho-analysis, but it's really much better, you know, that the memory should return of itself – gently and naturally. It's like a film in a hypo bath' (122). Forester has motives for keeping Digby in the dark, or at least keeping him incarcerated, but Digby inwardly acknowledges that he has no strong incentive for recovering his past: 'He was comfortable exactly as he was. Perhaps that was why his memory was slow in returning' (123). Earlier in the novel, Rowe's desire to forget the past is expressed in terms that seem to licence the destruction wrought on the wartime city: '[H]e was tied to London. Perhaps if every street with which he had associations were destroyed, he would be free to go […] After a raid he used to sally out and note with a kind of hope that this restaurant or that shop existed no longer – it was like loosening the bars of a prison cell one by one' (16–17). Unable to excise the memories from within himself, Rowe here expresses a wish to see destroyed instead the external prompts that cause those memories to return. Isolated in the hospital, Digby is apparently safe from such reminders, insulated also by his desire not to remember. However, there are indictors of the violence that may be attendant on the return of memory. This is expressed as anxiety when Digby, at the hospital, recognises, but cannot completely remember, Poole, the man sent to retrieve the cake from his flat: 'he didn't know the man but the whole obscurity of his past had seemed to shake – something at any moment might emerge from behind the curtain. [...] [H]e was apprehensive. Why should he fear to remember anything? "After all, I'm not a criminal' " (144).

The language here is reminiscent of the theatrical imagery used by Allingham to describe Campion's obscure past, but in the context of Greene's novel, it also calls to mind the blacked-out room in which Mrs Bellairs holds her séance, and where Rowe was framed for a murder that never actually happened. However, whilst Poole's insinuating comments raise an echo of the fears Rowe experiences when accused of murder at Mrs Bellairs's, Dr Forester's revelations have a more profound impact. Whilst confirming Johns' earlier comments about a gradual return of memory being the best prognosis for the amnesiac patient, an annoyed Forester reveals to Digby that in an earlier case he induced a patient's suicide: 'Life, you see, had become too much for him – and loss of memory was his escape. [...] I lost my temper. [...] I told Conway everything, and he killed himself that night. You see, his mind hadn't been given time to heal' (166). Digby attempts to differentiate between Conway's memory loss, apparently the result of a desire to escape from life, and his own amnesia, produced by commotional trauma, but what is also exposed here is the lack of absolute differentiation between the two. Digby's condition seems to be evidence of Dr Forester's assertion that 'We make our own insanity' (167), illustrating that predisposition can in fact affect one's reaction to an external assault – Anna, after all, appears to escape the bomb blast unscathed. But Forester's threats of violence towards Digby raise that spectre of therapy as damaging rather than palliative. Johns' hints about Forester's 'martyrdom' (125), an incident which almost led to him being struck off, together with fact that the doctor has written 'a pamphlet for the Ministry of Information, "The Psycho-Analysis of Nazidom" ' (135) and has an interest in spiritualism are all means by which Forester's authority is incrementally undermined.[16] When Forester demands that Digby look again at the newspaper photograph of Rowe, Digby begins to recover his knowledge not of Rowe's principal emotional crisis, his killing of his wife, but only of more recent events: 'his head was racked with pain as other memories struggled to get out like a child out of its mother's body [...] his brain reeled with the horror of returning life' (169–70). The imagery here reinforces the sense of memory's return as a violent process. Seeing the photograph has a similar effect to being addressed by name at the séance; in each case, what is experienced is an address from without that he does not wish to assimilate and which causes a visceral reaction. Faced with his own image in the photograph, he struggles to connect this to what he perceives about himself; similarly, his returning memories, although a part of him, are alien.

As I have suggested, Rowe's recovery is more problematic than either Campion's or Hambledon's, not least because of what he eventually decides to continue to conceal. Although Rowe seems to switch from being caught in events beyond his own control to being proactive, this is not an unequivocally positive outcome. The notion of a protagonist's behaviour being dictated by their inscription within a plot (in both senses) is a common feature of the thriller. Campion's predicament when he loses his memory is similar to the situation in which, for example, John Buchan's Richard Hannay finds himself in *The Thirty-Nine Steps* (1915); he is caught in a plot that is not of his own making and has to work hard to make the transition from hunted to hunter. John Mair's *Never Come Back* foregrounds more explicitly an awareness of the generic characteristics of the thriller, but, like Allingham and Greene, Mair cannot completely strip away the danger, despite the debunking. On the run after killing, ostensibly in self-defence, his erstwhile girlfriend Anna, Desmond Thane is sought by the mysterious Committee, for whom Anna was an agent. Escaping the Committee's clutches, Thane takes the risk of going back to London, only to be recognised by a girl while walking on Hampstead Heath:

> For an instant he thought of admitting his identity; then his habitual secrecy, accentuated still further by his experiences of the last week, got the better of him. [...] 'I'm Thane's cousin, you see, and this isn't the first time I've been mistaken for him [...]'
> The girl was disappointed.
> 'Oh, what a pity! I did hope you were him. It would have been such fun if I'd found him. [...] haven't you heard? He's lost his memory and disappeared.' (Mair 156)

Taking his cue from this presumption, spread around by his former employer, Thane decides that feigning loss of memory will be an effective way of both explaining his disappearance and putting himself into the care of the medical authorities, thus avoiding falling once more into the hands of the Committee.[17] He hands himself in for treatment and successfully denies knowledge of his estranged wife and his reviled employer, Poole,[18] but he is then horrified to discover that the doctor to whom he has been referred is Foster, one of the Committee members who had earlier incarcerated him. The performance he undertook for his wife and Poole is recast by Foster as a symptom of deep-seated mental disturbance, his assertions of sanity taken as having the opposite meaning: '[H]e at first simulated loss of memory to conceal the onset of his delusions' (197). This scenario, in which the judgement of a figure representative of the medical authorities outweighs any assertion on the side of the patient, indicates some of the suspicions of psychiatry and psychoanalysis that were prevalent at this period. It also illustrates the tension, identified by Janet Walker, between the need for conformity during wartime, a need which could itself be promoted by some types of psychotherapy, and the need to assert one's individuality, also within the therapeutic remit. (Walker 42) This ambivalence towards psychotherapy and its role in the formation or stabilisation of subjectivity is similar to that evoked in *The Ministry of Fear*, where, again, the notion of 'cure' is questioned through doubts raised about the credentials of the practitioner.

In two minds: *Hangover Square*

In the novels discussed so far, the contrast between different states of mind is not simply about normality versus disorder, but becomes, precisely, a means of interrogating the grounds by which normality is defined. The presence of charlatan doctors such as Greene's Dr Forester and Mair's Dr Foster places in doubt the explanatory powers of the metanarrative of medicine; indeed, in these novels, as in *Pray Silence* and *Traitor's Purse*, it is violence, in the form of either a shock revelation, the witnessing of a violent occurrence, or a physical blow, that holds the key to recovery, rather than medical treatment. In Hamilton's novel, the intersection of violence, memory loss and war is configured rather differently. For George Harvey Bone, Hamilton's protagonist, there is no recovery, only the self-inflicted violence of suicide. The focus therefore falls not on revealing the identity of the criminal, but on the anticipation of the crime. Whilst in Coles, Allingham and Greene the period of amnesia is an episode which serves to complicate both the character's understanding of himself and the structuring of the narrative, Bone vacillates throughout the novel between two states of mind which, initially at least, seem to be discrete. The transitions between them are increasingly violent, signalled by a '*Click!*' that is variously described as being like the switch from a silent film to a 'talkie' or 'the sound which a noise makes when it abruptly ceases' (Hamilton, *Hangover Square* 15). Whilst in his normal state of mind, Bone cannot remember what has happened during his 'dead' mood, and in his 'dead' mood he is overwhelmed by the *idée fixe* of murdering Netta Longden, the unsuccessful actress with whom he is infatuated but who treats him shoddily. Implicitly, one function of his 'dead' mood is to counter the feelings of inadequacy that he manages to keep at bay at other times.

One of the subtitles to the first edition of the novel was 'The Man with Two Minds' and the novel's epigraph is a definition of schizophrenia from a medical dictionary: 'a cleavage of the mental functions, associated with the assumption by the affected person of a second personality.' (Hamilton, *Hangover Square* 6; Comrie 797) In both his 'normal' and 'dead' moods, Bone does display some characteristics of schizophrenia: his wordplay on the name 'Netta' (27), his lack of emotional affect, and allusions to what could be auditory hallucinations (158) could all be seen as 'symptoms'. However, Hamilton's depiction of a man divided between two personalities owes more to popular figurative uses of the term 'schizophrenia', which emerged during the 1930s, than to the medical understandings of the disease. The figurative use, to imply the co-existence in an individual of opposing attitudes, infects the medical meaning, where the 'assumption of a second personality' happens not in the way Hamilton depicts it but more insidiously, with, for instance, an apparently rational individual gradually displaying increasingly irrational behaviour. Thus rather than assessing Bone as a 'case-study' of schizophrenia, it is more useful to focus on the end to which Hamilton puts his protagonist's various 'symptoms'.[19] The split between Bone's 'Two Minds' is not an absolute one; for example, whilst Bone does not know that his alter ego is bent on killing Netta, after a particularly humiliating night out, he, in his 'normal' state of mind, reflects angrily that he 'could smack [Netta's] face: he felt he could kill her' (79). His 'dead' mood is a way of keeping at bay this ambivalence towards Netta, but only by channelling these sentiments into an act of physical aggression.

The novel is not only concerned with Bone's psychological condition; it is also important to note the second subtitle of the first edition: 'A Story of Darkest Earl's Court in the Year 1939'.[20] An anthropological ambition is encoded in the phrase 'Darkest Earl's Court', which is resonant of both H. M. Stanley's *In Darkest Africa* (1890), and the adoption of the imagery of darkness by late-nineteenth century social explorers such as

William Booth, in, for example, *In Darkest England and the Way Out* (1890).[21] A contemporary parallel for the work of men such as Booth is identified in a review article which appeared in 1951 on the publication of Hamilton's *The West Pier*:

> Long before Mr. Tom Harrisson trained an eye, sharpened in Malekula, on the natives of Bolton, Mr. Hamilton was exploring the jungles of Earls Court, Soho and Bayswater with the field note-book of an anthropologist, noting drinking and sexual rituals, class-courtships and the role of the scapegoat in urban cliques. (Anon [Arthur Calder-Marshall], 'Patrick Hamilton's Novels' 564)[22]

The subtitle can be read, then, as an attempt to place the setting at both a temporal and geographical distance from the reader's frame of reference. However, as the parallel with Harrisson's Mass-Observation project implies, the strange becomes familiar; a review of *Hangover Square* suggested that the novel:

> gives a first-class description of the behaviour of the people who had a chance to make a new world between the two wars, and, indeed, of preventing the second one; it will indeed have a somewhat nightmare quality to most middle-class readers who reached maturity after the last war – it will bring up some carefully repressed memories with a painful clarity, in all probability. (West 186)

The two aspects of the novel expressed in the subtitle, the study of the 'man with two minds' and the examination of 'darkest Earl's Court' on the eve of war are therefore not separable from each other, just as 'Hangover Square' itself simultaneously suggests both a physiological condition and, as a corruption of 'Hanover Square', a location.

There is, then, a 'definite relationship between [Bone's] private tragedy and the enormous public tragedy of Europe' (Widdowson, 'Saloon Bar' 129). However, it is necessary to consider precisely how his 'schizophrenic' condition contributes to the exposition of this relationship. When he is his 'normal' self, Bone is aware, and becomes increasingly so through the course of the novel, that he is stifled by his present situation and would be glad to change it, especially if this could involve establishing a long-term relationship with Netta. He looks back on his past, specifically on his association with Bob Barton as 'the happiest [days] in his life' (56). His hopes for the future are circumscribed by the routine of attempting to make contact with Netta in which he appears to be trapped for much of the narrative: 'Every morning, after breakfast, wet or fine, cold or warm, he made this trip up the Earl's Court Road to look at the house in which she lived' (57). He acknowledges that, 'filthy idea' though it might be, a war could prove to be his salvation: 'he might be conscripted away from drinks, and smokes, and Netta' (31). This sense of debilitating repetition, of the entropy of Bone's daily life, can be contrasted with his perceptions when he is in his 'dead moods'. In these periods, his thoughts are almost exclusively future-oriented and there is little sense of his behaviour being governed by habit. Glum reflection, dithering over whether to make a phone call or have another drink, is replaced by action, as exemplified by the section of the narrative describing his behaviour on the return from the unsuccessful trip to Brighton. Without having to consider his actions consciously, he makes the arrangements for the murder of Peter and Netta, leaving his luggage at the station, buying the requisite bottle of gin and so forth: 'It was as though somebody had told him to do these things in just this order. Who had told him? [...] He remembered. What a fool he was – forgetting. This was his plan. He was obeying the plan he had worked out in the train' (188). Whilst Bone in his 'normal' state of mind wanders through Earl's Court recalling past triumphs and humiliations and contemplating what to do next, Bone in his 'dead' mood seems unable to think and act at the same time. The planning precedes the action, which is then carried out automatically.

One aspect of this plan does connect to Bone's past, indeed to an aspect of it that he does not consider during his 'normal' moods. Bone's plan involves not only killing Netta, but also leaving afterwards for Maidenhead: '[W]hy Maidenhead? Because he had been happy there with his sister, Ellen. They had had a splendid fortnight, and she had died a year or so later. He would go on the river again, and be at peace.' (18) The plan to murder Netta could be seen as a means of achieving reparation for the loss of his sister by taking another life. There is a similarity here with Arthur Rowe's desire for London, and with it his memories of his wife, to be destroyed; where Rowe wishes for a physical dismantling of the city, Bone wants to remove himself (and Netta) from its landscape. As in Rowe's reminiscences and dreams about his childhood, happiness seems to be both temporally and geographically elsewhere; in both cases, it proves to be little more than chimerical. When away from London and moderating his drinking, as during the first trip to Brighton, Bone feels optimistic and more determined than ever to leave behind his old way of life. He recognises that departing from both Netta and her milieu is the only answer: '[H]e could never get away from her so long as he was in Earl's Court. [...] Netta *was* Earl's Court now' (216). When he eventually gets to Maidenhead, and sees that it is 'just a town with shops, and newsagents, and pubs and cinemas' (279), his disappointment is not only a consequence of the mismatch between his happy associations and the actuality, but also because of the realisation that it is impossible to simply leave Earl's Court behind.

Bone's suicide might seem to be a way for Hamilton to avoid the moral implications of the murders of Netta and Peter; Bone deals out his own punishment and so there is no need for the law to pass judgement as it has in the case of Rowe. The issue of the rightness, or otherwise, of Bone's actions is complicated by the manner in which Netta and Peter are presented. In one of the occasional passages of third-person narration not either focused on Bone or focalized by him, the reader is presented with a description of Netta that leaves no doubt about her worthlessness as an object of desire:

> She was supposed to dislike fascism, to laugh at it, but actually she liked it enormously. In secret she liked pictures of marching, regimented men, in secret she was physically attracted by Hitler [...] She liked the uniforms, the guns, the breeches, the books, the swastikas, the shirts. [...] And somehow she was dimly aware of the class content of all this: she connected it with her own secret social aspirations and she would have liked to have seen something of the same sort of thing in this country. (129)

Netta's attraction to Peter fits this pattern because his class resentment and snobbery push him towards violence and fascist beliefs also. Although Netta evidently knows something of Peter's background, for Bone Peter is a more mysterious figure. Bone does know that 'Peter, of course, *was* a fascist, or had been at one time – used to go about Chelsea in a uniform' (32),[23] but also considers Peter as a figure without a history: 'Who was he, and where did he come from? He had always been there: he had known him as long as he had known Netta. And yet he knew nothing about him' (37). Later, Netta is described as having 'practically no vision of the future, and practically no awareness of the past' (131). This sense of being divorced from historical or even temporal considerations, aside from her own desires, is something Netta shares with Bone in his 'dead' moods, and implicitly, it is when he is most like them that he carries out the murder of Peter and Netta. Like the 'dead' mood, the ideology of fascism attempts to set itself apart from chronological time and focuses instead on the satisfaction of desires of a mythic or transcendent kind.

Widdowson suggests that the murder evidences Bone's wish to return to the pre-war world of Maidenhead, and the need, therefore to kill 'the types [...] of the actual contemporary world' (Widdowson, 'Saloon Bar' 133). But Bone himself, although he may acknowledge it only sporadically, is a part of that world. The action of the novel begins at Christmas 1938 and the climax takes place in September of the following year. At several points in the novel, Bone contrasts his own attitude towards appeasement with Peter's and Netta's; although he reluctantly confesses that war might provide a means of escape from his current situation, he expresses dissatisfaction with the appeasement process: '[H]ow [Peter and Netta] cheered old Umbrella! Oh yes, it was their cup of tea all right, was Munich. But it wasn't his. He didn't know much about politics, [...] but he knew that Munich was a phoney business' (31). Bone is portrayed not as a war-monger, but rather as a sceptic. However, many of the historical markers in the text emanate from the narrator rather than from Bone himself. Thus, at times, there is a sense of Bone being situated, without knowing it, within a complex network of historical events. Hamilton here plays on the reader's awareness of the fact that as the events of the narrative proceed, war itself moves closer, and also appeals to the reader's own memory, particularly in a passage which begins as a description of Leicester Square on a summer day:

> In the middle of the square the effigy of Shakespeare stared greyly out in the direction of the *Empire Cinema* with its bright advertisements of 'Good-bye, Mr Chips', with Robert Donat and Greer Garson. [...]
> Fine, fine, fine ... Blue and sunshine everywhere ...
> Fine for the King and Queen in Canada ...
> [...]
> Fine for the West Indian team ...
> Fine for the I.R.A. and their cloakrooms ...
> Fine for Hitler in Czechoslovakia ...
> [...] You couldn't believe that it would ever break, that the bombs had to fall (101).

This coupling of events that still have historical resonance ('Hitler in Czechoslovakia') with those of more ephemeral interest (the fortunes of the West Indian cricket team) echoes Bone's earlier attempt to sift relevant information from his newspaper. The allusion to the bombing campaign carried out on mainland Britain in 1939 by the IRA indicates the extent to which violence of a military kind refuses to be contained within the parameters of the war.[24] Even Greer Garson and Robert Donat will eventually be pressed into cinematic war service.[25] What is not clear is whether the narrator is implying that Bone or indeed anyone else at the time should have foreseen or could have averted what eventually transpired.

The ultimate conjunction of historical events with Bone's personal crisis occurs immediately after his murder of Netta and Peter. While Bone is preventing the murder scene from being disturbed by creating a web around the fixtures of Netta's flat with reels of cotton, he hears Chamberlain announcing the start of the war on the radio: 'Oh, so they were at it, were they, at last! Well, let them get on with it – he was too busy' (274). As I have noted, both word play – like Bone's play on 'net' – and auditory hallucinations, often of a persecutory kind, are characteristic of schizophrenia; here, Bone weaves an actual net around the flat, and the announcement of war signals the collapse of private into public violence. The end of Bone's personal struggle with Netta and Peter, the 'blond fascist' (273), pre-empts the start of official hostilities. Yet his action is also, implicitly, belated. Weeding out domestic fascism sooner, or at least not tolerating it in the way that Bone does for much of the novel, might have been more effective. Bone does not kill Netta and Peter out of any sense of patriotic duty, however, but because of his personal desire to return to happy days in Maidenhead. Soon, the killing of fascists will become a licensed occupation, but Hamilton implies that to believe that their removal could result in the recovery of some lost, idyllic version of England is misguided.

Treating memory

In the novels I have examined so far, memory loss is an integral part of the plot structure, influencing how the protagonist and, in turn, the reader, interprets information and events. Even when it takes a more peripheral role, it is often an index of the anxieties arising from the conditions of wartime. In Patricia Wentworth's *Miss Silver Intervenes* (1944), an instance of amnesia is used to reveal a complex blackmail plot. Meade Underwood believes that her fiancé Giles Armitage drowned when the boat on which they were returning from America was torpedoed. When she meets him in the street in London it is clear that he cannot remember their romance, and she is initially unwilling to hold him to their engagement, but, as in *The Ministry of Fear*, feelings of attraction transcend loss of memory: '[Giles] had the most extraordinary desire to look after her, to put the colour back in her cheeks and the light into her eyes, yet as far as he could remember he had never seen her before' (Wentworth, *Miss Silver Intervenes* 24). Giles, improbably, has lost his memory not for matters connected with his work, but only for the events of his personal life. This leaves him open to blackmail when Carola Roland, a fellow tenant in the flats where Meade lives, claims to have been married to him, providing as evidence his mother's wedding ring, a photograph of him and letters concerning a divorce settlement which he cannot remember making. Carola was in fact married to Giles' brother, who was killed at Dunkirk, and this part of the novel's plot, therefore expresses, in veiled form, some of the anxiety surrounding personal relationships in wartime.

In other novels from the period, which I will be considering in Chapter 4, a soldier believed dead proves to be alive, and his return causes trouble at home. Wentworth herself used a variation of this type of plot in *The Traveller Returns* (1948) when a woman thought to have been killed in France returns to claim her inheritance, but later proves to be an impostor. Whilst containing few direct references to the war, Josephine Tey's *Brat Farrar* (1949) also centres on a false claim to inheritance, with Brat's performance succeeding because he appears to 'remember' events from and information about his childhood, when in fact he is remembering facts that he has been told by an accomplice close to the family. Agatha Christie uses a similar device in *Taken at the Flood* (1948) where a woman who says she survived the destruction of her home in the blitz lays claim to an inheritance, only to be exposed as the housemaid, who has been exploiting the fact that her late mistress never met the relatives she is now attempting to swindle. Carola's actions in *Miss Silver Intervenes* also illustrate the fragility and uncertainty of wartime relationships, raising the possibility that, despite his assertions to the contrary, Giles, with whom Meade had a whirlwind romance, might indeed have secrets in his past. Giles's recovery of his memory is not depicted directly. After a confrontation with Carola he wakes up in the middle of the night able to remember the truth: 'I suppose it was really the shock of this business that brought my memory back. They all said a shock might do it, and by gum it did' (105). Carola, then, inadvertently effects Giles's cure, just as Dr Forester effects Digby's. This event occurs about halfway through the novel and the focus shifts to the central mystery, which involves Carola herself being blackmailed. Her marriage to Giles's brother was in fact bigamous, and there is therefore a kind of symmetry between Carola and Giles, with Carola wanting to forget her earlier attachments and Giles wanting to remember his. Memory thus takes on an ethical role, serving as a guarantee of personal integrity and casting in a new light Carola's question to Meade: 'Want to keep your memories? I don't. Fun while they last, but what's the good of remembering them?' (58) Carola wants to assert a kind of selectivity and control over memory which is both ethically dubious, and, ultimately, untenable.

Although Nicholas Blake did not make such extensive use of amnesia in his detective plots as the writers I have been discussing so far, his work generally shows both a fuller understanding of psychoanalysis and psychology and a similar concern with the potential manipulation of memory. In *The Case of the Abominable Snowman* (1941), Nigel Strangeways, Blake's investigating protagonist, attempts to challenge the negative stereotype of the psychoanalyst, and in particular the use of hypnotism, commenting of another character: 'Hereward's very naïf. He connects hypnotism with shady practices in back streets, or Doctor Mabuses – a black art to get possession of one's victim, soul and body' (64). Strangeways here refers to the Fritz Lang's *Dr Mabuse the Gambler* (1922), which, along with Robert Wiene's *The Cabinet of Dr Caligari* (1919), provided a cinematic paradigm of the deranged medical practitioner.[26] Later, however, Dr Bogan does indeed prove to be a charlatan, who, according to the narrator, exploits the gullibility of 'rich neurotics [...] ready to jump at a new craze' (168). Whilst in this and other novels, Blake asserts the utility of such psychoanalytic concepts as the Oedipus complex or repression, he falls back here on the stereotype of the dishonest practitioner, also taking the opportunity to criticise the doctor's over-credulous patients.

These and other examples of detective fiction are predicated on the idea that past events must be recalled in a timely and appropriate manner in order that present events might be elucidated. For the most part, the potential emotional sting of the recovery of memory is drawn because the regaining of memory will have a positive outcome both for the investigation and for the amnesiac individual, but in some instances, as in *The Ministry of Fear*, the potentially negative aspects of recall are exposed. Problematising memory in this way reveals the drawbacks in detective fiction's reliance on memory as the instrument of truth and is partly for this reason that a text like *The Ministry of Fear* has an ambivalent relationship to the genre. In Greene's novel, detection begins to take an inward path; the removal or sidelining of the detective figure and a refocusing of the plot on a protagonist's exploration of his or her memories is characteristic of much late-twentieth-century fiction, but it is also a strand of 1940s writing. Whilst Henry Green's *Caught* (1943), does not engage with crime fiction in the self-referential manner of *The Ministry of Fear*, it uses the memory (and forgetting) of crime as a means of exposing the complexity of wartime experience. Green frequently either displaces present perception by later remembrance or supplements one with the other. This can both signal a shift in the chronology of the narrative, and show how intervening events supersede earlier experience, as in this example: 'The next day Richard gave [his son] a bike Dy had bought for him. Many months later, at the height of the first Blitz, Roe could not remember how the child was given this present' (Green, *Caught* 22). Separated from his son by his job as an Auxiliary Fireman, Roe considers the impact of their being apart through reference to their now divergent memories: 'The boy would be building up memories peculiar to himself. The father had his own of that kind. He could not add to them' (30). As when Roe attempts to describe the effects of a raid to his sister Dy (177–8), he recognises that memory is what keeps us apart from each other; it is that which, especially in wartime, cannot be communicated effectively.

Similarly, Roe can only partially understand how his son might have felt when abducted from a department store by the sister of Roe's fire-service colleague Pye. This crime shadows the relationship between Roe and Pye, but another crime also surfaces in the course of the narrative. When Pye goes to the asylum to discuss his sister Prudence's condition with her doctor, the doctor suggests that a cure can only be achieved if the root of her illness, some traumatic event in her childhood, can be identified. The doctor gives his own excessively lucid and apparently unemotional account of the consequences for his own sister and himself of an accident she had in childhood, an account perhaps intended to serve as a model for Pye. However, when the doctor asks whether there were any 'boys round' (140) when his sister was young, Pye returns, as though by default, to the memory of a guilty sexual encounter from his own youth: '[Pye] saw it again as though it was before his eyes, which he now tried to draw away from the doctor's. He had never before thought of his sister's creeping separate from his own with Mrs Lane's little girl. In a surge of blood, it was made clear, false, that it might have been his own sister he was with that night' (140). None of this can be admitted to the doctor, despite his assertion that Pye's sister is 'just at a stage when a clue will make all the difference' (142). Pye does not see how admitting his own crime could facilitate his sister's recovery, and can only remain silent; he eventually takes his own life. Explaining Pye's suicide, Roe remarks that 'it was sex finished him off, and sex arising out of his authority' (196), believing that Pye had been living beyond his means in order to entertain women, but unbeknownst to Roe, his words could also refer to Pye's relations with his sister. Pye's suicide could be seen as a kind of personally administered rough justice but the potential effects of his actions on his sister, or of her actions on Roe's son, remain unspoken. Dorothy Cowlin's *Winter Solstice* (1942) has an apparently more positive outcome, but, like Green, Cowlin is concerned with establishing how an appropriate relationship to the past might be constituted when a crime has apparently been committed. This novel, accorded little notice on its publication, has received scant critical attention since, but in many respects, it is representative of the turn that the amnesia thriller would take in the later twentieth century. Here, amnesia is not a misfortune that befalls the central protagonist, but a constitutive factor; the recovery of lost memory is not a merely a means of complicating the plot; it *is* the plot. Alexandra Gollen, has been paralysed since the age of twelve following an unspecified illness in the wake of the death of her younger brother, Nick. For part of the narrative, it appears to the reader that she may be suppressing her murder of this boy, although his death eventually proves to have been an accident. Alexandra retains no memory of events before Nick's death; when Winifred, a young neighbour, comes to visit and tries to prompt Alexandra into remembering Nick, Alexandra feigns memory in order not to disappoint the other girl: she gives 'a creditable imitation of a suddenly returned memory' (Cowlin 33). Alexandra attempts to form memories of her brother retrospectively by 'carefully [collecting] all data concerning him and [storing] it in her clear, if scantily furnished mind, in order to deceive people into thinking that she *could* recall him' (33). This, however, like Brat Farrar's dissembling, is little more than a simulacrum of memory. Alexandra is constrained to relearn information about her brother in an emotionally void manner. Cowlin uses a model of memory based on repression; negative events from the past are presented as being unavailable to consciousness, with Alexandra's physical symptoms providing a shield against their recovery.

In this first part of the novel, a female visitor shows an interest in Alexandra's 'case' and suggests to Alexandra's older brothers that the girl's paralysis might indeed be a symptom: 'Sure she's not *shamming* [...]? I'm not suggesting *deliberate* sham. There's such a thing as sub-conscious shamming, you know. But there – Freud might never have existed so far as the doctors are concerned' (28). Intimidated by these forward comments, the brothers soon forget them, but this 'rather penetrating' (29) diagnosis is endorsed by the narrator and provides a clue to the means of Alexandra's recovery. Having been in a condition of stasis from the age of twelve, Alexandra will be unable to achieve maturity, and to escape from her atemporal world, until she returns to the originary trauma, the cause of her amnesia and paralysis. Alexandra's recovery is prompted by her infatuation with Iris Young whose free spirit (symbolized by the fact that she is an amateur aviatrix) provokes her to feel dissatisfied with her life. An intense desire to see a parade that she can hear passing in the street prompts her into the physical effort that overcomes her body's paralysis:

> Trombones ripped the world into scarlet tatters of glory; trumpets pierced it with silver lightning; human laughter fell like an orgy of smashed crockery […] Everything in the world was churning past that darkened window – but she must lie in bed, unable even to see it pass. […] [S]he dragged her body, trailing its shrunken, all but useless legs behind her, in an agony of sweat and heart-thuds, across the limitless flat world of worn linoleum. (82–3)

Notably, the manner in which the parade is described makes it seem frightening, apocalyptic almost, rather than beguiling. This description foreshadows the psychological struggle that Alexandra must undergo even as she regains her physical health; it also indicates the threatening nature of the outside world, despite the initial pleasures that it might provide.

The physical pain that Alexandra endures is matched by the violence of the recovery of her memory. Whereas in other novels I have considered, violence is often the spur to the end of a bout of amnesia, Alexandra's recovered memories not only manifest themselves in a violent way but are memories of violence that she witnessed as a child. Once she is able to leave the house, she goes into the town with Iris and her surroundings prompt the re-emergence of semantic memories; thus, for instance, despite being unable to consciously recall ever having taken a tram ride, Alexandra knows that she prefers to sit upstairs. Later, without conscious effort, she can recall a short cut that she took as a child, and although she is pleased at the reawakening of her knowledge of her surroundings, other memories give Iris pause:

> They stopped for a moment to look down at the river, fifty feet below, where slimy dark rocks and sooty warehouses made a narrow gorge for thick yellowish water, from which crept up a foul, chemical-and-sewerage smell which proved to be a key to a third portion of Alexandra's walled-up memory.
> 'Oh look!' she cried […] 'This is where we used to come to see the rats!' It was quite evident from her delighted tone that to see the rats had been one of the outstanding joys of her childhood.

> And that, mused Iris, as they resumed their way, that surely implied things about Alexandra's childhood that were not pleasant to think upon. Perhaps after all it would be as well not to stir the stagnant water of her memory, lest something worse than rats, some putrefying or obscene horror, should be disclosed. (95)

Iris seems here to consider the possibility that Alexandra might have been abused by her father, and that it would be better for her to remain in ignorance of this; certainly other images used in connection with Alexandra's recovery of memory, also suggest abjection: '[F]ragments of those blank thirteen years began to be vomited from time to time into her present memory [...] [Incidents] would turn up, like skulls in an old battlefield' (114; 185). It transpires that Alexandra's father was an alcoholic and that she witnessed his physical brutality towards her mother; but what her amnesia and paralysis have been masking is not an incident of violence towards her own person but what she subconsciously believes to be her own 'crime', her responsibility for the death of her baby brother. Her confused feelings towards a neighbour's baby are eventually decoded as signifying the ambivalence she felt towards Nick when obliged to take charge of him as a child. On a winter outing, a toboggan ride has a visceral effect on her; she falls unconscious and is transported back, finally, to the scene of Nick's death. He, it is revealed, fell out of her arms and under the wheels of a car when they were tobogganing on a cobbled street in the middle of town.

Alexandra is freed of any blame for the death but her dramatic reaction to it is itself diagnosed as symptomatic of conflicts already existing at the time of the accident: 'the normal healthy-minded sister would have got over it a lot sooner' (214). Although Alexandra seems to have found a soul mate by the end of the novel, Cowlin does not imply that the entry into adulthood will now be an easy one for her. The novel concludes with Alexandra and her new friend Donald out in the countryside together, but they can only be tentative in declaring their feelings towards each other and it is notable that one landmark they reach on their walk is a ruined cottage. Although there may be green shoots around it, the cottage appears as an emblem of Alexandra's damaged domestic circumstances, as well as foreshadowing the destruction of property that the coming war, a muted presence in the novel, will bring. Alexandra might have hope for the future, but the reader knows that re-entering the world will soon necessitate engaging in a conflict of a different kind.

Conclusion

Stephen Kern has argued that, through the course of the twentieth century, novels dealing with murder reflect the increasing complexity of available causal explanations, with novelists reflecting new developments in science and criminology in their murder plots. Kern identifies in particular a shift from the 'delightfully arrogant' (*Cultural History* 104) explanations of Sherlock Holmes, based on clearly identifiable and rational links between cause and effect, and modern texts that reflect a more complex world-view. During the twentieth century, there is an increasing recognition that 'personal identity evolves in time not additively, as a sum of memories, but psychodynamically, as the outcome of traumas and crises involving challenges to the autonomy of a self that appears to be increasingly fragmented and uncertain' (Kern, *Cultural History* 260). The novelists I have been discussing here recognise the potential impact of the events of wartime on the individual's autonomy, and in particular the extent to which the 'traumas and crises' of war necessitate a reconsideration of traditional plots. Amnesia, and the recovery of memory, can serve as a means of representing the fragmentation and uncertainty of wartime experience, and I have suggested that even where the gaps in memory (and therefore the plot) are eventually filled, there is often residual anxiety about the viability of such an urge to completion. Detective fiction might have traditionally served as a means of encompassing or controlling the apparently uncontrollable – violence, death – but in wartime, this function becomes both more urgent and more difficult.

3
Remembering the Country

In Alberto Cavalcanti's film *Went the Day Well?* (1943), the inhabitants of the village of Bramley End are visited by men of the Royal Engineers on manoeuvres in the area. From the lady of the manor to the postmistress, the villagers provide the army with billets and assistance, until a series of small clues begins to arouse suspicion: the rough manners and physical brutality of some of the soldiers attract attention; the vicar's daughter Nora (Valerie Taylor) notices that one of the soldiers writes his sevens 'the continental way'; an inquisitive evacuee finds a bar of chocolate embossed with the word 'Schokolade'. Eventually, the truth is revealed. These are German officers in disguise, sent to prepare the way for the invasion. They have had inside help from Oliver Wilsford (Leslie Banks), an apparently respectable villager, and, taking Bramley End hostage, they respond with violence to attempts to contact the outside world. Eventually, however, help arrives in the form of the Home Guard from a neighbouring village, and a pitched battle at the manor house sees off the threat of invasion.[1]

Although some contemporary reviewers felt that the film had missed its moment, with the height of the invasion scare having passed by the time of its release, what remains shocking is the sudden eruption of violence in such apparently idyllic surroundings. Cavalcanti gives a semi-documentary feel to the ambush and murder of the Bramley Home Guard contingent in a country lane, presenting the sequence in a concise series of brutal close-ups. Meanwhile, expressionist-influenced camera work underlines the disjunctive nature of scenes in which a domestic space becomes the site of violent action. Shot from a low angle within a shadowy and cramped *mise en scène*, the postmistress Mrs Collins (Muriel George), who is under guard to prevent her from using the post office switchboard to contact the outside world, hits her captor over the head with an axe while he sits at her kitchen table, only to be bayoneted by another soldier before she can get her message through. Similarly, in the final sequence, when soldiers stalk across the manicured lawns of the manor house to be met by gunfire, the women of the village are not slow to take up arms, with Nora shooting Oliver Wilsford at close range when she understands that her beau has been aiding the Germans all along. Such violence can be read either as emblematic of the extremes to which ordinary people would go to defend their home, or as a warning of the true meaning of 'total war'. The villagers of Bramley End might be using violence as a last resort, but they are nevertheless having to match the brute force of their invaders with equally brute force of their own.

There is another aspect of the film's structure which should be mentioned, however. It opens with a prologue delivered straight to camera by the verger (Mervyn Johns) who appears within the body of the film in a younger incarnation. Stressing the ordinariness of Bramley End, the verger notes its one unusual feature: the presence in the churchyard of a memorial which bears the names of a number of German soldiers: 'They wanted England these Jerries did, and this is the only bit they got.' At the end of the film, this prologue is matched with an epilogue, which again dwells on the village's memorial to the Germans. Thus although the action of *Went the Day Well?* is clearly marked as taking place in 1942 – when the film was made – it is framed by the prologue and epilogue as being in the remote past. The conceit of this frame is that the war is over, and the Germans defeated. Penelope Huston suggests that this device could be interpreted as a means of 'soothing [the] audience before getting down to the business of unsettling them' (12).[2] Certainly, framing the war as past, as a series of events that has already been memorialised, is a conceit that would appear to have straightforwardly reassuring intentions. Earlier in the film, a brief discussion between Oliver Wilsford and the German Commanding Officer, Ortler (Basil Sydney), takes place in front of a plaque in the church wall commemorating those who died in the 1914–18 war. That there will have been English dead, as well as Germans, to be commemorated at the end of the present conflict is a side issue here; what is important is that the church, the churchyard, and the village itself, embodied by the now aged verger, will still persist.[3]

The apparently enduring qualities of the English countryside are an important touchstone for many writers, but just as *Went the Day Well?* uncovers the potential for violence in the English village, so other representations are often ambivalent rather than simply nostalgic. I will examine the relationship between nostalgia and pastoral and will suggest why the depiction of the English countryside has particular potential for the production of writing that looks to the past. A selection of factual and semi-factual texts by writers including Margery Allingham and H. V. Morton will illustrate how, as in *Went the Day Well?*, attempts were made while the war was still in progress to assert the continuities of the countryside by emphasising its traditions, history and natural cycles. Through a combination of wartime chronicle and personal reminiscence, writers such as these attempt to champion the country as the repository for values that the war should be defending. The war thus serves to refocus ongoing debates about the past – and by extension, the future – of the countryside. Whilst Allingham's *The Oaken Heart* (1941) in particular takes the village as its focus, other writers centre instead on a different aspect of country life, the country house. This might be the seat of aristocrats or an upper-middle-class home, but in either case a reminiscing narrator or protagonist will often reflect on the effect that contact with such a household has had on their life. The house is rarely the site of unequivocal innocence or pleasure, though, and a critique of what it appears to represent will often be embedded in the narrative, in some cases through the use of gothic tropes such as haunting. These complicate looking back, as they imply that past events could return unbidden to threaten and disturb in the present.

Nostalgia and pastoral

Coined in the late seventeenth century to describe 'the physical symptoms of extreme homesickness' (Wagner 14), within about a hundred years the term 'nostalgia' is 'depathologized' and has a principally 'temporal rather than spatial orientation' (Dames 35). Rather than being a source of 'trauma or sickness', nostalgia becomes 'a poignant but harmless dip into reminiscence' (Dames 36). This does not mean that its original resonance is completely obliterated; both a conjunction of other times with other places, and an embedded sense of ambivalence towards an apparently 'harmless dip into reminiscence', are discernible in the twentieth-century writing I will examine here. As Michael Wood suggests, 'Nostalgia looks to the past, but it belongs to the present. Whatever its object or its content, it is a way of behaving *now*' (22).[4] An inability to place faith in the possibilities of progress into the future will exacerbate the turn to the past, or rather, to a nostalgic conception of it, which will centred around available artefacts, images or buildings. This aspect of nostalgia is expressed in William Sansom's short story 'Fireman Flower' (1944), when Flower is drawn to a room at the centre of a warehouse fire and finds not only an old friend but many familiar objects:

> there over by the table was the old silver teapot and Granny's crochet doily [...] he found himself wondering why this nostalgia should affect him so strongly [...] A sense of security lay about these pictures of the past [...] The past was more real than the present because the picture was clearly defined [...] nothing like the unstable present, which one could hardly understand at all. (233)

Eventually, however, Flower realizes that the price of stability will be the renunciation of love and other pleasures the future may hold; he therefore chooses to reject 'The past! That eiderdown!' (236).

As Sansom shows, an important aspect of nostalgia is its selectivity, a characteristic that means it can be considered not only as a form of memory, but equally as a form of managed forgetting that, in Nicholas Dames's view, performs the 'amelioration or cancellation of the past' (6). For Dames, discussing nineteenth-century literature, nostalgia 'is a socially binding form of memory, a memory for society' (15). The paradox here is that nostalgia is not dependent on individual experience; at their most powerful, nostalgic narratives draw in even those whose own lives are remote from the milieus depicted. Whilst nostalgia can be considered politically quiescent, it is important to recognize the importance of its ameliorative aspect at particular historical junctures. Nanette Aldred suggests that '[a]t times of political crises, British culture tends to turn to its rural roots as a motif of continuity [...] The land achieved an increased visibility because of its necessarily efficient cultivation during war' (118). The massive changes that British farming was undergoing in order to achieve this efficiency would necessarily be masked in representations that were more interested in the countryside as a concept than in agriculture as an activity.[5] Focusing on the comforting repetition of natural cycles could be a means of countering the threatening and unpredictable forward progress of political and military events. Although landscapes are, as Simon Schama has argued, 'constructs of the imagination projected onto wood and water and rock', it is important to recognise that 'once a certain idea of landscape, a myth, a vision, establishes itself in an actual place, it has a peculiar way of muddling categories, of making metaphors more real than their referents; of becoming, in fact, part of the scenery' (61). What emerges during the war years is a new version of an existing vision, adapted to react to (and against) new circumstances.

Contextualizing Paul Fussell's identification of the prevalence of the pastoral mode in First World War writing, Alan Howkins notes that 'in the years immediately before the Great War, sections of the artistic and intellectual elite had turned to the countryside, and to things rural, as the basis for a new England. The war seems to have speeded this process up' (*Death* 40). In the writing of Edmund Blunden, 'the horror and waste of the Flanders landscape is constantly set against a soothing and restoring land of England' (Howkins, *Death* 41); Howkins suggests that such sentiments were not confined to the literary elite. This vision of England is encapsulated in Hilaire Belloc's notion of the 'South Country', the heart of which, described by Belloc in his account of retracing the 'Old Road' from Winchester to Canterbury, are the chalk hills of the South Downs (190–91). However, the interwar years see an increasing interest in 'Deep England', a zone stretching from 'Hardy's Wessex to Tennyson's Lincolnshire, from Kipling's Sussex to Elgar's Worcestershire' but excluding 'the "Black Country" of the industrial Midlands and the north with its factories and windswept moors' (Calder, *Myth* 182). The 'Golden Country', which Winston Smith dreams of in *Nineteen Eighty-Four* (1949), belongs to the same lineage: 'The landscape [...] recurred so often in his dreams that he was never fully certain whether or not he had seen it in the real world' (32–33). Such conceptions of the countryside are often based on the notion that country society is 'an organic society, a "real" one, as opposed to the unnatural or "unreal" society of the town' (Howkins, 'Discovery' 63). It also, evidently, both springs from and fosters particular markers of English culture. Although many of the writers who depicted England in this way in the interwar years either were or had been, like Blunden, country-dwellers, such images take on particular point when their object is framed as being at either a spatial or temporal distance.[6] When a consideration of the countryside involves a critique of industrialisation, as represented by life in the city, these two aspects can be collapsed into each other so that the countryside, as it is now, is seen as a repository for the skills, virtues and values that the depredations of modernity are causing to vanish elsewhere. The countryside is not simply at a geographical remove from the city; it also represents a lost past. The village community can therefore become a synecdoche for the nation as it used to be.

Malcolm Chase sees the growth in popularity of often lavishly illustrated books about the English countryside in the period 1930–45 as an 'ultra-conservative' reaction to 'economic and social instability' (129). For Martin Wiener, Stanley Baldwin's 1924 pronouncement that 'England is the country and the country is England' (Baldwin 6) is key to explicating this reaction: 'This countryside of the mind was everything industrial society was not – ancient, slow-moving, stable, cozy, and "spiritual"' (Wiener 6). Looking to rural life, and specifically the rural past, is a symptom of anxiety about industrial progress and its social and psychological consequences. Ironically, as Glen Cavaliero notes, celebratory writing about the countryside encouraged new visitors to go there, in the process changing precisely what had been celebrated; 'the yearning for what was thought of as a simpler life led to the gradual complication of that life' (81).

Nostalgia might appear to be inherently conservative in that it champions looking back, a retrogressive rather than progressive movement. However, although some analyses of the rural past could lead to an emphasis on the squirearchy, or even a quasi-fascist focus on the land and soil, for others, forms of rural social organisation such as the guilds could offer a model for socialist development; either of these could be presented as 'natural' or 'organic'.[7] As Jeffrey Richards suggests: 'For the right the country meant the country house and the country church, the squire and the parson, and a deferential, hierarchical society. For the left it meant folk music, the village community, rural crafts and honest peasantry' (Richards, 'National Identity' 44). The inscription of these disparate ideologies onto rural life and the rural past illustrates the extent to which nostalgia presents 'not a choice but at least a temporary illusion of freedom from what historically happened' (Cavaliero 26). The countryside can appear to encapsulate 'priorities set by nature rather than current events' and during the war seemed to offer 'a timeless and indestructible conceptual retreat to those whose uncertain present was bombing raids, the rubble of destroyed cities, factory production lines and foreign battlefields' (Boyes 181).

Some of these tensions are exposed in Michael Powell and Emeric Pressburger's film *A Canterbury Tale* (1944), which, like *Went the Day Well?*, dramatises the effects of war on the countryside through some powerful visual conjunctions of the military and the rural. In one sequence, for example, the horse-drawn hay wagon being driven by the land girl Alison (Sheila Sim) is halted by three armoured personnel carriers that appear from the undergrowth and block her path. The film also reframes the pilgrimage to Canterbury as a literary and cultural trope of Englishness that still has relevance in wartime. However, it is in the depiction of the local magistrate and gentleman farmer Colpeper (Eric Portman) that the ideological ambivalence of nostalgic depictions of the countryside becomes most evident. The fervour of Colpeper's campaign to educate the locally stationed soldiers about country life leads him to take direct action to discourage relationships between the soldiers and women, including land girls, who are also contributing to the war effort. He is eventually revealed to be the 'glue-man', who has been pouring glue in women's hair to make them frightened of going out at night. The manner in which Colpeper is framed and lit at points in the film adds to the sense of mystery surrounding him. During his lecture, he is presented in silhouette against the circle of light cast by his magic lantern. He seems to have a halo, but the image is stark and he could equally be an anonymous demagogue at a political rally.[8] This image is broken when he moves and his eyes become illuminated; a reverse shot shows Alison looking up at Colpeper, apparently entranced by his paean to country life. As Ian Christie has noted, by the end of the film, 'the "bad" Colpeper of misogyny and resentment has been exorcised' through his contact with Alison and the film's other protagonists, whilst he appears to be 'responsible for the "blessings" conferred on Alison, Peter and Bob after they reach Canterbury and discover that they each have a future' (88). However, Colpeper's method of communicating his message is still morally questionable and the film raises doubts about whether the 'values that underlay the wartime appeal to a timeless England [...] could be impressed on townsfolk' (88). Whilst the landscapes shown throughout the film are beautiful, with Canterbury cathedral a prominent and undamaged landmark, these contrast starkly with the ruined townscape of Canterbury through which Alison walks towards the end of the film. The countryside might provide solace in the face of such destruction but it can only do so by temporarily masking present danger with reveries of the past or future hopes.

Topographical writing and the representation of Englishness

The question of what values the town and the country might respectively represent necessarily has an impact on how writers conceive of both progress, and, by extension, the type of civilisation the war is defending. Cities and towns can, occasionally, produce nostalgia. John Betjeman comments that an absence from England can lead the traveller to be selective in his recall: 'Even a town like Wolverhampton looks splendid through memory's telescope' (*English Cities* 7). Betjeman is usually careful to distinguish county towns from centres of industry and he prefers Cambridge to Oxford because it is less industrialised, but he does have praise for the civic buildings of Liverpool and Manchester, remarking that: 'To someone who likes people as well as buildings, the industrial towns are the hope and the life of England' (33).⁹ This does not prevent him from seeing the bombing of some cities as an opportunity rather than an unmitigated tragedy. According to Betjeman, 'Recent bombings have blown out a lot of very ugly stained glass' (16), and old towns have as much to fear from 'over enthusiastic "post war reconstruction" ' (42) as from Nazi bombing, which, whilst it might destroy the fabric, cannot obliterate a town's 'character' (16). Graham Greene, echoing Betjeman's *bêtes noires*, suggests in 1940 that 'the crated ground round Wolverhampton [...] those acres of abandoned cars round Slough [...] they all demanded violence' ('At Home' 447–8).¹⁰ He makes a more direct connection than does Betjeman between the spiritual and physical condition of the cities and their fitness for destruction: for Greene, civilisation is the 'cracked cup' (450) that was bound to break eventually. In *She Goes to War*, Catherine describes Liverpool in February 1941 as 'the abomination of desolation. Bombed or unbombed – in fact I think the bombed bits are better. It would be a good idea to remove all the people to safety and bomb at least seventy per cent of the town flat' (97). In late 1939, H. V. Morton spends a day 'motoring through the dreary, red-brick, industrial Midlands, a region always hideous and deformed, and now made even more horrible by the means taken to protect it' (*I Saw Two Englands* 238). Similar sentiments, if less explicitly expressed, underpin Vera Brittain's account of a visit to the Potteries in October 1940, before the worst of the raids on the Midlands had begun:

> I am shown a few places in which bombs have fallen. But these sporadic areas of devastation are difficult to distinguish from the débris normally caused in this district by 'wear and tear'. [...] [M]ore than once my commiseration is misplaced.
> 'You've had some trouble here!' I remark [...] and am cheerfully corrected by my escorts: 'Oh no! That wasn't done by bombs. It was like that long before the war!' (Brittain, *England's Hour* 174)

The city already looks like a war zone; according to this logic, the damage will be felt less here than in the countryside. Such a focus on the material shortcomings of the cityscape, emerging in writing from across the political spectrum, excludes the perspective of those for whom these cities and towns are home. Bombing is reconfigured as a depoliticised solution to a problem presented in largely topographical, rather than human, terms.

According to Malcolm Chase, towards the end of the war, the writer H. J. Massingham described Nazism as 'wholly an urban movement';

England could avoid such degradation because of the 'greater depth and rootedness' of its traditions and 'richer cultural inheritance' (qtd. in Chase 131). As early as 1929, however, Massingham suggested that the industrial world had already declared war on the country: 'with the coming of the Railway Age, followed in furious sequence by the Motor and the Bungaloid Age of to-day, [...] Englishmen began to impose themselves on the English countryside in the spirit of conquering aliens' ('England' 298).[11] In 1942, the left-wing philosopher C. E. M Joad uses similarly martial imagery to describe what happened to the countryside in the years preceding the war: 'London burst like a bomb and scattered its debris far and wide over the faces of Surrey and Kent, and presently over that of Sussex' ('Face' 335).[12] Joad was certainly not against opening up the countryside to visitors but wanted greater control to be exercised over residential developments. The coastal railway routes are described by Joad as having 'accumulated little ganglions of vulgarity around their stations, as an alien body thrust into the flesh accumulates a zone of inflamed tissue around its place of entry' ('Face' 335). The conjunction of organic and mechanical imagery is echoed by Patrick Hamilton, who describes London as a monster which breathes by sucking up working men and women 'through an infinitely complicated respiratory apparatus of trains and termini into the mighty congested lungs' only to exhale them again at the end of the working day (*Slaves* 3).[13] Massingham echoes the ambivalence towards civilisation and progress expressed by Joad and Hamilton, and by Greene, and in 1942 predicts an inexorable reconfiguration of society: 'The complexity of our society is too heavy a burden for it to bear. [...] [I]ts movement, abrupt or gradual, will be katabolic and towards simplification. In that sense, its direction will be from the modern towards the mediaeval, unless the disintegration is more radical' (*Remembrance* 117–8).[14] (It should be noted that if the word 'mediaeval' is used in an evaluative way here, the value placed on it is a positive one; Massingham refers to the age 'that perfected the guild system and created the Early English style' [*English* 135]). The elevation of the countryside to an emblem of what the war is being fought to defend re-emphasizes the importance of addressing the existing anxieties about the preservation of the countryside that are expressed here.

As might be expected from the stark assertion of its title, C. Henry Warren's *England is a Village* (1940) also situates the true values of Englishness in the rural way of life, but like Massingham and Joad, he inveighs against the damage that was already being done to country life before the outbreak of war. During the hard winter of 1939–40, the narrator, who lives in an Essex village that he refers to as 'Larkfield', reflects that being sequestered from the outside world by heavy snowfall gives a glimpse of how life used to be 'in the days before it began to ape (not very successfully) the towns' (18). Aping the town means having modern conveniences such as 'radio and electric light and tinned food', all of which encourage 'dependence' on the outside world (18). Similarly, Warren deplores the fact that the village children have to travel into the town to go to school, as this means they have less time to learn the ways of the countryside and more opportunity to visit 'the sixpenny stores and the cinemas' (75). This is the outcome of the change that Flora Thompson sees beginning during the 1880s. In *Lark Rise* (1939), she reflects on the decline of traditional country games: 'Of all the generations that had played the games, that of the eighties was to be the last. Already those children had one foot in the national school and one on the village green' (143). Mass production and centralization are the enemy of individuality and 'character', and it is not difficult to see how Warren's lament for the assault on the values of the countryside could be read as a critique of the conditions that have led to war: the countryside is constructed as pre-industrial, pre-capitalist and, therefore, pre-war. However, in the preface he added before the book's publication in May 1940, by which time the hard winter has been succeeded by spring, Warren attempts to emphasize not what the countryside has lost to the town, but what the towns, and the nation as a whole, can learn from communities like Larkfield: 'it is from the ashes (if such must be) of the Larkfields of England that our phoenix strength shall rise [...] The best of England is a village' (ix). Implicitly, even the ashes of a village are potentially more fruitful than a town or city, from which no such spiritual rebirth could spring.

If for some writers the war on the countryside was declared well before 1939, in *The Oaken Heart: The Story of an English Village at War* Margery Allingham gives a more nuanced account of the relationship between village life in the pre-war and in wartime. Written and published in 1941, principally for an American readership, this text is a memoir that aims to give a sense not just of Allingham's own concerns and feelings but of the life of the village itself. It covers the period from about 1938 until early 1941, and one of its peculiarities is the extent to which even the events of two or three years prior to the time of writing are placed at a temporal distance. For example, Allingham tends to use the phases 'in those days' or 'at that time', which exacerbate the remoteness of what is being described: 'In those days Hitler was said to resemble Charlie Chaplin [...] at that time we knew nothing about gas at all [...] [a]t that time [...] the damage looked as though it was going to be a great deal worse' (*Oaken Heart* 31, 55, 101). This emphasizes how much has happened in this relatively short space of time; it also encourages Allingham to view her own and her neighbours' actions and attitudes with a degree of hindsight that at times amounts to 'backshadowing'. This is the term used by Michael André Bernstein to describe a narrative or part of a narrative in which 'shared knowledge of the outcome of a series of events by narrator and listener is used to judge the participants in those events *as though they too should have known what was to come*' (16). Allingham's case is different in that there is a presumed identity between the narrator and the participant, but at times, she certainly seems to judge herself for not seeing what was to come (and, by, implication, for not being better prepared). For example, Allingham describes how the news of plans to evacuate city-dwelling children to the countryside 'almost mitigated some of the cold dread of the casualty lists which must lie behind the mind of everyone who has to stay at home' (*Oaken Heart* 66); but she then adds: 'When I remember what did happen when the war proper began I cannot help laughing at us a little and I fancy most of Auburn joins me' (68). Thus, her memory of the villagers' reaction to the evacuation plans is overlaid with, and inextricable from, her knowledge of what happened when these plans were executed: the villagers found themselves having to cope not just with children but with a number of nursing and expectant mothers.

However, Allingham in not simply 'laughing' at the naïveté of herself and her fellow villagers; there is also an implicit comment here on the amount of information that was made available to them. She does not deny that, prior to the war, local concerns could often overshadow national issues; the campaign to prevent the closure of the village school means that the village does not hear 'the first rumblings of the war' (12). What becomes clear as the text progresses is the extent to which the village has to adapt to the demands being made nationally. Compromises are made: 'Auburn put "Gas" and "First Aid" where it wanted them, tucked in between the whist drives and the Women's Institute and other meetings' (85). Having asserted early on in the text that the village is not idyllic or 'complacently picturesque' (9), Allingham nevertheless stresses its sense of its own identity, history and traditions, albeit that these are not completely insulated from change. Yet at times Allingham regrets the adaptability that the villagers display:

> The process of hardening up is imperceptible. After the first effort the mental and spiritual muscles get going on their own. The unbelievable

gradually becomes a commonplace. The gas-mask loses its nightmare shape and becomes no more ugly than an umbrella. But there is a loss in all this as well as a gain. It seemed such a mercy and yet such a pity at the time, I remember. (83)

Implicitly, accustoming oneself to things which had seemed 'unbelievable' can point to an erosion of spiritual values, just as the London women who are accustomed to hot running water and Woolworths are somehow inauthentic (200).[15] Allingham wishes to preserve a record of the kind of innocence that allowed the gasmasks to seem so shocking in the first place.

Allingham's sentiments are akin to those expressed by Edward Glover, President of the British Psycho-Analytical Society during the war and government advisor on civilian morale, when he depicts the effects of war on the 'cottager's wife'. Glover uses this figure to illustrate that an individual's 'war aims' might seem to be very personal, but that underpinning the cottager's wife's desire that Hitler should not smash her cups and saucers is a 'deep devotion to her family' and a 'deep attachment to all the simple things that go to make up her picture of England' including 'the children's cricket pitch on the village green, the church steeple [...], the local omnibus service, the cinema, the garden fence over which she can gossip' (Glover 16). This is a more inclusive picture of village life than, for instance, Warren's, but as Gillian Swanson argues, it not only situates the woman firmly in the family, but also suggests that 'the emotional fervour of love of country derives from love of family' (75). Preserving this apparently organic, and depoliticised, connection between family and the country (very different, in Glover's view, from the manner in which the family is made to serve the state under Nazism) can itself be a valuable aspect of wartime morale. To judge from Allingham's account, introducing benighted townswomen to these virtues is a worthy war aim in itself.

Allingham does not imply that the village has been completely isolated from the nation up until this point. Frequent references are made to earlier experiences of war, although Allingham recognises that the impact of the current war is likely to be very different. Thinking back to the First World War (she was ten in 1914), Allingham comments: 'War simply meant death to me; a soldier galloping up on a fat grey horse to kiss my tearful nurse goodbye over the wall under the chestnut trees, and then death [...] death final, empty and away somewhere' (25). This 'empty' death, represented by 'casualty lists in very small type' (25) is supplemented by the tales of veterans, 'reminiscences told on the sea-wall or on the benches outside the pubs, or published in books and coming round in the library vans' (27). This detail of the library van seems to me to emphasise the remoteness of the experiences being described; they have to be 'imported' to the village, or exist on its fringes, on the bench outside, rather than inside, the pub. The usefulness of the earlier conflict as a point of reference is limited; whilst air attack is not completely unknown, a Zeppelin having 'come down in a village not far away in the last war' (42), the villagers have also learned of the devastation caused by bombing raids in Spain and China.[16] Although the locality of the village is affected by air raids, it is only late on in the text, during a visit to London in the autumn of 1940, that Allingham is confronted with the extent of the devastation bombing could cause.

Having visited her publisher, she decides to stop off on the way back to the railway station to buy some toffee from Madame Caporelli's shop. Heading there, she compares one damaged street to the image, used in silent films to represent the passage of time, of a tree blossoming and then immediately being stripped by a winter wind. Then she reaches her destination:

> I had been prepared for damage along the way but I had not envisaged anything so local or so complete. Here was no winter apple-tree. The whole plant had been tugged up by the roots and cut into firewood. Whole sections of the not very beautiful but familiar façade were exactly as usual, and then, where there should have been a restaurant or a bookshop or a tailor's or a sports outfitters, there was suddenly just a great clean-sided hole with chaos in its mouth. (337)

The completeness of the destruction is particularly striking to Allingham; it is notable that she uses a quasi-natural image to express this, as though temporarily closing the gap between country and city, but this cannot disguise the violence that has been done to a familiar metaphor. This recalls an earlier passage in which London is itself seen as a collection of villages, exciting the admiration of the country dwellers: 'The old villages in the East End took it first, but the central ones had it too' (324). This image is echoed in Elizabeth Bowen's description, relating to the same period, of the bombed city reconstituting itself as a cluster of villages ('London 1940' 22–3); in Allingham's text, it suggests not only a kinship between country and city dwellers but also the belief that it is the values and spirit of the village that will pull the city through. Allingham writes about village life from the perspective of one who has lived in the village for a number of years, has family connections with the region, and is actively involved in its daily life. She is therefore in a strong position from which to monitor and describe the impact on the village of the events of the war. Embedding into her descriptions an element of temporal perspective ('in those days'), emphasizes the impact those events have had, whilst simultaneously attempting to weave them into the existing story of the village. The war has caused changes, just as the closure of the village school would, but these can be absorbed and understood, even if, at the distance of only two or three years, memory exposes a lack of understanding of their possible scope, and even if there is uncertainty about what the future might hold.

The preservation, through narrative, of particular aspects or images of England expresses both a concern that these might be lost and a belief that they are, precisely, valuable enough to be preserved. H. V. Morton, best known for his book *In Search of England* (1927), and for a series of books about London, including *The Heart of London* (1925), attempts a similar kind of proleptic memorialisation of England in *I Saw Two Englands*, first published in October 1942 (by which time *In Search of England* had reached its twenty-eighth edition). Morton's book describes two journeys around England, one undertaken in May 1939, the second in October of the same year. He describes why he decided to go on the first journey in terms that, retrospectively, express a degree of fatalism, tinged with a glimmer of hope:

> I thought […] it would be a good thing to get away from London. No one knew what was going to happen, and it was pointless to go on listening to theories and speculations. If war should come, I said to myself, I should dearly love to have had a last glimpse of pre-war England – the second pre-war England of my generation – and if, after all, it did not come, what could be finer than a journey through England in the Spring? (Morton, *I Saw* 2)

Inevitably, the pleasures of the 'journey through England in the Spring' are tainted with anxieties about what might be to come, and, as this extract indicates, Morton was old enough to have served in the earlier conflict and, therefore, has this as a personal point of reference in a way that Allingham, only a child in 1914, does not.[17] For much of the first part of the book, dealing with his pre-war journey, Morton's references to the current political situation press at the margins of the narrative. He travels to various historic sites and country seats throughout Kent, Sussex, and Oxfordshire, and gives accounts of the key events that have occurred in these places, but in the interstices of these descriptions are acknowledgements that preparations are underway for a new historical departure. For example, in Maidstone, Morton visits a building that was formerly the palace of the Archbishop of Canterbury. It has since, 'by one of the merry chances not uncommon in the career of an ancient building in England' been transformed into a 'Maternity Welfare Centre' (48). Morton has some wry comments to make about this change of use, although he suggests, after touring the building, that 'it does not appear to resent the Maternity Centre; in fact it seems to like it' (49). What upsets him more are other changes that the building is undergoing; carpenters are installing partitions in the tithe barn to make it fit for use by the ARP, and 'gas chambers' (air-raid shelters) are also being constructed. 'Gas chambers in a priceless mediaeval tithe barn, and a clinic in my Lord of Canterbury's palace! No one can say that Maidstone neglects its antiquities' (50). Coupling the 'gas chambers' and the clinic together in this way as examples of 'neglect' serves to mask the fact that the former, at least, is in fact a pragmatic means of preparing for an anticipated eventuality. Morton wishes to preserve what he can of the spirit of 'my Lord Canterbury's palace' in its original incarnation, stripping away later accretions and returning to its first historical use. Implicitly, he seems to express the hope that this original function will outlast the later ones in public memory.

The itinerary for this first journey is only loosely planned, with Morton travelling by car and stopping off at a variety of towns and villages as the fancy takes him. His second journey, begun in mid-October 1939, is, as he describes it, 'a circumscribed tour' (189–90); he goes armed with letters of introduction from various Ministries, as well as petrol coupons and gas mask: 'I was conscious that in the twinkling of an eye all had changed. Gone was the careless, easy-to-see England that had been technically at peace for so long. It was another England I should see, an England technically at war' (189). This time, Morton intends to record not an England that might be passing, but England as it is now; perhaps inevitably, however, there are points at which even this part of the narrative looks back. A visit to Salisbury Plain provokes the following reaction:

> Memories of long ago – indeed, so long ago that they seem like the memories of someone else – assailed me as I saw the wide spaces of the Plain in the early morning [...] Now and then the bang of a trench mortar sounded from a far hill; machine-guns stammered for a second on distant ranges; and the whole Plain was alive, as it was in 1914–18, training the youth of England to defend its birthright. [...] It was

different on the Plain in the last War, as I remember it. Sitting beside me now in the car was a child with a captain's stars on his shoulders [...] and to him I confided some of my memories of the Plain [...] The child looked at me with the expression of one who sees before him a veteran of Agincourt. (203–04)

The place itself is familiar, but the type of activities being carried out are strange to Morton, who reflects, for instance, on how far aviation has developed in the interwar years, and surprises his guide with memories of cavalry training. Whilst Morton's historical knowledge helped him to find his bearings in the castles, houses and villages he visited on his earlier journey, his memories of his own war experience are not so helpful when it comes to making sense of the scene on Salisbury Plain. Yet, just as the tithe barn remains beneath the partitions that have been erected to transform its use, so the Plain itself, 'the rabbits scurrying round their burrows, the clouds wheeling above the open landscape' (203), endures. Finding this apparent sameness amidst the change seems as important to Morton here as it does on his earlier journey.

In the book's Postscript, Morton compares the defence of England against invasion in 1942 with earlier times when the country appeared to be in peril; an appeal to the community of the village necessitates leaping back in time beyond the First World War. Morton is involved in his village Home Guard, and reflects that, in the countryside in particular, one becomes aware of a history of local defence:

> I think one is peculiarly conscious of this in a country district full of old farm-houses which have been standing for centuries: buildings whose panelling conceals secret rooms, whose wide chimneys lead to "priests' holes", whose windows have known the tap of a secret code in the night, whose barns and outhouses have stabled many a strange horse and have concealed many a mysterious rider. [...] Danger has skipped us for a century or two; and now we are back in Danger. (287)

Morton appeals here to a cultural memory that dates back to the middle-ages and also encompasses the English Civil War. The movement here is similar to that which Simon Featherstone identifies in one of J. B. Priestley's 'Postscript' broadcasts from June 1940. Featherstone shows that Priestley's transformation of the village into 'an emblematic fiction of the nation' is 'derived in part from literary sources', particularly the works of Thomas Hardy (158) The establishment of this literary continuity 'means the true and menacing presence of the First World War is elided' (Featherstone 157), and the Napoleonic Wars, as represented in Hardy's *The Dynasts* are foregrounded instead.[18] In his description of his involvement in the Home Guard, Morton chooses reference points from earlier in history, priests' holes and secret panelling, which tend to give a romanticized gloss to the invasion threat. Later, he describes how, when on fire-watching duty he fills the time 'with memories of those lovely places in England which I shall not see again until the war is over' (289–90). He lists the places he remembers at such times, implying an active and repeated remembering of many of the places he visited earlier in the book, and finally reflecting that in defending his own 'few square miles' (290) he is, implicitly, defending the rest also. Morton is thus standing guard over a particular vision of England, one that is encapsulated by his own darkened village, but which is guaranteed by his memory of other places. The possibility that the towns he loves might be damaged is not admitted here, but even if it were, it would seem likely that, in a similar way to Betjeman, Morton would place a strong belief in the endurance, if not of the materiality, then of the spirit of those places. Like Allingham, Morton makes a concerted effort not only to preserve the present for the benefit of the future, but also to preserve a particular vision of the past. Whilst Allingham is concerned to de-sentimentalize life in the English village, Morton attempts to contextualize present threats of invasion in relation to the geographical, topographical and even architectural evidences of earlier conflicts. This cultural memory is preferred to his own personal memories of the First World War, which are both too proximate and too dissonant to provide a useful point of reference.

Both Allingham and Morton are concerned with the potential and actual impact of the war on country communities, but not all narrative memorializations of the English countryside present it in positive terms. Denton Welch, whose semi-autobiographical novel *In Youth is Pleasure* (1945) attracted the attention of Edith Sitwell, wrote a journal from 1942 until his death in 1948. Welch was thirty-three when he died; he was left semi-invalid after being knocked off his bicycle in 1935. From this time, Welch lived in the Kent countryside, and for the most part used the events of his life prior to the accident as source material for his novels and short stories. The journal itself is often retrospective, rather than a record of day-to-day events. Although much of it was probably not intend for publication, one section in particular, written in 1943 and extracted from the manuscript and published separately as *I Left my Grandfather's House* in 1958, bears examination as a self-contained narrative. Looking back to 1933, Welch describes a walking holiday that took him from Sussex to the West Country. This piece of writing is obviously very different from both *The Oaken Heart* and *I Saw Two Englands*; Welch does not have the stated purpose of recording pre-war England for future generations, and he makes no explicit references to the conflict that was well underway at his time of writing. But, just as in the rest of his journal he cannot, despite his relative seclusion, keep the war completely at bay, so in this long retrospective section, there are clues to the threat that may lie ahead.

Welch certainly does not produce a hymn to the beauties of the English countryside; he has an eye for the grotesque and the abject. On the South Downs, near the start of the trip, he sees a small, isolated cottage in the distance and decides to investigate:

> Even at some distance it looked deserted. […] I climbed over one of the gaps and let myself into the cottage. There was still a door to one of the openings; the place where the handle had been was black and smooth and greasy from many hands. The main room had the same disgusting quality about it […] There were fish bones on the floor, and excrement. Over the mantelpiece someone had scrawled an obscene couplet […] I thought of the tramps and vagabonds stopping at the derelict house for one night of their never ending journey. […] One day it would all come down, I thought. (Welch, *I Left* 28–9)

There are ruined cottages in Allingham's village also, but none quite so revolting as this. Whilst Welch is certainly not immune to the beauties of the landscape, this kind of incident, like a cloud passing over the sun, often casts its shadow on his narrative. His own walking holiday is contrasted with the 'never ending journey' of the tramps who have left their mark on the house. They, and the cottage itself, seem emblematic of irredeemable decay, not just of Welch's own mortality, an ever-present concern given the state of his health at the time of writing, but of society's rotten underbelly. In contrast to Morton's occasionally ironic but generally restrained account of leisurely travels, Welch recounts a catalogue of embarrassing encounters with strange people, and on occasion despairs at being able to find a bed for the night. At one point, after being turned away from a cottage he decides that: 'English people [are] the most inhospitable and boorish on the face of the earth' (64). More surprisingly, he also admits to gaps in his memory of his itinerary: 'I […] walked on to Castle Cary, I think because I liked the name. From here my journey is lost; I can remember nothing until I emerged in the market place at Dunster. I do not understand this blank, but as I look at the map no name strikes any chord at all' (65). Whilst Morton is at pains to list those places which deserve preservation in both individual and national memory, Welch admits freely that some places are completely unmemorable, to him at least.

The soldiers who occasionally emerge from the landscapes in Welch's journal, and with whom he makes often tentative conversation, are reminders both of the war that threatens to impinge on his life, and of his own existence on the fringes of society; this seems to be, at least in part, where their allure resides. Whilst the militarisation of the landscape could be threatening, Welch tends to neutralise this threat by his manner of depicting the army personnel he encounters; writing in March 1943 about a walk in the country, he comments: 'I came to soldiers practising manoeuvres. The first two I came on wore leaves and twigs stuck into netting stretched over their tin hats. The effect was wild and pastoral and fancy-dress. The careful, camouflage greens looked specially chosen for their prettiness' (Welch, *Journals* 60–61).[19] Whilst this description might seem inappropriately fanciful, there is perhaps not such a difference between Welch's identification of a 'pastoral' aspect to the camouflage, and Morton's placing of himself in a genealogy stretching back to Agincourt. To defend the land and its history, one must, either spiritually or indeed literally, become part of it.

Country houses as sites of memory

When neither village life nor the itinerary of a traveller are the focus in discussions of the countryside, the country house can provide a means of examining the interaction – or lack of interaction – between a group of individuals, often a family, and their surroundings. Accounting for the continuing use of the country house in literature of the war years, Richard Gill suggests that: 'In an era of travelers, wanderers, seekers, the house remains a "still point" in an overturning world [...] The fictional house may then become for both writers and readers alike a surrogate for something missed; and an imaginative act may recover, at least temporarily, the feeling of community that has been lost' (Gill 16). In particular, the 'violence and apprehension of the late thirties and forties helped to dissolve the satirical view prevailing during the previous years and prompted writers [...] to undertake [...] reorientation and reassessment' (194). So, for example, Evelyn Waugh moves from the ironic depiction of Hetton, the seat of the Lasts in *A Handful of Dust* (1934), described by a guidebook as '*entirely rebuilt in 1864 in the Gothic style and* [...] *now devoid of interest*' (17), to the elegiac portrayal of Lord Marchmain's residence in *Brideshead Revisited* (1945). The action of a number of the novels to be discussed here takes place not in seats of the aristocracy like Brideshead but in houses that have more modest pretensions, but the functions that Gill identifies often remain. Thus, in Jocelyn Playfair's *A House in the Country* (1944), Brede Manor becomes home to a disparate community of evacuees and refugees, but appears to retain few of the social or economic functions that the epithet 'manor' might suggest.

Novels such as Waugh's and Playfair's reflect the changing fortunes of the country house in this period. Alun Howkins reminds us that, in the interwar years, the degree of influence the country house had on its surroundings varied from place to place:

> For example, while many areas of Surrey remained rural in 1921 they were already within the orbit of a newer suburban world where the traditional 'norms' of agricultural society were considered unimportant in reality [...] On the other hand, in more purely agricultural districts, for instance rural Oxfordshire, it is clear from some accounts that an active elite presence, often seen as a nineteenth-century phenomenon, continued important throughout the inter-war period. (Howkins, *Death* 57)

Country life was increasingly seen as offering leisure opportunities for those who could afford to move there and Edwardian and inter-war houses often had little or no economic relationship with the land. 'New' money provided the opportunity to buy into some of the traditions and pleasures of country life, although this would not always convince those whose connection to the land was an ancestral one. Thus, in Nancy Mitford's *The Pursuit of Love* (1945), the banker Sir Leicester Kroesig is treated with disdain by Linda and her cousin Fanny, used to the 'cruel woods' at Alconleigh. Driving into Surrey, Linda predicts that, 'The garden at Planes [Sir Leicester's house] will be a riot of sterility, just you wait' (Mitford, *Pursuit* 16–17). Sure enough, 'every tree [appears] to be entirely covered with a waving mass of pink or mauve tissue-paper. [...] The whole effect was of a scene for musical comedy, and it exactly suited Sir Leicester, who, in the country, gave a surprisingly adequate performance of the old English squire. Picturesque. Delightful' (74–5).

Writing in 1941 for William Collins' popular 'Britain in Pictures' series (in which Betjeman's book on cities and small towns, and Edmund Blunden's on the English village also appeared), Vita Sackville-West also expresses the importance of an organic connection between the country house (and, by extension, its inhabitants) and the immediate locale.

For example, she explains her decision not to hyphenate the phrase 'country house':

> I want to emphasise that the house is essentially part of the country, not only *in* the country, but part of it, a natural growth. [...] [I]t should agree with its landscape and suggest the life of its inhabitants past or present, should never overwhelm its surroundings. The peculiar genius of the English country house lies in its knack of fitting in. (Sackville-West 7–8)

She therefore deplores houses that seem merely to be ostentatious gestures by rich men – Castle Howard in Yorkshire, designed by Vanbrugh, falls into this category. She prefers, to the work of 'a single eminent architect' (9), the accretion over a number of years of different additions and decorations, both inside and out. In an analysis of this attitude to the country house, Patrick Wright suggests that

> this interior is a place of 'synecdoche', where the whole is always greater than the sum of its parts [...] If the continuities of ancestral residence were to be broken, then the associational magic would die. [...] The ancestral magic haunting the interior of the English country house was so potent it could even make ordinary household junk [...] glow with special significance. (*Journey* 90–1)

Taking this accumulative, organic view of the past leaves no space for questioning the value of what is actually being preserved; instead, the house and its contents appear to be inexorably bound together, the one imbuing the other with its aura. To achieve this it is, according to Susan Stewart, 'necessary to obliterate the object's context of origin' but the result is a sense of self that is apparently 'capable of transcending the accidents and dispersions of historical reality' (158). Sackville-West expresses an anxiety that the war is likely to compound the existing problems faced by the country house, and accelerate its disintegration and dispersal of its contents. Turning a house into a government department or a school might preserve its fabric, but for Sackville-West, under these conditions the house will cease to be an organism; the continuity of family habitation will have been broken. This is the post-war fate of Cranmer, in Mollie Panter-Downes's *One Fine Day* (1947), given over to 'something which called itself the National Trussed' (106).[20] The 'fresh-cheeked, full-bodied Cranmer stock' has 'dwindled and thinned into Edward' (115) the last of the line, whose wife appears to be unable to have children. Ironically, meanwhile, in the village, 'people like those awful Porters bred and bred like rabbits in their dreadful cottage' (118). The latest Porter baby, fathered by a Pole, has a 'round and noble head' (56), a sign that perceptions of aristocracy and indeed Englishness have been permanently altered by the war.

Sackville-West's own family home had been used as a model by Virginia Woolf in *Orlando* (1928), and Woolf also chose a country house as the setting for *Between the Acts* (1941). Locating the action on the brink of the war that was ongoing while she was writing, Woolf communicates the conflicting forces of *'Unity – Dispersity'* (Woolf, *Between* 119) to which Pointz Hall is subject. The view still coincides with the description from the Guide Book of 1833: 'No house had been built; no town had sprung up' (34); but later at the pageant, visitors gossip about 'That hideous new house at Pyes Corner [...] And those bungalows! – have you seen 'em?' (47) 'Some', we are told, 'had been there for centuries, never selling an acre. On the other hand there were the new-comers, the Manresas, bringing the old houses up to date, adding bathrooms' (47). Changes might not be immediately perceptible, but they have happened, and will continue to happen. The problem of how to situate oneself and one's memories not only in relation to such local changes, but within the course of historical events is pointed up by the depiction of Mrs Swithin. After reading a history book, she reflects on life before man, when there were 'rhododendron forests in Piccadilly' (8), an image that implies the difficulty of conceiving of what came before to the exclusion of what came after. She is also given to remembering incidents that have a strong connection to the house itself: 'she remembered her mother – her mother in that very room rebuking her [...] "but in a very different world," as her brother would remind her' (8–9). The pageant might imply that people in the past were, as Mrs Swithin suggests, only 'you and me and William dressed differently' (104), or that, as the vicar asserts, 'We act different parts; but are the same' (114). However, the power of memory to guarantee continuity of individual subjectivity is placed in doubt, when Mrs Swithin reflects: ' "Ever since I was a child I've felt ..." A film fell over her eyes, shutting off the present. She tried to recall her childhood; then gave it up' (91). When she asks Isa whether she agrees with the vicar's assertion of the continuity of human nature, Isa has to suspend judgement: ' "Yes," Isa answered. "No," she added. It was Yes, No. Yes, yes, yes, the tide rushed out embracing. No, no, no, it contracted' (127). Neither unity nor dispersity are satisfactory positions, and Isa's uncertainty reflects the anxiety of the immediate pre-war, and the sense of living under threat, a threat represented by the aeroplane that flies over the pageant, and which had been fulfilled by the time the novel was published.

In other examples, the decline of the country house is associated with the narrator or protagonist coming to maturity as an individual; remembering, therefore, is often fraught with difficulties. At the start of the second book of *Brideshead Revisited*, Charles Ryder reminds the reader of the implications of the novel's subtitle, which promises to reveal his 'sacred and profane' memories: 'My theme is memory, that winged host that soared about me one grey morning of war-time' (196).[21] However, if memory here visits in the form of angels, this image is immediately succeeded by a much more mundane one, as Ryder compares his memories to 'the pigeons of St Mark's' usually present 'singly, in pairs' (196), but now filling the sky like a cloud. Although such contrasting images convey the sense that effects of memory can be experienced with greater or lesser degrees of intensity at different times, Ryder's past is presented in the novel as a largely chronological narrative that for the most part does not betray its origin as an act of recollection. Only occasionally is the reader reminded that Ryder is relating events with the benefit of hindsight, as when, for example, having described his first visit to Brideshead, Ryder asks rhetorically: 'could I have known then that it would one day be remembered with tears [...]?' (37) The pleasure and pain of the events of Ryder's early life are more pointed precisely because of their persistence in his memory, and their melancholy is exacerbated by the wretched condition of Brideshead when Ryder returns, and the mismatch between his experience of the place now and his memory of how it was then.

Memory is therefore not only an aspect of how the novel is structured but also part of its subject matter; indeed Ryder's career prior to his army service has been built on another form of memorialisation:

> I became an architectural painter. [...] I loved buildings that grew silently with the centuries, catching and keeping the best of each generation [...] In such buildings England abounded, and, in the last decade of their grandeur, Englishmen seemed for the first time to become conscious of what had been taken for granted, and to salute their achievement at the moment of extinction. [...] After my first exhibition I was called to all parts of the country to make portraits of houses that were soon to be deserted or debased. (198–99)

Ryder is therefore able to profit from the economic decline that is causing the destruction of these properties; describing his paintings of them as 'portraits' and using the word 'extinction' suggests a belief, similar to Sackville-West's, in the organic nature of the relationship between these houses and their surroundings.[22] Yet these are qualities that, in the abstract, cannot ultimately furnish Ryder with the 'inspiration' (199) that fed him while he worked on his first commission, a series of paintings of the interior of the Flytes' London seat, Marchmain House. A generalized sense of nostalgia or regret cannot provide the same emotional charge as a personal loss, this despite the fact that Ryder becomes wealthy on the proceeds from his 'three splendid folios – *Ryder's Country Seats, Ryder's English Homes*, and *Ryder's Village and Provincial Architecture*' (199). There is an apparent acknowledgement here of the difficulty of bridging the gap between individual and cultural memory. Ryder states that he believes these houses to be important, the repositories of the 'best of each generation', but he has to make them his own before presenting them back to the folio-buying public. His name, implicitly, is the guarantee of their worth and interest, and his abandonment of this project seems to be a way of acknowledging the tenuous nature of this guarantee.

Ryder's paintings are a means of materializing memory, or, at least, giving the processes of memory a material prompt. Similarly, lying under a tree smoking after they escape from Oxford to the countryside in a borrowed car early on in the narrative, Sebastian Flyte remarks to Ryder: 'Just the place to bury a crock of gold [...] I should like to bury something precious in every place where I've been happy and then, when I was old and ugly and miserable, I could come back and dig it up and remember' (23). Flyte's later fate – alcoholism and retreat to a monastery – perhaps belies the consolatory properties of memory that are asserted here, although Flyte does not suggest that such remembering would necessarily restore his happiness. Memory has the doubleness encapsulated in the motto on the skull in Charles's Oxford rooms, *Et in Arcadia Ego*. This can be read either a reassurance ('Even *I* have reached Arcadia') or a threat ('Even in Arcadia, there is no escape from me'); memory could be a consolation, but it could also prove a torment. By the end of the novel, contemplating the mess that the previous Company have left behind at Brideshead, Ryder is unable to give a proper response to Hooper's observation that: 'It doesn't seem to make any sense – one family in a place this size' (303). Ryder cannot ultimately do more than assert what he himself gained from his 'romance' with the Flytes and with Brideshead: his own faith, signified by the lamp burning once more in the chapel.

The ambivalence of nostalgia, in particular the recognition that it is predicated on loss, and the added point that country house life has for those who glimpse it only as it is passing, is also found in lesser-known novels from this period. In L. P. Hartley's *The Sixth Heaven* (1946), set in the early 1920s, Eustace is invited to a weekend party at the home of the Staveleys, the local gentry and long an object of fascination for him; his position as an outsider is broadly analogous to Charles Ryder's. Hartley excels in the depiction of awkwardness and self-doubt and this novel does not have the elegiac tone of *Brideshead Revisited*, or indeed of Hartley's *The Go-Between* (1953), but in one incident, Eustace is apparently shown to have a greater sense of affinity with the family's history than Dick, the son of the house, does. Eustace finds a ruined chapel in the grounds of the house, but his conversation there with Dick is interrupted by Dick's act of casual vandalism:

> [Dick] leaned over the font and, taking hold of a bit of masonry that stuck out, tooth-like, from the gash in its side, wrenched the fragment off.
> To Eustace it was as if the stone cried out, and he could not hide the pain he felt.
> 'Don't distress yourself,' said Dick, smiling, 'it would have had to come off, anyhow. I'm just forestalling wind and weather.' He threw the fragment playfully at Eustace, who caught and put it in his pocket. (Hartley, *Eustace* 388)

There have already been indications, both implicit and explicit, that Dick has fascist or quasi-fascist sympathies, but this incident is not simply another marker of his destructive tendencies. Dick has explained to Eustace that the beautiful ruin was itself manmade: 'at the time of the Reformation the Staveley of the day became such an ardent Protestant that he pulled the chapel down and used the stones for building purposes' (386). His action is a reminder, to the reader if not to Eustace, that the apparent spirit of place that Eustace experiences at the chapel has a specific historical cause. Just as the earlier Staveley destroyed part of his own heritage, so might future generations. This vignette is a signal of the violence that is still to come at the time when the narrative is set, but has happened at the time of the novel's publication. Eustace's small attempt to preserve a piece of this past induces pathos, but is also futile.

The respective class positions of Eustace and Charles Ryder contribute to them being situated as outsiders to the world of the country house. In each case, their concern for both the past and the future of the house and what it represents appears to equal or even exceed that of the family members who invite them in. Philip Larkin's novel *A Girl in Winter*, begun in 1944, and published in 1947, focuses on an upper-middle-class rather than aristocratic household, but here too an outsider figure is used as a means of assessing the worth and durability of the values and attitudes depicted. In this novel, a detailed description of a single day in the life of Katherine Lind, a refugee from mainland Europe working in a provincial English library during the Second World War,[23] is interrupted by a description of the visit she made to England as a schoolgirl to visit her pen-pal, Robin Fennel, and his family. Katherine has recently made renewed contact with the Fennels, after reading a newspaper notice announcing the death of Robin's sister's child, and is expecting to hear from Robin. The novel culminates in him visiting her flat and in a belated and uneasy consummation of the relationship that failed to flourish some years earlier. The description of Katherine's visit to the Fennels' country home both compounds the reader's curiosity about what the eventual outcome of Robin and Katherine's meeting will be and evokes a strong sense of an outsider's perceptions of England, and, indeed, the English past.

Larkin, like Waugh and Hartley, is attuned to the effects of modernity on country life. When Katherine expresses her surprise, passing through Kent on the way to Oxfordshire, at the extent to which the county is built up, Mr Fennel agrees with her that there are 'too many houses [...] it's the same all over England – good arable land being turned into pasture, pasture turning into housing estates. It'll be the ruin of us' (Larkin, *Girl* 79). He is similarly dismissive of industrialisation: 'Suppose there's another war? What are we going to live on? Christmas crackers and ball-bearings?'(79) (The question of where ordinary people should live or work does not feature in his critique.) When Katherine is taken to see the village in which the Fennels' house stands, it is clear that the depredations of modernity have reached even here: 'She looked curiously round the sides of cottages [...] From occasional doorways came dance music from Radio Luxembourg, and she could see dimly through the lace curtains on the windowsill mass-produced china figures and Sunday newspapers, read by men in shirt sleeves' (94–5). Katherine admits to Robin and his sister, Jane, that this contrasts with the 'white cottages' and 'very old church' (95) that she expected, but she apparently feels a certain respect for the evidence of the villagers' lived experience. Unlike Mr Fennel, she is prepared to adjust her preconceptions to meet reality; what she sees becomes more important than what she has learned from books. Similarly, she becomes exasperated by Robin's 'tourist guide' commentary when they visit Oxford, and wishes to extract a more personal resonance from what she sees around her:

> [T]here was a grave in the churchyard that fascinated her, ornate and Jacobean, with four angels, an urn, and a grinning skull, all worn away by the continual weather that had beaten it for three hundred years. She did not ask Robin whose it was, and dreaded lest he should tell her. (157)

This small detail, detached from any specific historical or biographical narrative, constitutes one of the memories of the trip that has most significance for her. Robin's anecdotes about Civil War battles and local eccentrics are a poor substitute for a more personal expression of emotion. Katherine, like Eustace in Hartley's novel, forges a private connection with the English past; the grave can have a meaning for her despite the fact that she is an outsider.

The imminent visit from Robin, now in the army, provokes in Katherine a reassessment of her situation. The lack of information about the circumstances of her leaving her homeland, and the detailed description of her library routine, create the sense that she is living in the present, having been unable to fully absorb the impact of either her distant or more recent past: 'To live from day to day, as she had been doing, shut out the past, but it shut out the future too [...] All the time she had been behaving as if everything would suddenly snap back to normal, if she could only hang on a little longer' (182). However, Larkin does not allow the reunion between Katherine and Robin to provide a simple means of reclaiming the past and asserting hope for the future. As a soldier, Robin, pragmatically, is not prepared to plan too far ahead, and any resolution of the romance plot is deferred. A young woman living in transitory circumstances, Katherine realizes that her fate is not completely in her own hands; asserting an understanding of the past – or indeed of the present as it becomes the past – cannot disguise the impact that is likely to be wrought by events beyond her control.

For the older female protagonist of Jocelyn Playfair's *A House in the Country* (1944), hopes for the future are rooted not only in the successful actions of combatants but in the management of the domestic sphere. Cressida has been left in charge of Brede Manor, which is now home to various evacuees, refugees, and servicemen, while Charles, the manor's owner is away on active service. Cressida's husband Simon was friends with Charles; Charles was involved in Simon's death in a car accident but absolved of blame. When Cressida recalls being brought to Brede by Simon, she expresses a sense of immediate attachment to the house that appears to predetermine her later attachment to its owner:

> [Cressida] remembered sweeping through village after village at the terrifying speed Simon always maintained [...] Brede Somervel had just been another village, and then those high iron gates had come suddenly into view [...] Cressida [...] had been shaken by a sense of familiarity so strong that she felt recognition rather than mere admiration when the house came in sight for the first time. Ridiculous, impossible and only half-coherent words had sung in her head. Mine ... mine ... it's mine ... it's always been mine ... (Playfair 117–18)

The exigencies of wartime allow Cressida to take charge of the house and the war increases her investment in and attachment to the building and its surrounds; she is able to adapt to wartime conditions without losing a sense of the spirit of her home. These reflections about her first visit occur when Cressida is fire-watching, and, as she remembers how Charles offered to let the house to Simon, 'reality asserted itself, and six bombs fell upon Brede Somervell in as many seconds' (119). Paradoxically, the remainder of the evening, following the raid, is not described directly as it happens, nor is Cressida able to reconstruct a coherent narrative of events later. Her memory of arriving at the house is lyrical but has a dream-like quality; reality asserts itself when the bombs fall:

> The rest of that night was never perfectly clear in Cressida's memory. She did remember kneeling beside Northeast [whose cottage was bombed], digging and scraping until her hands bled. She remembered cutting herself on what turned out to be the corrugated-iron roof of old Northeast's pathetic home-made air-raid shelter. [...] She remembered men with picks and shovels, and other men with a stretcher. [...] She remembered having her bleeding hands washed at the First Aid Post. (122–23)

The repetition of the phrase 'she remembered' suggests that her memory of the aftermath of the bombing is fractured, implying that she was unable to fully take in what was happening at the time. There is a stark contrast between this staccato listing of events and her description of arriving at Brede, so perfect that it seems predestined. The traumas of war interrupt her pleasant reminiscences of the past and it is unclear how these different experiences can be bound together. Ironically, when

Charles eventually arrives home on leave, having been missing at sea for some days, he feels alienated from an England that appears not to have suffered enough; Cressida may have a strong sense of her own involvement in the war effort, but ultimately, like Larkin's Katherine and Robin, she and Charles must each fight their own war. Having declared his love for Cressida, Charles departs at the end of the novel, and, again, romantic closure has to be deferred.

Each of these novels attempts to acknowledge the limits of nostalgia, either through the use of a narrator who is now 'older and wiser', or through the introduction into a nostalgic, memorial narrative of the dissonant voice of history. On the surface, Dodie Smith's *I Capture the Castle* (1949), which Smith began in 1940, put aside until 1945, and completed in late 1947, eschews such a leavening of nostalgia. Although the title has echoes of the chivalric or the fairy-tale, 'capturing', in the parlance of the teenaged narrator, Cassandra, means representing, or, more precisely, preserving in writing for the future. Therefore, although the novel is written as a diary, with sections describing the narrator's surroundings and feelings at the very moment of writing, a large part of it is concerned with 'capturing' events that she believes she may wish to revisit at some future date. This is a more thoroughgoing version of the proleptic nostalgia represented in the novels I have discussed so far; where Katherine or Eustace attempt to preserve an image or object in memory, Cassandra makes a written record. A successful playwright during the 1930s, Smith spent the war years in America and felt that setting a novel in the past was one way to avoid being out of step with the temper of contemporary Britain (Grove 163–4). The text is thus an *aide mémoire* writ large; its action takes place in the mid-1930s, largely in the castle, a ruined survival in the grounds of a country house of more recent and more opulent design. Cassandra's father, Mortmain, a writer with one successful experimental novel under his belt, is having difficulty producing a follow-up and the family struggle for money until Cassandra's sister Rose becomes engaged to Simon, the young American heir to the estate in which the castle stands.

Cassandra's journal is itself evidence of her own desire to become a writer, and it is partly for this motive, as well as for more personal reasons, that she wishes to perfect her abilities at 'capturing' her surroundings. Her own pleasure in the challenge of such representation is contrasted with the difficulty her father has in putting pen to paper. He has been unable to write since a spell in prison following an assault on his wife, an incident that is portrayed in a relatively light-hearted fashion by Cassandra (Smith, *I Capture* 4–5). Simon suggests that Mortmain's spell in prison must provide the key to his writer's block and that Mortmain should be encouraged to recall this time:

> I think a psycho-analyst would say the trouble lay much further back than those few months in prison – but that prison might have brought it to the surface. He'd certainly explore that period thoroughly – make your father remember every detail of it; in a way, he'd have to be put back in prison. (142)

Cassandra takes Simon at his word and, with the help of her younger brother, incarcerates her father in a ruined tower in the hope that he will rediscover his creativity. This rough-and-ready behavioural therapy appears to have results, although Cassandra is confused by the novel her father eventually produces. Evidently, her father's modernist style – named 'Enigmatism' by Simon – is far removed from her own developing aesthetic. Whilst her father has immersed himself in children's books and magazines in order to attempt to recreate the perceptions of childhood, she prefers to observe what is around her now, even though she too is aware of the potential short-comings of realistic representation. In fact, as Nicola Humble points out, having 'taken the sting out of the experimental highbrow' through its depiction of Mortmain's writing, 'the novel even borrows some of its devices; notably an insistence on the materiality of text' (33).

The shortcomings of the available means of representation are particularly pronounced where memory is concerned, and the recognition of this undercuts the often nostalgic tone of much of the novel. One example of this occurs when Cassandra and Rose have an afternoon in the village with Simon and his cousin Neil. Sitting outside the local pub, they can hear the children singing in the school nearby:

> They were doing rounds [including] 'Sumer is icumen in' which is my very favourite tune – when I learnt it at school it was part of a lesson on Chaucer and Langland, and that was one of the few times when I had a flash of being back in the past. While I listened to Miss Marcy's children singing I seemed to capture everything together – mediaeval England, myself at ten, the summers of the past and the summer really coming. I can't imagine ever feeling happier than I did for those moments. (152–3)

When Cassandra describes having 'a flash of being in the past', she uses an image reminiscent of photography to describe what appears to be the memory of an epiphany. It is not immediately clear whether 'those moments' refers to when she first learned the song herself, or to her sentiments on hearing it again now; this is perhaps appropriate, in that the song itself conjures for her such a multi-faceted past, one that has historical and personal aspects. But, Simon, who has little personal knowledge of the village, also appears to be overwhelmed by both its beauty, and, inseparable from this, its history, feelings which he too expresses in terms of a wish to simultaneously preserve and represent. He wishes he could paint pictures of what he sees, and stares 'all around, as if he were trying to memorize things' (153). Pleasure in the present has in some way to be supplemented by the possibility of its future recovery or repetition; it has to be captured, either in painting, or in an active exercise of memory. Attempting to 'memorize things' is thus paradoxically both a means of preserving the evidence of the past for the future and an attempt to still the passage of time.

This double movement is even more pronounced in Cassandra's description of Midsummer Evening and the encounter that she has with Simon, who is by this stage engaged to her sister. In a nod to her classical namesake, Cassandra begins her account by foreshadowing the upset that will be the sequel to the pleasurable events she is about to describe: 'I must set it down to-day so that I shall have it for ever, intact and lovely, untouched by the sadness that is coming' (199). She hopes that she will be able to preserve these events from what is to come after, as though to keep causes separate from effects. The events of the evening have a 'strange, remembered quality' (199) and are therefore imbued with inevitability or predestination, a sense of 'fitness' that serves, temporarily to mask the fact that what Cassandra describes is an inappropriate moment of intimacy with her sister's fiancé. The repeated or reiterated quality of the events is compounded by the fact that Cassandra and her sister have a tradition of performing a quasi-pagan ceremony at midsummer; owing to Rose's absence in London on a visit to her future in-laws, Cassandra must this year perform it herself. The ritual is expressive of the cyclical, and therefore repetitive, aspect of time; it also has a particular relationship to Englishness. Explaining the ceremony to Simon, who arrives just as she is about to perform it, Cassandra reflects that the American 'was one of the few people who would really find the Midsummer rites romantic – that he'd see them as a link with the past and that they might even help with those English roots he wants to strike' (210). Simon may be able to forge a connection with England, but he must first understand England's past. However, although Cassandra tells Simon that on a previous occasion she and

Rose summoned 'an elemental' from out of the mist around the castle during the ceremony, the romantic encounter between Simon and Cassandra happens not at the castle but in the more civilized surroundings of the house, where he takes her for supper. Whilst Simon considers the rites to be of anthropological interest, it is signal that Cassandra's initiation into the adult rituals of illicit courtship should take place at the house, and that leaping around the bonfire and 'elementals' should be replaced by dancing on the terrace to music from the gramophone.

At the end of the novel, Smith resists the definitive closure that could have resulted from rectifying Simon and Rose's mistake and pairing Simon instead with Cassandra. Rose reveals that she became engaged to Simon only because of his wealth; she leaves for America with his cousin Neil. Simon leaves England also, and there is hope, but not certainty, that he and Cassandra might be united on his return. Notably, the novel ends just as Mortmain's reputation is being revived with his new work, which opens with the repeated phrase, 'The cat sat on the mat', intended to evoke the consciousness of a child learning to read and write. In imitation of this, although dubious about its literary effects, Cassandra ends her journal with the repeated phrase, addressed to Simon, 'I love you, I love you, I love you' (342). Remembered feelings and situations are finally displaced by an emotion expressed in the present, and the child's first words find a parallel in Cassandra expressing adult emotions for the first time. Apart from leaving some doubts about what might eventually happen to Cassandra and Simon, Smith also leaves the issue of how to successfully 'capture' events and feelings unresolved. Cassandra, like her father, falls back on a linguistic cliché after spending the whole of the proceeding narrative painstakingly searching for the best means to preserve her feelings. Perhaps what this present tense ending expresses, even if its exploration is beyond the immediate scope of the narrative, is a degree of scepticism, detectable also in the other novels I have examined here, about the consolations that looking back might provide.

Haunted Houses

The memories that are evoked or formed at these houses can painful or disturbing, but the houses themselves are often depicted in language that connects them to the fantasies of childhood, and specifically, to fairy tales. Thinking back to her family's initial arrival at the castle, Cassandra describes how the overgrown brambles along the path 'claw[ed] at the car as if trying to hold it back – I remember thinking of the Prince fighting his way through the wood to the Sleeping Beauty' (Smith 28). Similarly, on her arrival at Brede, Cressida sees the manor's grounds as 'magically lovely, enclosed by gates that were the barriers of fairyland' (Playfair 118). Meanwhile, for Charles Ryder, the very word 'Brideshead' is 'a name so familiar [...], a conjuror's name of such ancient power, that at its mere sound, the phantoms of those haunted late years began to take flight' (21). This type of language appeals to a particular archetype of the enchanted castle, emerging from the apparently ahistorical (or at least, dehistoricised) fairy tale narratives of childhood, and appealing to an innocent sensibility; but, as in Cassandra's description of brambles clawing at the car, it can also have a more sinister side. The fairy tale castle can also be a place of gothic horrors, as represented in a literary continuum that includes 'Bluebeard', Charlotte Bronte's *Jane Eyre* (1847) and Daphne Du Maurier's *Rebecca* (1938). In the latter, the destruction of Manderley seems to be the only way to exorcise Rebecca's ghost, but it is the unnamed narrator and her husband Maxim who are left to wander the country, rootless, like a pair of latter-day Ancient Mariners. Indeed, as Avril Horner and Sue Zlosnik note, 'Rebecca is only a ghost in so far as she is a powerful memory for the novel's characters' (25), who are unable to accommodate the disruption of the family line and the family home that she embodies. The language of haunting can be a powerful, albeit often sinister way, of expressing the persistence of the past in the present, and, therefore, of establishing a sense of continuity of habitation that can be an important aspect of the country house.

'[A] gothic tale of hatred and betrayal, the tormented mother's desperate attempts to reclaim her daughter immersing three generations in hatred and revenge, and in their dreadful consequences, suicide, incest, madness and despair' (Hastings 243). Selina Hastings' summary of Rosamond Lehmann's *The Ballad and the Source* (1944), is a fair description of the events with which the novel is concerned. Wendy Pollard suggests that these gothic aspects provoked unease in a number of male critics when the novel was published (Pollard 113–18), but the effects of the manner in which these are narrated have also to be taken into account. The first-person narrator of the novel, Rebecca, does not experience any of this drama directly, but instead is a narratee, fascinated by the history of Sybil Jardine's family, which is related to her by the aptly named Sybil herself, by the servant Tilly, and by Maisie, Sybil's granddaughter. This narrative technique tends to water down some of the excesses of the plot, not least because of Rebecca's shocked reaction to some of what she hears; but importantly, Rebecca is herself looking back, recalling, in a prodigious feat of memory, conversations that took place some years previously. Yet Rebecca acknowledges that her account is constrained by the exigencies of memory: 'Looking back into childhood is like looking into a semi-transparent globe within which people and places lie embedded. A shake – and they stir, rise up, circle in interweaving groups, then settle down again. There are no dates' (Lehmann, *Ballad* 27). This lack of historical or chronological rootedness adds to the mythical quality of the story Sybil tells. Rebecca cannot clearly remember the times or dates when she met with Sybil, but what Sybil told is clearly imprinted.

Many of their conversations take place at Sybil's house, The Priory, reached from Rebecca's home by a shortcut through a graveyard, where, on her way for her first visit, Rebecca picks some 'plump and prosperous' violets:

> When I wondered why they should grow so exceptionally fat in that one spot, Mademoiselle [the governess] answered in a dry way that no doubt they had rich soil to nourish them; and I saw the dead stretched out under me in the earth, feeding these flowers with a thin milk drawn from their bones. (9)

Before Rebecca has even met Sybil, then, the notion of a symbiotic, or even parasitic relationship between the living and the dead is established. Later, in a more sinister version of this image of the dead emerging into the land of the living, Rebecca recalls her attempts to extract information from Tilly, who was at one time employed by Sybil:

> Her memory, for the old days microscopically accurate, had well-nigh ceased to function with regard to the events of the last ten years; but I had somehow at last managed to tap where buried forms and voices could still be heard, alive, tapping and calling back from underground. (93)

This image suggests the extent to which the events and people she describes are still, in Tilly's memory at least, alive; but the notion of a premature burial is a sinister one. Their voices may be audible, but these people will only ever be ventriloquised by Tilly or Sybil, or indeed Rebecca herself. Whether recovering their stories is a positive, recuperative act is very much open to question. As Judy Simons suggests, although '[n]ostalgia constitutes a creative act', Rebecca, grown older, is 'less confident about her ability to judge the moral complexities she encounters from the simple perspective of childhood' (Simons 103–04). What she hears about the family leads Rebecca to believe that rather than learning from the past and progressing, successive generations are simply repeating the mistakes of their forebears: 'It [...] went on and one, like a curse. Liar begot liar; and all their road, forward and back, far back, was cratered with disastrous pits of guilt, haunted by ruinous voices crying vengeance' (Lehmann, *Ballad* 82).[24]

Rebecca hears the final instalments of the Sybil's feud with her daughter from Maisie, who comes to stay at The Priory during the First World War, while Sybil is in France. Rebecca is by now no longer a child and Maisie's continuation of the story undercuts some of the flourishes of Sybil's version. As Maisie's ad hoc Christmas party wears on, Rebecca imagines Sybil as the 'Enchantress Queen in an antique ballad of revenge' (238). Sybil is not simply the narrator of her family history but an actor in it, one whose motives often appear to be clouded and sinister. Rebecca has earlier questioned her initial belief that she was in some way specially chosen by Sybil to be her interlocutor, feeling that is 'presenting a part she had rehearsed a hundred times', and seeing herself 'as one of a long shadowy series of confidential audiences, all gazing, listening, as spellbound, as gratified as I' (110). This scepticism goes some way towards undercutting Sybil's power as a storyteller; Sybil is indeed a grotesque figure, whose own behaviour is itself reprehensible. By the end of the novel, she is still in self-imposed exile in France; The Priory will eventually be inherited by Maisie, but she asserts she will never have children: 'There's madness in my family' (272). Her prediction of her brother Malcolm's death in the war is fulfilled and thus it appears that only the family's story will survive. The novel concludes with Rebecca's dream, a vision of Sybil locked out from The Priory, but still exercising a powerful hold; the persistence of this form of survival, then, is not to be underestimated.

The Christmas party at The Priory foreshadows the installation of the next generation in the house, but this is something that Maisie asserts will never actually come about. If in this novel the older generation is temporarily displaced by younger, in Henry Green's *Loving* (1945) it is the servants who displace the family during their absence. Jeremy Treglown notes that the novel has often been described as 'an ironic fairy tale' (Treglown, *Romancing* 165); it begins 'Once upon a day' and ends 'happily ever after'. Such a description, as Treglown also points out, detracts from the political aspects of Green's analysis of life an Irish 'Big House' and the 'happily ever after' ending is belied by the fact that Raunce and Edith, whose union is described in this fashion, have left for an England that is at war. Commenting later on her depiction of her family's house in Ireland in *Bowen's Court* (1942), Elizabeth Bowen suggests that haunting is not an appropriate image for the way in which previous generations continue to inhabit the house:

> With the end of each generation, the lives that submerged here were absorbed again. With each death, the air of the place had thickened: it had been added to. The dead do not need to visit Bowen's Court rooms – as I said, we had no ghosts in that house – because they already permeated them. (Bowen, *Bowen's Court* 451)[25]

The dead impress themselves on the house, just as in Sackville-West's description their clutter serves as relics. In the final part of Elizabeth Goudge's trilogy *The Eliots of Damerosehay* (1938–51), a visitor to the house senses the presence of children in the garden, 'wraiths, not necessarily of the dead but of vanished childhood' (507). These presences echo events from earlier novels in the trilogy, and one of these spectral children lives on in the house as an adult. Green, similarly, attempts to convey the sense that the air of Kinalty has been 'thickened' by past inhabitants, who are not revenants because they never left. Raunce, the Head Footman promoted to butler after the death of Eldon, the previous incumbent, at one point comes upon the maids Kate and Edith dancing in the ball room to music from the gramophone:

> They were wheeling wheeling in each other's arms heedless at the far end where they had drawn up one of the white blinds. Above from a rather low ceiling five great chandeliers swept one after the other almost to the waxed parquet floor reflecting in their hundred thousand drops the single sparkle of distant day, again and again red velvet panelled walls, and two girls, minute in purple, dancing multiplied to eternity in these trembling pears of glass. (Green, *Loving* 57)

The girls' dance is a subversive gesture, in that they are inhabiting a space that was not intended for them, and which contrasts with their own cramped quarters, but they also appear, momentarily, to embody all those who have ever danced in this room, refracted 'to eternity' in the chandelier. Rod Mengham suggests that the 'rotations of the waltz do not comprise a sequence of movements with start and finish but an open, self-perpetuating form which rebounds further into the faceting of the chandelier' (148). Not merely reflected, the girls are contained in the 'trembling pears of glass'. It is as though the room itself will now always retain the memory of them and their movements, just as it reflects back the image of others.

Later, the girls decide to entertain Albert, the cook's nephew (or possibly her son) evacuated from England, and the children of the house, by playing a game of blind man's buff. The site they choose for this game is the sculpture gallery, a 'complete copy of Greek temple' hidden amidst the 'great Gothic pile' of Kinalty (Green, *Loving* 103): 'Their cries reverberated round the Gallery. [...] [T]his immemorial game went on before witnesses in bronze in marble and plaster, echoed up and down over and over again' (107). The echo here has a similar effect to the multiple reflections in the chandelier, implying that this 'immemorial' game could, potentially go on forever, and that it will somehow be preserved in the fabric of the building. Bowen describes the Big Houses as places in which 'something important occurred once, and seems, from all evidence, to be occurring still' (*Bowen's Court* 20). In Green's novel, not just the important but the trivial contributes to the aura of the house; the two servant girls in particular appear to inhabit the building with an ease that belies their status. But there are also reminders of the fragility of its fabric. At one point, it is described as a house that 'had yet to be burned down' (56), an ironic nod towards the fate of many Big Houses. If the house can be a repository for memory, it can also be reinscribed politically by an act of terrorism or an act of war.

Conclusion

The threat of destruction overshadows a number of the houses described in these novels; even if their fabric remains undamaged, the way of life that they have contained and indeed enabled, is often seen to be under threat. It is perhaps not surprising that landscape, rather than architecture, could be more readily made to symbolize the survival of the country beyond the war. Antonia Lant's comments on the representation of Britain in wartime films have relevance for literature also. She argues that although 'the few miraculous wartime architectural survivals' such as St Paul's Cathedral provided visual emblems of resistance to the 'iconography of urban destruction [...] [l]andscape imagery provides the best visual antidote to war, for the continuity it evokes' (49). Yet the evocation of continuity is achieved at a price; the fact that the war did change both the landscape and the way of life of the countryside has to be elided. Where authors are alert to the realities of country life, the problem becomes how to accommodate, and record, the changes that the war is bringing. As Allingham's memoir shows, in wartime, even the recent past can seem historically distant. Looking back therefore contains, and expresses, the not inconsiderable anxieties about what further changes the future might hold, changes against which the materiality of the landscape cannot provide protection.

Some of these texts might appear to hark back to a time before memory, and the depiction of the what is remembered, were rendered problematic by both developments in psychology and modernist explorations of consciousness. Looking nostalgically to the past and imbuing buildings and objects with emblematic force might seem to be a way of denying the fears, traumas and politically realities of which that past was also comprised. A petrified version of the earlier times, reliable and unchanging, insulates the past against troubling reinterpretation. But there is a twofold danger in condemning nostalgic representations as 'inauthentic': firstly, there can be a presumption that writers are not aware of the selectivity that such representations involve; secondly, it implies that there can be a completely 'authentic' representation of the past. Many of the novels I have examined here introduce disjunctive elements that undercut any sense of complacency in their depiction of the processes of memory, and certainly for many protagonists, whilst the act of remembering might appear to be painless and, in narrative terms, unproblematic, the impact of what is remembered on the present is often disturbing. Rather than merely irresponsible escapism, nostalgia can be seen as an explicable symptom in troubling and difficult circumstances, and writers are often aware of both its potential and its limitations as a representational form.

4
In Time of War

Discussing how a disparate group of factory workers perceives the passing of the war, the narrator of Inez Holden's 1941 novel *Night Shift* observes that: 'The few months ago in war-time soon became "the old days" so that already we looked back on the first months of war as on remote memories of adolescence' (115–16). These remarks illustrate how the routine of work in the factory distorts the perception of time; the events of only a few months ago seem remote. Even while the war was still in train, however, the identification of its different phases could give a shape to experience and memory. Events such as the retreat from Dunkirk, the Battle of Britain, or the Normandy landings were understood and depicted, at the time, as important turning points in the conflict, whilst many writers, particularly those living in London and other large cities, were attuned to the fluctuations of the air war.[1] In this chapter, I will be focusing on works published after the end of the conflict, some of them begun while it was still in progress, which attempt to assess what the impact of the war has been or will be. The difficulties inherent in this task are illustrated in Stevie Smith's novel *The Holiday*, written during the war years but only published in 1949. Smith decided to update the novel's action and delete references to the war being ongoing; her narrator Celia comments: 'It is a year or so after the war. It cannot be said that it is war, it cannot be said that it is peace, it can be said that it is post-war; this will probably go on for ten years' (13). The social, cultural and psychological impact of the events of the war cannot be contained within the temporal span of 1939–45. Shaping the key events of wartime into a narrative could be reassuring, but, as I will show, there is also a contrary drive, to forget the past and look to the future.

A number of commentators in the immediate post-war years expressed concern at the effects that the desire to depict the war and its aftermath appeared to be having on the development of the novel. In some respects, this debate mirrors discussions from the start of the war about the role of the writer in the war effort. As I suggested in the introduction, the question of engagement, specifically whether it would be possible for writers to preserve a sense of their own aesthetic in the face of political events in the outside world, and the practical question of whether it would be possible for authors to continue to produce extended prose works under war conditions, were key issues. In the immediate post-war, many literary figures again confronted the question of what the writer's appropriate relation to the wider political scene might be. In his reviews and articles for the *Times Literary Supplement*, R. D. Charques often expressed disappointment with the lack of imagination being displayed in contemporary literature and decried the predilection he identified for 'the documentary transcription of personal experience' and 'the discussion of political ideas' (Anon. [R. D. Charques], 'Imagination' 149). Marie Scott-James, in *Time and Tide*, similarly lamented: 'What a pity it is that so many contemporary novelists bury their real story beneath a mass of irrelevant topical detail. A short history lesson on every alternate page' ('New Novels', 29 October 1945 882). She also complained that few novels 'have been touched by the creative imagination' ('New Novels', 26 January 1946 88). For Charques, this issue is exacerbated by, but does not have its roots in, the war. Discussing interwar writing in an article from November 1945, he identifies what he believes to be a damaging trend for writers 'no longer to write novels, but rather to write novels about free will or coal mining or divorce reform' (Anon [R.D. Charques], 'The English Novel' 554). Charques therefore fears for the future vitality of the novel if content takes precedence over formal, aesthetic and imaginative concerns. Frank Swinnerton, whilst sharing Charques view that the novel had gone into decline before the outbreak of war, blames Darwin and Freud, whose influence has 'paralysed what used to be called the mythopoetic faculty' (32). The Darwinian or Freudian metanarratives leave to little to the writer's creative powers, and like Charques, Swinnerton calls for a revival of the imagination, which he believes to have been swamped by writers' desire to display their education (33).

Others, whilst seeming to be in sympathy with some of these sentiments, placed the perceived problem into context. In her contribution to a debate on 'The Future of Fiction' published in *New Writing and Daylight* in 1946, Rose Macaulay argues that the war has 'clogged and stunned imagination, and intellectual activity has been paralysed' (73), with the effects on younger writers being particularly acute. Macaulay suggests, however, that whilst the effects on the individual of the 'perils, discomforts, fears, [and] adventures' (73) of war may be profound, the war itself is a 'limited experience' which she does not expect to have a 'great or lasting' (73) influence on fiction. Writing in May 1948, P. H. Newby, himself a novelist, identified the depiction of childhood and war as two of the most popular subjects for new novels:

> But what else can we expect? If, for the moment, we think of childhood as the period when reality breaks in upon illusion [...] and if by war we mean the special emotional climate of the past ten years, it will be seen that for the young writer, at least, there is not much else to write about. This, surely, is the limiting factor in the novel to-day.
> ('New Novels' 440)

Like Macaulay, Newby sees the war as restricting creativity, doubting whether novels emerging from the war could have a lasting impact on the development of the form. Other writers too expressed scepticism about the potential longevity of novels about the war, implying that such works could only be of transitory interest, if they were of interest at all. Rosamund Lehmann, writing in 1946, believed that it was 'too soon' for any 'great war novel' to have appeared. When it did emerge, she argued, it would be from 'some country whose inhabitants have undergone a great communal death and rebirth' ('Future' 6–7), implying that the experience of war in Britain, not being of this nature, was not profound enough to produce a 'great war novel'. From the perspective of the early 1970s, V. S. Pritchett put it more bluntly: 'the war [...] was like a car smash or pile-up. English writing did not vanish but for years the experience exhausted us mentally and physically' (*Midnight* 227).

A key question then, seems to be how to overcome the traumatic impact of this 'car smash' and engage with 'the times' in a manner that does not result in political or sociological observation becoming subservient to artistic concerns, and without producing works that will have little resonance beyond the immediate historical context. One younger commentator, the novelist and essayist Alex Comfort, who had a particular concern with the manner in which violence, and what he saw as an increasingly brutalized society, affected literature, suggested that one way of tackling the overwhelming scale of world events was to focus on their effects on particular individuals:

> For me at any rate, the solution which presents itself is to concentrate on the fixed-points, as one might look away from a fire to allow one's

sight to settle down – the soldier in his pillbox watching Hitler's body burn, disliking the smoke, wondering if he will get a sanitary fatigue afterwards, and whether his wife has been killed [...] not the viewpoint of the man who in going to be executed, or even of the firing squad. (76)

Comfort audaciously chooses a German soldier as his example here, emphasizing his concern with a humanism that cuts across national boundaries, and exposing the disjunction between individual subjectivity and the scope of history. Yet it is only through the individual's experience of it that the historical event can be made graspable. As Elizabeth Bowen commented: 'through the particular, in war-time, I felt the high voltage current of the general pass' ('Postscript' 224). Comfort's example is also useful because it points to one of the common themes in the novel in the post-war period. Many writers were concerned not only to depict their own or others' war experiences but to expose the difficulty of making the transition from the army to civilian life, or from war to peacetime. These are not firmly entrenched binary oppositions, however: not only the soldier but also the soldier's wife is in danger.

Some works from this period do deal schematically with the social issues of wartime, or strain towards political commentary. However, whilst 'stock' figures such as the returning serviceman or prisoner of war feature in many of the novels that I will be discussing here, the manner in which their memories of the war and the effects of this on their reassimilation into civilian society are depicted varies widely. Writers show differing degrees of understanding of the potential psychological condition of war veterans and their possible treatment, and this inevitably has an impact on the level of complexity with which the subjectivity of these individuals is depicted. Authors including Nigel Balchin, H. E. Bates and Henry Green are interested in presenting the psychological damage (often a memory disorder) wrought on soldiers by the war. Whilst Balchin, in *Mine Own Executioner* (1945), attempts to engage with current medical discourse and treatment methods, Bates, in *The Purple Plain* (1947) and Green, in *Back* (1946), have a more oblique approach to the possibility of reintegration or cure. In Balchin's realist novel the psychoanalyst's consulting room is the site of a process of remembering that is intended to have cathartic effects, but in Green's novel, patterns of repetition and forgetting seem liable to stall a recovery that the protagonist is initially unable to admit is necessary. Bates' protagonist, meanwhile, can overcome the shock of losing his wife during the Blitz and his subsequent lack of interest in living only when his involvement in a plane crash puts his own life in danger.

The power of developing cultural narratives of war experience is exemplified by novels dealing with instances of imposture, where individuals lay claim to a past, often of a heroic nature, that is not actually their own. Works including Betty Miller's *On the Side of the Angels* (1945) and Elizabeth Taylor's *A Wreath of Roses* (1949) show the allure of such heroic narratives to both the deceiver and the deceived. Whilst the impostors can usually be labelled as suffering from a psychological disorder of some kind, often itself a product of war experience, such narratives raise important questions about memory and authenticity. Elizabeth Bowen's *The Heat of the Day* (1949) also displays a concern with the interface between domestic and public deception, exposing the complicated relationship between war experience, subjectivity and dissembling. There are implications here for cultural as well as individual memory; once memory is admitted to be open to distortion or denial, the reassuring power of cultural memory is subtly eroded.

War and the post-war

A number of writers, then, choose to address the role of memory in either effecting or indeed blocking the transition from wartime to postwar. At the most mundane level comes the recognition that it will not be possible to simply switch back from one's wartime way of life to one's pre-war role; authors are often attentive both to the changes that active service has wrought and to how civilians have had to adapt and change. A Mass–Observation study published in 1944 showed that individuals who could remember the aftermath of the last war were anxious that the 'high hopes and broken promises, [...] enormous unemployment figures and [...] "war heroes" selling matches or singing in the streets' (Mass–Observation 25) of that period should not be replicated, even if this meant delaying the release of individuals from the services. The plans for social reform contained in the Beveridge Report did not necessarily foster optimism, and Ian McLaine suggests that 'public cynicism underlay the initial excitement' (182) that the report provoked. Although the Beveridge Report did find its way into some prisoner of war camps, David Rolf argues that, isolated as they were from the social changes happening at home, 'prisoners' fears of mass unemployment did not recede; they were still locked into the crippling experience of the 1930s' means test, "dole" queue and closed factory gates' (127). Even for those who had not undergone the trauma of imprisonment, adjustments would be both necessary and difficult. Niamh Baker points out that whilst some women who had undertaken war work in factories were probably glad to give up having to combine long working hours with the difficulties of organising the wartime domestic economy (such as queuing for food), work had at least provided women with opportunities to share their troubles (5–7). But as Jenny Hartley notes, 'War, although potentially emancipatory for women, could never be their congenial habitat. It brought separation, suffering and death', and, in any case, 'women's place in the public ranks of war was always seen as temporary' (11).

N. H. Reeve suggests that the 'uneasy-homecoming syndrome is so ubiquitous [in the post-war period] as to have become a virtual cliché' (162). The 'first novel of demobilization' (Allen 148), Robert Henriques *The Journey Home*, was published in December 1944, and as early as June 1945 R. D. Charques could label J. B. Priestley's *Three Men in New Suits* 'conventional' (Anon [R. D. Charques], 'Demobilized' 257): one ex-soldier's wife has left him for a GI, another man becomes involved with a girl working at a local factory. In many instances, though, the manner in which the uneasy homecoming, and the returnee's relationship to the past are depicted transcends or attempts to challenge emerging stereotypes. Not all authors who consider this topic engage explicitly with the discourses of medicine or psychology, but many do attempt to tackle, however obliquely, the issue raised bluntly in Olivia Manning's *Artist Among the Missing* (1949): 'Neurosis is a sort of occupational disease of war' (175). Even among individuals, either soldiers or civilians, who do not suffer from anything diagnosable, it is debatable whether there is ever a 'normal' or unproblematic resumption of civilian life. 'You can't live under unnatural conditions like this and not go mad' (23), comments one of the protagonists in Richard Mason's *The Wind Cannot Read* (1947), reflecting on his experiences after the retreat from Burma. A further key issue here is how to forge some kind of continuity between the wartime self and the post-war self, and the manner in which the individual's memories of wartime experience are introduced into narratives concerned primarily with the post-war can be revealing.

In Priestley's novel, Alan, from a wealthy upper-middle-class family, Herbert, whose family are farmers, and working-class Eddie, all face a similar sense of disorientation on their return. For Alan, this is expressed as a kind of psychic splitting:

> The sight of the old house split Alan into two men. One, who had been born there, recognised with affection every window pane and worn brick, and simply came home. The other, who had been away for years and had fought his way from the African desert into the

middle of Europe, stared at this rambling old building, huddled deep into its green island hillside, and began to wonder what this remote place meant to him. If one man came home, the other still arrived at a billet at the end of a long march. (Priestley, *Three Men* 16)

Past associations cannot supersede the intervening experiences that have rendered his home strange to Alan. He tries to explain his disorientation to his mother, who hopes he will be able to pick up his life again where he 'dropped' it: 'Alan shook his head. "I don't think it's like that, you know. Life's not a walking-stick or something – that you can drop or pick up. My life's been going on – inside me –"' (25) Alan's urge to put the psychological lessons of war to work in the post-war world culminates in a rousing speech at the end of the novel, when he advises his fellow ex-servicemen to look forward rather than returning 'to the muddle of the pre-war time' (150). He wishes in particular to prevent a repetition of the events through which he has passed, a message reinforced by Priestley in his *Letter to a Returning Serviceman* (1945), where he warns Bob, the imagined recipient of the letter: 'They tell us that history does not repeat itself. All I can say is that history just now is trying its hardest. The 1918–19 pattern is distinctly visible. Once more you are being told to take it easy and all will be well' (5). This essay concludes on an apocalyptic tone, with Priestley warning of the destruction that could be wrought by the atom bomb (32). For Alan, learning from the past means looking not to the pre-war but to the positive lessons that can be gleaned from his wartime experiences, and specifically from the commonality of purpose that he shared with his fellow soldiers. Alan's rhetoric is also intended to buoy up Eddie and Herbert who have returned to crises among their own families. Herbert's relations expect his commitment to the family farm; Eddie's wife leaves him for another man, causing him to reinterpret their relationship and discover, retrospectively, evidence of her unfaithfulness.

Whilst Priestley emphasizes that the experience of war has changed his protagonists, it is evident that their sense of disorientation on returning is compounded by the unexpected changes that have been undergone by those they left behind. The tension between change and stability is dramatised in a different way in *The Captive Heart* (1946), identified by Robert Murphy as the first film focusing on British prisoners of war (Murphy 212). (Notably, in order to provide a socially diverse cast of soldiers, this particular camp houses both officers and ordinary soldiers.) Karel Hasek (Michael Redgrave), a Czech political prisoner, has escaped from a concentration camp. He finds the body of a dead English soldier,

Geoffrey Mitchell, and steals his identity documents. Under this assumed persona, he is taken prisoner with a group of officers and men from other regiments; fortuitously, he spent some of his childhood in England and therefore speaks unaccented English. He manages to quell the suspicions of his fellow prisoners, but then a letter arrives from Geoffrey Mitchell's wife (played by Redgrave's wife, Rachel Kempson). It transpires that Mitchell's marriage was in difficulty; in order to disguise his ignorance about Mitchell's family affairs and home life, and as a means of escaping from the routine of life in the camp, Hasek replies to the letter, explaining the change in his handwriting by an injury, and asking Mrs Mitchell to 'carry on writing as though I were a stranger'. In the camp, he tells her, 'The future is remote, the present empty, even the past begins to feel unreal.' Mrs Mitchell's response stresses that, despite the influx of evacuees to their village, the cycle of life there continues as it always did: 'Everything's changed and yet nothing's changed. There's the whistle of the 4.35 half an hour late as usual. [...] There's still cricket on Saturday afternoons [...] Beyond the river you can see the first vivid green of the larches and the bluebell wood.'[2] From Mrs Mitchell writing, the action cuts to Hasek reading; the images of village life to which her letter provides the voice-over are intended to be temporally parallel to events in the camp, but the manner in which they are presented means that Hasek can partake, indirectly, of what, for Mitchell, would be memories.

However, when Mrs Mitchell asks whether they will be able to recapture the happiness of the early days of their marriage, Hasek is obliged to attempt to disabuse her, whilst still being unable to reveal his true identity. He accurately tells her, 'I have no place in your past or your future, Celia. You must think of your husband as dead.' Their wartime correspondence has created a perpetual present, one that is underpinned by her evocation of a vision of England that emphasizes its essentially unchanging nature. After his release, Hasek goes to visit Mrs Mitchell and tell her the truth. She is initially horrified, but he tells her, 'It was as if you were offering me a new world.' Mrs Mitchell's portrayal of England has won over the displaced person; but her England, far from being 'new' is in fact a repository of deeply rooted values. The imposture carried out by Hasek – a kind of long-distance version of the Shakespearean 'bed-trick'– becomes a means of displacing the idea that England might have undergone, or might need to undergo, any fundamental change itself. Mrs Mitchell eventually overcomes her shock and admits that she has fallen in love with this new version of her husband; but despite his origin in war-torn continental Europe, he will simply provide the means for her to restart her marriage at the point at which it failed the first time.

This film is a variation on what Sue Harper has called the 'Enoch Arden' theme, in which 'a loved one who is presumed dead returns unexpectedly' (214 n.29). Michael Redgrave also starred in *The Years Between* (1946), the screen version of Daphne Du Maurier's 1944 play which features another a version of this plot; the unexpected return of Michael Wentworth, who was reported killed, scotches both his wife's incipient love affair with another man and her political ambitions. Even worse, it transpires that Wentworth was on a secret mission in mainland Europe and knew that his wife would be deceived into believing him dead in order to preserve his cover. Harper suggests that films with this type of plot:

> were popular because they enabled audiences to rehearse a number of responses in the postwar period. They could admit fears that those who returned from the war would be permanently changed; they could recognise the desire that those who were dead would return home in a stranger's guise; and they could enjoy the provision of an alibi for having loved strangers, in that they might thereby have been entertaining angels unawares. (214 n.29)

In Tennyson's poem *Enoch Arden* (1864), however, pathos arises from the fact that, on returning from the desert island on which he has been stranded for many years, Arden decides not to disrupt the apparently idyllic life that his wife is now living with their childhood friend. Writers and film-makers of the late 1940s generally chose dramatic confrontation over self-sacrifice. Helen Ashton's novel *The Captain Comes Home* (1947) makes explicit use of the Enoch Arden theme in that her protagonist John Crowe, believed dead after the withdrawal from the Greek mainland, survives on an island with the help of sympathetic locals. His eventual confrontation with Robert Slater, the man who is now married to his wife Phyllis, results in Crowe being put on trial for assault. This gives Ashton the opportunity to present medical and legal testimony about Crowe's state of mind that essentially stands as a substitute for self-expression on his part. Whilst Crowe's ordeal on the island is depicted directly, at the start of the novel, once he returns home Crowe slips out of focus, and much of the novel is concerned instead with the difficulties of readjustment that are faced by another local couple. Phyllis is shown to have been an unsuitable match in any case, and the satisfactory conclusion of the legal proceedings coincides with the end of the novel, meaning the conflicts that resulted in the case in the first place are never really addressed.

The use of the island in this novel and the prison camp in *The Captive Heart* means that the protagonists switch not from active service to home life, but from a state of hiatus, an intermediate space between war and peace. This perhaps diminishes the difficulty that the writer might otherwise face in depicting men who are in or have been in combat situations but it can also result in imprisonment being used for symbolic reasons rather than being depicted realistically. This is to some extent the case with Monica Dickens' *The Happy Prisoner* (1946), but although her cast of characters does include a man released from a prison camp in Japan, the prisoner of the title is Oliver North, who is confined to bed at home, having lost a leg and suffered damage to his heart when hit by a shell-splinter at Arnhem. Oliver's confinement alters his perception of the world: retrospection has become 'one of his favourite ways of passing the time' (Dickens 8). Whilst he previously hoped to move away from the family home and work in London, his illness means that he will never be able to cope with life in the city, and he reverts to 'his boyhood's inclination towards the land' (78). With any progress forward severely circumscribed by his injuries, and confined for much of the novel to a single room, Oliver becomes a confidant for many of his family members, the intersection of a network of other people's stories.

The account he delivers to his new nurse, Elizabeth, of the events leading up to his own injuries, is tinged with moments of comedy, and delivered as though it has been often rehearsed. He tells, for instance, how he felt when he regained consciousness after being hit:

> When I came to, I was being gently rocked; I thought I was a baby in my cradle. I swear it. I'm not just making that up because I've read that you get a subconscious mother-craving *in extremis*, though I did read that afterwards and was gratified to think I'd run so true to form. Actually, I was in a small boat. (47)

Oliver's glossing of this incident, attempting to separate what he felt then from what he learned afterwards, creates the impression that he has a good deal of insight into his condition. However, the self-conscious reference here to a 'mother-craving' is significant, as Oliver has in many respects been forced to regress to a childlike, dependent condition. He is also, implicitly, feminized by his injuries, an effect compounded by the way in which he becomes a sounding board for his sisters, remaining static whilst they demonstrate their mobility.[3] At one point,

Oliver is visited in rapid succession by his younger sister Violet, whose wedding is approaching, and his older sister Heather, whose husband has recently been released by the Japanese:

> In a moment, [Violet] burst into Oliver's room, her hair dishevelled [...] 'Can I borrow your trench-coat, Ollie?' she asked breathlessly. [...] His next visitor was Heather, in an overall, with her head tied up in Oliver's silk invasion map of Germany. 'I've just had a row with Ma,' she stated, taking one of his cigarettes. (196–97)

The small details of the borrowed trenchcoat and the invasion map used as a headscarf serve to emphasize that the gender roles within the household have been disturbed both by the war, and by the more immediate consequences of Oliver's injury. Because he, the main protagonist, is bed-bound for the bulk of the narrative, action in the novel is almost all reported to him rather than shown directly. Thus Heather's husband John confides in Oliver about an affair that he had in Melbourne on his way home from the Far East, Heather herself explains why she first ran away with another man and then came back, and even the reticent Elizabeth eventually tells him about her estrangement from her father. Oliver does win the affections of Elizabeth, who decides to throw over her rich fiancé in Oliver's favour, but as soon as he has finished his declaration, she has to resume her role as his carer, as the emotional exertion has been too much for him. Despite his gradual recovery through the course of the book, it is evident that, whilst the war might have provided him with the opportunity to demonstrate his masculinity and break free of the influence of his often overbearing mother, it also scotches his ambitions. Ending the narrative with Oliver still an invalid fixes the novel in Stevie Smith's 'post-war'; recovery, both personal and social, is still a future prospect.

Recovering (from) the war

Oliver North's illness does have psychological aspects; he is prone to both depression and to bad dreams. His brother-in-law John apparently disappoints the family by failing to fit the stereotype of the released prisoner of war, although Dickens perhaps implies that he has devised strategies for keeping the worst memories at bay:

> His waiting time in Australia had repaired the ravages of what had been one of the better Japanese prison camps. Violet wanted horror

stories from him, but [...] [a]lthough he spoke of boredom and hunger and of brewing the same tea-leaves a dozen times and then tossing for who should eat the leaves, he made none of it seem uncomfortably real. Oliver thought that if he had had to suffer several months in a Japanese prison camp he would have made a much better story out of it than this. (141)

Although there are few, if any, signs elsewhere in the novel of some fundamental trauma being masked by John here, Oliver's reaction is worth noting, because it contains the presumption that John has indeed selected and ordered his experiences, thus explaining why the end result is not suitably horrific. (It could be argued that the casual nastiness of the detail about the tea-leaves is in fact as awful as any more explicit account of brutality.) Dickens' depiction of John fits with the description of returning prisoners in Guy Morgan's memoir *Only Ghosts Can Live* (1945): 'to-morrow we would become leisurely anecdotes across a dinner-table, pub-corner bores; to-day we were first editions. Each was in process of dramatising the story he had to tell, knowing that for a short time, each in his own home circle, would have the spotlight on him' (162). John, understandably, chooses to focus on a relatively circumscribed series of events, and what he decides not to share can never be estimated; in fact, his big secret proves to be the affair he had in Melbourne, itself a life-affirming, if adulterous, gesture in the aftermath of danger.

Both Morgan and Dickens recognise the limits to communication between former service personnel and civilians. According to Ben Shephard, both former prisoners and their families were advised against the discussion of life in captivity: 'Ex-prisoners were told not to upset their relatives by talking about their experiences to them, and their next-of-kin were instructed in official pamphlets not to ask about them' (321). The treatment of those returning from the Far East presented particular problems, because relatively little was known about conditions in the Far Eastern camps until the end of the war. The mysterious and unspeakable nature of prisoner experiences with the Japanese are communicated obliquely in Mary Renault's *North Face* (1949), where Miss Fowler, weighing up Neil, a new arrival at the boarding house, misinterprets the physical evidence: 'His deep tan, combined with his spareness, had suggested tuberculosis until she noticed that his condition was too hard for this. Provisionally, she decided that he might have been a prisoner with the Japanese. There was a certain look about his eyes' (24). Neil's reticence is an important aspect of her romanticised consideration of him; his refusal to tell her about his war record in fact conceals a domestic intrigue rather than any more refined form of torture. Whilst in *The Happy Prisoner*, imprisonment in the Far East allows John's experiences to remain beyond the realms of speculation, in Nigel Balchin's *Mine Own Executioner*, incarceration by the Japanese serves a different purpose. Life in European camps could be portrayed, as it is in *The Captive Heart* as a round of 'goon-baiting' and Red Cross parcels, punctuated by the occasional rush of melancholy; in Balchin's novel, the emphasis is on brutal treatment and isolation, factors which eventually lead to the psychic dissolution of the former prisoner.[4]

Balchin's central protagonist, Felix Milne, is a psychotherapist who has become disillusioned with both his marriage and his private patients, who, for the most part are 'rich, unhappy people, chiefly women, who're incurably normal and want something done about it' (Balchin, *Mine Own* 16). He is approached by the wife of Adam Lucian, a former Spitfire pilot; Lucian has made one attempt to kill his wife and she believes that his problems stem from his war experience. Milne appears to be the ideal choice as he is a lay analyst, having chosen to go into training analysis rather than completing his medical studies, and Lucian has a phobia of the medical profession. Balchin goes to some lengths to make Lucian's war experience atypical; notably, Lucian is deprived of many of the resources that are usually believed to have lessened the possibility of neurosis, particularly camaraderie. As a fighter pilot, he works alone, and the nature of his captivity is also unusual. Shot down in Burma, he is not sent to a prison camp, but is instead kept in isolation by the platoon of Japanese soldiers who capture him. They break his leg to prevent him escaping, but when this heals, he manages to make his getaway, killing a Japanese soldier in the process. Milne decides to use drug therapy as a means of encouraging Lucian to discuss the details of his captivity, because, like John in *The Happy Prisoner*, Lucian is reluctant, in ordinary conversation, to go beyond the truncated and emotionally detached version that he has created for himself. Under the influence of sodium thio–pentane, he reveals that, tortured by his captors, he gave away military secrets, and Milne identifies this as one cause of Lucian's anxiety.

In having Milne use drug therapy, Balchin shows an awareness of developments in the treatment of war neurosis that took place during the course of the war, and like other novelists of the time, including Jack Aistrop in *Pretend I am a Stranger* (1949) and Gilbert Frankau in *Michael's Wife* (1948), displays ambivalence towards this particular technique. The effects of sodium amytal, a drug similar to that used by Milne and initially administered as a means of calming down combatants returning from Dunkirk, were observed by William Sargant, a psychiatrist who was sceptical of orthodox Freudian methods of analysis:

> The injections had strange side-effects [...] a soldier might suddenly recover suppressed memories of the gruesome experiences that had caused or hastened his breakdown, and relive them before us. After this discharge of pent-up emotions, especially battle terrors and possibly rage against their officers, soldiers would suddenly improve. (Sargant 88)

For Sargant, then, the cathartic effect of the drug is a useful side effect, which can contribute to a soldier's recovery; this did not mean, however, that soldiers would be able to cope if confronted again with similarly stressful combat situations. As Ruth Leys argues, Sargant's 'conceptualization of abreaction was ambiguous through and through' (196). Whilst at times he emphasised the importance of the patient integrating the recovered material into conscious memory, elsewhere he stresses simply the expulsion of the trauma, with drug treatment a means of discharging pent-up emotions rather than a precursor to a fuller analysis that might facilitate the reintegration of the traumatic incident into the individual's life-history. Milne decides that he will be unable to carry out a successful analysis until Lucian has told him about his war experiences, but his use of drug therapy is complicated by the fact that he is not a fully qualified doctor and has to ask his colleague Garsten to oversee his use of the drug. Garsten has had previous experience of using similar drugs on war casualties: 'We hadn't time for long-term analyses, of course. [...] They were all right if there was no strain. But I think they'd have come apart in your hand if they'd gone back into battle.' (166) He also warns Milne that he was able to treat his patients soon after the traumatic incident, whereas there has been a longer time-lapse in Lucian's case: 'these delayed fuse jobs are rather the devil as a rule' (167).

Lucian is not suffering from amnesia but is simply reluctant to discuss his time in the jungle because of his shame at having given away military secrets. Recovering from the effects of the drug he asks Milne, 'Did I spill the beans? [...] I told you the lot, didn't I?' (148) His aggressive behaviour has resulted from the strain of a conscious act of concealment, rather than from repression. However, the revelation of Lucian's wartime experience is only the start, and Milne determines to carry out further analysis. Apparently taking his cue from the idea that a breakdown in a traumatic situation is liable to be precipitated by 'constitutional factors',[5] Balchin posits that the revelation of Lucian's war trauma causes a resurfacing of a more fundamental conflict. Balchin reconfigures the incident in Burma as a catalyst for the resurgence of Lucian's unresolved Oedipus complex; having initially mistaken his wife for a Japanese, he finally kills her in the belief that she is his 'unfaithful' mother. Milne at first diagnoses Lucian as 'schizoid' and therefore treatable, but by the end of the novel, he believes that his patient has descended into full-blown schizophrenia, a condition beyond his therapeutic remit. But Balchin's attempts at portraying medical procedure in a realistic way seem to collapse towards the climax of the narrative when, as Charques commented wryly: 'Following upon the discovery that Lucian had loved his mother and hated his father there is a roof-top chase.' (Anon [R.D. Charques], 'Psycho-analyst' 461)[6] This culminates in Lucian's suicide. Aside from Lucian himself, there are few indications that the action of the novel is taking place in the aftermath of a conflict and there is little or no sense of the physical damage wrought on London or of any other disruption that the war might have caused. Lucian personifies the inassimilable residue of the conflict; it is perhaps not surprising that his character collapses under the weight of this representational burden. A further reason for this collapse is that Balchin is attempting to examine not only Lucian's state of mind, but also the pressures on clinical psychology and psychiatry as medical practices in the period prior to the establishment of the National Health Service. As in many of his other novels, personal crises are set against a background of institutional conflicts, and this compounds Lucian's relative marginalisation; Milne's struggles, as much as Lucian's, are the focal point.

Balchin returned to the figure of the physically and psychically damaged war veteran in his 1949 novel *A Sort of Traitors*, a thriller based around a research laboratory and depicting the emerging tensions of the cold war. Bill, who works at the lab, becomes involved with his colleague Lucy; she lives with Ivor, formerly her boyfriend, who has had to have both arms amputated after an RAF training accident and is deeply embittered. Although important in terms of his initiation of the spy plot, persuading Bill to reveal secret information to a spy, Ivor is in many respects a peripheral character, as much of the action is centred on tensions among the staff at the lab. Balchin seems unable to incorporate Ivor into the post-war socio-political scene, and his brutal excision from the plot – he commits suicide prior to the climax of the novel – seems emblematic of this. Balchin's most successful novels are *Darkness Falls From the Air* (1942) and *The Small Back Room* (1943), featuring protagonists who have to deal with both the exigencies of daily life in wartime and their own involvement in the 'war effort'. These novels use few, if any, breaks with forward-moving chronology; reflecting on the past is relegated in favour of coping with problems in the present. Balchin's novels of the later 1940s appear to reveal the untenability of this approach in the immediate post-war period. Both Lucian and Ivor embody the irruption into the present of past events that have been insufficiently assimilated and understood.

Balchin's explicit use of the discourse of psychoanalysis to explain one man's reaction to the events of war can be contrasted with H. E. Bates's *The Purple Plain* (1947), set in Burma in 1945. This novel also features a pilot who has psychological problems, but here, recovery is achieved not through the intervention of a representative of the medical profession but through a configuration of repetition. Forrester has been left deeply disillusioned by his wife's death in a London air raid on the evening of their wedding. Having overcome his initial suicidal thoughts, he is subject to occasional flashes of memory which appear to assault his senses; dining with Mrs McNab and some refugee woman at the local mission, he is overcome by the sight of the women's dresses and the sound of them practising Easter hymns. The singing, initially resonant of childhood, leads him inexorably to more recent memories of a traumatic nature: 'The past, leaden and bright, divulged suddenly the harsh remembrance he could not bear' (Bates, *Purple Plain* 68). However, the women living at the mission have themselves been traumatised by the destruction of their community. The mother of Anna, a Burmese girl with whom Forrester gradually falls in love, has not spoken since being uprooted from her home, and only regains her powers of speech in the aftermath of the air raid which occurs on the night of the dinner.

The 1954 film version of *The Purple Plain* emphasizes the parallel between this raid and the one in which Forrester's wife was killed. Anna (Win Min Than) is buried by falling branches, and a shot of her hand emerging from the wreckage is a visual echo of a shot of Forrester's wife's hand, the climax of his dream about the earlier raid. The parallel is also pointed up by the use in both sequences of reverse shots to the shocked face of Forrester (Gregory Peck), accompanied by dramatic music. Rescuing Anna thus becomes a means of compensating for having been unable to save his wife. The film maintains the hallucinatory nature of Forrester's perceptions as depicted in the novel; immediately before the raid, Forrester sees 'the face of Anna [...] A shadow seemed to go over it in the lamplight and for an awful moment it reappeared, unforgettably frightening, as the face he had loved long ago in England' (72). Then, shielding her from the bombs as they fall, he asserts, 'It shan't happen.

Not again. I won't let it happen. I won't let it' (72). This substitution allows Forrester to overcome some of the guilt he feels about his wife's death, but his recovery does not end with his rediscovery of the ability to love. The second half of the novel describes how Forrester, together with his young navigator Carrington and Blore, an older officer, attempt to survive after their plane crashes in an inaccessible and inhospitable part of the country. This protracted episode, during which Blore kills himself and Forrester has to care for the injured Carrington, can be compared to Lucian's epic trek through the jungle in *Mine Own Executioner*, but whereas Lucian's escape serves principally as an indicator of his 'toughness', Forrester is shown to grow in compassion even as his strength fails. Despite knowing that Blore has killed himself, he maintains, for Carrington's benefit, the fiction that the other man has gone on ahead, and, as the situation deteriorates, he appears to take strength from his memories of events at the mission, recalling Mrs MacNab's description of what Anna experienced: 'He remembered all she had said about the girl being afraid. It had made him feel very small. It had made him begin to look outside himself' (208). Implicitly, Forrester is enabled to continue by his recollection of how much Anna has experienced. Perhaps inevitably, she is a figure who comes to have a symbolic importance that outweighs the attention given to her actual social, cultural and familial situation. Forrester's determination to stay with her in what he has hitherto found an inhospitable country can be read as a means of evading his own experiences and his own past by allying himself to an alien and, to him, ineffable, culture. Whilst the outcome for Forrester might be more positive (in that he survives), he, like Lucian, is unable to fully assimilate past traumas until he has confronted new ones.

The confusion of what is being recollected with what is being perceived, characteristic of the hallucinations Forrester experiences, occurs in a more extreme fashion in other novels from this period. As in *The Purple Plain*, this technique can be used to signal that particular events from the past have been insufficiently assimilated and that they must be confronted, either through the construction of a narrative or through some form of re-enactment. In James Hanley's *Emily* (1948), set during the later part of the war, John Lennor, who is home on leave from Burma, goes to see his son Willie, who has suffered severe psychological damage during an air raid. On his way home from this visit, Lennor begins hallucinating that a Japanese soldier has taken the place of the bus conductor, and the passengers have turned into monkeys. What is notable here is that these hallucinations are not initially marked as such but are simply presented as Lennor's perceptions: 'A bus pulled up on the corner. Lennor stopped dead, staring at it. Monkeys were coming down the staircase from the top deck. The Jap called "Hurry along, please," caught Lennor's eyes, smiled at him' (Hanley, *Emily* 96). There are few details given about Lennor's experiences abroad; Willie's trauma stands as a proxy for his own, and there is only a tenuous sense of resolution at the end of the novel. A perhaps more conventional use of the trauma – repetition – recovery model appears in Stuart B. Jackman's *Portrait in Two Colours* (1948). Simon Calder has trouble accustoming himself to life back at home after serving in the Middle East, but the cause of his anxiety is only revealed when, having been to collect a hire car, he believes his friend Alan, who was killed in action, is in the car with him: 'He drove quite slowly, feeling his way. He switched off the dash-light and listened to the tyres on the hard surface. And he felt Alan move and stretch his legs under the dashboard beside him' (Jackman 87). Alan's presence beside him is not signalled as being remembered and therefore takes on the quality of a hallucination. Calder crashes the car, and, during his recuperation, which forms the second part of the novel, the upsetting events leading to Alan's death are recounted. The use of hallucination as a means of introducing past events into a forward-moving narrative results in a disconcerting blurring of perception and memory, and this is exacerbated by the largely realistic idiom in which these incidents are described. The inability to distinguish between the perceived and the remembered not only threatens the individual's mental balance, but also makes it difficult to consign past events to the past: when will the war end?

Remembering to forget: *Back*

A key example of how such experiments with the depiction of perception can be used to great effect in exposing the difficulties of reintegration is Henry Green's *Back* (1946), set in 1944 and featuring a returned prisoner of war, Charley Summers, who, as well as suffering psychical damage, has lost a leg.[7] If in Balchin's novels, the war is figured as a kind of excess, represented not only in the nature and degree of ex-servicemen's psychological and physical injuries but also in their melodramatic suicides, in *Back*, the excess is largely linguistic. During Charley's absence, his married lover Rose has died, and one of the features of the novel is the persistence of her name, which at times appears to spring at Charley from everywhere:

> He fled Rose, yet every place he went she rose up before him; in florists' windows; in a second-hand bookseller's with a set of

Miss Rhoda Broughton, where, as he was staring for her reflection in the window, his eyes read a title, 'Cometh up as a flower' which twisted his guts; [...] from a wireless shop, a record through loud speakers of 'Honeysuckle Rose.' (Green, *Back* 52–3)[8]

The fixation is heightened when Charley apparently mistakes Rose's half-sister Nancy for Rose herself. As Mark Rawlinson has noted, Charley is a 'prisoner of his imaginative work on memory' (203); however, Charley's continuing belief that Nancy is Rose is not only the result of his belief in his own imagination, but is also a consequence of his refusing to believe, or remember, what Nancy repeatedly asserts – that she is *not* Rose. Charley's disorder, if it can be named in this way, is therefore not only about remembering and elaborating memory into a more acceptable version, but also about what he forgets. Nancy herself finds it a burden to be a 'sort of walking memory to other people [...] It's only natural I suppose, but you men, that used to know her I mean, with her red hair you all talk about, I suppose you're dead easy to think only of yourselves?' (71) This comment not only compounds Charley's belief, at this point, that Nancy is working as a prostitute, but is also a reminder of the fact that his mistake has a selfish aspect that constitutes an attack on Nancy's subjectivity.

Charley's propensity to forget is stressed from the start of the novel when he goes to visit Rose's grave. The sound of geese cackling is likened to an explosion he once witnessed: 'he felt what he had seen until the silence which followed, when he at once forgot' (4). There is an ambiguity here, and it is not clear whether what Charley forgets is what he has seen now, or what he saw then, although both could be implied, as he is left only with a sense of having 'been warned' (4). Entering the churchyard, Charley encounters a young child on a tricycle, who means nothing to him, and whom he also immediately forgets; when he then meets Rose's husband James, he discovers that the child was Rose's son, and could therefore also be his own. He is appalled that 'the first sight of the boy had meant nothing. Because one of the things he had always hung on to was that blood spoke, or called, to blood' (9). What Green portrays here is, in many respects, a not unusual pattern of the registration and immediate dismissal of external information that appears to have no relevance; only retrospectively does the encounter with the child take on significance. Charley's frustration seems to stem from his inability to recognize the importance of the encounter when it was happening; knowing now is too late. Belated knowledge also underpins the occasional allusions Charley makes to his injury, caused by his not having seen a sniper, 'the gun beneath a rose' (3); here too, understanding arrived too late. The pursuit of Nancy could therefore be understood as a misguided attempt to recapture his relationship with Rose, to make up for his inability to know that her death would intervene.

Charley is not the only one prone to forgetting; the child Ridley is described by his father as having a very poor memory, unable to remember simple errands: 'there are times I send him for something, and he forgets all about it while he's on the way' (81). Ridley might emblematise a future generation shorn of the past, but for the fact that the older generation share his deficiency. When Mr Grant, Rose and Nancy's father, falls ill towards the end of the narrative, Nancy goes to help nurse him and explains to Charley, who has come to visit, that Mr Grant has confused her with Rose. What Nancy forgets is that this is the same mistake that Charley himself has made. Paradoxically, Mr Grant's illness precipitates the recovery of his wife's memory. When Charley first goes to visit them on his return home – because, as well as being Rose's secret lover during her marriage, he was her fiancé, and a family friend, prior to it – Mrs Grant believes that he is her brother, returned from the First World War. However, there are hints that this forgetting, apparently caused by the death of her daughter, was in fact a conscious tactic. Going to see her after her recovery, Charley asks Mrs Grant whether she recalls his previous visit: ' "I don't know whether I do or I don't," she replied, and he was horrified to find a sudden look of sly cunning begin to spread over her placid face' (170). Whilst her doctor attempts to explain her condition by reference to the familiar notion of a 'blackout' being drawn, or 'surplus' material being 'thrown overboard' (154), both the look that makes Charley uneasy, and her recovery when it is no longer advantageous to be ill suggest that this 'forgetting', too, has a deliberate aspect.

Mrs Grant's mistaking of Charley for her brother not only parallels his own confusion of Rose and Nancy, but is also echoed by other references to the last war in the novel. Charley's landlady, one of his colleagues at work, and even, indirectly, Nancy, contextualize his behaviour by comparing him to casualties from the First World War. That this parallel is reiterated in fact serves to underline its inadequacy, just as the doctor's explanation of Mrs Grant's memory loss falls short. Looking back to before is an unsatisfactory means of attempting to understand what is happening now, but it is also easier than confronting present problems more directly. Michael North has suggested that Charley's creative 'amendments of the past' are largely 'self-serving' (127); similarly, turning to comparisons with those who returned damaged from the First World War is a means for those with whom Charley comes into contact to avoid having to directly address his particular situation. Resorting to the existing paradigm of the returning soldier is therefore, in its own way, self-serving. James, similarly, offers Charley an account of an eighteenth-century French case of monomania which appears to have parallels with Charley own, but as Treglown suggests, the 'romantic implausibilities' of that text are experienced by Charley as 'psychosis' (*Romancing* 186). Charley's fellow returnee, Middlewitch, appears to offer an alternative model for recovery, having apparently adapted himself to life in wartime London, and warns Charley against introspection. This, he claims, will only 'perpetuate the conditions you've lived under, which weren't natural' (26), but from Charley's perspective, Middlewitch's apparent ease in the new situation of wartime London only means that he too is dismissive of Charley's own inability to settle back down again.

Green is only ever oblique about the nature of Charley's sufferings during his time abroad;[9] Charley's final confrontation – or missed confrontation – with his memories is spurred when, from the room downstairs where he is supposed to be sleeping, he hears Mrs Grant and Nancy attempting and failing to revive the dying Mr Grant:

> [Mrs Grant] was yelling now. 'Gerald.' After which the most frightful sobbing. 'Gerald darling, Father, where are you?'; then, in a sort of torn bellow, 'Father,' then, finally, 'Come back,' and the culmination of all this was about to remind Summers of something in France which he knew, as he valued his reason, that he must always shut out. He clapped hands down tight over his ears. He concentrated on not ever remembering. On keeping himself dead empty. [...] But he won free. He mastered it. And, when he took his streaming hands away, everything was dead quiet. (183)

Treglown suggests that this moment signals an 'easing of [Charley's] obsession with the past' (*Romancing* 191); but Green eschews the type of confrontation with, or re-enactment of past events that writers such as Balchin and Bates posit as a means of recovery. Rather than serving as a catalyst for the revelation of the nature of Charley's trauma, Mr Grant's death, and Charley's overhearing of the women's cries, have to stand in its place. Charley's strategy for keeping his pain at bay is deliberate, rather than involuntary, forgetting, and in the light of this, his behaviour throughout the novel is explicable; the narrative is a series of attempts to either master involuntary associations, or deliberately reconstruct an albeit counterfactual version of events. By leaving Charley's trauma undefined, Green suggests both its very inexpressibility and the extent to which it remains a barrier between himself and others. At the very end of the novel, Charley bursts into tears at the sight of Nancy waiting in bed for him, a reaction which suggests that he has recognised that Rose is dead, but which also underlines to Nancy that she has 'taken on' (207) a man who is still deeply scarred. Mourning, it is implied, may be superseded by consummation, but perhaps Nancy can never supersede Rose. At the conclusion of *Back*, a détente, rather than an understanding appears to have been achieved; within the narrative, the war still continues, and hope for the future is held in suspense.

Impostures

If Green pointedly denies the reader the type of revelations that are at the core of a novel like *Mine Own Executioner*, other writers challenge such melodramatic plotstructures through the use of protagonists who lay claim to a past, and particularly a war record, that is not their own. In *The Captive Heart*, Hasek impersonates another man in order to save his own life; the protagonists of other texts have less positive motivations. Elizabeth Taylor's *A Wreath of Roses* (1949) is one key example here and the trope of imposture is also central to Betty Miller's *On the Side of the Angels* (1945), which, although it was completed in early 1944, uses the figure of an impostor to look towards the long-term consequences on society of the violence of war. Denton Welch based his short story 'Brave and Cruel' (1949) on events surrounding the arrival of a confidence trickster in the village where he was living.[10] Laying claim to a false past, usually portrayed in these texts as a form of self-aggrandisement, can also be a means of attempting to fit oneself into the prevalent discourses of war, even if in actuality one has been excluded from them. On a narrative level, it can also be a way through which the power of such discourses can be interrogated. What status does a 'true' war story have if an invented one seems equally credible and has equal impact?

Any act of imposture has a dialogic element. The particular claims made by the impostor have to be received in the desired way by the community into which the impostor attempts to fit. Some of these texts imply that the impostor satisfies a particular need on the part of those who are deceived. Fantasies can be realised, images from the news or from feature films can become flesh. Both Miller and Welch emphasize the importance of the impostor displaying signifiers of military prowess that are recognisable to his victims. Neil Herriot in *On the Side of the Angels* masquerades as a Commando, and is marked out by his green beret. When Claudia and her sister Honor are introduced to him, it is clear that they consider him to be a cut above the 'ordinary' soldiers with whom they have hitherto had contact: '[Claudia] saw the Commando flash on his sleeve: she looked at him with interest and respect. So did Honor who, smiling, spoke to him for the first time. "You're the only Commando soldier I've seen in the flesh [...] Usually I only see them on news-reels –"' (Miller, *On the Side* 40).[11] Herriot's allure is compounded for the two women by the fact that Claudia's fiancé has been invalided out of the army, and Honor's husband has been seconded to a medical corps; neither are fulfilling the stereotypical role of the man of action. In Welch's story, set soon after the end of the war, the impostor Micki Beaumont, who claims to have been in the RAF, buys a book about the air war, a record of a military march, and 'a spotted scarf, of a pattern much favoured by pilots [...] It was as though Micki had gone out to collect three symbols of his past career' (Welch, 'Brave and Cruel' 478).[12] Whilst military uniform is a signifier of conformity and a means of 'subduing personality', the Commando flash and the RAF scarf serve as a means of guaranteeing, falsely, 'the authority of a status' (Bryant 137). Such imposture therefore threatens the integrity of uniform's signifying power.

Mrs Bellingly, who introduces Micki to the village community, interprets his often impulsive behaviour as a consequence of his war service: 'He can't keep still a moment. While he's talking, he prowls up and down and uses his whole body to accentuate his meaning. Poor boy! He must have had frightful experiences as a pilot' (457). However, Welch's narrator David, and other inhabitants of the village, are suspicious of Micki from the outset. After Micki becomes engaged, on the strength of a week's acquaintance, to a local girl called Elizabeth, Mrs Charles, a neighbour, expresses her views to David:

'But does no one realize that the man's an impostor, an out-and-out rogue?'
[...] 'I think I've explained so much away by telling myself to remember that he landed on his head,' I answered.
'I don't believe he's ever even been up in an aeroplane.'
'But I've seen a photograph of him in his uniform with the wings plainly visible.'
'What does that prove?' Mrs Charles rapped out. (486)

Starting from a position of scepticism that is rooted in notions of 'proper' conduct, Mrs Charles will not allow his alleged past to excuse Micki's outré behaviour. After Micki's exposure as a fraud and incipient bigamist, Mrs Bellingly reconstructs recent events to paint herself in a more favourable light, claiming to have seen through Micki all along: 'Everything which did not fit in with this new picture was glossed over, or ruthlessly suppressed' (503). This reshaping of events even in their immediate aftermath is a way for Mrs Bellingly to avoid confronting her own deception, but also means she can reassert her sense of order in the wake of what appeared to be a refreshing, but then proved a dangerous, disturbance. Later, hearing that Micki has attempted to contact Katherine again, Mrs Bellingly expresses her surprise: ' "Life is so amazingly mixed and confused, isn't it?" "Yes, people won't stay in their appointed places, they flow about like anything," I agreed' (508). This comment expresses a sense of uncertainty in the face of the potential shift in social and moral values that the war appears to have engendered, and that Micki represents.[13] The figure of the airman might have had romantic and daring associations, but attempting to integrate these into the post-war world proves difficult.

Miller similarly uses the impostor as a means of addressing the difficulty of squaring the values of the pre-war, and potentially post-war, with the values of wartime. Indeed, as Jenny Hartley has argued, 'Miller finds the attractions of war embedded in Western culture' (174). The novel explicitly debates the problematic attraction of violence, embodied in this instance by Neil Herriot. Walking home with Claudia as an air raid is about to begin, Herriot expresses his belief that the confrontation with potential death that is an integral part of war is something to be embraced, exhilarating rather than frightening:

> [Claudia] sensed the excitement in his voice. Momentarily, it roused her: she felt an answering thrill in her own nerves. At once, she was ashamed: ready to disown her own response. There was something debased in this, she thought. It was wrong to feed on danger: to take to peril as to an aphrodisiac ... (64)

The irony here lies in the fact that Herriot's own excitement is only really vicarious; he has never had to face the danger of combat to which he lays claim. But Claudia, although she does agree to betray her fiancé Andrew and go away with Herriot, is not completely credulous. When Herriot mentions the names of actions in which he has allegedly taken part, 'Vaagso' and 'Dieppe', she feels a 'momentary discomfort' (96–7); later, when she has an assignation with Herriot in Oxford, she worries on a number of occasions that he is either not going to keep their appointment or that he is going to abandon her. Two different types of subterfuge – the illicit sexual liason, and Herriot's claim to war experience – become blurred. Miller seems to imply that it could never be a case of Claudia believing in her desires, over and above her belief in Herriot's war stories; her desire is too deeply tied up with his claims about the vitality of his experiences. After Herriot's exposure, Andrew, as yet unaware of the extent of her treachery, but in the knowledge that she was attracted to Herriot, analyses the effects of Herriot's imposture on those who had contact with him in the following way:

> We create a fiction out of our own desires. The fiction in this case happened to be the Commando hero: the killer, tough, unscrupulous; outside the bounds of ordinary convention. A fiction so attractive to the law-abiding that we chose in its favour to ignore the reality: the fact that a Commando is a Commando precisely because he can be relied upon to conduct himself in a manner not less, but infinitely more disciplined and responsible than the average citizen. (232)

Andrew thus attempts to dispel the notion that the Commando is an appropriate repository for those desires that are 'outside the bounds'; what he does not suggest, however, is how else such desires, which war both creates and attempts to regulate, might be dissipated.

Part of Miller's aim is to show that Herriot's pose is in many ways simply a more extreme version of a type of performance that is widespread; as Hartley has noted, other men in the novel seem to have been transformed through the adoption of a uniform, whilst local girls make themselves up in the semblance of movie stars (Hartley 174–5). Yet Miller also implies that although such performances might be the product of wartime conditions, it is difficult to know how they will signify once the conflict ends. Herriot's imposture is ultimately seen as pathetic rather than pathological; a family man with a steady job and a good Home Guard record, he cannot resist the lure of deeper involvement in the war, even if this has to be feigned. A more sinister instance of pretence and refiguring of the past is found in Taylor's *A Wreath of Roses*. Richard Elton not only claims a war record that is not his own but uses this to obscure the fact that he has committed a murder. But Taylor's handling of Elton's encounters with Camilla, who meets him when she is on her way to visit her friend Liz, means that a situation that could descend into melodrama is used instead as a way of considering both the lure of violence and the problems of a desire for certainty and continuity in the immediate post-war. Reeve has noted a number of explicit and implicit references to Virginia Woolf's *To the Lighthouse* (1927) in this novel. Frances, with whom Liz and Camilla are staying, is an artist; Camilla shares her name with one of Woolf's protagonists; and Taylor appears to 'oscillate between yearning for a harmonising vision' of the sort represented by Lily Briscoe's painting in *To the Lighthouse*, 'and an exasperated dismissal of the falsity of any such thing' (Reeve 161). Indeed, Taylor's exploration of the failure of memory to provide this harmonising vision also bears comparison to Woolf's in *Mrs Dalloway* (1925); like Woolf's First World War veteran Septimus Smith, Elton and Camilla find memory to be a source of discomfort rather than the repository of a unified sense of self.

Camilla and Elton are initially brought together when they witness an act of violence; as they wait for their train, a man throws himself off the railway bridge. This provides the pretext for Elton to strike up conversation with her, but Camilla has already interpreted the suicide as a portending ill: 'To her shocked mind, it seemed that the death she had witnessed was not to be so easily left behind as the train moved forward; but that it would go along with her' (Taylor, *Wreath* 4). What she has seen cannot simply be confined to the past, and has more than a merely contingent relationship to what is to come. Taylor also obliquely reminds the reader that violence, and particularly violent death, are not confined to wartime; but her experience does not increase Camilla's sensitivity to other, further removed, horrors. She notices Elton reading the newspaper account of a murder: 'Camilla could see the photograph of a dark girl, smiling, amidst the descriptions (she supposed) of violent despatch, dismemberment and ludicrous parcelling-out in luggage-office, lift-shaft or canal' (9). This could indeed be an account of the murder committed by Elton himself; although Camilla might be sceptical about the sensationalist manner in which the event is probably recounted, she is more accepting of the self-conscious fiction which comprises Elton's account of his war experience. On hearing that he has come back to his childhood home to write a war memoir, she is initially uninterested: '("The war and his experience in it," she thought. "Unreadable")' (6). She nevertheless feels obliged to ask for further details:

'What were you? What did you do?'
'Dropped by moonlight half-way across France. Sat between Gestapo men in trains, with my transmitter in a case on the rack above, hid in cellars while they searched for me overhead ...' he broke off, looking excited, as if he were listening to this story, not telling it ... 'Oh, the sound of those footsteps going up and down, wandering away, but always coming back [...] And it all being so much like the books I read

as a boy – passwords, disguises, swallowing bits of paper, hiding others in currant buns ...'
'So *that* is the sort of man who did it!' she thought, staring back at him.
'You must have great nerve,' she suggested, trying in this to find an excuse, a reason, for the emptiness in his eyes. (7)

Elton employs a kind of double-bluff when he frames his experiences as having been like books he read as boy; foregrounding their fictive nature is a means of deflecting attention from the fact that he is indeed recounting only what he has read rather than what he has been through. Notably, he avoids the first-person pronoun in this passage. Camilla's response shows that his gamble – presuming that she would be familiar enough herself with such narratives to take them as true regardless of who was enunciating them – has paid off. She collaborates in his self-fictionalisation when she attempts to account for his lack of affect. Unwittingly, she embellishes his story, bringing him and it into line. Her attitude is thus similar to Mrs Bellingly's in 'Brave and Cruel'; she is taken in because she wants to believe. Reeve suggests that Elton's stories about both the war and his childhood, have 'a fluency and consistency which might ordinarily make them suspect, but which for precisely those qualities exert a seductive power over the unfulfilled or the embittered by change, in search of similarly watertight narratives for themselves' (163–4). Camilla's belief in Elton's stories is at odds with the difficulty she has in articulating her own past; prompted later by Elton to recall an old love affair, she hesitates: 'how could she? The nineteen-forties impinged on the nineteen-twenties; such darkness lay over the nostalgia that it seemed not sweet but meaningless' (158). There can be no 'pure' recall; Elton's fabulations represent the most extreme kind of work on memory, but Camilla herself fails to fully articulate this important episode from her past.

As I have indicated, the strand of the novel concerning the painter Frances and her visitor Morland Beddoes provides Taylor with the opportunity to consider further the relationship between memory and art. Having corresponded with Frances while he was a prisoner of war, Beddoes comes to meet her for the first time, although not without trepidation, especially when Camilla tells him that Liz, who modelled for a painting by Frances that Beddoes owns, is also staying. He explains:

> Think of a picture you know very well, perhaps you have been familiar with it for years. It is static, unchanging. The world lies frozen inside

the frame. As if a hand pulled a lever and all the traffic stood still. [...] That Bar at the Folies-Bergère! Suppose the barmaid awoke from that frozen moment – the moment which we are so accustomed to, which has lasted so many years – took up the rose and smelt it, lifted her hands from the marble and poured out a glass of Bass! All the mirrors would splinter, the world disintegrate, the moment fly away into thin air. [...] I feel that Liz will break all the glass for me in the same way. (133–4)

Beddoes believes that Frances's painting helped him see the world in a new manner and that this vision will be shattered if he meets Liz in the flesh. The painting, a representation of a particular moment in time, can transcend that moment through his viewing of it, but time cannot be allowed to reflect back on the painting; to be reminded that the subject has grown older would destroy what the painting means to him. Frances, who is on the brink of giving up painting when Beddoes arrives, partly because of her ill health, and partly because of disillusionment, sees the process from a different perspective: 'She had no way to turn. There is no past for an artist. What is done is cast away, good only for the time of its creation. Work is the present and the immediate future; but her immediate future was a blank' (237). What has been sustaining for Beddoes proves to have become a trap for Frances; Taylor here exposes the difficulty, for the artist, of how to move forward from the moment of vision, a difficulty Woolf evades in *To the Lighthouse* by having the novel end with Lily completing her painting. Frances believes that her previous manner of painting no longer fits the reality of the contemporary world, whilst Beddoes appears to see her work as a relief from brutality. When he remarks that life is 'loving-kindness and simplicity, and it lay there all the time in your pictures' she retorts that he is wrong, that life is 'darkness, and the terrible things we do to one another, and to ourselves. [...] [a]nd paintings don't matter. They are like making daisy-chains in the shadow of a volcano' (170). Having experienced war and incarceration, Beddoes wishes to salvage some fragments of humanism through the contemplation of Frances's art; but what she emphasises is that her belief humanity has also been shaken. Art and the artist cannot be unaffected by the shock of world events.

Beddoes does however see through Elton's imposture, although he does not share his suspicions soon enough to save Camilla from a final frightening encounter with Elton. At an abandoned cottage, Elton asks Camilla to pretend they are newly-weds, just moved in; but the place is a ruin, with the atmosphere of a crime scene. He confesses that he has committed a murder, attempting to justify, or at least contextualize his actions by telling her that acts of cruelty where the only way of resisting a stultifying provincial childhood. Again, Taylor does not allow violence to be hermetically sealed within the bounds of wartime, and again, Elton attempts to create a fable about his own past, a placeholder for whatever his real memories might be. Alone with him, Camilla finally realizes how she has been deceived, and how she has deceived herself: 'The other world, the world of violence, of people in newspapers, crept round about her, a world she had scarcely believed in. Parting the leaves to look for treasure, love, adventure, she inadvertently disclosed evil, and recoiled' (250). That 'other' world is not 'other' at all; she could be the next victim. But Elton has wanted her not for that purpose, but as a participant in his self-fabulation. Now she has heard his story, and refused to take any further part in it, she finds she can leave. By pointing to Camilla's willingness to become involved with Elton, her desire to 'part the leaves', Taylor implies not that Camilla is foolish, or naïve, or deserved to be exploited, but that the narratives with which she was wooed are indeed beguiling, even though there is an undertow of violence beneath the *Boys' Own* surface. Taylor asks how, in the context of the developing and solidifying mythologies of war, individual experience can be held separate from cultural inscription.

'Re-read me backwards': Elizabeth Bowen's *The Heat of the Day*

The complex relationship between narratives of war experience, subjectivity and dissembling is at the core of Elizabeth Bowen's novel *The Heat of the Day*, a novel which, like Taylor's, has plot elements that might appear to be more at home in genre fiction. Discussing *The Heat of the Day* in a pamphlet on Bowen published in 1952, Jocelyn Brooke explained that the plot, which 'might almost, one feels, have been conceived by Mr. Graham Greene or by Mr. Nigel Balchin', is combined with a structure and style that produces the effect of the novel 'being composed of a number of fragments' (*Elizabeth Bowen* 25). This Brooke saw as a 'bold attempt to supply an aesthetic equivalent to the actual breaking-up of urban life under the stress of war' (25–6). The style and structure of the novel occlude the spy plot, but Bowen constantly presses at the question of the individual's relationship to the events of war, a question at the heart of the act of espionage. Like Allingham in *The Oaken Heart*, Bowen uses a form of backshadowing to create a sense of temporal perspective that can emphasize the extent to which protagonists are attempting to retain autonomy in the midst of events that are beyond their control. Whilst the action of the novel is centred on the winter of 1942–43, in the opening chapters Bowen reverses the chronology. Beginning in September 1942 with Harrison's meeting with Louie in the park and his visit to Stella to inform her of her lover Robert's treachery, the action moves back to May 1942 and the funeral of Stella's husband's Cousin Francis, where Stella and Harrison first meet, and finally reaches September 1940, and the start of Stella and Robert's relationship. The description in Chapter Five of how the autumn of 1940 looks from a distance of two years militates against both the clichés of a wartime romantic encounter and memory as a recuperative process:

> That autumn of 1940 was to appear, by two autumns later, apocryphal, more far away than peace. […] [T]hat particular psychic London was to be gone for ever; more bombs would fall, but not on the same city. War moved from the horizon to the map. […] The first generation of ruins, cleaned up, shored up, began to weather – in daylight they took their places as a norm of the scene […] For Stella, her early knowing of Robert was associated with the icelike tinkle of broken glass being swept up among crisping leaves, and with the charred freshness of every morning. She could recapture that 1940 autumn only in sensations; thoughts, if there had been any, could not be found again. (Bowen, *Heat of the Day* 92–3)

There is ambivalence, if not nostalgia, in the association of Robert with, in Bowen's deliberately dissonant phrases, 'the icelike tinkle' of broken glass and the 'charred freshness' of the morning. The war, as exemplified by bombing, is spatially and temporally removed, but living under the threat of bombing is, paradoxically, preferable to becoming acclimatized to the war as an ongoing, distant event. When death is a present reality, life is itself valued more. Thus the signifiers of destruction are also the things that remind her of the exhilaration of the early days of their relationship, but Stella's inability to separate their first meetings from the aftermath of this destruction, and the fact that these events are experienced as 'sensations' rather than 'thoughts', can be understood, retrospectively, as a sign of the blunting of responses induced by life in the city at war.

Bowen's telescoping back from 1942 to 1940 and forwards again in this passage is mirrored at the end of the novel. Following Robert's death after his fall from the roof of Stella's flat, the movements of the protagonists over the next two years are rapidly sketched in: 'Stella moved across

London [...]; Harrison vanished from London; [...] Roderick [...] obtained his commission in the autumn of 1943. [...] Connie [...] found herself returned to the foreground by the renewal of enemy air attacks on London early in 1944' (301). Bowen then returns to the immediate aftermath of Robert's death, specifically his inquest, during which Stella has to give an account of their relationship. But although she claims to 'remember everything ... Is it unusual? I have a good memory' (302), her account is necessarily selective. Following her evidence at the inquest, the events of 1942–44 are described again:

> 1942, still with no Second Front, ran out [...] February [1943], the Germans capitulated at Stalingrad; [...] War's being global meant it ran off the edges of maps; it was uncontainable [...] 1944 was the year in which there could not but be the Second Front [...] Reflections were cut short by the renewal of air attacks on London – a five-night February season to be known as the Little Blitz. (307–8)

This is more than simply a device to rush the narrative forward to the point at which Bowen wishes to resume the stories of her protagonists. Bowen separates off this catalogue of historical events from the protagonists' activities, with Robert's inquest as a hinge. In fact, these public and private events are inextricably entwined. Stella wishes to retain a separation between her relationship with Robert and his espionage activities but the structure of the narrative at this point raises doubts about the viability of this manoeuvre.[14]

Stella's public retelling in the courtroom of her life with Robert is a reminder of his comment during their final meeting: 'You'll have to re-read me backwards, figure me out' (270). Maud Ellmann argues that 're-reading backwards' is 'precisely what a psychoanalyst would do' (160), and suggests that Bowen endorses Ernest Jones's analysis of espionage, which he attributes to a crisis of masculinity. Stella and Robert's visit to Robert's family's home in the countryside is important in this respect, and also provides a counter-point to Stella's visit to Ireland. Implicitly, the seeds of Robert's treachery are to be found in his upbringing; as Jacqueline Rose suggests, like Woolf in *Three Guineas*, 'Bowen believes that you can run a line between fascism in Europe and the comfortable self-deceptions, the relations of power and deceit, which hold in the average English drawing-room'(77).[15] Robert's actions can be read as a covert and misguided attempt to assert himself in the face of his overwhelming female relatives. When he takes Stella to meet his mother, her domestic tyranny is expressed in a manner that has a comical edge. In reply to Stella's comment that she drinks a lot of tea, Mrs Kelway remarks that they have it only once a day, 'otherwise we might not have enough for guests' (113), exposing the 'smug economies of the home front' (Anon [Francis Wyndham], 'Climate' 152).

More revealing about the nature of Robert's relationship with his family is the description of his room at the top of the house. Aside from the 'fictions of boyishness', including collections of butterflies and birds' eggs, Stella sees 'sixty or seventy photographs, upwards from snapshots to crowded groups […] All the photographs featured Robert. […] [H]e was depicted at every age' (116). He assures her that he was not responsible for putting the pictures up, although he hasn't removed them either, but rather than serving as a form of prosthetic memory, reminding him of himself at different stages of his life, the photographs make him feel alienated. When Stella remarks that the room feels 'empty', he replies: 'Each time I come back again into it I'm hit in the face by the feeling that I don't exist – that I not only am not but have never been. […] If to have gone through motions ever since one was born is, as I think now, criminal, here's my criminal record' (117–18). Implicitly, Robert's current activities have an authenticity for him that is lacking in this visual account of his earlier life. The photographs, together with the furniture and other objects in the room, represent to him the fiction by which he was expected live, but which he is now challenging. His secret activities therefore serve a similar psychic and narrative function to the acts of imposture in Taylor's and Miller's novels. Re-reading him backwards will produce not a coherent narrative, but one that, like the wall of photographs from different points in his life, is a patching together of fragments that can only ever produce an illusion of continuity.

Stella has a different experience of memory during her visit to Ireland following her son Roderick's inheritance of Mount Morris from Cousin Francis. Her last visit to the house was on her honeymoon, when Roderick was conceived, but when she arrives there, she is surprised at the recognition the building awakens in her: '[I]t rose to the surface in her, as though something weighting it to the bottom had let go. Expectancy rather than memory from now on guided her […] [S]he seemed to perceive on all sides round her, and with a phantasmogoric clearness, everything that for the eye the darkness hid (165–66). Stella appears to re-experience, rather than remember the Mount Morris. The image of the house rising from the bottom is echoed later when Stella, at Roderick's request, asks if there is a boat, only to be told that Cousin Francis had it sunk as a precaution. When it is eventually raised, it is found to be 'decayed' (313); but Stella's knowledge of the house appears to be perfectly preserved, even though it is depicted as being of a hallucinatory or super-sensory nature. Describing her wartime stories 'Ivy Gripped the Steps' and 'The Inherited Clock', Bowen comments that the past 'discharges its load of feeling into the anaesthetized and bewildered present' (Bowen, 'Postscript' 221). Memory is conceived not as a movement from the present into the past but as the emergence of the past in the present. Emanating from the mind, this past is more real than 'reality' itself. Such hallucinations are not, however, evidence of 'mental peril' (Bowen, 'Postscript' 218); rather, they are a 'saving resort on the part of the characters: life, mechanized by the controls of war-time [...] had to complete itself in *some* way' (Bowen, 'Postscript' 219). The most notable example of this occurs in 'Mysterious Kôr', but as Rose suggests, for much of *The Heat of the Day* also, and especially in the description of Stella's first evening at Mount Morris, Bowen 'hovers just this side of hallucination' (81).

Whilst her own earlier experience of the house is important to Stella, she also wonders what the future might hold for Roderick. He is unattached, and she attempts to imagine her daughter-in-law: 'since Stella having no daughter could not conjure up youthfulness other than her own, the daughter-in-law curled forming like ectoplasm out of Stella's flank' (175). An image of futurity – imagining who Roderick might marry – is undercut by Stella's mediumistic fashioning of this bride, who is modelled on her young self. Stella's own sentiments are projected onto this projection:

> Yes, this for the bride would be a room to be first marvelled at, then changed. [...] For instance, here [...] was one picture to banish [...] a liner going down in a blaze with all lights on [...] '*Nearer my God to Thee: The Titanic: 1912.*' The significance of this drawing-room picture of Cousin Nettie's would never be known. (176)

These comments are strange inasmuch as the significance of the picture, historically speaking, is self-evident; what is puzzling is why Nettie, Francis's eccentric wife, should have chosen to put it up when presumably she has no personal connection with the event it depicts. Later, however, Roderick himself seems to raise a counter to these sentiments, echoing Morland Beddoes' view of the enduring nature of art. Discussing Robert's death with his mother, Roderick remarks, 'Robert's dying of what he did will not always be there, won't last like a book or picture: by the time one is able to understand it it will be gone, it just won't be there to be judged.' (300) In the light of these comments, Stella appears to have mistaken the durable for the transitory – even Nettie's magazine picture has more chance of being understood in the future than Robert's actions.

During Roderick's visit to Nettie at her nursing home Wistaria Lodge, a journey he makes in order to explain that he is now the owner of Mount Morris, he notices the pictures that Nettie has up in her room: 'Mrs Tringsby's original choice of pictures, of a rural innocuous kind, had been supplemented by [...] a bevy of tinted pictures of children; all, it seemed, engaged innocently in some act of destruction – depetalling daisies, puffing at dandelion clocks, trampling primrose woods' (209–10). No photograph of Mount Morris is on display, and when Roderick asks Nettie about this, she explains: ' "[W]hy should I want a picture of anything I have seen? Don't *you* think," she said, "it is a little odd that they could expect anyone to be so forgetful?" ' (210)[16] For Nettie, pictures function in an oblique, rather than straightforwardly representational way; just as the destructive children signal a form of rebellion against Mrs Tringsby, the owner of Wistaria Lodge, so the picture of the Titanic could be seen to symbolise the 'sinking' of her marriage to Francis. Stella's sense of the familiarity of Mount Morris on her arrival there would appear to support Nettie's suggestion that memory needs no supplementation from external, visual prompts. In some respects, Stella and Nettie are a matching pair; both have had unsuccessful marriages, and both are passed over in favour of Roderick so far as succession to the ownership of Mount Morris is concerned. It is also Nettie who reveals to Roderick that, rather than his mother leaving his father, as he had thought, his father had already left to live with the woman who had nursed him after the First World War. Stella's attempt to create her past in her own image is foiled by Nettie who, from behind the protective mask of eccentricity, is able to reveal the truth.

As well as the uncovering of the remote past, *The Heat of the Day* also articulates, through the figure of Louie Lewis, another strand of thinking about how the current conflict might be remembered or might influence the working of memory. Louie, who attempts to chat-up Harrison in the opening chapter of the novel, is described as having 'with regard to time, an infant lack of stereoscopic vision; she saw then and now on the same plane; they were the same. To her everything seemed to be going on at once' (17). This flattened perception of time seems to be a cruder version of Stella's hallucinatory experience of the introjection of the past into the present. It also becomes important later when, under the influence of her friend Connie, Louie starts to take an interest in the war, or at least the war as conveyed in newspaper reports, but finds herself at a disadvantage, 'owing to having begun in the middle; she never quite had the courage to ask anyone, even Connie, how it had all begun – evidently one thing must have led to another, as in life; and whose the mistake had been in first place, or how long ago, you would not care to say' (151). The papers make the war seem manageable and give Louie a sense of involvement and inclusion, although Bowen here seems cynical about her lack of understanding of the causes of the conflict, and equally so when Louie, bowing to her friend's superior knowledge, asks, 'But isn't much to be learned from the lessons of history, Connie?' (155) It should perhaps be Stella and Robert who ask such a question; they, along with Harrison, seem, paradoxically, furthest detached from the events of war that Louie reads about. After Louie encounters Stella and Harrison in a subterranean café, she has a sudden insight about Stella's personality: 'Mrs Rodney walked like a soul astray. Those three words reached Louie imperatively, as though spoken – memory up to now had been surface pictures knocked apart and together by the heavings of a submerged trouble' (248–9). This image recalls not only the pictures of Robert jostling on the wall at Holme Dene, but also the photograph of the Titanic at Mount Morris, the 'surface pictures' like fragments of an ice floe 'knocked apart and together.' The 'surface picture' is also a reminder of the photograph of Louie's husband Tom that, she promises him in her letters, she looks at each day. In fact, this is a 'misrepresentation'; although she might lift the photograph to dust the mantelpiece, '[t]o see [...] is not to look' (158–9). It is when thinking again about Stella, after parting from her, that Louie's ideas about the other woman achieve the level of insight implied by the phrase 'a soul astray'. Again, Bowen seems to prioritize an inward-looking, self-reflexive version of remembrance over one that which may be contained in the external form of the photograph. What has also to be grasped, for Stella, is the extent to which the conditions of wartime might damage or impair this inner vision.

The novel ends not with the end of the war but with Louie watching returning bombers, and then showing her baby a flight of swans as they pass overhead. Kristine Miller suggests that '[b]y connecting the birth of the baby with the rebirth of peace in England, the novel integrates domestic life and politics on the site of a war-torn shelter' ('Even a Shelter' 152). Louie's child is illegitimate, but she is preserving the fiction that he is the son of her husband Tom, who has, fortuitously, been killed in action. This piece of domestic deception undercuts any idealism that might tinge the parallel Miller describes; Bowen's novel ends when news of the Normandy landings has just been received, and questions about the political future of Britain remain, for her protagonists, in suspense.

For Bowen, this suspense and uncertainty has to be held in balance with the desire for artistic completion and closure. In this respect, she, like many of the other writers I have discussed here, recognises and engages with the difficulty of representing the war, and specifically the memory of the war, that commentators of the time identified.

Conclusion: looking back, looking forwards

Perhaps ironically in view of her own achievement, in an article published in May 1945, Elizabeth Bowen was among those who expressed a degree of pessimism about the ability of novelists to encompass the war in fiction: 'for the novelist, perspective, and also a term of time in which to relate one experience to another, are essential – I suggest that we should not expect any *comprehensive* war novel until five, even ten years after hostilities cease.' ('Short Story' 16) The shifting perspectives and fractured chronology of *The Heat of the Day* emphasize the recalcitrance of the events of wartime; it would seem unlikely that these could ever be given *'comprehensive'* form. Even for the individual, relating one experience to another is a process fraught with uncertainties; Bowen certainly appears to doubt the effectiveness of memory as a means of suturing events into a whole. The expectation, implied by Bowen and expressed by other commentators, that the war could be encapsulated in a small number of key works was over-optimistic given its scope. Looking to the example of the First World War was misleading, as even those texts that are considered representative of the earlier conflict only actually represent small glimpses of it. Yet small glimpses can themselves challenge or supplement developing cultural narratives about the war years. There are novels from this period that that focus on arguing a case rather than stretching the parameters of the novel as a form. However, many of the authors I have been discussing find creative ways of attempting to encompass the war within a narrative, and memory is a key locus for this. Whether using a medical model of memory within a realistic framework, as Balchin does, or conceiving of memory in a manner more reminiscent of modernism, as Green does, authors show an awareness of the power of memory as an often problematic focal point for the depiction of the disturbances to subjectivity that characterize wartime.

Conclusion

In *Nineteen Eighty-Four* (1949), Winston Smith tries to find a witness to provide a truthful narrative of pre-Revolutionary life, to counter the version that, in his job at the Ministry of Truth, he helps construct. The response he receives from the old man he meets in the prole quarter leads him to despair; it would indeed appear that individual memory is unable to preserve what the Ministry of Truth is destroying:

> the few scattered survivors from the ancient world were incapable of comparing one age with another. They remembered a million useless things, a quarrel with a work-mate, a hunt for a lost bicycle pump, the expression on a long-dead sister's face, the swirls of dust on a windy morning seventy years ago: but all the relevant facts were outside the range of their vision. (96)

However, shortly after indulging in these pessimistic reflections, Winston returns to Mr Charrington's shop and buys the glass paperweight that he later describes to Julia as 'a little chunk of history that they've forgotten to alter. It's a message from a hundred years ago, if one knew how to read it' (152). During their illicit meeting in the room over the shop, Julia is able to supply some further lines to the song 'Oranges and Lemons', first mentioned to Winston by Mr Charrington, although Winston has to explain to her what a lemon is (153). The significance that Winston attributes to both the song and the paperweight as points of resistance against the imposition from above of a narrative of the past raises the question of how 'the relevant facts' might be defined. Winston has been using the wrong frame of reference, and it is precisely in the 'million useless things', like the rhyme and the paperweight, that the lived past resides.

The fragility of these messages from the past is emphasised when, during the raid on the room over the shop, the paperweight is smashed and a voice from the telescreen mockingly chants the final two lines of the song. Perhaps ideological re-inscription has had its effect on these things too. This pessimism, all the greater because of the glimpse of an escape that Winston has experienced during the novel, can be contrasted with the depiction of memory in Storm Jameson's *Then We Shall Hear Singing* (1942). Jameson's novel, like Orwell's is a dystopian fiction, set after a German victory in an unnamed, and apparently largely rural, European country. Dr Hesse plans to impose the rule of the invaders by eliminating the 'higher functions' (17) of the brains of the men of fighting age, thereby destroying their memories, but the regional Governor has qualms about this plan: 'I don't like to think of men losing their past. The memory of a nation costs too much to make. [...] It puts a frightful responsibility on the rest of us. [...] We shall have to carry their past and future for them' (27). If Orwell appears to doubt whether individual memory can survive without some form of collective memory to guarantee it, Jameson here suggests that collective memory itself cannot arise without the memory work of individuals. This would help explain why the Ministry of Truth's efforts are so barren and hollow; they have no grounding in lived experience. Jameson also expresses greater optimism about the potential for a national memory to survive in the event of the type of dictatorial rule that she depicts in the novel. Crucially, Dr Hesse underestimates the power of the memories of the elderly and of children, and one elderly woman, Anna, voices a belief in the extreme durability of memory:

> The day they took our country it broke into a million pieces under their hands. A piece may be as large as a field with its vines growing across it, or as small as a shadow on a ceiling or a grave in some village they won't let us visit. But any of them is safe with the man or woman or child who remembers it exactly. When the time comes to bring them into the sunlight and fit them together, not one will be missing. (Jameson, *Then* 35)

Later, Anna asserts that memories can hide 'in things, in a cup, a piece of stone, in our earth itself, in the grass' (220). Implicitly, even if an object is broken, or land ploughed up or evacuated, it can still function as a repository for memory, so long as there are people who believe in the importance of remembering. Jameson seems to offer hope in a dark time, asserting that those countries that are living under Nazi occupation will be able to retrieve their history; Orwell offers glimpses of hope only to suggest that dictatorial regimes will always be more powerful than individual gestures.

These two novels project futures in which the past is contested; they therefore raise the question of how their own time, the time of writing, will be remembered. As Peter Middleton and Tim Woods have argued, 'texts are forms of prosthetic social memory by which readers increase and correct their own limited cognitive strengths and participate in a public memorial space. Textual memory also looks forward' (5). The novels I have been examining in this book tell us about how writers during the 1940s conceived of the past, and can also give a sense how they conceptualised the process of memory. But, no less than these explicitly dystopian fictions, they also project a sense of what these writers felt was worthy of preservation for the future. As the mythic and historical narratives of the war with which we are now familiar were in the process of formation, another narrative, a narrative formed by and reflecting upon memory, was laying its own claim to those events. Sometimes this narrative supports the now familiar ideological tropes of the 'spirit of the Blitz', the 'brave airman', and so forth; sometimes it poses a challenge to what we thought we knew about wartime. Memory can express continuity and transcendence, or change and disjunction; an epiphanic moment of sublime insight can be reconfigured as trauma. Tracing the manner in which memory is depicted in the fiction of this period helps to expose that, whether engaged with modernism, realism or genre writing, writers were continually struggling with the question of how to depict a wartime subjectivity. This is not to say that the development of the novel reached a standstill; on the contrary, this was an important moment for the reassessment and reinvigoration of the novel. Critics at the time and since might argue that no new school or movement emerged during this period, but, as Damon DeCosta has argued, the characterisation of the Second World War as 'a literary hiatus [...] has resulted more from scholars looking for what isn't there than from their critical examination of what is' ('Literary Response' 7).

The nature of any narrative of memory will be inflected by the cultural and historical circumstances from which it arises. Despite their highly disparate cultural and historical contexts, and the different understandings of memory and literary techniques that they bring to bear, some striking intertextual resonances with 1940s fiction emerge in the works of early-twenty-first century authors. The novelists of the 1940s often displayed a grasp of psychoanalytical or medical conceptualisations of memory, and, as in the case of Brittain's *Account Rendered* or

Bell's *Martin Croft*, introducing a practitioner to speak for and explain such ideas was one way of providing the reader with assistance in the assessment of the protagonist's behaviour. Whilst similar tactics are sometimes employed in contemporary fiction, the voice of medical authority is more likely to be treated sceptically, and new conceptions of memory are in evidence. Neurological models, which can bring into focus the tenuous nature of the connection between the individual body and its memories, and indeed the fragility of the faculty of memory, have drawn authors' attention. This can serve as a means of re-mystifying memory, and can problematize models, such as the psychoanalytic, that rely on memory being transformed into interpretable narratives. Thus for example, in Liz Jensen's *War Crimes for the Home* (2002), the narrator, Gloria, suffers from Alzheimer's disease, and is therefore battling against the deterioration of her capacity for recalling the events of her wartime youth. Jensen compounds these difficulties, because Gloria also suffers from a form of imposed memory loss, the result of the work of the stage hypnotist Zedorro. This somewhat outlandish plot twist in fact represents darkly ironic wish-fulfilment on the Gloria's part; her desire to forget then is countered by her inability to remember now. For the lay person, the effects of science and magic can seem equally incomprehensible; the opposition of the two is complicated by Zedorro's use of what, in other circumstances, could be a legitimate therapy. Gloria is suspicious of Dr Kaplan, recruited by her children to help her recover this memory, but the narrative ultimately endorses his efforts and the very act of remembering is shown to have therapeutic effects.

Gloria works in a munitions factory, and acknowledges the gulf between her war experience and that of her GI boyfriend and his fellow soldiers: 'I didn't have no war like Izzi's war, or any man's war [...] The war I had, it was my little war, a woman's war, a nobody's war' (212). However both she and they are part of the same conflict; the 'big war outside' and the 'little war at home' (93) are simply different perspectives on the same event. This question of whether boundaries can or should be drawn between combatants and those who did not fight also concerns Michael Frayn in his novel *Spies* (2002). Like Jensen's, Frayn's narrator, Stephen, is looking back to his experience of wartime, but whereas Gloria was a young woman during the war years, Stephen was a child. Frayn also disturbs the process of recall through a style of narration that depicts memory as elusive and malleable: 'What I remember, when I examine my memory carefully, isn't a narrative at all. It's a collection of vivid particulars. [...] Certain individual moments, which seem to mean so much, but which mean in fact so little until the hidden links between them have been found' (32). However, whilst the events Stephen remembers are depicted in confusing and sometimes repeated fragments, he, as an adult, is able to give them the meaning that was inaccessible to him when he was a child, identifying the 'hidden links' and creating the narrative. Accuracy of interpretation can compensate for the shortfalls in the accuracy of recall. Like Jensen, Frayn ultimately provides the reader with a sense of a clear picture of past events emerging from the fog of memory.

Frayn's plot centres on the revelation that the activities of Mrs Hayward, the mother of Stephen's friend Keith, interpreted by the boys as meaning that she is a German spy, concealed the fact that she was aiding her brother-in-law, Keith's Uncle Peter, a deserter from the RAF in hiding in the locality. This, together with the revelation that Stephen is in fact half German–Jewish, allows Frayn to discuss the moral relativism of the war, as when Stephen reflects that members of his father's family were killed during Allied air raids, 'by Uncle Peter, or by his colleagues in Bomber Command' (229). Frayn thus engages critically with a familiar element of wartime and post-war cultural mythology. Similarly, the revelation of Stephen's origins, hidden during wartime, allows Frayn to point to other, less familiar, aspects of wartime life such as the experiences of refugees or internees. This desire to engage with and question the established narratives of wartime was already discernible during the war years; contemporary authors have developed a variety of strategies for elucidating the complexities of our relationship to what happened 'then'. Ian McEwan's *Atonement* (2001) introduces a 'remembering' narrator only at the climax of what on the surface appears to be a realist, retrospective fiction. McEwan poses questions about the status of realism as a literary form, and in particular its role in contributing to and shaping our understanding of the past, and also makes explicit an implicit reference to the literary culture of the 1940s. Part way through the third section of the narrative, which describes her experiences as a nurse in London at the period of the Dunkirk landings, Briony, who has submitted a story to *Horizon*, receives a response initialled 'C.C', rejecting the story but suggesting some changes that might be made to it. From the description of the story contained in the letter, it is clear that what Briony submitted is what the reader has already read as the first part of the novel, with the changes incorporated. The letter mentions that Elizabeth Bowen has read Briony's manuscript, reinforcing the echo of *The Heat of the Day* in an earlier description of London: 'In those days of May, before the story from France was fully understood, before the bombing of the city in September, London had the outward signs, but not yet the mentality, of war.' (287) This foreshadowing, which occurs shortly before Briony has to help care for the injured from Dunkirk, is a reminder that the narrator, and by extension the reader, is positioned at an historical distance from the events described; the narrator, unlike Briony, is able to predict how events will progress.

This sense of the narrator's omniscience is part of what is interrogated by the novel's coda, a section of first-person narration appended after the conclusion of the body of the narrative, which itself ends with the legend 'BT London 1999' (349). It is revealed that Briony is not only a protagonist within but also the 'author' of the preceding narrative, which constitutes her atonement for her false accusation against Robbie Turner. In the narrative, having been released from prison and joined the army, Robbie survives Dunkirk and is reunited with Briony's sister Cecilia, but in the coda, Briony reveals the full extent of her crafting of the story, suggesting that a 'realistic' depiction of events could have had a quite different outcome. The narrator alludes to early drafts that were 'pitiless. [...] I can no longer think what purpose would be served if, say, I tried to persuade my reader, by direct or indirect means, that Robbie Turner died of septicaemia at Bray Dunes on 1 June 1940, or that Cecilia was killed in September of the same year by the bomb that destroyed Balham Underground station' (370). Briony has already revealed that she is suffering from a form of dementia that is causing her memory to fail (354), and now asserts that she is happy that, once all the witnesses have gone, they will exist only as her 'inventions' (371), that, on paper at least, events will have a positive outcome. McEwan poses questions about how narratives convince us of their truth; Briony's narrative apparently shies away from actuality, but it also exposes the process by which individuals become subject to history through an attempt to 'rescue' them from its depredations.

'[A]lways there is some more war to be written about' (Smith, *The Holiday* 8). These examples of creative engagement with the literary and historical past demonstrate both a continuing fascination with the Second World War, and how new ways of conceptualising memory can be explored or critiqued through formal experiment. The writers I have discussed in the body of this book turned to memory for a variety of reasons: as a means of understanding the present crisis through comparisons with the past; as a means of attempting to provide reassurance about the integrity of the subject at a time when individuals were under physical and emotional threat. The recovery of lost memory could be a way to provide narrative completion, recovering the past at a time when the future was parlous. Both their attitudes towards war and their conceptions of memory have since been overlaid with new paradigms, some of which are alluded to in the novels I have discussed in this conclusion. Whilst contemporary narratives of memory can be situated as part of a wider engagement with memory in contemporary culture, it is nevertheless striking that memory has become, once again, a key to understanding the events of the Second World War. This is testimony not just to the continuing rethinking and reconsideration of the war, but also to the literary legacy of earlier writers. This legacy cannot easily be quantified; it is perceptible not only in the way that those writers attempted to depict their time for their time, but also in their influence on the way in which the war has entered cultural and literary memory.

Notes

Introduction

1. Alfred Hitchcock's question in response to criticism of his film *Stage Fright* (1950) is relevant here: 'So why is it that we can't tell a lie through a flashback?' (Truffaut 158) The (apparently) material depiction of the past would appear to guarantee its factuality. As Thomas Sutcliffe notes, part of what is at stake here is the disruption a particular kind of pact between the audience and the film-maker (11).
2. *Look at All Those Roses* appeared in 1941; of the stories collected in *The Demon Lover* (1945), 'The Demon Lover' appeared in *The Listener* in November 1941, 'Happy Autumn Fields' in *The Cornhill* in November 1944 and 'Mysterious Kôr' in *Penguin New Writing* in November 1944.
3. I will be focusing on new works published during the 1940s, but it is interesting to note Henry Reed's comments, from an essay of 1946, on the fortunes in wartime of 'classic' writers: 'Anthony Trollope has regained some of the enormous popularity he enjoyed in his own day [...] Joseph Conrad is beginning to revive [...] D. H. Lawrence is, for the moment, all but forgotten' (8). As influences on contemporary writers, Reed identifies Thomas Hardy, James Joyce and 'Henry James, who has entered on a period of popularity which he never attained in his lifetime' (9).
4. In a discussion of 1980s television adaptations of texts from the 1930s including Vera Brittain's *Testament of Youth* (1933) Roger Bromley identifies a similar shift in relation to the status of realism: 'At their moment of original publication many of these [works] were welcomed as radical cultural interventions in a political struggle over poverty, injustice and unemployment. They were hailed for their "realism". The problem is that the "realism" of that period, in the costume drama of television adaptation, becomes the "romanticism" of ours' (112).
5. The 'Mystic Writing-Pad', which Freud uses as an analogy for the workings of memory, cannot be considered an 'advanced technology' but it has elements which prove useful in developing this classical analogy. See Sigmund Freud, 'A Note Upon the "Mystic Writing Pad" ' (1924).
6. Structurally, the novel takes the type of disruption of chronology favoured by Isherwood in *The Memorial* to an extreme, leaving Huxley open to Nicholas Murray's accusation, appropriate in the context of the present discussion, that there is a 'scissors and paste quality in the flashbacks and fast forwards' (157) he uses here. In another novel from the same year, Graham Greene's *A Gun for Sale*, the killer Raven appears to have a 'photographic' memory: 'His eyes, like little concealed cameras, photographed the room instantaneously' (2–3). This serves both as a sign of his coldness and lack of emotion, and as a means of keeping at bay more painful memories from his past.
7. Daniel Schacter notes that in 1977 psychologists identified a particular type of memory experience which they named 'flashbulb memory'. These occur

in relation to shocking or traumatic events and it appears to the subject that their memory 'preserves or "freezes" whatever happens at the moment we learn of the shocking event' (*Searching* 195). Such memories are, however, subject to deterioration, although not to the same extent as emotionally neutral memories from the same period.

8. Such comparisons between cinema and memory are based on the notion that both are essentially realist forms of representation; they forget that, as Matt K. Matsuda explains, for an early film maker such as Méliès, 'the realism of cinema was neither science nor "objective" witnessing, but a truth of illusions, a reality of tricks and simulations' (170). Pointing to the use of the word by takers of hallucinogens, Ruth Leys notes that 'flashbacks' are often considered by researchers in psychology to have 'imaginative and role-playing dimensions' (242). For the most part, the writers I am discussing here presented memory in a realist fashion, although as I will show, there were exceptions.

9. Of Freud's works, Woolf is only known to have read *Moses and Monotheism*, which appeared in English in 1939, although it is highly likely that she would have had a general acquaintance with the Freudian ideas that were in circulation during the 1920s and 1930s. As regards the accessibility of Freud's work in English, translations of *Beyond the Pleasure Principle* and *Introductory Lectures* appeared in 1922. Writing in 1946, the literary critic H. V. Routh makes particular note of the appearance of the latter (135). Pelican editions of *New Introductory Lectures* and *The Psychopathology of Everyday Life* were published in 1934 and 1938 respectively. The latter text deals with one memory-related concept that has achieved continuing wide currency, parapraxes, or what later became known as 'Freudian slips'.

10. Literature was of course not the only sphere in which these new concepts had an impact. Gillian Swanson notes that 'psychological studies of family, marriage and parenting conducted through the 1930s informed the monitoring of civilian morale' during the war years, and that, for example, '[c]laims concerning the centrality of the relationship between mother and child to emotional well-being [...] gained new emphasis during the war' (74).

11. The kinds of techniques recommended for improving the reader's social or employment prospects could also be used for other purposes. The music-hall entertainer 'Mr Memory', in Alfred Hitchcock's adaptation of John Buchan's *The Thirty-Nine Steps* (1935), is based on an actual turn-of-the-century act who performed under the name 'Datas', and specialised in answering the audience's questions about sporting events and famous trials, and who, like Mr Memory, had the catch-phrase, 'Am I right, Sir?' Datas' autobiography is unrevealing about the techniques he used to enable him to remember this information but it seems unlikely that he suffered from the hypertrophied memory with synaesthesia that afflicted Sherashevsky, the subject of A. R. Luria's study *The Mind of a Mnemonist* (1968). Sherashevsky, whose performances involved the reproduction of lists of random words or abstract symbols provided by the audience, found that the associations particular words and sounds had for him made it difficult for him to follow a conversation or read a sentence from beginning to end without 'irrelevant' memories intruding.

12. Wells however could not endorse the ideas about immortality and wrote a scathing commentary on Dunne's *The New Immortality* (1938) in 'The Immortality of Mr. J. W. Dunne' (1939).

13. In Priestley's novel *Bright Day* (1946), the process of memory is presented rather differently when Gregory Dawson, a screen-writer, sets out to deliberately recall a series of events from his past after an encounter with some former acquaintances. This act of recall is linear (although there are some gaps) and non-spontaneous, and Gregory stops and starts his memory as though it were a film: 'At that point [...] I deliberately stopped remembering. It was late, and I got up to prepare for bed' (71).
14. As Keith Williams notes, Greene also appealed to Dunne's theories about dreaming to describe the experience of seeing the film *Son of the Sheik* (1926) after the death of its star, Rudolph Valentino: 'The man is moving on the screen and at the same time he is dead and magnificently and absurdly entombed' (qtd. in Williams 112).
15. Later in his search for an explanation, the narrator visits his friend who is reading *The New and the Old Self* by Doctor Birinus Hals-Gruber: 'I opened it at random and read a bit. There was a lot about the *Sesame Impulse* and the *Agamemnon-Reflex* which made, as they say, fascinating reading. But I couldn't relate Miss Hargreaves to any of it' (147). Indeed, her appearance remains resistant to any rational explanation.
16. J. W. N. Sullivan, reviewing *An Experiment with Time* for the *Times Literary Supplement* describes Dunne's explanation of these phenomena as 'very obscure' but nevertheless asserts that 'it is evident that our ordinary notion of time as a moving present separating a non-existent past from a non-existent future must be given up.' (659). As Michael H. Whitworth shows in *Einstein's Wake*, Sullivan was an important populariser of new scientific ideas, including Einstein's theories, throughout the 1920s.
17. Ian Hamilton notes that Connolly had changed his mind by May 1942, and argued that '[i]nstead of writing, writers should spend their spare time reading' (135).
18. For a discussion of the way in which the Communist Party of Great Britain shifted its position in relation to the war during 1939–41, see Angus Calder, *The Myth of the Blitz* 77–89.
19. As Jeremy Treglown notes, the editorial in the same issue of the *TLS* was critical of Cecil's sympathetic attitude towards those who might wish, despite unfavourable circumstances, to continue to inhabit an 'ivory tower' (Treglown, '*The Times Literary Supplement*' 142). George Orwell also reflected on the issue of escapism in his 'London Letter to the Partisan Review' written in April 1941: 'I don't see any tendency to escapism in current literature [...] If I could get the time and mental peace to write a novel now, I should want to write about the past, the pre-1914 period, which I suppose comes under the heading of "escapism"' (115).
20. In the course of the series, Lehmann does single out for praise two writers who Henry Reed classed as 'young novelists' in his 1946 study, although both were over thirty when the war broke out: F. L. Green, best known for *Odd Man Out* (1945), and Nigel Balchin, author of *Darkness Falls From the Air* (1942) and *The Small Back Room* (1943). The 1946 film adaptation of Green's novel, directed by Carol Reed and featuring James Mason is probably now better known than the original. Balchin has also fallen into critical neglect, but I discuss his novel *Mine Own Executioner* (1945) in Chapter 4 below.

21. Harrisson opens his article on war books with a lengthy (and initially unacknowledged) quotation from *The Aerodrome*, and later comments: 'I imagine most of it was written before the war. Yet he captures, more nearly than anyone else so far, the tense struggle of the 1940's' (422).
22. For example, as I have noted, Elizabeth Bowen began *The Heat of the Day* (1949) in 1943 but did not finish it until after the war, and Philip Larkin's *A Girl in Winter*, completed in August 1945, was not published until February 1947. In one of the letters exchanged with Graham Greene and V. S. Pritchett published in edited form in 1948 in the *Partisan Review* as 'The Creative Life in Our Time: An Exchange of Letters', Bowen also noted that in the immediate post-war period, established writers suffered from 'the complete *non-existence* of all our earlier written books. That is to say, they do not exist commercially: owing to the paper shortage they are out of print' (Bowen, 'Why Do I Write?' 226).
23. Manning's novel was first published privately and anonymously as *The Middle Parts of Fortune* in 1929. The reviewer is here referring to an expurgated version that appeared the following year; Manning's name was added to the title page in 1943. The original, unexpurgated version was republished in 1977. See Niall Ferguson's introduction to *The Middle Parts of Fortune* vii–xviii. As early as 1933, 'war books' could be debunked in the opening of A. G. Macdonell's *England, Their England* (1933): 'From Chapter 2 to the end there will be no terrific descriptions of the effect of a chlorine gas cloud upon a party of nuns in a bombarded nunnery [...] There will be no streams of consciousness, chapters long, in the best style of Bloomsbury, describing minutely the sensation of a man who has been caught in a heavy-howitzer barrage [...] there are going to be no long passages in exquisite cadences [...] about the quietness of life in billets in comparison with life during a trench mortar bombardment' (7).

1 Remembering the Last War

1. I discuss this particular comparison further in Chapter 3 below.
2. In *Homage to Catalonia* (1938), writing of events he witnessed 'less than seven months' previously in Spain, Orwell notes that 'it is a period that has already receded into enormous distance. Later events have obliterated it much more completely than they have obliterated 1935, or 1905, for that matter' (2).
3. Bell had wanted to go and fight, and became an ambulance driver instead as a concession to his concerned mother.
4. Having been on the receiving end of aerial bombardment in Spain, Romilly joined the Canadian Air Force in 1940, and was killed in action in November 1941. See Jessica Mitford, *Hons and Rebels* 221–7.
5. Even less nostalgic depictions of the war could be socially quiescent; Rosa Maria Bracco has shown that in a large body of interwar middlebrow writing, novelists 'offer an assessment of the common tragic experience of war' whilst communicating and reinforcing what they saw to be 'essential social values' (64).
6. See Croft, *Comrade Heart* 106–24 for Swingler's involvement in these campaigns.

7. Antony Beevor suggests that the fact that many of the key commanders of the New Zealand forces on Crete were First World War veterans had a deleterious effect on their conceptions of the battle: 'Their notions of warfare had been formed by hard pounding in the trenches of Flanders. Yet the Battle of Crete, a revolutionary development in warfare, was to be a contest in which fast reactions, clear thinking and ruthless decisions counted most.' (100–01)
8. Mackenzie estimates that in mid-1940, First World War veterans probably averaged about 35 per cent of Home Guard intake across all ranks, with the average age of recruits approximately 35 years: 'celebrated cases such as Thomas Walton, who lied about his age and joined the LDV at the age of 84 and had served in the Sudan, were the exception rather than the rule' (37–8). In *The Life and Death of Colonel Blimp*, during a montage sequence detailing Clive Candy's Home Guard career, a page from Wintringham's *Picture Post* article of 21 September 1940 is shown in doctored form, with Candy's (Roger Livesey's) face replacing Wintringham's own in a picture spread of 'Some of the Men who Teach at the Home Guard School' (17).
9. See also George Orwell, 'Boys' Weeklies' and Michael Paris, *Warrior Nation* 153–4. In Waugh's *A Handful of Dust* (1934), one of items in the 'gallery representative of every phase of [Tony Last's] adolescence' is a 'framed picture of a dreadnought (a coloured supplement from *Chums*), all its guns spouting flame and smoke' (16). In Orwell's *Coming Up for Air* (1939), *Chums* is one of the papers that the working-class grammar school boy George Bowling remembers taking with him to read while fishing (77).
10. For Waugh's description of his own involvement with the Commandoes on Crete (an interesting intertext to Pargeter's *She Goes to War*), see his 'Memorandum on LAYFORCE' (1941). Waugh also returns to these events in *Officers and Gentlemen* (1955), the second volume of his trilogy *The Sword of Honour*. For a discussion of these contrasting accounts, see Angus Calder's 'Mr Wu and the Colonials' (1997). For more on the literary representation of Commandoes, see Chapter 4 below.
11. In the film *The Gentle Sex* (1943), the elderly Mrs Sheridan (Mary Jerrold), the mother of Anne Lawrence's (Joyce Howard's) fiancé, reveals to a surprised Anne and her ATS friends that she drove an ambulance in the First World War and was injured at Étaples. This causes Anne to regret her hasty comments about the potential social changes that might arise from women's active involvement in the current war.
12. Whilst managing to avoid giving details of the novel's ending, R. D. Charques warned prospective readers that it was 'rather a let-down' (Anon [R. D. Charques], 'Keep it Dark' 469).
13. See Robert Graves and Alan Hodge 66–70 for an account of the career of Horatio Bottomley, 'the patriot of patriots and the ablest recruiting agent in the country' (67).
14. The split between Paula as the true love of Smithy, and Paula as the 'trophy' wife of Rainier can be compared to the split between Chris's first love Margaret and his aristocratic wife Kitty in Rebecca West's *The Return of the Soldier* (1918). Condensing these two functions into a single individual means that Hilton can mask the fact that Smithy/Rainier may now have to confront pain and loss, and also means that 'reuniting' him with Paula cancels out the potential complexities of her own position. West's novel ends on

a highly ambivalent note; Kitty regains her husband, but for this to happen, Chris has had to remember the loss of his son, and the horrors of war.
15. Reviewing *England's Hour* (1941), Brittain's account of the impact of the Blitz, Graham Greene suggested that 'the book might have been called more accurately "Brittain's Hour" ' ('A Pride' 178). Similar criticisms have been levelled at *Testament of Youth*; see for instance, Claire M. Tylee, *The Great War and Women's Consciousness* 209–23.
16. Miller's wife Betty Miller also shows an interest in the psychological effects of war in her novel *On the Side of the Angels* (1945), which I discuss in Chapter 4 below.
17. Brittain was spurred to write the novel following the trial of Leonard Lockhart, a General Practitioner, who was imprisoned in November 1939. Lockhart was found guilty but insane on the charge of murdering his wife, and had apparently committed the crime whilst in a dissociated state of mind. Lockhart was released in 1942, and Brittain was forced to rewrite the novel, which had originally been called 'Day of Judgment', and to change its protagonist's occupation when, having read the manuscript in early 1943, Lockhart made objections. See Berry and Bostridge 456–7, and, for a report on the verdict, Anon, 'Doctor Guilty, but Insane' (1939). The novel as we now have it was completed in September 1944 but was not published in Britain until a year later.

2 Damaged Minds: Crime and Detection

1. In relation to Italy, David Forgacs notes that 'a considerable amount of material of foreign origin' including 'American films and comics, French films and detective stories [and] British crime novels [...] remained in circulation [for most of the war] despite pressures from various quarters' (78). Martin Kitchen, discussing censorship of literature in Nazi Germany, suggests that official disapproval of Anglo-American detective stories had its roots in the fact that 'these books suggested that Scotland Yard was every bit as good as the German police, or an American gumshoe as cunning as the Gestapo. Goebbels tried to encourage German writers to try their hand at detective stories that would show Himmler's men as "the best police force in the world" ' (280).
2. Dorothy L. Sayers makes a similar point in relation to the historical development of the detective story in an essay from 1929. See '[Introduction to] The Omnibus of Crime' 55–6.
3. Although Priestman discusses *The Ministry of Fear* in this context, most of his examples from the 1940s are of American *noir* fictions, such as John Franklin Bardin's *Devil Take the Blue-Tail Fly* (1948). According to one of his biographers, Patrick Hamilton, whose popular stage play *Gaslight* (1938) employs elements of Victorian stage melodrama, 'toyed with the idea of writing a three-volume Victorian thriller *à la* Wilkie Collins' (Jones 225) before embarking on *Hangover Square*.
4. In *Crooked House* (1949), Agatha Christie warns against remembering conventions too well when eleven-year-old Josephine Leonides perpetrates a crime, and eventually precipitates her own death, by drawing on what she

has read: 'All she had to do was to avoid leaving fingerprints and the slightest knowledge of detective fiction would teach her that. And everything else had been a mere hotch-potch, culled at random from stock mystery stories.' (188)
5. The golden age is usually defined as the period between the publication of Agatha Christie's first novel *The Mysterious Affair at Styles* (1920) and the appearance of Dorothy L. Sayers last novel, *Busman's Honeymoon* (1937), although E. C. Bentley's *Trent's Last Case* (1913) is sometimes identified as the inaugural example.
6. Certainly Symons' prediction of the demise of the detective as protagonist was far from the mark. John Scaggs has shown how many devices associated with the 'golden age' or even earlier detective writing, such as the locked room mystery and the detective as 'reasoning machine' have re-emerged, not always with an ironic twist, in contemporary novels and television crime series. See Scaggs 33–54.
7. A longer version of this account of the development of the novel appears in Greene's *Ways of Escape* 93–100. Greene notes that the 'funny' aspect fell by the wayside long before the book was completed. His typology seems to refer to the works of Freeman Wills Crofts, whose Inspector French stories often rely on the mechanics of, for example, railway timetables, Dorothy L. Sayers *The Nine Tailors* (1934) in which campanology plays an important part, and Agatha Christie's or Ngaio Marsh's country house murders. Michael Innes (the pseudonym of J. I. M. Stewart) had published several of his quirky detective novels featuring Inspector Appleby by the time of Greene's journey in late 1941. *The Secret Vanguard* (1940) uses the device of a character unwittingly overhearing a secret message being passed, but despite its country house setting, *Hamlet, Revenge!* (1937) seems more likely to have influenced Greene, not least because its plot is a combination of spy story and detective story. Both Greene and his brother Hugh were collectors of detective stories from their youth, and Brian Diemert suggests A. E. W. Mason's *At the Villa Rose* (1910), which features a murder at a séance, as another possible influence on *The Ministry of Fear* (153).
8. The idea that a detective story could adequately represent the experience of wartime is debunked in Richard Mason's *The Wind Cannot Read* (1947). The narrator's friend Peter announces: 'I've been writing a book. [...] It's going to be the great book of the war. An epic. What *All Quiet on the Western Front* was to the last war, and *For Whom the Bell Tolls* to the Spanish War, my book will be to World War Two. Unfortunately I can't make up my mind whether it shall be *The War Office Murder*, or *One of Our Bodies is Missing*' (81). When the book is completed, it is in fact an account of a wartime escape from France over the Pyrenees (165).
9. Writing about the interwar years, Alison Light suggests that '[w]hodunits could be just the answer to that lack of capacity for concentrated thinking which plagued the returned soldier [...] whodunits were perhaps the literature of emotional invalids, shock-absorbing and rehabilitating, like playing endless rounds of clock patience' (71).
10. A film version of the novel was released in 1948. It was banned from exhibition by many local authorities but Ross McKibbin notes that '[i]n those areas where it was shown it broke all records' (441 n.76). An incident in Mary Renault's *North Face* (1949), indicates the continuing allure of the novel. On

holiday in a boarding house and short of reading material, Miss Fisher looks among the sofa cushions: 'She had noticed, the evening before, that this was where Miss Lettice Winter put her copy of *No Orchids for Miss Blandish* when her mother came into the room. Miss Fisher had heard interesting accounts of it, and it might still be there' (46). Unfortunately, it isn't. In Nevil Shute's *The Chequer Board* (1947), hospitalized Commando Corporal Brent finds *True Tales of Adventure* 'thin watery, stuff' (37) compared to his own experiences and decides to 'ask sister if she's got one with more ginger in it [...] Girls and that. Maybe they'll have a copy of *No Orchids for Miss Blandish*, or one o'them' (37). Notably, *No Orchids* also makes use of amnesia as a plot device. Having been terrorised and drugged by her captors, Miss Blandish emerges unable to remember her own name and this is symbolic of the brutalisation she has undergone.

11. Orwell identifies the reactionary aspects of these novels, but Andy Croft notes that during the 1930s, the idea that the thriller reinforced the existing order was challenged by writers on the left, including Patrick Hamilton's brother Bruce (*Red Letter Days* 185–97).

12. In a discussion of Agatha Christie, Gillian Gill distinguishes between material and logical clues, connecting the former to the Holmesian tradition of deduction from visible signifiers, and the latter to a focus on the underlying motivation for a crime, a technique often employed by Hercule Poirot and Miss Marple. Christie, she argues, uses both together (38–9).

13. Later, in 1943, the National Savings Committee began a poster campaign featuring the 'Squander-bug' in an attempt to encourage saving rather than spending.

14. The nature and cause of the Major's own illness is unclear. His apparent paranoia eventually proves to have a grounding in actuality when the belongings of Jones the private detective are found buried on an island in the asylum's grounds. The Major's age is unspecified, but his disorder evidently dates from the current conflict, and an allusion to a fellow-soldier who 'they got [...] on the beach' (160) implies that he was involved in the evacuation of Dunkirk.

15. This is usually the case even in contemporary examples of the 'amnesia thriller' which often display a thorough understanding of the psychological effects of trauma; see for example Minette Walters, *The Dark Room* (1995) and Nicci French, *Land of the Living* (2003).

16. Kenneth Richmond, the Jungian analyst by whom Greene was treated in 1921, was also a spiritualist, but Greene never seems to have expressed any particularly negative sentiments about him personally. See Sherry 92–108.

17. Agatha Christie uses the device of feigned amnesia in a non-parodic way in her novel *The Secret Adversary* (1922). A young woman claims not to be able to remember being handed secret papers by a fellow-passenger before the evacuation of the *Lusitania*, in order to prevent the papers falling into the wrong hands. Her performance is believed because her captors are incredulous that a young girl could have read enough to be able to dissemble such a disorder successfully. Jared Cade suggests that this plot could explain Christie's own apparently amnesiac interlude in 1925 (126).

18. Mair was a journalist and reviewer who worked for *The New Statesman* and *John O'London's Weekly*, and the original portrayal of the editor in *Never Come Back* led to the withdrawal of the first edition of the book. In a letter written

to John Hayward shortly after Mair's death on an RAF mission in 1942, Stevie Smith summed up the controversy: 'there was a fine fuss about [the novel], because John had awful rows with *John O'London* and its then editor [...] and it all came out in the book – not quite all though, because I remember they settled it out of court' (Smith, *Me Again* 283). See also Julian Symon's introduction in Mair v–xiii.

19. For a discussion of the persistent belief, fostered by the figurative use of the term, that schizophrenia is characterised by swings between two discrete personalities, Jekyll and Hyde style, see Trevor Turner, 'Schizophrenia' (1995). In the period under discussion, even Nicholas Blake, generally well-informed on such issues, implies that it might be possible for a 'schizophrenic' to commit a murder whilst inhabited by one personality, and then not remember these events the next day (Blake, *Malice* 164).
20. The current paperback edition of the novel has only the subtitle: 'A Story of Darkest Earl's Court'.
21. Joseph Bristow comments: 'Booth's analogy is, by his own admission, rather strained but it plainly indicates how the dark continent served as a vivid metaphor for the insanitary world that plagued the late Victorian social conscience' (131).
22. This anthropological bent is also evidenced by Hamilton's collecting of newspaper cuttings about famous crimes, which may have contributed, in particular, to the characterisation of *The Gorse* trilogy's Ernest Ralph Gorse. See Jones 303. See also note 10 in Chapter 4 below.
23. Peter might have gone around this particular part of London in a uniform because in 1933 the British Union of Fascists converted a former teacher training college situated in Chelsea into their headquarters, known as Black House, 'a combination of barracks and social club' (Pugh 134). Following the 'Battle of Cable Street', a confrontation between fascists, anti-fascists and the police which took place on 4 October 1936 in the East End of London, the 1936 Public Order Act banned the wearing of uniforms to signify membership of political organisations. The law could be to some extent finessed, though, as an ordinary black shirt was not classed as a uniform and could still be used to indicate party membership in some circumstances (Pugh 173–6). According to Hamilton's friend Claud Cockburn, the portrayal of Peter led to suspicions among Cockburn's friends in the Communist Party; Bill Rust, editor of the *Daily Worker*, apparently decided that such realism could only be the result of having had dealings with the British Union of Fascists. Evidently, a meeting with Hamilton soon dispelled these concerns. Although he never joined the Communist Party, Hamilton shared many of its beliefs (Jones 256).
24. 'The I.R.A. and their cloakrooms' could be a specific reference to a bomb planted in the left-luggage office at King's Cross railway station in July 1939, which caused a fatality. See Fisk 72–4.
25. Their principal contributions had not been made at the time of *Hangover Square*'s publication, but would include, for Garson *Mrs Miniver* and *Random Harvest* (both 1942) and for Donat *Perfect Strangers* (1945).
26. Lang also directed the film *The Ministry of Fear* (1944), and Greene was disappointed that he omitted the asylum scenes.

3 Remembering the Country

1. The Graham Greene short story on which the film is based, 'The Lieutenant Died Last: An Unrecorded Victory in 1940' (1940) paints a rather less idyllic picture of the village. Potter, the name itself somewhat less redolent of pastoral fruitfulness than Bramley End, is 'only one public-house [...] one cash store and post office [...] a small tin-roofed church [...] half a dozen cottages' (46–7). Although Potter has a manor house, this is not inhabited. The rescuer of the village in the story is the poacher, Bill Purves, who single handedly wipes out the invading force, whilst hearkening back 'forty years to South Africa and an ambush on the veldt' (52). A poacher called Purvis does figure in the film, but rather less prominently; played by Edward Rigby, he loses his life while facilitating the escape of George (Harry Fowler), an evacuee, who raises the alarm in the next village. Notably, whilst the film ends abruptly with the rescue of the village, followed by a brief epilogue, in the story, the impact on Purves of his actions are at least implied. He finds a photograph of a baby in the pocket of the lieutenant he kills and keeps this as a 'souvenir [...] Sometimes he took it out of a drawer and looked at it himself – uneasily. It made him – for no reason that *he* could understand – feel bad' (58–9). Clive Coultas also notes differences in the portrayal of the invaders; the depiction of the Nazis as 'amateur bunglers' in the story 'probably arose out of the phoney war period. By the time of the film, in 1942, they had turned into ruthless paratroopers' (98).
2. Houston also notes that the prologue and epilogue are included in the shooting script and were not added on when the film was complete 'by which time optimism could have been more justified' (12).
3. The proleptic nature of this memorialisation is similar to that found in Winston Churchill's speech of 18 June 1940: 'Let us therefore brace ourselves to our duty and so bear ourselves that if the British Commonwealth and Empire lasts for a thousand years, men will still say, "This was their finest hour" ' (Churchill 207). We, now, can create the conditions in which this positive remembering will happen. Mark Rawlinson, who also notes that '[t]he Second World War was fought with an eye on posterity's memory', suggests that there is an echo of Hitler's 'millenial rhetoric' (2) in this speech.
4. Wood also comments on the prevalence of a nostalgic construction of the Second World War during the mid-1970s (24–5).
5. For a description of the impact of the war on British farming, particularly the effects of new government regulations, see Sadie Ward, *War in the Countryside* (1988).
6. In a letter to Ethel Smythe in January 1941, written from Rodmell in Sussex, Virginia Woolf comments: 'You never shared my passion for [London]. Yet its what, in some odd corner of my dreaming mind, represents Chaucer, Shakespeare, Dickens. Its my only patriotism: save one vision, in Warwickshire one spring [May 1934] when we were driving back from Ireland and I saw a stallion being led, under the may and the beeches, along a grass ride; and I thought that is England' (*Leave the Letters* 460). Gillian Beer notes that Woolf expresses 'the sense of herself as exile' here (168); for me this coalesces in the use of the word 'that', rather than 'this': 'that is England', but she is distanced from it.

7. For a detailed discussion of the politics of discourse on the English countryside in this period, see Matless, *Landscape and Englishness*, especially Part II 'Organic England' (103–70) and Part III 'Landscapes of War and Reconstruction' (173–264).
8. I would agree with Robert Murphy that Portman is 'a disturbing presence even in [...] films [...] where he plays good characters' (108).
9. In 1957, Betjeman was a founder member of the Victorian Society, established to campaign for the preservation of examples of Victorian architecture, then considered out of fashion.
10. Betjeman's poem 'Slough', with the infamous opening line 'Come, friendly bombs, and fall on Slough', was published in *Continual Dew* (1937).
11. For other objections to the bungalow, see Matless 40–1, 48–9. As Ross McKibbin has noted, the use of the word 'Bungaloid' condemns both a particular style of housing and its inhabitants, an elision that he also identifies in the descriptions of new housing developments of different kinds in George Orwell's *Coming Up for Air* (McKibbin 79). A number of the stories from V. S. Pritchett's *It May Never Happen* (1945) also use descriptions of either bungalows or new estates as a means of evoking sites of spiritual or emotional desolation. See for instance 'The Sailor', 'Pocock Passes' and 'Aunt Gertrude'.
12. In *The Untutored Townsman's Invasion of the Country* (1946), Joad develops the arguments of this article and also argues against the army's appropriation of parts of the Dorset coast. See also Patrick Wright, *The Village that Died for England* (1995).
13. At the end of *Mr Stimpson and Mr Gorse*, written in 1951 but set in 1928, Hamilton describes how cars, 'so strongly resembling beetles if seen from the air, finally took complete control of the country, the countryside, the villages, the roads, the towns and the entire lives of the human beings who dwelt or moved therein' (*Gorse Trilogy* 562). Eventually the beetles begin 'to kill men, women and children at a furiously increasing pace – practically at random' (564). Hamilton's jaundiced view of motor-travel could have been fostered by the serious injuries he suffered when he was run over in 1932.
14. The word 'katabolic' (or 'catabolic') refers to a destructive metabolism.
15. In an article published in May 1940, Beverley Nichols describes the transformation that country life could bring about for previously city-dwelling members of the Women's Land Army. Forsaking make-up and hair dye, 'these city girls become purified by their work on the land' (qtd. in Sonia O. Rose 213). C. E. M. Joad, also quoted by Rose, hoped that exposure to country life could have a similar effect on evacuees (212). See also C. Henry Warren 31. As David Matless puts it: 'The assumption is that while the city would be horribly bewildering to a country child, the country should be a place of pleasant unfamiliarity to the city child; not a place of boredom, loneliness and dullness.' (181–2) Richard Titmuss, writing soon after the war, stressed the disjunction between the environment that evacuated town-dwellers might be used to and that to which they were transferred in pragmatic terms: 'An environment which produces a higher infant mortality rate than Tokyo does not generally rear children who can come to terms with life in an Ayrshire village' (132).
16. In her 1940 memoir, M. V. Hughes notes that the village on the outskirts of London to which she moves at the end of the First World War 'owes its

development, from a hamlet into an embryo township, entirely to an unpleasant arrival from the sky'; Cuffley is placed 'on the map' after a Zeppelin is brought down there in 1916 (Hughes 11). This text is also interesting for its depiction of inter-war life in a village that, despite being isolated and lacking many amenities, is nevertheless close enough to London for Hughes' children to travel there daily by train to go to school, and for them to consider themselves still a 'London family'.

17. Michael Bartholomew points out that the details of Morton's service during the First World War are unclear but that he was probably not posted abroad (52).
18. See also Mark Connelly, *We Can Take It!* 60–61 for the use of analogies with the Napoleonic Wars in newspapers and magazines of the time. As Featherstone notes, Priestley was one of a group of 'politically anomalous' writers, including Siegfried Sassoon, John Lehmann and Henry Reed who discussed *The Dynasts* during the war years; comparisons were often drawn between the Home Guard and Hardy's 'Bang-Up-Locals' (157). A contributory factor to interest in Hardy at this time was that the centenary of Hardy's birth fell on 2 June 1940, towards the end of the Dunkirk evacuations. Another interesting example of the use of pre-twentieth century reference points in the representation of England in wartime is Warwick Deeping's *The Man Who Went Back* (1940). This is a time travel narrative in which the protagonist is transported back to an ancient Britain that is fending off an invasion from the Saxons. Despite acknowledging that the notion of history repeating itself is a cliché, the narrator is nevertheless struck by similarities between his present and the past in which he finds himself:

    > That babbling little beast Goebbels! Russia. Chaos hanging over one by a thread! How like was the pattern in this island world into which I had been translated. Beauty, order, peace, crops and herds, farmsteads, orchards, and into it spilling this savagery, this wolf spirit, slaying, destroying, fouling. Was the higher order always to fall before the lower? Was the planned violence of Totalitarianism any better than the savagery of these other Teutons? Did the wheel always turn and find itself crushing our dreams in muck and blood? (70).

19. An earlier, abridged edition of the journals was published in 1952. The editor on that occasion was Jocelyn Brooke, whose own writings display a fascination for the relationship between the soldier and the landscape. For example, in *The Goose Cathedral* (1950), he remembers how, as a child, he imagined a breed of 'wild' soldiers, 'nesting in the undercliff [...] half-human, half-animal, smooth-faced fauns with putteed legs and (protruding from their khaki-covered buttocks) small white tails like the scuts of rabbits' (*The Orchid Trilogy* 340).
20. The National Trust had existed since the 1890s, but as Patrick Wright notes, large country houses became a concern after 1934 when the economic threats to their survival were becoming evident. 'At this time the trust only owned two such buildings [...] By 1945 the number had risen to seventeen.' (*Journey* 79). See also Helen Ashton's *The Captain Comes Home* (1947); Wilchester Castle is not of sufficient historical interest to the National Trust, and the protagonists debate whether a new housing estate on the land will be an improvement or not (198–99).

21. In editions of the novel up until its 1960 revision, the body of the text was divided in a prologue and epilogue, both entitled 'Brideshead Revisited', with two central sections, subtitled 'The Sacred and Profane Memories of Charles Ryder: Et in Arcadia Ego' and 'The Sacred and Profane Memories of Charles Ryder: A Twitch Upon the Thread', thus giving increased prominence to the novel's subtitle.
22. In his preface to the 1960 re-issue of the novel, Waugh admits that at the time when it was written it seemed that English country houses were 'doomed to decay and spoliation' and that in the depiction of Brideshead he therefore 'piled it on rather' ('Preface' 8). However, like Sackville-West, he expresses some ambivalence towards the idea that, if it were preserved, 'Brideshead today would be open to trippers, its treasures rearranged by expert hands' ('Preface' 8).
23. Katherine's nationality, and the circumstances of her arrival in England are not given by Larkin, although her name and other small clues imply that she is either German or Austrian. Tom Paulin suggests that this lack of specificity diminishes the effectiveness of Larkin's portrayal of an outsider's view of the English, because we have little sense of the co-ordinates from which Katherine takes her bearings (240–2).
24. In *The Sea-Grape Tree* (1976), her belated sequel to *The Ballad and the Source*, Lehmann, who had become interested in spiritualism following her daughter's death in 1958, develops the trope of voices calling from the past by having Rebecca visited by the spirit of the now dead Sybil.
25. In this 'Afterword' to the original text, Bowen was writing when Bowen's Court no longer existed; she had been forced to sell it in 1960 and the new owner demolished it soon afterwards.

4 In Time of War

1. See for instance Mollie Panter-Downes, *London War Notes 1939–1945* (1971), which describes civilian reactions to these and other wartime events.
2. Reviewing the film for *Time and Tide*, Helen Fletcher describes Mrs Mitchell's letters as 'partly *The Times* fourth leader, partly the parish magazine, and partly *Punch*. [...] Anyway they got her a new husband' (320). A more sympathetic assessment comes from Roger Manvell in *Britain Today*, who notes the involvement of former prisoner of war and writer Guy Morgan in scripting the film (35–6).
3. In wartime, a 'mobile woman' was one who, having been called up for war service, was liable to be moved to a posting in any part of the country. The sisters are not mobile in this sense, but in her study *Blackout*, Antonia Lant forges connections between this specific meaning of 'mobile' and women's changing status in wartime that are relevant here: 'The term "mobile" clearly had both a literal and a metaphorical meaning, the metaphorical resting on the literal. The category of woman was on the move: it was impossible to pin down with certainty.' (86)
4. Shephard notes the conclusions reached by T. F. Rodger, a psychiatrist attached to Mountbatten's South East Asia Command, about the effects of imprisonment in the east. Rodger suggested in 1945 that those who had been imprisoned by the Japanese displayed fewer adverse reactions than those

who had been in captivity elsewhere, and 'considered this to be due in large measure to the contempt which British soldiers were able to feel for the Japanese and the absence of any feeling that the enemy was a man of similar outlook and cultural background to themselves' (qtd. in Shephard 319). There was also a belief that because for much of the war, officers were not separated from their men in Japanese camps, it was possible for *esprit de corps* to be maintained. However, as Shephard also argues, this optimistic picture was belied by the fact that psychiatric conditions in the released men were often initially masked by the effects of starvation, ill-treatment and tropical diseases. In relation to the racially based aspect of Rodger's argument, Abram Kardiner and Herbert Spiegel suggested in 1947 that, in combat situations at least, the soldier tends 'to empathize with the enemy soldiers he is fighting' (34); soldiers fighting in the Mediterranean were more likely to express hatred of the Japanese than were the troops actually engaged in combat in the Pacific. The authors continue that: 'The positive relatedness to his own group is much more important than [the soldier's] negative relatedness to the enemy' (35).

5. Discussing attitudes towards war veterans during the inter-war period, Peter Barham argues that 'constitutional factors' were commonly invoked from the late 1920s onwards as a means of 'disengaging the connection between war service and disability [...] [I]f mentally disordered servicemen were all disturbed before the event, then there was clearly no need to give them pensions; and from the fact they were all inherently off-balance, it followed that they had no lessons to teach the rest of society about the conditions of modern warfare, and could conveniently be excised from the mainstream cultural narrative.' (Barham, 305–6) A sub-plot of Frankau's *Michael's Wife* deals with the attempt of Michael, a journalist and First World War veteran, to expose these inequities of the pension system during the Second World War whilst simultaneously dealing with his own and his wife's psychological problems. George Sava's *Land Fit for Heroes* (1945) depicts the failed attempts of a veteran, in the early 1920s, to be granted compensation for the after-effects of gas inhalation.

6. In the 1947 film of *Mine Own Executioner*, the re-emergence of a conflict from Lucian's childhood is signalled when, walking the streets prior to the murder of his wife, he attempts to tear down an advertising poster featuring a baby's face, while an off-key version of 'Rock-a-bye Baby' is heard on the soundtrack.

7. The first exchange of sick and wounded prisoners between Britain and Germany occurred in October 1943, and further repatriations took place throughout 1944. As Green's novel illustrates, and as David Rolf describes, coming home was often a difficult transition: 'After being away for so long many ex-POWs were strangers in their own homes; they were confused by rationing and much of their general information on home conditions was not up-to-date. They felt easily embarrassed in company, were irritated by the noise of children and often felt they were being watched by, and were suspicious of, their neighbours.' (Rolf 191) For a description of the efforts made to minimise the psychological shock of returning, see Ahrenfeldt.

8. Discussing *Back*, Jeremy Treglown notes that the use of the rose as a symbol is one reason why Green's '[c]ontemporaries were strongly reminded of T. S. Eliot' (*Romancing* 187). For an exploration of the use of the rose in T. S. Eliot's *Little Gidding* (1942), see Knowles 100–31.

9. Gerard Barrett suggests that Charley 'may have suffered a sexual violation in the camps or an extreme form of deprivation, such as solitary confinement', and implies that Charley's injured leg could symbolize castration, or at least sexual impotence, but, as Barrett admits, such speculation about what happened to Charley is less important than the 'oblique [...] way it is expressed' (170–1).
10. For Welch's diary entries concerning the events on which the story is based, see *The Journals of Denton Welch* 99–108. The culprit in this instance was sentenced to three months hard labour for impersonating an officer. Perhaps the most notorious example of such an impostor is Neville Heath, who was hanged in September 1946 for the sexual assault and murder of two women in the summer of that year, and who masqueraded as an RAF officer, despite having been dismissed from the Air Force in 1935, at one point styling himself 'Group-Captain Rupert Brooke'. Heath is one model for Patrick Hamilton's Ralph Gorse, who featured in *The West Pier* (1951), *Mr Stimpson and Mr Gorse* (1953), and *Unknown Assailant* (1955). These novels are set in the inter-war years; in *Mr Stimpson and Mr Gorse*, Gorse claims to have served during the First World War in order to impress one of his victims, one in a series of false identities he adopts in the course of the trilogy. Gorse's claim to be an RAF officer is a central conceit of *The Charmer*, an adaptation of *Mr Stimpson and Mr Gorse*, made by London Weekend Television and screened in 1987, in which the action is moved forward in time to include the Second World War.
11. Like RAF pilots, Commandoes are often depicted in literature of this period in a manner which emphasises the alluring danger of their chosen role. Commandoes are individualists, outsiders and recklessly brave. The young mill owner David Oldroyd in Phyllis Bentley's *The Rise of Henry Morcar* (1946), who is executed after attempting to start an anti-Nazi revolt in an unnamed European country, is one example of this type. However, other authors are, like Miller, more ambivalent about the type of personnel such a force might attract. See for instance the confidence trickster David Hunter in Agatha Christie's *Taken at the Flood* (1948): 'I'm Irish. But like all the Irish, I like fighting. The Commandoes held an irresistible fascination for me' (72). In Nevil Shute's *The Chequer Board* (1947), Douglas Brent, who has been a Commando during the war, takes a job as a 'Wall of Death' rider: 'It was a job that a Commando or a Paratrooper would have turned to naturally [...] full of bravado and noise and glamour' (244).
12. Stephen Bungay explains why pilots preferred to wear scarves rather than ties: 'The summer temperature of the Channel rarely rose above 14 c which gave a downed pilot a survival time of about four hours. If he happened to be wearing regulation dress, his survival time was far shorter, though, as the collar of the Standard Officer's Van Heusen shirt shrank in contact with sea water and throttled the wearer. The wearing of silk scarves [...] which many outside Fighter Command thought a mere affectation was a life-saving measure, and also prevented chafing when turning the neck to look behind' (68).
13. As I noted in Chapter 2 above, imposture not related to the military was a means of expressing similar social anxieties in detective fiction from this period.

14. Heather Bryant Jordan suggests that Bowen herself hesitates over 'the distinction between being a traitor and a spy. In the effort to separate these two concepts (a task of particular immediacy for her [owing to her involvement in intelligence-gathering in Ireland for the British government]) she struggled to fashion Robert into an abstraction.' (156) As many Bowen scholars have noted, Jack Lane and Brendan Clifford present a highly subjective and often inaccurate account of Bowen's wartime activities in *Elizabeth Bowen: 'Notes on Eire'* (1999). More useful in terms of contextualizing her reports is Robert Fisk, *In Time of War* (1983).
15. The key difference here is that Woolf exposes a parallel between the dominance of men in the home and their dominance in aspects of public life, although she does not deny that women too can be belligerent or tyrannous. Drawing this connection between the domestic and the political could provide a response to readers, including Rosamund Lehmann, who express discomfort at the nature of Robert's allegiances: 'What bothers me a little is that I cannot see why he shouldn't have been a Communist and therefore pro-Russian, pro-Ally, rather than pro-"enemy"' (qtd. in Glendinning 151). Robert's treachery has specific social roots; his choice of allegiance also prevents him from becoming a romantic figure. See also Gill Plain, *Women's Fiction* 169.
16. Nettie's comments here echo a discussion that occurs in Ivy Compton-Burnett's *Parents and Children* (1941). Fulbert's children discuss his decision to take with him a photograph of his wife Eleanor, but not one of them, when he goes travelling abroad:

> 'He will not forget us,' said Luce in a peaceful tone.
> 'No, dear, but that is not the point of a photograph,' said Eleanor. 'It gives a sort of companionship, an illusion of the presence of the person.'
> 'The real presence must be a shadowy one in that case,' said Regan.
> (174–5)

Here, as in *The Heat of the Day*, photographs are important for their symbolic, rather than indexical, meaning.

Bibliography

Adam, Ruth. *Murder in the Home Guard*. London: Chapman & Hall, 1942.
Ahrenfeldt, Robert H. 'Rehabilitation and Civil Resettlement of Repatriated Prisoners of War'. *Psychiatry in the British Army in the Second World War*. London: Routledge and Kegan Paul, 1958. 226–50.
Aistrop, Jack. *Pretend I am a Stranger*. London: Dennis Dobson, 1949.
Alberti, Johanna. 'A Time for Hard Writers: The Impact of the War on Women Writers'. *'Millions Like Us'? British Culture in the Second World War*. ed. Nick Hayes and Jeff Hill. Liverpool: Liverpool University Press, 1999. 156–78.
Aldgate, Anthony and Jeffrey Richards. 'What a Difference a War Makes: *The Life and Death of Colonel Blimp*'. *Best of British: Cinema and Society from 1930 to the Present*. 2nd ed. London: I. B. Tauris, 2002. 79–93.
Aldred, Nanette. '*A Canterbury Tale*: Powell and Pressburger's Film Fantasies of Britain'. *A Paradise Lost: The Neo-Romantic Imagination in Britain 1935–55*. ed. David Mellor. London: Lund Humphries, 1987. 118–24.
Alldritt, Keith. *Modernism in the Second World War: The Later Poetry of Ezra Pound). T.S. Eliot, Basil Bunting and Hugh MacDiarmuid*. New York: Peter Lang, 1989.
Allen, Walter. 'New Novels'. *Time and Tide* 17 February 1945: 148.
Allingham, Margery. *Black Plumes*. 1940. Harmondsworth: Penguin, 1966.
——. *Coroner's Pidgin*. 1945. London: Heinemann, 1974.
——. *More Work for the Undertaker*. 1949. Harmondsworth: Penguin, 1991.
——. *The Oaken Heart*. 1941. Ingatestone: Sarsen Publishing, 1987.
——. *The Tiger in the Smoke*. 1952. London: Hogarth, 1987.
——. *Traitor's Purse*. 1941. Harmondsworth: Penguin, 1960.
Anon. 'Doctor Guilty, but Insane'. *The Times* 20 November 1939: 3.
Anon. [Arthur Calder-Marshall]. 'Patrick Hamilton's Novels'. *Times Literary Supplement* 7 September 1951: 564.
Anon. [R. D. Charques]. 'Demobilized'. *Times Literary Supplement* 2 June 1945: 257.
——. 'The English Novel Between the Wars'. *Times Literary Supplement* 24 November 1945: 553–55.
——. 'Imagination and the Crisis'. *Times Literary Supplement* 30 March 1946: 149.
——. 'Keep it Dark: *Random Harvest* by James Hilton'. *Times Literary Supplement* 20 September 1941: 469.
——. 'Psycho-analyst at Work: *Mine Own Executioner*'. *Times Literary Supplement* 29 September 1945: 461.
——. 'The Urge to Write'. *Times Literary Supplement* 4 August 1945: 367.
Anon. [Marie Hannah]. 'Vision in Burma'. *Times Literary Supplement* 6 December 1947: 625.
Anon. [Julian Maclaren-Ross]. 'Heroes of Our Time'. *Times Literary Supplement* 8 May 1953: 300.
Anon. [J. W. N. Sullivan]. 'Dreaming of the Future'. *Times Literary Supplement* 29 September 1927: 659.
Anon. [Geoffrey West]. 'Lost Horizon'. *Times Literary Supplement* 28 September 1933: 648.

Anon. [Francis Wyndham]. 'The Climate of Treason'. *Times Literary Supplement* 5 March 1949: 152.
Antze, Paul and Michael Lambek. 'Introduction: Forecasting Memory'. *Tense Past: Cultural Essays in Trauma and Memory*. ed. Paul Antze and Michael Lambek. New York: Routledge, 1996. xi-xxxviii.
Ashton, Helen. *The Captain Comes Home*. London: Collins, 1947.
Auden, W. H. 'The Guilty Vicarage'. 1948. *The Dyer's Hand and Other Essays*. London: Faber & Faber, 1963. 146–58.
—— and Christopher Isherwood. *The Ascent of F6: A Tragedy in Two Acts*. London: Faber & Faber, 1936.
Baker, Frank. *Miss Hargreaves: A Fantasy*. 1940. Leyburn: Tartarus Press, 2004.
Baker, Niamh. *Happily Ever After? Women's Fiction in Postwar Britain, 1945–60*. New York: St Martin's Press, 1989.
Balchin, Nigel. *Darkness Falls From the Air*. 1942. London: Cassell, 2002.
——. *Mine Own Executioner*. 1945. London: Fontana, 1959.
——. *The Small Back Room*. 1943. London: Cassell, 2000.
——. *A Sort of Traitors*. 1949. London: Pan Books, 1969.
Baldwin, Stanley. 'England'. *On England and Other Addresses*. London: Philip Allen, 1926. 1–9.
Bardin, John Franklin. *Devil Take the Blue-Tail Fly*. 1948. Harmondsworth: Penguin, 1988.
Barham, Peter. *Forgotten Lunatics of the Great War*. New Haven and London: Yale University Press, 2004.
Baron, Alexander. *From the City, From the Plough*. 1948. London: Mayflower Books, 1972.
Barrett, Gerard. 'Souvenirs from France: Textual Traumatism in Henry Green's *Back*'. *The Fiction of the 1940s: Stories of Survival*. ed. Rod Mengham and N. H. Reeve. Basingstoke: Palgrave, 2001. 169–84.
Bartholomew, Michael. *In Search of H. V. Morton*. London: Methuen, 2004.
Bartlett, Frederic. *Remembering: A Study in Experimental and Social Psychology*. Cambridge: Cambridge University Press, 1932.
Bates, H. E. *Fair Stood the Wind for France*. 1944. Harmondsworth: Penguin, 2005.
——. *The Modern Short Story: A Cultural Survey*. London: Thomas Nelson and Sons, 1941.
——. *The Purple Plain*. 1947. London: Cassell, 2001.
Baxendale, John and Chris Pawling. *Narrating the Thirties: A Decade in the Making: 1930 to the Present*. Basingstoke: Macmillan, 1992.
Beckett, Samuel. *Proust*. 1931. London: John Calder, 1965.
Beddoe, Deirdre. *Back to Home and Duty: Women Between the Wars 1918–1939*. London: Pandora, 1989.
Beer, Gillian. 'The Island and the Aeroplane: The Case of Virginia Woolf'. *Virginia Woolf: The Common Ground*. Edinburgh: Edinburgh University Press, 1996. 149–78.
Beevor, Antony. *Crete: The Battle and the Resistance*. London: John Murray, 1991.
Bell, Adrian. 'Introduction'. *The Open Air: An Anthology of English Country Life*. London: Faber & Faber, 1936. 9–17.
——. 'English Tradition and Idiom'. *Scrutiny* 2.1 (June 1933): 45–50.
Bell, Josephine. *Martin Croft*. London: Longmans, Green & Co, 1941.
——. *The Port of London Murders*. 1938. Harmondsworth: Penguin, 1955.

Belloc, Hilaire *The Old Road from Canterbury to Winchester*. 1904. London: Constable, 1952.
Bendit, Phoebe D. and Laurence J. Bendit. *Living Together Again*. London: Gramol, 1946.
Bennett, Andrew and Nicholas Royle. *Elizabeth Bowen and the Dissolution of the Novel*. Basingstoke: Macmillan, 1995.
Bentley, Phyllis. *The Rise of Henry Morcar*. 1946. London: Victor Gollancz, 1966.
Bergonzi, Bernard. *Wartime and Aftermath: English Literature and Its Background 1939–60*. Oxford: Oxford University Press, 1993.
Bergson, Henri. *An Introduction to Metaphysics*. 1903. Trans. T. E. Hulme, 1912. Indianapolis, IN: Hackett Publishing Company, 1999.
Bernstein, Michael André. *Foregone Conclusions: Against Apocalyptic History*. Berkeley, CA: University of California Press, 1994.
Berridge, Elizabeth. *Tell it to a Stranger: Stories from the Forties*. London: Persephone Books, 2000.
Berry, Paul and Mark Bostridge. *Vera Brittain: A Life*. London: Pimlico, 1996.
Betjeman, John. *English Cities and Small Towns*. London: Collins, 1943.
———. *John Betjeman's Collected Poems*. ed. Lord Birkenhead. London: John Murray, 1958.
Bingham, Adrian. *Gender, Modernity, and the Popular Press in Inter-War Britain*. Oxford: Clarendon Press, 2004.
Bion, Wilfred. 'The "War of Nerves": Civilian Reaction. Morale and Prophylaxis'. *The Neuroses in War*. ed. Emanuel Miller. London: Macmillan, 1940. 180–200.
Blake, Nicholas [Cecil Day Lewis]. *The Beast Must Die*. 1938. London: Hogarth Press, 1989.
———. *The Case of the Abominable Snowman*. 1941. Harmondsworth: Penguin, 1954.
———. *The Head of a Traveller*. 1949. London: Pan Books, 1955.
———. *Malice in Wonderland*. London: Collins, 1940.
———. 'School of Red Herrings'. *Diversion: Twenty-Two Authors on the Lively Arts*. ed. John Sutro. London: Max Parrish, 1950. 58–69.
Bloch, Ernst. 'A Philosophical View of the Detective Novel'. 1960. *The Utopian Function of Art and Literature: Selected Essays*. Trans. Jack Zipes and Frank Mecklenburg. Cambridge. Mass: The MIT Press, 1988. 245–64.
Bloom, Harold, ed. *Elizabeth Bowen*. New York: Chelsea House, 1987.
Bluemel, Kirsten. *George Orwell and the Radical Eccentrics*. New York: Palgrave, 2004.
Blunden, Edmund. *English Villages*. 1943. London: Prion, 1999.
Blythe, Ronald, ed. *Components of the Scene: Stories, Poems and Essays of the Second World War*. Harmondsworth: Penguin, 1966.
Boston, Anne, ed. *Wave Me Goodbye: Stories of the Second World War*. 1988. Harmondsworth: Penguin, 1989.
Bottome, Phyllis. *London Pride*. 1941. London: Faber & Faber, 1956.
Bowen, Elizabeth. *Bowen's Court & Seven Winters: Memories of a Dublin Childhood*. 1942, 1943. 2nd ed. 1964. London: Virago, 1984.
———. 'The Cult of Nostalgia'. *The Listener* 9 August 1951: 225–26.
———. 'The Demon Lover'. *The Collected Stories of Elizabeth Bowen*. Harmondsworth: Penguin, 1986. 661–66.
———. *The Heat of the Day*. 1949. London: Vintage, 1998.
———. 'London, 1940'. 1950. *The Mulberry Tree: Writings of Elizabeth Bowen*. ed. Hermione Lee. London: Virago, 1986. 21–25.

Bowen, Elizabeth. 'Postscript by the Author'. 1944. *The Demon Lover and Other Stories*. London: Jonathan Cape, 1952. 216–24.
——'The Short Story in England'. *Britain Today* 109 (May 1945): 11–16.
——. 'Why Do I Write?' *The Mulberry Tree: Writings of Elizabeth Bowen*. ed. Hermione Lee. London: Virago, 1996. 221–29.
——, Graham Greene and V. S. Pritchett. 'The Creative Life in Our Time: An Exchange of Letters'. *Partisan Review* 15.11 (1948): 1175–89.
Bowlby, John. *Forty-Four Juvenile Thieves: Their Characters and Home-Life*. 1944. London: Ballière, Tindall & Cox, 1946.
Boyes, Georgina. *The Imagined Village: Culture, Ideology and the English Folk Revival*. Manchester: Manchester University Press, 1993.
Bracco, Rosa Maria. *Merchants of Hope: British Middlebrow Writers and the First World War, 1919–1939*. Providence and Oxford: Berg, 1993.
Bristow, Joseph. *Empire Boys: Adventures in a Man's World*. London: Harper Collins, 1991.
Brittain, Vera. *Account Rendered*. London: Macmillan, 1945.
——. *Born 1925*. London: Macmillan, 1948.
——. *England's Hour*. 1941. London: Futura, 1981.
——. *Testament of a Peace Lover: Letters from Vera Brittain*. ed. Winifred and Alan Eden-Green. London: Virago, 1988.
——. *Wartime Chronicle: Diary 1939–1945*. London: Victor Gollancz, 1989.
Bromley, Roger. *Lost Narratives: Popular Fictions, Politics and Recent History*. London: Routledge, 1988.
Brooke, Jocelyn. *Elizabeth Bowen*. London: Longmans. Green & Co, 1952.
——. *The Orchid Trilogy*. 1948–50. Harmondsworth: Penguin, 1981.
Brooks, Peter. *Reading for the Plot: Design and Intention in Narrative*. Oxford: Clarendon Press, 1984.
Bryant, Clifton D. *Khaki-Collar Crime: Deviant Behaviour in the Military Context*. New York: Free Press, 1979.
Buchan, John. *The Thirty-Nine Steps*. 1915. Oxford: Oxford University Press, 1993.
Buchanan, Tom. *Britain and the Spanish Civil War*. Cambridge: Cambridge University Press, 1997.
Bungay, Stephen. *The Most Dangerous Enemy: A History of the Battle of Britain*. London: Aurum Press, 2000.
Burt, Cyril. 'Psychology in War-Time'. *Spectator* 21 August 1942: 166–7.
——, ed. *How the Mind Works*. London: George Allen and Unwin, 1933.
Cade, Jared. *Agatha Christie and the Eleven Missing Days*. London: Peter Owen, 2000.
Cadogan, Mary and Patricia Craig. *The Lady Investigates: Women Detectives and Spies in Fiction*. Oxford: Oxford University Press, 1986.
——. *Women and Children First: The Fiction of the Two World Wars*. London: Victor Gollancz, 1978.
Calder, Angus. 'Mr Wu and the Colonials: the British Empire's Evacuation from Crete'. *A Time to Kill: The Soldier's Experience of War in the West 1939–1945*. eds, Paul Addison and Angus Calder. London: Pimlico, 1997. 129–46.
——. *The Myth of the Blitz*. London: Pimlico, 1992.
Calder-Marshall, Arthur, et al. 'Why Not War Writers? A Manifesto'. *Horizon* 4.22 (October 1941): 236–39.

Cattell, Raymond B. *Your Mind and Mine: An Account of Psychology for the Inquiring Layman and the Prospective Student.* London: George G. Harrap, 1934.
Cavaliero, Glen. *The Rural Tradition in the English Novel 1900–1939.* Basingstoke: Macmillan, 1977.
Ceadel, Martin. *Pacifism in Britain: The Defining of a Faith.* Oxford: Clarendon, 1980.
———. *Semi-Detached Idealists: The British Peace Movement and International Relations, 1854–1945.* Oxford: Oxford University Press, 2000.
Cecil, David. 'The Author in a Suffering World'. *Times Literary Supplement* 11 January 1941: 18–20.
Chapman, James. 'British Cinema and "The People's War".' *'Millions Like Us'? British Culture in the Second World War.* ed. Nick Hayes and Jeff Hill. Liverpool: Liverpool University Press, 1999. 33–61.
Chase, James Hadley. *No Orchids for Miss Blandish.* 1939. London: Corgi, 1977.
Chase, Malcolm. 'This is no claptrap: this is our heritage'. *The Imagined Past: History and Nostalgia.* ed. Malcolm Chase and Christopher Shaw. Manchester: Manchester University Press, 1989. 128–46.
——— and Christopher Shaw. 'The Dimensions of Nostalgia'. *The Imagined Past: History and Nostalgia.* ed. Malcolm Chase and Christopher Shaw. Manchester: Manchester University Press, 1989. 1–17.
Chibnall, Steve. 'Pulp Versus Penguins: Paperbacks Go To War'. *War Culture: Social Change and Changing Experience in World War Two.* ed. Pat Kirkham and David Thoms. London: Lawrence & Wishart, 1995. 131–49.
Christie, Agatha. *The Body in the Library.* 1942. London: Harper Collins, 2000.
———. *Crooked House.* 1949. Harmondsworth: Penguin, 1953.
———. *Five Little Pigs.* 1943. London: Fontana, 1988.
———. *The Hollow.* 1946. London: Harper Collins, 2002.
———. *The Moving Finger.* 1943. London: Harper Collins, 2002.
———. *N or M?* 1941. London: Harper Collins, 1999.
———. *One Two, Buckle My Shoe.* 1940. London: Harper Collins, 2002.
———. *The Secret Adversary.* 1922. London: Pan Books, 1970.
———. *Taken at the Flood.* 1948. London: Harper Collins, 2002.
Christie, Ian. ' "History is Now and England": *A Canterbury Tale* and its Contexts'. *The Films of Michael Powell: International Perspectives on an English Film Maker.* ed. Ian Christie and Andrew Moor. London: BFI, 2005. 75–93.
Churchill, Winston S. 'The Finest Hour'. *The War Speeches of the Rt. Hon. Winston S. Churchill Volume I.* ed. Charles Eade. London: Purnell, 1951. 198–207.
Clark, Jon et al. eds. *Culture and Crisis in Britain in the Thirties.* London: Lawrence and Wishart, 1979.
Clune, Maggie, Gary Day and Chris Maguire. 'Decline and Fall? The Course of the Novel'. *Literature and Culture in Modern Britain Volume Two 1930–1955.* ed. Gary Day. London: Longman, 1997. 50–69.
Coles, Manning. *Drink to Yesterday.* Introduction by T. J. Binyon. 1940. London: Dent, 1984.
———. *Pray Silence.* 1940. London: Hodder & Stoughton, 1950.
A Combatant [Goronwy Rees]. 'Letter: Why Not War Writers?'. *Horizon* 4.24 (December 1941): 437–8.
Comfort, Alex. *The Novel and Our Time.* London: Phoenix House, 1948.

Compton-Burnett, Ivy. *Parents and Children*. 1941. London: Victor Gollancz, 1961.
Comrie, John D., ed. *Black's Medical Dictionary*. 14th ed. London: Adam and Charles Black, 1937.
Connelly, Mark. *We Can Take It! Britain and the Memory of the Second World War*. London: Pearson, 2004.
Connolly, Cyril. *The Condemned Playground: Essays 1927–1944*. London: Routledge, 1945.
——. *Enemies of Promise*. 1938. Harmondsworth: Penguin, 1961.
——. 'The Ivory Shelter'. *New Statesman and Nation* 7 October 1939: 482–83.
Corcoran, Neil. *Elizabeth Bowen: The Enforced Return*. Oxford: Oxford University Press, 2004.
Coultas, Clive. 'British Cinema and the Reality of War'. *Britain and the Cinema in the Second World War*. ed. Philip M. Taylor. Basingstoke: Macmillan, 1988. 84–100.
Cowlin, Dorothy. *Winter Solstice*. 1942. London: Merlin Press, 1991.
Croft, Andy. *Comrade Heart: A Life of Randall Swingler*. Manchester: Manchester University Press, 2003.
——. *Red Letter Days: British Fiction in the 1930s*. London: Lawrence & Wishart, 1990.
Cunningham, Valentine. *British Writers of the Thirties*. Oxford: Clarendon Press, 1988.
——, ed. *Spanish Front: Writers on the Civil War*. Oxford: Oxford University Press, 1986.
Dames, Nicholas. *Amnesiac Selves: Nostalgia, Forgetting, and British Fiction, 1810–1870*. New York: Oxford University Press, 2001.
Datas [J. W. M. Bottle]. *Datas: The Memory Man by Himself*. London: Wright & Brown, 1932.
Davin, Dan. *For the Rest of Our Lives*. London: Nicholson & Watson, 1947.
Dear, I. C. B., ed. *The Oxford Companion to the Second World War*. Oxford: Oxford University Press, 1995.
DeCoste, Damon Marcel. 'The Literary Response to the Second World War'. *A Companion to the British and Irish Novel 1945–2000*. ed. Brian W. Shaffer. Oxford: Blackwell, 2005. 3–20.
——. 'Modernism's Shell-Shocked History: Amnesia, Repetition and the War in Graham Greene's *The Ministry of Fear*'. *Twentieth Century Literature* 45.4 (Winter 1999): 428–51.
Deeping, Warwick. *The Man Who Went Back*. London: Cassell, 1940.
De-La-Noy, Michael. *Denton Welch: The Making of a Writer*. London: Viking, 1984.
Denning, Michael. *Cover Stories: Narrative and Ideology in the British Spy Thriller*. London: Routledge and Kegan Paul, 1987.
Dickens, Monica. *The Happy Prisoner*. 1946. Harmondsworth: Penguin, 1965.
Dicks, H.V. *Fifty Years of the Tavistock Clinic*. London: Routledge and Kegan Paul, 1970.
Diemert, Brian. *Graham Greene's Thrillers and the 1930s*. Montreal: McGill-Queen's University Press, 1996.
Du Maurier, Daphne. *Rebecca*. 1938. London: Pan, 1975.
——. *The Years Between*. 1944. London: Victor Gollancz, 1945.
Dunne, J. W. *An Experiment with Time*. 1927. 2nd ed. London: A & C. Black, 1929.
——. *The Serial Universe*. London: Faber & Faber, 1934.

Ellmann, Maud. *Elizabeth Bowen: The Shadow Across the Page*. Edinburgh: Edinburgh University Press, 2003.
Evans, Gareth Lloyd. *J.B. Priestley – The Dramatist*. London: Heinemann, 1964
Featherstone, Simon. 'The Nation as Pastoral in British Literature of the Second World War'. *Journal of European Studies* 16 (1986): 155–68.
Fedorowich, Kent and Bob Moore, ed. *Prisoners of War and their Captors in World War II*. Oxford: Berg, 1996.
Fentress, James and Chris Wickham. *Social Memory*. Oxford: Blackwell, 1992.
Fernback, David. 'Tom Wintringham and Socialist Defence Strategy'. *History Workshop Journal* 14 (1982): 63–91.
Finn, Ralph L. *Return to Earth*. London: Hutchinson, 1945.
Fisk, Robert. *In Time of War: Ireland, Ulster and the Price of Neutrality 1939–45*. London: André Deutsch, 1983.
Fletcher, Helen. 'Films'. *Time & Tide* 6 April 1946: 320.
Flora, Joseph M., ed. *The English Short Story 1880–1945: A Critical History*. Boston, MA: Twayne Publishers, 1985.
Forgacs, David. *Italian Culture in the Industrial Era 1880–1980: Cultural Industries, Politics and the Public*. Manchester: Manchester University Press, 1990.
Forster, E. M. 'English Prose between 1918 and 1939'. 1944. *Two Cheers for Democracy*. 1951. London: Edward Arnold, 1972. 266–77.
Foster, Kevin. *Fighting Fictions: War, Narrative and National Identity*. London: Pluto Press, 1999.
Frankau, Gilbert. *Michael's Wife*. London: Macdonald, 1948.
Frankau, Pamela. *The Willow Cabin*. 1949. London: Reprint Society, 1951.
Frayn, Michael. *Spies*. 2002. London: Faber & Faber, 2003.
French, Nicci. *Land of the Living*. London: Michael Joseph, 2002.
Freud, Anna and Dorothy T. Burlingham. *War and Children*. 1943. Westport, CT: Greenwood Press, 1973.
Freud, Sigmund. *Beyond the Pleasure Principle*. 1920. *The Standard Edition of the Complete Works of Sigmund Freud Volume XVIII*. Trans and ed. James Strachey. London: Hogarth Press and the Institute of Psycho-analysis, 1955. 1–64.
——. *Moses and Monotheism*. 1937–8. Trans. Katherine Jones. London: Hogarth Press and the Institute of Psycho-analysis, 1939.
——. *New Introductory Lectures on Psycho-analysis*. Trans. W. J. H. Sprott. London: Hogarth Press, 1934.
——. 'A Note Upon the "Mystic Writing Pad"'. 1924. *The Standard Edition of the Complete Works of Sigmund Freud Volume XIX*. Trans and ed. James Strachey. London: Hogarth Press and the Institute for Psychoanalysis, 1961. 227–32.
——. *The Psychopathology of Everyday Life*. 1901. Trans. A. A. Brill. Harmondsworth: Penguin, 1938.
——. 'The "Uncanny"'. 1919. *The Standard Edition of the Complete Works of Sigmund Freud Volume XVII*. Trans and ed. James Strachey. London: Hogarth Press and the Institute of Psycho-analysis, 1957. 217–56.
Fussell, Paul. *The Great War and Modern Memory*. Oxford: Oxford University Press, 1975.
——. *Wartime: Understanding and Behaviour in the Second World War*. New York: Oxford University Press, 1989.
Genette, Gerard. *Narrative Discourse*. Trans. Jane E. Lewin. 1972. Oxford: Basil Blackwell, 1980.

Gervais, David. *Literary Englands: Versions of 'Englishness' in Modern Writing.* Cambridge: Cambridge University Press, 1993.
Gill, Gillian. *Agatha Christie: The Woman and Her Mysteries.* London: Robson Books, 1999.
Gill, Richard. *Happy Rural Seat: The English Country House and the Literary Imagination.* New Haven and London: Yale University Press, 1972.
Glendinning, Victoria. *Elizabeth Bowen: Portrait of a Writer.* 1977. London: Phoenix, 1993.
Glover, Edward. *The Psychology of Fear and Courage.* Harmondsworth: Penguin, 1940.
Gorra, Michael. *The English Novel at Mid-Century: From the Leaning Tower.* New York: Macmillan, 1990.
Goudge, Elizabeth. *The Eliots of Damerosehay.* 1938–51. London: Hodder and Stoughton, 1957.
Graves, Robert and Alan Hodges. *The Long Week-End: A Social History of Great Britain 1918–1939.* 1940. New York: Norton, 1994.
Green, F. L. *Odd Man Out.* 1945. Harmondsworth: Penguin, 1948.
Green, Henry. *Back.* 1946. London: Harvill, 1998.
———. *Caught.* 1943. London: Harvill, 2001.
———. *Concluding.* London: Hogarth Press, 1948.
———. *Doting.* London: Hogarth Press, 1952.
———. *Loving.* 1945. Harmondsworth: Penguin Books, 1953.
———. 'The Lull'. *New Writing and Daylight* Summer 1943: 11–21.
———. *Nothing.* London: Hogarth Press, 1950.
———. *Pack my Bag: A Self-Portrait.* 1940. Harmondsworth: Penguin, 1992.
———. *Surviving: The Uncollected Writings of Henry Green.* ed. Matthew Yorke. London: Chatto & Windus, 1992.
Greene, Graham. 'At Home'. *Collected Essays.* London: Bodley Head, 1969. 447–51.
———. *The Confidential Agent.* 1936. London: Heinemann, 1961.
———. *The End of the Affair.* 1951. Harmondsworth: Penguin, 1975.
———. *A Gun for Sale.* 1936. London: Heinemann, 1961.
———. *The Heart of the Matter.* 1948. London: William Heinemann and the Bodley Head, 1971.
———. 'The Lieutenant Died Last: An Unrecorded Victory in 1940'. 1940. *The Last Word & Other Stories.* London: Reinhardt Books, 1990. 46–59.
———. *The Ministry of Fear.* 1943. London: William Heinemann and the Bodley Head, 1973.
———. *Mornings in the Dark.* ed. David Parkinson. London: Carcanet, 1993.
———. *The Pleasure-Dome: The Collected Film Criticism 1935–1940.* ed. John Russell Taylor. London: Secker & Warburg, 1972.
———. 'A Pride of Bombs'. *The Spectator* 14 February 1941: 178.
———. *Ways of Escape.* London: Bodley Head, 1980.
Gregory, Adrian. *The Silence of Memory: Armistice Day 1919–1946.* Oxford and Providence: Berg, 1994.
Grove, Valerie. *Dear Dodie: The Life of Dodie Smith.* London: Chatto & Windus, 1996.
Haaken, Janice. *Pillar of Salt: Gender, Memory and the Perils of Looking Back.* New Brunswick: Rutgers University Press, 1998.

Hacking, Ian. *Rewriting the Soul: Multiple Personality and the Sciences of Memory*. 1995. Princeton: Princeton University Press, 1998.
Halbwachs, Maurice. *On Collective Memory*. ed. and trans. Lewis A. Coser. Chicago, IL: University of Chicago Press, 1992.
Hamilton, Ian. *The Little Magazines: A Study of Six Editors*. London: Wiedenfeld and Nicholson, 1976.
Hamilton, Patrick. *Gaslight: A Victorian Thriller in Three Acts*. 1939. London: Constable and Company, 1999.
——. *The Gorse Trilogy*. 1951–55. Harmondsworth: Penguin, 1992.
——. *Hangover Square*. 1941. Harmondsworth: Penguin, 2001.
——. *Impromptu in Moribundia*. 1939. Nottingham: Trent Editions, 1999.
——. *The Slaves of Solitude*. 1947. Harmondsworth: Penguin, 1999.
Hanley, James. *Emily*. London: Nicholson and Watson, 1948.
——. *No Directions*. 1943. London: Andre Deutsch, 1990.
Hanson, Clare. *Short Stories and Short Fictions, 1880–1980*. Basingstoke: Macmillan, 1985.
Hapke, Laura. 'An Absence of Soldiers: Wartime Fiction by British Women'. *Visions of War: World War II in Popular Literature and Culture*. ed. M. Paul Holsinger and Mary Anne Schofield. Bowling Green: Bowling Green State University Popular Press, 1992.
Hardy, Thomas. *The Dynasts. The Complete Poetical Works of Thomas Hardy Volume IV* and *Volume V*. ed. Samuel Hynes. Oxford: Clarendon Press, 1995.
Harman, Claire. *Sylvia Townsend Warner: A Biography*. London: Chatto and Windus, 1989.
Harper, Sue. *Picturing the Past: The Rise and Fall of the British Costume Film*. London: BFI, 1994.
Harrisson, Tom. *Living Through the Blitz*. 1976. Harmondsworth: Penguin, 1990.
——. 'War Books'. *Horizon* 4.24 (December 1941): 416–37.
Hartley, Jenny. *Millions Like Us: British Women's Fiction of the Second World War*. London: Virago, 1997.
Hartley, L. P. *Eustace and Hilda: A Trilogy*. 1944–47. London: Putnam, 1958.
——. *The Go-Between*. 1953. Harmondsworth: Penguin, 1958.
Hastings, Selina. *Rosamond Lehmann*. London: Vintage, 2003.
Haycraft, Howard. *Murder for Pleasure: The Life and Times of the Detective Story*. 1941. New York: Carroll and Graf, 1984.
Henriques, Robert. *The Journey Home*. London: William Heinemann, 1944.
Hepburn, Allan. *Intrigue: Espionage and Culture*. New Haven, CT and London: Yale University Press, 2005.
Hewison, Robert. *Under Siege: Literary Life in London 1939–1945*. London: Quartet Books, 1979.
——. *In Anger: Culture in the Cold War 1945–60*. 1981. Rev. ed London: Methuen, 1988.
Hillary, Richard. *The Last Enemy*. 1942. London: Pan, 1960.
Hilton, James. *Goodbye, Mr Chips*. London: Hodder & Stoughton, 1934.
——. *Lost Horizon*. 1933. Basingstoke: Macmillan, 1972.
——. *Random Harvest*. 1941. London: Pan Books, 1948.
Holden, Inez. *It was Different at the Time*. London: John Lane and The Bodley Head, 1943.
——. *Night Shift*. London: John Lane, 1941.

Holton, Robert. *Jarring Witnesses: Modern Fiction and the Representation of History*. Brighton: Harvester Wheatsheaf, 1994.
Horner, Avril. and Sue Zlosnik. *Daphne Du Maurier: Writing, Identity and the Gothic Imagination*. Basingstoke: Macmillan, 1998.
Household, Geoffrey. *Rogue Male*. 1939. London: Orion Books, 2002.
Howkins, Alun. *The Death of Rural England: A Social History of the Countryside since 1900*. London: Routledge, 2003.
——. 'The Discovery of Rural England'. *Englishness: Politics and Culture 1880–1920*. ed. Robert Collis and Philip Dodd. London: Croom Helm, 1986. 62–88.
Hughes, M. V. *A London Family Between the Wars*. 1940. Oxford: Oxford University Press, 1985.
Humble, Nicola. *The Feminine Middlebrow Novel, 1920s to 1950s: Class, Domesticity and Bohemianism*. Oxford: Oxford University Press. 2001.
Huston, Penelope. *Went the Day Well?* London: BFI Publishing, 1992.
Huxley, Aldous. *After Many a Summer*. 1939.
——. *Eyeless in Gaza*. 1936. Harmondsworth: Penguin, 1975.
——. *Those Barren Leaves*. London: Chatto & Windus, 1925.
——. *Time Must Have a Stop*. London: Chatto & Windus, 1945.
Hynes, Samuel. *The Auden Generation: Literature and Politics in England in the 1930s*. London: The Bodley Head, 1976.
Iles, Francis. *Malice Aforethought*. 1931. London: Orion, 1999.
Ingelbien, Raphaël. *Misreading England: Poetry and Nationhood Since the Second World War*. Amsterdam: Rodopi. 2002.
Ingman, Heather. *Women's Fiction between the Wars: Mothers, Daughters and Writing*. Edinburgh: Edinburgh University Press, 1998.
Ingram, Kevin. *Rebel: The Short Life of Esmond Romilly*. London: Weidenfeld and Nicholson, 1985.
Innes, Michael. *Death at the President's Lodging*. 1936. Harmondsworth: Penguin, 1966.
——. *Hamlet, Revenge!* London: Gollancz, 1937.
——. *The Secret Vanguard*. 1940. Harmondsworth: Penguin, 1959.
Isherwood, Christopher. *Goodbye to Berlin*. 1939. London: Hogarth Press, 1966.
——. *Lions and Shadows: An Education in the Twenties*. 1938. London: Methuen, 1985.
——. *The Memorial: Portrait of the Family*. 1932. London: Hogarth Press, 1960.
Jackman, Stuart B. *Portrait in Two Colours*. London: Faber & Faber, 1948.
James, Clive. 'Prisoners of Clarity – 1: Nigel Balchin'. *New Review* 1.1 (1974): 64–72.
James, William. *The Principles of Psychology*.1890. New York: Dover Publications, 1950.
Jameson, Storm. 'A Crisis of the Spirit'. 1941. *The Writer's Situation and Other Essays*. Basingstoke: Macmillan, 1950. 136–63.
——. *Then We Shall Hear Singing: A Fantasy in C Major*. London: Cassell, 1942.
Janis, Irving L. *Air War and Emotional Stress: Psychological Studies of Bombing and Civil Defence*. New York: McGraw-Hill, 1951.
Jensen, Liz. *War Crimes for the Home*. London: Bloomsbury. 2002.
Joad, C. E. M. 'The Face of England: How it is Ravaged and How it may be Preserved'. *Horizon* 5.29 (May 1942): 335–50.

Joad, C. E. M. *The Untutored Townsman's Invasion of the Country*. London: Faber & Faber, 1946.
———. *What is at Stake, and Why Not Say So?* London: Victor Gollancz, 1940.
Johnson, Pamela Hansford. *Avenue of Stone*. 1947. Basingstoke: Macmillan, 1973.
Johnstone, Richard. *The Will to Believe: Novelists of the Nineteen-Thirties*. Oxford: Oxford University Press, 1982.
Jones, Nigel. *Through a Glass Darkly: The Life of Patrick Hamilton*. London: Abacus, 1993.
Jordan, Heather Bryant. *How will the Heart Endure? Elizabeth Bowen and the Landscape of War*. Ann Arbor, MI: University of Michigan Press, 1992.
Joseph, Michael. *The Adventure of Publishing*. London: Allan Wingate, 1949.
Kaplan, Sydney Janet. 'Rosamond Lehmann's *The Ballad and the Source*: A Confrontation with "The Great Mother"'. *Twentieth Century Literature* 27.2 (1981): 127–45.
Kardiner, Abram and Herbert Spiegel. *War Stress and Neurotic Illness*. New York: Paul B. Hoeber, 1947.
Kee, Robert. *A Crowd is not Company*. 1947. London: Phoenix Press, 2000.
Kern, Stephen. *A Cultural History of Causality: Science, Murder Novels, and Systems of Thought*. Princeton, NJ: Princeton University Press. 2005.
———. *The Culture of Time and Space 1880–1918*. Cambridge, MA: Harvard University Press, 1983.
Kettle, Arnold. *An Introduction to the English Novel Volume II: Henry James to 1950*. 1953. London: Hutchinson, 1976.
Kitchen, Martin. *Nazi Germany at War*. London: Longman, 1995.
Klein, Holger, et al eds. *The Second World War in Fiction*. Basingstoke: Macmillan, 1984.
Knight, Stephen. *Form and Ideology in Crime Fiction*. London: Macmillan, 1980.
Knowles, Sebastian D. G. *A Purgatorial Flame: Seven British Writers in the Second World War*. Philadelphia, PA: University of Pennsylvania Press, 1990.
Kushner, Tony. *We Europeans? Mass-Observation, 'Race' and British Identity in the Twentieth Century*. Aldershot: Ashgate, 2004.
Lachmann, Renate. *Memory and Literature: Intertextuality in Russian Modernism*. Trans. Roy Sellars and Anthony Wall. 1990. Minneapolis, MN: University of Minnesota Press, 1997.
Lakoff, George and Mark Johnson. *Metaphors We Live By*. Chicago, IL: Chicago University Press, 1980.
Landsberg, Alison. 'Prosthetic Memory: the Ethics and Politics of Memory in an Age of Mass Culture'. *Memory and Popular Film*. ed. Paul Grainge. Manchester: Manchester University Press, 2003. 144–61.
Lane, Jack and Brendan Clifford. *Elizabeth Bowen: 'Notes on Eire': Espionage Reports to Winston Churchill, 1940–2; With a Review of Irish Neutrality in World War 2*. Millstreet: Aubane Historical Society, 1999.
Lant, Antonia. *Blackout: Reinventing Women for Wartime British Cinema*. Princeton, NJ: Princeton University Press, 1991.
Laplanche, Jean and Jean-Betrand Pontalis. *The Language of Psychoanalysis*. 1973. Trans. Donald Nicholson-Smith. London: Karnac Books, 1988.
Larkin, Philip. *A Girl in Winter*. 1947. London: Faber & Faber, 1982.
———. *Jill*. 1946. London: Faber & Faber, 1986.
Lassner, Phyllis. *British Women Writers of World War II: Battlegrounds of their Own*. Basingstoke: Macmillan, 1997.

Lassner, Phyllis. *Elizabeth Bowen*. Basingstoke: Macmillan, 1990.
Lee, Hermione. *Elizabeth Bowen*. Rev. ed. London: Vintage, 1999.
Leese, Peter. *Shell Shock: Traumatic Neurosis and the British Soldiers of the First World War*. Basingstoke: Palgrave. 2002.
Lehmann, John. *The Ample Proposition: Autobiography III*. London: Eyre & Spottiswoode, 1966.
———. 'The Armoured Writer – I'. *New Writing and Daylight* Summer 1942: 153–60.
———. 'The Armoured Writer – II'. *New Writing and Daylight* Winter 1942–3: 165–76.
———. 'The Armoured Writer – III'. *New Writing and Daylight* Summer 1943: 170–80.
———. 'The Armoured Writer – IV'. *New Writing and Daylight* Winter 1943–4: 162–68.
———. *I am my Brother: Autobiography II*. London: Longmans, 1960.
———. *The Whispering Gallery: Autobiography I*. London: Longmans, Green & Co, 1955.
Lehmann, Rosamond. *The Ballad and the Source*. 1944. London: Virago, 1993.
——— 'The Future of the Novel?' *Britain Today* 122 (June 1946): 5–11.
———. *The Gypsy's Baby & Other Stories*.1946. London: Virago, 1982.
———. *The Sea-Grape Tree*. 1976. London: Virago, 1982.
Lewis, Alun. 'Private Jones'. *The Last Inspection and Other Stories*. 1942. London: George Allen and Unwin, 1947. 21–43.
Lewis, Cecil Day. *The Buried Day*. London: Chatto & Windus, 1960.
Lewis, Jeremy. *Penguin Special: The Life and Times of Allen Lane*. London: Viking, 2005.
Lewis, Margaret. *Edith Pargeter: Ellis Peters*. Bridgend: Seren, 1994.
Leys, Ruth. *Trauma: A Genealogy*. Chicago, IL: University of Chicago Press, 2000.
Liddell, Robert. *A Treatise on the Novel*. London: Jonathan Cape, 1947.
Light, Alison. *Forever England: Femininity, Literature and Conservatism Between the Wars*. London: Routledge, 1991.
Limentani, A. 'The Psychoanalytic Movement During the Years of the War 1939–1945 According the Archives of the I. P. A'. *International Review of Psychoanalysis* 16.1 (1989): 3–13.
Lindsay, Jack. *Beyond Terror: A Novel of the Battle of Crete*. London: Andrew Dakers, 1943.
Luria, A. R. *The Mind of a Mnemonist: A Little Book about a Vast Memory*. 1968. Trans. Lynn Solotaroff. Cambridge, MA: Harvard University Press, 1987.
McAleer, Joseph. *Popular Reading and Publishing in Britain 1914–1950*. Oxford: Clarendon Press, 1992.
Macaulay, Rose. 'The Future of Fiction'. *New Writing and Daylight* September 1946: 71–4.
———. *The World My Wilderness*. 1950. Harmondsworth: Penguin, 1958.
McCracken, Scott. *Pulp: Reading Popular Fiction*. Manchester: Manchester University Press, 1998.
Macdonell, A. G. *England, Their England*. 1933. London: Picador, 1983.
McEwan, Ian. *Atonement*. 2001. London: Vintage, 2002.
Mackenzie, S. P. *The Home Guard: A Military and Political History*. New York: Oxford University Press, 1995.
McKibbin, Ross. *Class and Cultures: England 1918–1951*. Oxford: Oxford University Press, 1998.

McLaine, Ian. *Ministry of Morale: Home Front Morale and the Ministry of Information in World War II*. London: George Allen & Unwin, 1979.

Maclaren-Ross, Julian. *Collected Memoirs*. ed. Paul Willetts. London: Black Spring Press, 2004.

Mair, John. *Never Come Back*. 1942. Introduction by Julian Symons. Oxford: Oxford University Press, 1986.

Mandler, Peter. 'Against "Englishness": English Culture and the Limits to Rural Nostalgia, 1850–1940'. *Transactions of the Royal Historical Society*. Sixth Series VII (1997): 155–75.

Manning, Frederic. *The Middle Parts of Fortune: Somme and Ancre, 1916*. 1930. Introduction by Niall Ferguson. Penguin: Harmondsworth, 2000.

Manning, Olivia. *Artist Among the Missing*. London: William Heinemann, 1949.

Manvell, Roger. 'Recent Films'. *Britain Today* 122 (June 1946): 35–6.

Marsh, Jean. *Death Stalks the Bride*. London: John Long, 1943.

Marsh, Ngaio. *Death and the Dancing Footman*. 1942. London: Collins, 1984.

Maslen, Elizabeth. *Political and Social Issues in British Women's Fiction, 1928–1968*. Basingstoke: Palgrave. 2001.

Mason, A. E. W. *At the Villa Rose*. 1910. London: Hodder and Stoughton, 1940.

Mason, Richard. *The Wind Cannot Read*. London: Hodder & Stoughton, 1947.

Massingham. H. J. 'England Laid Waste'. *The Heritage of Man*. London: Jonathan Cape, 1929. 294–310.

——. *The English Countryman: A Study of the English Tradition*. 1942. London: B. T. Batsford, 1943.

——. *A Mirror of England: An Anthology of the Writings of H. J. Massingham*. ed. Edward Abelson. Bideford: Green Books, 1988.

——. *Remembrance: An Autobiography*. London: Batsford, 1942.

Mass-Observation. *The Journey Home*. London: John Murray, 1944.

Matless, David. *Landscape and Englishness*. London: Reaktion Books, 1998.

Matsuda, Matt K. *The Memory of the Modern*. New York: Oxford University Press, 1996.

Mengham, Rod. *The Idiom of the Time: The Writings of Henry Green*. Cambridge: Cambridge University Press, 1982.

Menninger, William L. *Psychiatry in a Troubled World*. New York: Macmillan, 1948.

Meyers, Jeffrey. *Graham Greene: A Revaluation*. Basingstoke: Macmillan, 1990.

Middleton, Peter and Tim Woods. *Literatures of Memory: History, Time and Space in Postwar Writing*. Manchester: Manchester University Press, 2000.

Miller, Betty. *Farewell Leicester Square*. 1941. London: Persephone Books, 2000.

——. *On the Side of the Angels*. 1945. London: Virago, 1985.

Miller, Kristine A. ' "Even a Shelter's Not Safe": The Blitz on Homes in Elizabeth Bowen's Wartime Writing'. *Twentieth Century Literature* 45.2 (1999): 138–58.

——. 'The War of the Roses: Sexual Politics in Henry Green's *Back*'. *Modern Fiction Studies* 49.2 (2003): 228–45.

Mitford, Jessica. *Hons and Rebels*. 1960. London: Orion, 2000.

Mitford, Nancy. *The Pursuit of Love with Love in a Cold Climate*. 1945, 1949. London: Hamish Hamilton, 1985.

Montefiore, Janet. *Men and Women Writers of the 1930s: The Dangerous Flood of History*. London: Routledge, 1996.

Moor, Andrew. *Powell and Pressburger: A Cinema of Magic Spaces*. London: I. B. Tauris, 2005.

Moore, John. *The Brensham Trilogy*. 1946–48. Oxford: Oxford University Press, 1985.
Moore, Reginald and Woodrow Wyatt, eds,. *Stories of the Forties Volume I*. London: Nicholson & Watson, 1945.
Moretti, Franco. 'Clues'. *Signs Taken for Wonders: Essays in the Sociology of Literary Forms*. 2nd ed. London: Verso, 1983. 130–56.
Morgan, Guy. *Only Ghosts Can Live*. London: Crosby Lockwood, 1945.
Morgan, Janet. *Agatha Christie: A Biography*. London: Collins, 1984.
Morton. H. V. *I Saw Two Englands: A Record of a Journey Before the War, and After the Outbreak of War, in the Year 1939*. London: Methuen, 1942.
———. *In Search of England*. 1927. London: Methuen, 1943.
Motion, Andrew. *Philip Larkin: A Writer's Life*. London: Faber & Faber, 1993.
Muggeridge, Malcolm. *The Thirties: 1930–1940 in Great Britain*. 1940. London: Collins, 1967.
Munton, Alan. *English Fiction of the Second World War*. London: Faber & Faber, 1989.
Murphy, Robert. *British Cinema and the Second World War*. London: Continuum, 2000.
Murray, Nicholas. *Aldous Huxley: An English Intellectual*. London: Little, Brown, 2002.
Nalbantian, Suzanne. *Memory in Literature: From Rousseau to Neuroscience*. Basingstoke: Palgrave, 2003.
Newby, P. H. 'New Novels'. *New Statesman and Nation* 29 May 1948: 440–1.
———. *The Novel 1945–1950*. London: Longmans. Green and Co., 1951.
Noakes, Lucy. *War and the British: Gender and National Identity 1939–91*. London: I. B. Tauris, 1998.
North, Michael. *Henry Green and the Writing of his Generation*. Charlottesville, VA: University Press of Virginia, 1984.
Orwell, George. 'Boys' Weeklies'. *The Collected Essays, Letters and Journalism of George Orwell Volume I: An Age Like This 1920–1940*. ed. Sonia Orwell and Ian Angus. London: Secker and Warburg, 1968. 460–485.
———. *A Clergyman's Daughter*. 1935. Harmondsworth: Penguin, 1990.
———. *Coming Up for Air*. 1939. Harmondsworth: Penguin, 1969.
———. *Homage to Catalonia*. 1938. Harmondsworth: Penguin, 2003.
———. 'London Letter to *Partisan Review*'. 15 April 1941. *The Collected Essays, Journalism and Letters of George Orwell Volume II: My Country Right or Left 1940–1943*. ed. Sonia Orwell and Ian Angus. London: Secker & Warburg, 1968. 112–23.
———. 'London Letter to *Partisan Review*'. 17 August 1941. *The Collected Essays, Letters and Journalism of George Orwell Volume II: My Country Right or Left 1940–1943*. ed. Sonia Orwell and Ian Angus. London: Secker and Warburg, 1968. 145–54.
———. 'Looking Back on the Spanish War'. *The Collected Essays, Journalism and Letters of George Orwell Volume II: My Country Right or Left 1940–1943*. ed. Sonia Orwell and Ian Angus. London: Secker and Warburg, 1968. 249–67.
———. 'My Country Right or Left'. *The Collected Essays, Letters and Journalism of George Orwell Volume I: An Age Like This 1920–1940*. ed. Sonia Orwell and Ian Angus. London: Secker and Warburg, 1968. 535–40.
———. *Nineteen Eighty-Four*. 1949. Harmondsworth: Penguin, 2000.

——. 'Raffles and Miss Blandish'. *The Collected Essays, Journalism and Letters of George Orwell Volume III: As I Please 1943–1945*. ed. Sonia Orwell and Ian Angus. London: Secker & Warburg, 1968. 212–24.
Otis, Laura. *Organic Memory: History and the Body in the Late Nineteenth and Early Twentieth Centuries*. Lincoln and London: University of Nebraska Press, 1991.
Palmer, Jerry. *Thrillers: Genesis and Structure of a Popular Genre*. London: Edward Arnold, 1978.
Panter-Downes, Mollie. *One Fine Day*. 1947. London: Virago, 1985.
——. *London War Notes 1939–1945*. ed. William Shawn. New York: Farrar, Strauss and Giroux, 1971.
Pargeter, Edith. *Ordinary People*. London: William Heinemann, 1941.
——. *She Goes to War*. 1942. London: Headline, 1989.
——. *Warfare Accomplished*. 1947. London: Headline, 1990.
Paris, Michael. *Warrior Nation: Images of War in British Popular Culture, 1850–2000*. London: Reaktion Books, 2000.
Paulin, Tom. 'She Did Not Change: Philip Larkin'. *Minotaur: Poetry and the Nation State*. London: Faber & Faber, 1992. 233–51.
Peake, Mervyn. *The Gormenghast Trilogy*. 1946–59. London: Vintage, 1999.
Pelman Institute. *The Pelman System of Mind and Memory Training*. London: Pelman Institute, n.d.
——. *Pelmanism: The Pelman System for the Training of Mind, Memory and Personality Lessons I–IX*. London: Pelman Institute. n.d.
Pick, Daniel. *War Machine: The Rationalisation of Slaughter in the Modern Age*. New Haven, CT: Yale University Press, 1993.
Piette, Adam. *Imagination at War: British Fiction and Poetry, 1939–1945*. Basingstoke: Papermac, 1995.
Plain, Gill. *Twentieth-Century Crime Fiction: Gender, Sexuality and the Body*. Edinburgh: Edinburgh University Press, 2001.
——. *Women's Fiction of the Second World War*. Edinburgh: Edinburgh University Press, 1996.
Plato. *Theaetetus*. Trans. Robin A. H. Waterfield. Harmondsworth: Penguin, 1987.
Playfair, I. S. O. et al. 'The Loss of Crete'. *The History of the Second World War United Kingdom Military Series: The Mediterranean and Middle East Volume II: 'The Germans Come to the Help of their Ally'*. London: HMSO, 1956. 121–51.
Playfair, Jocelyn. *A House in the Country*. London: Persephone Books, 2002.
Pollard, Wendy. *Rosamond Lehmann and Her Critics: The Vagaries of Literary Reputation*. London: Ashgate, 2004.
Porter, Dennis. *The Pursuit of Crime: Art and Ideology in Detective Fiction*. New Haven and London: Yale University Press, 1981.
Priestley, J. B. *Bright Day*. 1946. London: Reprint Society, 1948.
——. *English Journey*. 1934. London: William Heinemann, 1968.
——. *An Inspector Calls and Other Plays*. Harmondsworth: Penguin, 2000.
——. 'Introduction'. *Two Time Plays: Time and The Conways and I Have Been Here Before*. London: William Heinemann, 1937. 7–13.
——. *Letter to a Returning Serviceman*. London: Home & Van Thal, 1945.
——. *Midnight on the Desert: Chapters of Autobiography*. London: Readers' Union and William Heinemann, 1940.
——. *Postscripts*. London: William Heinemann, 1940.

Priestley, J. B. *Three Men in New Suits*. 1945. London: Allison & Busby, 1984.
Priestman, Martin. *Crime Fiction: From Poe to the Present*. Exeter: Northcote House, 1998.
Pritchett, V. S. *The Complete Short Stories*. London: Chatto & Windus, 1990.
——. *Midnight Oil*. London: Chatto & Windus, 1971.
Pugh, Martin. *Hurrah for the Blackshirts! Fascists and Fascism in Britain Between the Wars*. London: Jonathan Cape, 2005.
Radstone, Susannah. 'Working with Memory: An Introduction'. *Memory and Methodology*. ed. Susannah Radstone. Oxford and New York: Berg, 2000. 1–22.
Rau, Petra. 'The Common Frontier: Fictions of Alterity in Elizabeth Bowen's *The Heat of the Day* and Graham Greene's *The Ministry of Fear*'. *Literature and History* 14.1 (2005): 31–55.
Rawlinson, Mark. *British Writing of the Second World War*. Oxford: Oxford University Press, 2000.
Reed, Henry. *The Novel Since 1939*. London: Longmans, Green and Co, 1946.
Reeve, N. H. 'Away from the Lighthouse: William Sansom and Elizabeth Taylor in 1949'. *The Fiction of the 1940s: Stories of Survival*. ed. Rod Mengham and N. H. Reeve. Basingstoke: Palgrave, 2001. 152–68.
Renault, Mary. *The Charioteer*. 1959. New York: Vintage Books, 1987.
——. *The Friendly Young Ladies*. 1944. London: Virago, 1985.
——. *North Face*. London: Longmans, 1949.
'R. G. G.' and G. Ronald Hargreaves. 'The Differential Diagnosis of the Psychoneuroses of War'. *The Neuroses in War*. ed. Emanuel Miller. London: Macmillan, 1940. 85–104.
Richards, Jeffrey. 'National Identity in British Wartime Films'. *Britain and the Cinema in the Second World War*. ed. Philip M. Taylor. Basingstoke: Macmillan, 1988. 42–62.
—— and Dorothy Sheridan. *Mass-Observation at the Movies*. London: Routledge and Kegan Paul, 1987.
Rolf, David. *Prisoners of the Reich: Germany's Captives 1939–1945*. London: Leo Cooper, 1988.
Rose, Jacqueline. 'Bizarre Objects: Mary Butts and Elizabeth Bowen'. *Critical Quarterly* 42.1 (2000): 75–85.
Rose, Nikolas. *The Psychological Complex: Psychology, Politics and Society in England, 1869–1939*. London: Routledge and Kegan Paul, 1985.
Rose, Sonia O. *Which People's War? National Identity and Citizenship in Britain 1939–1945*. Oxford: Oxford University Press, 2003.
Rose, Stephen. *The Making of Memory*. London: Bantam, 1993.
Ross, Alan. *The Forties: A Period Piece*. London: George Weidenfeld & Nicholson, 1950.
Routh, H. V. *English Literature and Ideas in the Twentieth Century: An Inquiry into Present Difficulties and Future Prospects*. London: Methuen, 1946.
Rowland, Susan. *From Agatha Christie to Ruth Rendell: British Women Writers in Detective and Crime Fiction*. Basingstoke: Palgrave, 2001.
Russell, Bertrand. *Which Way to Peace?* London: Michael Joseph, 1936.
Sackville-West, Vita. *English Country Houses*. London: Collins, 1941.
Salaman, Esther. *A Collection of Moments: A Study of Involuntary Memories*. London: Longman, 1970.
Sansom, William. *The Blitz: Westminster at War*. 1947. Oxford: Oxford University Press, 1990.

———. *The Body*. 1949. Harmondsworth: Penguin, 1959.
———. 'Fireman Flower'. 1944. *Fireman Flower and Other Stories*. London: Chatto & Windus in association with the Hogarth Press, 1952. 196–255.
Sargant, William. *The Unquiet Mind: The Autobiography of a Physician in Psychological Medicine*. London: Heinemann, 1967.
Sayers, Dorothy. L. '[Introduction to] The Omnibus of Crime'. 1929. *Detective Fiction: A Collection of Critical Essays*. ed. Robin W. Winks. Woodstock: Foul Play Press, 1988. 53–83.
Scaggs, John. *Crime Fiction*. London: Routledge, 2005.
Schacter, Daniel. *Searching for Memory: The Brain, the Mind and the Past*. New York: Basic Books, 1996.
———. 'Memory Distortion: History and Current Status'. *Memory Distortion: How Minds. Brains and Societies Reconstruct the Past*. ed. Daniel Schacter. Cambridge, MA: Harvard University Press, 1995. 1–43.
Schama, Simon. *Landscape and Memory*. London: Fontana, 1995.
Schimanski, Stefan and Henry Treece, eds. *Leaves in the Storm: A Book of Diaries*. London: Lindsay Drummond, 1947.
Schudson, Michael. 'Dynamics of Distortion in Collective Memory'. *Memory Distortion: How Minds. Brains and Societies Reconstruct the Past*. ed. Daniel Schacter. Cambridge, MA: Harvard University Press, 1995. 346–64.
Schwartz, Joseph. *Cassandra's Daughter: A History of Psychoanalysis*. 1999. New York: Penguin, 2001.
Scott-James, Marie. 'New Novels'. *Time and Tide* 20 October 1945: 882, 884.
———. 'New Novels'. *Time and Tide* 26 January 1946: 88.
Scott-James, R. A. *Fifty Years of English Literature 1900–1950*. Rev. ed. London: Longmans, 1955.
Sellar, W. C., and R. J. Yeatman. *And Now All This*. London: Methuen, 1932.
Sheffield, G. D. 'The Shadow of the Somme: The Influence of the First World War on British Soldiers' Perceptions and Behaviour in the Second World War'. *Time to Kill: The Soldier's Experience of War in the West 1939–1945*. ed. Paul Addison and Angus Calder. London: Pimlico, 1997. 29–39.
Shelden, Michael. *Friends of Promise: Cyril Connolly and the World of* Horizon. London: Minerva, 1990.
Shephard, Ben. *A War of Nerves: Soldiers and Psychiatrists 1914–1994*. London: Pimlico. 2002.
Sherry, Norman. *The Life of Graham Greene Volume 1 1904–1939*. London: Jonathan Cape, 1989.
Sherwood, Roy. *Things We Should Know About Mind*. London: Rider & Co, 1936.
Shute, Nevil. *The Chequer Board*. 1947. London: Heinemann, 1974.
———. *Most Secret*. 1945. London: Mandarin, 1991.
———. *No Highway*. 1948. London: Pan Books, 1979.
Sillars, Stuart. *British Romantic Art and the Second World War*. Basingstoke: Macmillan, 1991.
Silverstein, Marc. 'After the Fall: The World of Graham Greene's Thrillers'. *Novel* 22.1 (1988): 24–44.
Simons, Judy. *Rosamond Lehmann*. Basingstoke: Macmillan, 1992.
Sinclair, Andrew. *War Like a Wasp: The Lost Decade of the Forties*. London: Hamish Hamilton, 1989.
Small, Helen. 'The Unquiet Limit: Old Age and Memory in Victorian Narrative'. *Memory and Memorials, 1789–1914: Literary and Cultural Perspectives*. ed.

Matthew Campbell, Jacqueline M. Labbe and Sally Shuttleworth. London: Routledge, 2000. 60–79.

Smith, Dodie. *I Capture the Castle*. 1949. London: Virago, 1996.

Smith, Stevie. *The Holiday*. 1949. London: Virago, 1980.

——. *Me Again: The Uncollected Writings of Stevie Smith*. ed. Jack Barbera and William McBrien. London: Virago, 1981.

Sorabji, Richard. *Aristotle on Memory*. London: Duckworth, 1972.

Spender, Stephen. *The Destructive Element: A Study of Modern Writers and Beliefs*. London: Jonathan Cape, 1935.

——. *World Within World*. 1951. London: Readers' Union, 1953.

Spicer, Andrew. *Typical Men: The Representation of Masculinity in Popular British Cinema*. London: I. B. Tauris, 2003.

Stannard, Martin. *Evelyn Waugh: No Abiding City 1939–1966*. London: J. M. Dent, 1992.

Starns, Penny Elaine and Martin L. Parsons. 'Against their Will: The Use and Abuse of British Children during the Second World War'. *Children and War: A Historical Anthology*. ed. James Marten. New York: New York University Press, 2002. 266–78.

Stewart, Susan. *On Longing: Narratives of the Miniature, the Gigantic, the Souvenir, the Collection*. Durham, NC: Duke University Press, 1993.

Stewart, Victoria. ' "War Memoirs of the Dead": Writing and Remembrance in the First World War'. *Literature and History* 14.2 (Autumn 2005): 37–52.

Stone, Martin. 'Shellshock and the Psychologists'. *The Anatomy of Madness: Essays in the History of Psychiatry*. ed. W. F. Bynum. Roy Porter and Michael Shepherd. London and New York: Tavistock Publications, 1985. 242–71.

Stonebridge, Lyndsey. 'Bombs and Roses: The Writing of Anxiety in Henry Green's *Caught*'. *The Fiction of the 1940s: Stories of Survival*. ed. Rod Mengham and N. H. Reeve. Basingstoke: Palgrave, 2001. 46–69.

——. *The Destructive Element: British Psychoanalysis and Modernism*. Basingstoke: Macmillan, 1998.

Struther, Jan. *Mrs Miniver*. 1939. London: Virago, 1991.

Sullivan. J. W. N. 'Dreaming of the Future'. *Times Literary Supplement* 29 September 1927: 659.

Summerfield, Penny. 'Approaches to women and social change in the Second World War'. *What Difference Did the War Make?* ed. Brian Brivati and Harriet Jones. Leicester and London: Leicester University Press, 1993. 63–79.

Sutcliffe, Thomas. *Watching*. London: Faber & Faber, 2000.

Swanson, Gillian. ' "So much money and so little to spend it on": Morale, Consumption and Sexuality'. *Nationalising Femininity: Culture, Sexuality and British Cinema in the Second World War*. ed. Christine Gledhill and Gillian Swanson. Manchester: Manchester University Press, 1996. 70–90.

Swinnerton, Frank. 'The Decay of the Novel'. *The Spectator* 10 July 1942: 32–33.

Symons, Julian. *Bloody Murder: From the Detective Story to the Crime Novel*. London: Faber & Faber, 1972.

Talbott, John E. 'Soldiers, Psychiatrists, and Combat Trauma'. *Journal of Interdisciplinary History* 27.3 (Winter 1997): 437–54.

Taylor, D. J. *Orwell*. London: Chatto & Windus, 2003.

Taylor, Elizabeth. *At Mrs Lippencote's*. 1945. London: Peter Davies, 1968.

———. *Palladian*. 1946. Chatto & Windus, 1969.
———. *A View of the Harbour*. 1947. London: Virago, 1995.
———. *A Wreath of Roses*. 1949. London: Virago, 1994.
Taylor, John Russell. *Hitch: The Life and Work of Alfred Hitchcock*. London: Faber & Faber, 1978.
Tennyson, Alfred. 'Enoch Arden'. 1864. *Tennyson: Poems and Plays*. ed. T. Herbert Warren. Rev. Frederick Page. Oxford: Oxford University Press, 1975. 117–29.
Terdiman, Richard. *Present Past: Modernity and the Memory Crisis*. Ithaca, NY and London: Cornell University Press, 1993.
Tey, Josephine. *Brat Farrar*. 1949. London: Pan Books, 1959.
Thompson, Flora. *Lark Rise to Candleford*. 1939–43. Harmondsworth: Penguin, 1979.
Thomson, Mathew. 'Psychology and the "Consciousness of Modernity" in Early Twentieth-century Britain'. *Meanings of Modernity: Britain from the Late-Victorian Era to World War II*. ed. Martin Daunton and Bernhard Rieger. Oxford and New York: Berg, 2001.
Thomson, Robert. *The Pelican History of Psychology*. Harmondsworth: Penguin, 1968.
Thorogood, Julia. *Margery Allingham: A Biography*. London: Heinemann, 1991.
Tilsley, Frank. 'Reassurance'. *The Spectator* 12 January 1940: 41–2.
Titmuss, Richard M. *Problems of Social Policy*. London: HMSO & Longmans, Green & Co, 1950.
Todd, Barbara Euphan. *Miss Ranskill Comes Home*. 1946. London: Persephone, 2003.
Todorov, Tsvetan. 'The Typology of Detective Fiction'. 1966. *Modern Criticism and Theory: A Reader*. ed. David Lodge. Harlow: Longman, 1988. 157–65.
Toynbee, Philip. 'The Decline and Future of the English Novel'. *New Writing and Daylight* Winter 1943–44: 35–45.
———. 'Experiment and the Future of the Novel'. *The Craft of Letters in England*. ed. John Lehmann. London: The Cresset Press, 1956. 60–73.
———. *Friends Apart: A Memoir of Esmond Romilly and Jasper Ridley in the Thirties*. 1954. 2nd ed. London: Sidgwick & Jackson, 1980.
Treglown, Jeremy. *Romancing: The Life and Work of Henry Green*. London: Faber & Faber, 2000.
———. 'The Times Literary Supplement in the Second World War and How to Fill Some Gaps in Modern British Cultural History'. *Grub Street and the Ivory Tower: Literary Journalism and Literary Scholarship from Fielding to the Internet*. ed. Jeremy Treglown and Bridget Bennett. Oxford: Clarendon.Press, 1998. 135–50.
Troy, William. 'Virginia Woolf and the Novel of Sensibility'.1932. *Virginia Woolf. To the Lighthouse: A Casebook*. ed. Morris Beja. London: Macmillan, 1970. 85–89.
Truffaut, Francois with Helen C. Scott. *Hitchcock*. London: Secker & Warburg, 1968.
Turim, Maureen. *Flashbacks in Film: Memory and History*. New York: Routledge, 1989.
Turner, Barry and Tony Rennell. *When Daddy Came Home: How Family Life Changed Forever in 1945*. London: Hutchinson, 1995.
Turner, Trevor. 'Schizophrenia'. *A History of Clinical Psychiatry: The Origin and History of Psychiatric Disorders*. ed. German E. Berrios and Roy Porter. London and Brunswick: Athlone Press, 1995.

Tylee, Claire M. *The Great War and Women's Consciousness: Images of Militarism and Womanhood in Women's Writings 1916–64*. Basingstoke: Macmillan, 1990.
Wagner, Tamara S. *Longing: Narratives of Nostalgia in the British Novel, 1740–1890*. Lewisburg: Bucknell University Press, 2004.
Walker, Janet. *Couching Resistance: Women, Film and Psychoanalytic Psychiatry*. Minneapolis, MN: University of Minnesota Press, 1993.
Wallace, Diana. *The Women's Historical Novel: British Women Writers, 1900–2000*. Basingstoke: Palgrave, 2005.
Walters, Minette. *The Dark Room*. Basingstoke: Macmillan, 1995.
Ward, Sadie. *War in the Countryside, 1939–1945*. Batsford: Newton Abbot, 1988.
Warner, Rex. *The Aerodrome*. 1941. Oxford: Oxford University Press, 1985.
Warner, Sylvia Townsend. *A Garland of Straw and other Stories*. London: Chatto & Windus, 1943.
———. *The Museum of Cheats and other Stories*. London: Chatto & Windus, 1947.
Warren, C. Henry. *England is a Village*. 1940. London: Eyre and Spottiswoode, 1941.
Watson, Colin. *Snobbery with Violence: English Crime Stories and their Audience*. 1971. London: Methuen, 1987.
Waugh, Evelyn. *Brideshead Revisited*. London: Chapman and Hall, 1945.
———. *A Handful of Dust*. 1934. London: Chapman and Hall, 1961.
———. 'Memorandum on LAYFORCE. July 1940–July 1941'. 1941. *The Diaries of Evelyn Waugh*. ed. Michael Davie. London: Wiedenfeld and Nicolson, 1976. 489–517.
———. 'Preface'. *Brideshead Revisited*. 1945. Rev. ed. 1960. Harmondsworth: Penguin, 2003. 7–8.
———. *Put out More Flags*. 1942. London: Chapman and Hall, 1967.
———. *Sword of Honour*. 1952–61. Harmondsworth: Penguin, 1999.
Welch, Denton. 'Brave and Cruel'. 1949. *Fragments of a Life Story: The Collected Short Writings of Denton Welch*. ed. Michael De-La-Noy. Harmondsworth: Penguin, 1987. 456–518.
———. *I Left My Grandfather's House*. London: Allison & Busby, 1984.
———. *The Journals of Denton Welch*. ed. Michael De-la-Noy. Harmondsworth: Penguin, 1987.
———. *A Voice Through a Cloud*. 1950. Harmondsworth: Penguin, 1983.
Wells, H. G. 'The Immortality of Mr. J. W. Dunne'. *The Nineteenth Century and After* 125. 743 (January 1939): 13–17.
———. 'The Queer Story of Brownlow's Newspaper'. 1932. *The Man with a Nose and the Other Uncollected Short Stories of H.G. Wells*. ed. J. R. Hammond. London: Athlone Press, 1984. 25–42.
———. *The Shape of Things to Come*. 1933. London: Penguin, 2005.
Wentworth, Patricia. *Latter End*. 1949. London: New English Library, 2001.
———. *Miss Silver Intervenes*. 1944. London: New English Library, 1999.
———. *The Traveller Returns*. London: Hodder and Stoughton, 1948.
West, A. P. 'New Novels'. *The New Statesman and Nation* 23 August 1941: 186.
West, Rebecca. *The Return of the Soldier*. 1918. London: Virago, 1996.
Westmacott, Mary [Agatha Christie]. *Absent in the Spring*. 1944. London: William Collins 1971.
———. *Giant's Bread*. 1930. London: Fontana, 1983.
Whitworth, Michael H. *Einstein's Wake: Relativity, Metaphor, and Modernist Literature*. Oxford: Oxford University Press, 2004.

———. 'Virginia Woolf and Modernism'. *The Cambridge Companion to Virginia Woolf*. ed. Sue Roe and Susan Sellars. Cambridge: Cambridge University Press, 2000. 146–63.
Widdowson. Peter 'Between the Acts? English Fiction in the Thirties'. *Culture and Crisis in Britain in the Thirties*. ed. Jon Clark et al. London: Lawrence and Wishart, 1979. 133–64.
———. 'The Saloon Bar Society: Patrick Hamilton's Fiction in the 1930s'. *The 1930s: A Challenge to Orthodoxy*. ed. John Lucas. Sussex: Harvester Press, 1978. 117–37.
Wiener, Martin. *English Culture and the Decline of the Industrial Spirit, 1850–1980*. Cambridge: Cambridge University Press, 1980.
Williams, Charles. *All Hallows Eve*. London: Faber & Faber, 1945.
Williams, Eric. *The Wooden Horse*. London: Collins, 1949.
Williams, Keith. *British Writers and the Media, 1930–45*. Basingstoke: Macmillan, 1996.
——— and Steven Matthews, eds. *Rewriting the Thirties: Modernism and After*. London: Longman, 1997.
Wintringham, Tom. 'Against Invasion: The Lessons of Spain'. *Picture Post* 15 June 1940: 9–24.
———. 'The Home Guard Can Fight'. *Picture Post* 21 September 1940: 9–17.
Wood, Michael. 'You Can't Go Home Again'. 1974. *Arts in Society*. ed. Paul Barker. London: Fontana, 1977. 21–30.
Woolf, Virginia. *Between the Acts*. 1941. Harmondsworth: Penguin, 1992.
———. 'The Leaning Tower'. 1940. *Collected Essays Volume 2*. Hogarth Press, 1966. 162–81.
———. *Leave the Letters Till We're Dead: The Letters of Virginia Woolf Volume VI: 1936*–1941. ed. Nigel Nicholson and Joanna Trautmann. London: Hogarth Press, 1980.
———. 'Modern Fiction'. 1919. Rev. 1925. *The Crowded Dance of Modern Life: Selected Essays Volume Two*. ed. Rachel Bowlby. Harmondsworth: Penguin, 1993. 5–12.
———. *Mrs Dalloway*. 1925. Oxford: Oxford University Press, 1999.
———. *Orlando*. 1928. Oxford: Oxford University Press, 1998.
———. 'Three Guineas'. 1938. *A Room of One's Own / Three Guineas*. ed. Michele Barrett. Harmondsworth: Penguin, 1993. 115–321.
Wright, Patrick. *A Journey Through Ruins: The Last Days of London*. London: Paladin, 1992.
———. *On Living in an Old Country: The National Past in Contemporary Britain*. London: Verso, 1985.
———. *The Village that Died for England: The Strange Story of Tyneham*. London: Chatto & Windus, 1995.
Yonge, Charlotte. *The Little Duke: or Richard the Fearless*. 1845. London: Blackie, 1891.
Young, E. H. *Chatterton Square*. 1947. London: Virago, 1987.
Ziegler, Philip. *London at War 1939–1945*. London: Mandarin, 1996.
Zwerdling, Alex. *Orwell and the Left*. New Haven and London: Yale University Press, 1974.

Filmography

Brief Encounter. Dir. David Lean. Cineguild, 1945.
A Canterbury Tale. Dir. Michael Powell and Emeric Pressburger. Archers, 1944.

The Captive Heart. Dir. Basil Dearden. Ealing, 1946.
The Charmer. Dir. Alan Gibson. London Weekend Television, 1987.
Dangerous Moonlight. Dir. Brian Desmond. RKO, 1941.
Dead of Night. Dir. Cavalcanti, Charles Crichton, Robert Hamer, Basil Dearden. Ealing, 1945.
Fires Were Started. Dir. Humphrey Jennings. Crown Film Unit, 1943.
The Gentle Sex. Dir. Leslie Howard, Maurice Elvey. Two Cities, 1943.
Gone with the Wind. Dir. Victor Fleming. MGM, 1939.
Hangover Square. Dir. John Brahm. TCF, 1945.
The Life and Death of Colonel Blimp. Dir. Michael Powell, Emeric Pressburger. Archers, 1943.
Listen to Britain. Dir. Humphrey Jennings. Crown Film Unit, 1941.
The Man in Grey. Dir. Leslie Arliss. Gainsborough, 1943.
Mine Own Executioner. Dir. Anthony Kimmins. London Films, 1947.
The Ministry of Fear, Dir. Fritz Lang. Paramount, 1944.
Mrs Miniver. Dir. William Wyler. MGM, 1942.
The Purple Plain. Dir. Robert Parrish. Two Cities, 1954.
Random Harvest. Dir. Mervyn Le Roy. MGM, 1942.
Stage Fright. Dir. Alfred Hitchcock. Warner, 1950.
The Thirty-Nine Steps. Dir. Alfred Hitchcock. Gaumont British, 1935.
Went the Day Well? Dir. Alberto Cavalcanti. Ealing, 1942.
The Years Between. Dir. Compton Bennett. Sydney Box, 1946

Index

Novels are listed under the name of the author, films under their titles.

Adam, Ruth
   Murder in the Home Guard, 63
Adler, Alfred, 10
Aistrop, Jack
   Pretend I am a Stranger, 144
Alberti, Joanna, 18
Aldred, Nanette, 97
Allingham, Margery
   The Oaken Heart, 66, 96, 103–7, 111, 160
   Traitor's Purse, 65–6, 68–9, 74–6, 77, 78, 79
amnesia, *see* memory
Ashton, Helen
   The Captain Comes Home, 40–1
Auden, W. H.
   'The Guilty Vicarage', 61, 63
   and Christopher Isherwood, *The Ascent of F6*, 4

Baker, Frank
   Miss Hargreaves, 12, 177 n.15
Baker, Niamh, 136–7
Balchin, Nigel, 177 n.20
   Darkness Falls from the Air, 146
   Mine Own Executioner, 135, 144–6, 148, 153
   The Small Back Room, 146
   A Sort of Traitors, 146–7
Baldwin, Stanley, 98
Bardin, John Franklin
   Devil Take the Blue-Tail Fly, 180 n.3
Barham, Peter, 188 n.5
Barrett, Gerard, 189 n.9
Bartholomew, Michael, 186 n.17
Bartlett, Frederic
   Remembering, 10
Bates, H. E.
   Fair Stood the Wind for France, 73
   The Purple Plain, 135, 147–8
Baxendale, John, 1
Beckett, Samuel, 8–9
Beer, Gillian, 184 n.6
Beevor, Antony, 179 n.7
Bell, Josephine
   Martin Croft, 42–4, 49, 50, 170–1
Bell, Julian, 22

Belloc, Hilaire, 98
Bentley, E. C.
   Trent's Last Case, 181 n.5
Bentley, Phyllis
   The Rise of Henry Morcar, 189 n.11
Bergonzi, Bernard, 2
Bergson, Henri, 7–8
Bernstein, Michael André, 104
Betjeman, John, 100–1, 110, 113, 185 n.9, 185 n.10
Beveridge Report, 136
Bion, Wilfred, 50
Blake, Nicholas, 62, 64
   The Case of the Abominable Snowman, 88
   Malice in Wonderland, 183 n.19
   see also Lewis, Cecil Day
Bloch, Ernst, 63–4
Blunden, Edmund, 98, 113
   Undertones of War, 18
Booth, William
   In Darkest London and the Way Out, 82
Bowen, Elizabeth, 2–3, 135, 167
   Bowen's Court, 129, 187 n.25
   'The Demon Lover', 53–5, 56, 175 n.2
   The Demon Lover, 175 n.2
   'Happy Autumn Fields', 175 n.2
   The Heat of the Day, 2, 136, 160–7, 172
   'The Inherited Clock', 164
   'Ivy Gripped the Steps', 164
   Look at All Those Roses, 175 n.2
   'Mysterious Kôr', 164, 175 n.2
Bristow, Joseph, 183 n.21
British Union of Fascists, 183 n.23
Brittain, Vera, 33, 45
   Account Rendered, 21, 45–52, 53, 170, 180 n.17
   Born 1925, 52, 53
   England's Hour, 101, 180 n.15
   Testament of Youth, 46, 175 n.4
   Wartime Chronicle, 45
Bromley, Roger, 175 n.4
Brooke, Jocelyn, 186 n.19
   Elizabeth Bowen, 160
   The Goose Cathedral, 186 n.19

214   Index

Buchan, John, 61
  The Thirty-Nine Steps, 79
Buchanan, Tom, 22, 26–7
Bungay, Stephen, 189 n.12
Burt, Cyril, 10

The Cabinet of Dr Caligari, 88
Cade, Jared, 182 n.17
Calder, Angus, 177 n.18
A Canterbury Tale, 99–100
The Captive Heart, 138–40, 141, 144, 153
Cavaliero, Glen, 99
Ceadel, Martin, 21, 47
Cecil, David, 14
Chapman, James, 16–17
Charques, R. D., 18, 19, 133, 137, 146, 179 n.12
Chase, James Hadley
  No Orchids for Miss Blandish, 63, 181 n.10
Chase, Malcolm, 98, 101–3
Childers, Erskine, 61
Christie, Agatha, 12, 58, 62, 181 n.7, 182 n.12
  Crooked House, 180 n.4
  Five Little Pigs, 60
  The Mysterious Affair at Styles, 181 n.5
  The Secret Adversary, 182 n.17
  Taken at the Flood, 87
Christie, Ian, 100
Churchill, Winston, 184 n.3
Clifford, Brendan, 190 n.14
Clune, Maggie, 2
Cockburn, Claud, 183 n.23
Coles, Manning
  Drink to Yesterday, 67–8, 70, 73–4
  Pray Silence, 66–8, 70–1, 75
Collins, Wilkie
  The Moonstone, 58–9
Comfort, Alex, 134–5
Commandoes
  depiction of in 1940s writing, 34–5, 153–4, 155–6, 179 n.10, 189 n.11
Compton-Burnett, Ivy, 13
  Parents and Children, 190 n.16
Connelly, Mark, 186 n.18
Connolly, Cyril, 14, 177 n.17
Conrad, Joseph, 175 n.3
Cowlin, Dorothy
  Winter Solstice, 59, 90–2
Croft, Andy, 3–4, 25, 182 n.11
Cunningham, Valentine, 4, 25

Dames, Nicholas, 97
Dangerous Moonlight, 51
Datas (J. W. M. Bottle), 176 n.11

Davin, Dan
  For the Rest of Our Lives, 25–6
Day, Gary, 2
DeCoste, Damon, 72, 170
Deeping, Warwick
  The Man Who Went Back, 186 n.18
Dickens, Monica
  The Happy Prisoner, 141–3, 144
Diemert, Brian, 72, 181 n.7
Donat, Robert, 85–6, 183 n.25
Dr Mabuse the Gambler, 88
Du Maurier, Daphne
  Rebecca, 38
  The Years Between, 140
Dunne, J. W.
  An Experiment with Time, 12–13, 41
  The New Immortality, 176 n.12

Eliot, T. S., 14, 188 n.8

Featherstone, Simon, 109–10
Finn, Ralph L.
  Return to Earth, 31
First World War, 22–5, 27, 28, 30, 32–6, 37–9, 42, 43, 44, 46, 47, 48, 49, 52, 53–4, 55–7, 95, 105–6, 151, 178 n.23, 179 n.7, 179 n.8
Fisk, Robert, 190 n.14
flashbacks, 2, 7, 176 n.8
  see also memory
Fletcher, Helen, 187 n.2
Forgacs, David, 180 n.1
Forster, E. M., 9, 14
Foster, Kevin, 24
Frankau, Gilbert
  Michael's Wife, 144, 188 n.5
Frayn, Michael
  Spies, 171–2
French, Nicci
  Land of the Living, 182 n.15
Freud, Sigmund, 9, 133, 176 n.9
Fussell, Paul, 32, 33, 98

Garson, Greer, 85, 183 n.25
Genette, Gerard, 7
The Gentle Sex, 179 n.11
Gide, André, 14
Gill, Gillian, 182 n.12
Gill, Richard, 112
Glover, Edward, 105
Gone With the Wind, 17
Goudge, Elizabeth
  The Eliots of Damerosehay, 129
Graves, Robert, 10, 11, 179 n.13

Green, F.L., 177 n.20
Green, Henry, 18
  Back, 135, 149–53
  Caught, 17, 88–90
  Loving, 128–30
Greene, Graham, 12, 160
  'At Home', 101
  A Gun for Sale, 61
  'The Lieutenant Died Last', 184 n.1
  The Ministry of Fear, 17, 59, 60–1, 65, 66, 69, 72, 74, 76–9, 80, 83, 86, 88

Haaken, Janice, 10
Hamilton, Bruce, 182 n.11
Hamilton, Ian, 177 n.17
Hamilton, Patrick, 183 n.22, 183 n.23, 185 n.13
  Gaslight, 180 n.3
  The Gorse Trilogy, 183 n.22, 185 n.13
  Hangover Square, 59, 66, 80–6, 180 n.3
  The Slaves of Solitude, 102
Hanley, James
  Emily, 148–9
Hardy, Thomas
  The Dynasts, 110, 111, 186 n.18
Harper, Sue, 140
Harrisson, Tom, 16, 17, 20, 82
Hartley, Jenny, 3, 54, 137
Hartley, L. P.
  The Go-Between, 118
  The Sixth Heaven, 118, 119, 120
Hastings, Selina, 126
Haycraft, Howard, 58, 59, 61
Heath, Neville, 189 n.10
Henriques, Robert
  The Journey Home, 137
Henschel, George, 48, 51
Hepburn, Allan, 61
Hewison, Robert, 16, 18
Hilton, James, 4, 12, 33, 57
  Lost Horizon, 4, 41
  Random Harvest, 21, 36–42, 44
Hitchcock, Alfred, 175 n.1, 176 n.11
Hodge, Alan, 11
Holden, Inez
  Night Shift, 31, 132
Home Front, 18, 50
Home Guard, 32, 94, 109–10, 179 n.8
Horizon, 14–15, 16
Horner, Avril, 126
Howkins, Alan, 98, 113
Hughes, M. V., 185 n.16
Hulton, Edward, 32
Humble, Nicola, 1, 4

Huxley, Aldous
  After Many a Summer, 4
  Eyeless in Gaza, 6, 175 n.6
  Those Barren Leaves, 9

Iles, Francis
  Malice Aforethought, 10
inferiority complex, 10
Ingman, Heather, 9
Innes, Michael
  Hamlet, Revenge!, 181 n.7
  The Secret Vanguard, 181 n.7
Irish Republican Army (IRA), 85, 183 n.24
Isherwood, Christopher, 11, 24, 57
  Goodbye to Berlin, 6
  Lions and Shadows, 4–5, 23–4
  The Memorial, 4–5
  and W. H. Auden, *The Ascent of F6*, 4

Jackman, Stuart B., 149
James, Henry, 175 n.3
James, William, 7–8
Jameson, Storm
  Then We Shall Hear Singing, 169–70
Jensen, Liz
  War Crimes for the Home, 171–2
Joad, C. E. M., 102, 185 n.12, 185 n.15
John O'London's Weekly, 182 n.18
Jordan, Heather Bryant, 190 n.14
Joyce, James, 14, 175 n.3

Kardiner, Abram, 187 n.4
Kern, Stephen, 7–8, 60, 93
Kitchen, Martin, 180 n.1
Knowles, Sebastian, 18

Lachmann, Renate, 3
Landsberg, Alison, 13
Lane, Jack, 190 n.14
Lang, Fritz, 88
Lant, Antonia, 130, 187 n.3
Larkin, Philip
  A Girl in Winter, 118–20, 122
Lassner, Phyllis, 46
Lawrence, D. H., 175 n.3
Lehmann, John, 15–16, 17–18, 19, 61
Lehmann, Rosamond, 134
  The Ballad and the Source, 126–8
  The Sea-Grape Tree, 187 n.24
Lewis, Alun
  'Private Jones', 27
Lewis, Cecil Day, 23
  see also Blake, Nicholas

216 Index

Lewis, Margaret, 27
Leys, Ruth, 145, 176 n.8
The Life and Death of Colonel Blimp, 32
Light, Alison, 13, 60, 181 n.9
Lindsay, Jack
   Beyond Terror, 26
Local Defence Volunteers (LDV), *see* Home Guard
Luria, A. R.
   The Mind of a Mnemonist, 176 n.11

McAleer, Joseph, 3, 35
Macaulay, Rose, 4, 133–4
McCracken, Scott, 63–4
Macdonell, A.G.
   England, Their England, 178 n.23
McEwan, Ian
   Atonement, 172–3
Macguire, Chris, 2
Mackenzie, S.P., 179 n.8
McKibbin, Ross, 181 n.10, 185 n.11
McLaine, Ian, 136
Mair, John, 182 n.18
   Never Come Back, 59, 71–2, 79–80
The Man in Grey, 17
Manning, Frederick
   Her Privates We, 18, 173 n.23
Manning, Olivia
   Artist Among the Missing, 137
Mansfield, Katherine, 4
Manvell, Roger, 187 n.2
Marsh, Jean
   Death Stalks the Bride, 63
Marsh, Ngaio, 181 n.7
   Death and the Dancing Footman, 63
Maslen, Elizabeth, 27
Mason, A. E. W.
   At the Villa Rose, 181 n.7
Mason, Richard
   The Wind Cannot Read, 137, 181 n.8
Massingham, H. J., 101–2
Mass-Observation, 16, 82, 136
Matless, David, 185 n.7, 185 n.11, 185 n.15
Matsuda, Matt K., 176 n.8
Matthews, Steven, 4
memory
   amnesia, 16, 36, 47, 50, 51, 57, 58, 61, 65, 72, 73, 75, 77, 86–8, 90–1, 171, 182 n.17
   cultural, 3, 13, 42, 109, 136, 168–70
   déjà vu, 12, 41
   and film, 2, 6, 75
   'flashbulb', 175 n.7
   and haunting, 53–5, 126, 129
   involuntary, 8–9
   mnemonists, 176 n.11
   nostalgia, 13, 31, 77, 95, 96–7, 99, 100, 117–18, 122–4, 161
   and photography, 2, 6, 163, 164–5
   recovery of, 37–8, 61, 68, 70, 74, 76, 79, 92, 145
   'storehouse' model of, 10, 75
   and trauma, 8, 40, 42, 70, 73, 121, 145
   see also flashbacks
Mengham, Rod, 129
Metz, Christian, 7
Middleton, Peter, 170
Miller, Betty,
   On the Side of the Angels, 136, 153–4, 155–6, 163, 180 n.16
Miller, Emanuel, 46
Miller, Kristine, 166
Mine own Executioner, 188 n.6
The Ministry of Fear, 183 n.26
Mitford, Jessica
   Hons and Rebels, 178 n.4
Mitford, Nancy
   The Pursuit of Love, 113
modernism, 1, 3, 4, 8, 17, 131, 170
Montefiore, Janet, 5
Moore, George, 14
Moretti, Franco, 63–4
Morgan, Guy
   Only Ghosts Can Live, 143
Morton, H. V., 96, 107
   I Saw Two Englands, 101, 107–10, 111, 112
Mrs Miniver, 45
Muggeridge, Malcolm, 10
Munton, Alan, 15–16, 18
Murphy, Robert, 138, 185 n.8
Murray, Nicholas, 175 n.6

National Trust, 114, 186 n.20
Nazi-Soviet Non-Aggression Pact (Molotov-Ribbentrop Pact), 14, 25
Newby, P. H., 2, 19, 134
New Writing and Daylight, 15, 16, 17–18, 133
Nichols, Beverley, 185 n.15
No Orchids for Miss Blandish, 181 n.10
nostalgia, *see* memory

Oedipus complex, 9, 146
Orwell, George, 32, 57, 177 n.19
   A Clergyman's Daughter, 10
   Coming up for Air, 8–9, 179 n.9
   Homage to Catalonia, 178 n.2
   'Looking Back on the Spanish Civil War', 21–2, 24
   'My Country Right or Left', 24–5

Orwell, George – *continued*
  Nineteen Eighty-Four, 13, 98, 168–9, 170
  'Raffles and Miss Blandish', 62–3
Otis, Laura, 6, 7
Owen, Wilfred, 22

pacifism, 33–4, 47
Panter-Downes, Mollie, 33
  One Fine Day, 114–5
Pargeter, Edith
  Ordinary People, 33–4
  She Goes to War, 27–31, 101
Pawling, Chris, 1
Peace Pledge Union (PPU), 47
Peck, Gregory, 147
Pelmanism, 10–11
Picture Post, 32
Piette, Adam, 3
Plain, Gill, 3, 60, 62, 63, 64
Plato, 5
Playfair, Jocelyn
  A House in the Country, 113, 120–22, 126
Pollard, Wendy, 126
Portman, Eric, 99, 185 n.8
Powell, Michael, 32, 99
Pressburger, Emeric, 32, 99
Priestley, J. B., 20, 32–3, 41, 109
  Bright Day, 177 n.13
  I Have Been Here Before, 12
  Letter to a Returning Serviceman, 138
  Three Men in New Suits, 137–8
  Time and the Conways, 12
Priestman, Martin, 58, 61
Pritchett, V. S., 134, 185 n.11
Proust, Marcel, 8
Punch, 9
The Purple Plain, 147

Random Harvest, 36
Rawlinson, Mark, 3, 150, 184 n.3
Redgrave, Michael, 138, 140
Reed, Henry, 175 n. 3
Rees, Goronwy, 15
Reeve, N. H., 137, 158
Renault, Mary
  North Face, 143–4, 181 n.10
Richards, Jeffrey, 99
Richmond, Kenneth, 182 n.16
Rodger, T. F., 187 n.4
Rolf, David, 136
Romilly, Esmond, 22–3, 178 n.4
Rose, Jacqueline, 162
Rose, Stephen, 5–6, 7
Routh, H. V., 176 n.9
Rowland, Susan, 62, 65, 71

Royal Air Force (RAF)
  depiction of airmen in 1940s writing, 29–30, 144, 154, 172, 189 n.10, 189 n.11
Russell, Bertrand, 20

Sackville-West, Vita, 113–14, 115
Sansom, William, 18
  'Fireman Flower', 96–7
Sargant, William, 145
Sassoon, Siegfried, 22, 34
Sava, George
  Land Fit for Heroes, 188 n.5
Sayers, Dorothy L., 62, 180 n.2
  Busman's Honeymoon, 181 n.5
  The Nine Tailors, 181 n.7
Scaggs, John, 181 n.6
Schachter, Daniel, 175 n.7
Schama, Simon, 97
schizophrenia, 81, 146, 183 n.19
Scott-James, Marie, 133
Sellar, W. C.
  and R. J. Yeatman, *And Now All This*, 9
Sheffield, G. D., 23
shell shock, 39, 43, 50, 53, 69
Shephard, Ben, 143
Shute, Nevil
  The Chequer Board, 181 n.10, 189 n.11
Sitwell, Edith, 110
Small, Helen, 50
Smith, Dodie
  I Capture the Castle, 122–6
Smith, Stevie, 182 n.18
  The Holiday, 132, 173
Socrates, 5
Son of the Sheik, 177 n.14
Spanish Civil War, 20, 21–3, 24–31
The Spectator, 33
Spiegel, Herbert, 187 n.4
Stage Fright, 175 n.1
Stanley, H. M.
  In Darkest Africa, 81
Stewart, Susan, 114
Stone, Martin, 50
Struther, Jan, 45
Sullivan, J. W. N., 177 n.16
Sutcliffe, Thomas, 175 n.1
Swanson, Gillian, 105
Swingler, Randall, 25
Swinnerton, Frank, 133
Symons, Julian, 59–60, 62, 65

Talbott, John, 8
Taylor, Elizabeth
  A Wreath of Roses, 136, 153, 156–60

Tennyson, Alfred (Lord Tennyson)
  Enoch Arden, 140
Tey, Josephine
  Brat Farrar, 87
  The Thirty-Nine Steps, 176 n.11
Thompson, Flora, 103
Tilsley, Frank
  'Reassurance', 33
Time and Tide, 133, 187 n.2
Times Literary Supplement, 18, 133, 177 n.19
Titmuss, Richard, 185 n.15
Toynbee, Philip, 22–3, 28, 57
Treglown, Jeremy, 128, 152, 177 n.19
Trollope, Anthony, 175 n.3
Troy, William, 8
Turim, Maureen, 7
Tylee, Claire M., 180 n.15

Valentino, Rudolph, 177 n.14

Walbrook, Anton, 51
Wallace, Edgar, 58
Walters, Minette
  The Dark Room, 182 n.15
Ward, Sadie, 184 n.5
Warner, Rex
  The Aerodrome, 17
Warren, C. Henry, 102–3
Waugh, Evelyn
  Brideshead Revisited, 35–6, 112–13, 116–17, 118, 126
  A Handful of Dust, 112, 179 n.9
  'Memorandum on LAYFORCE', 179 n.10
  Officers and Gentlemen, 179 n.10
  Put Out More Flags, 34–5, 36
Welch, Denton
  'Brave and Cruel', 153, 154–5, 158
  I Left My Grandfather's House, 110–12
  In Youth is Pleasure, 110

Wells, H. G.
  'The Queer Story of Brownlow's Newspaper', 11–12, 176 n.12
  The Shape of Things to Come, 11–12
Went the Day Well?, 94–5
Wentworth, Patricia
  Miss Silver Intervenes, 86–7
  The Traveller Returns, 87
West, Rebecca
  Return of the Soldier, 179 n.14
Whitworth, Michael H., 6, 8, 177 n.16
Widdowson, Peter, 3, 5, 82, 85
Wiener, Martin, 98–9
Williams, Keith, 2, 4, 177 n.14
Wintringham, Tom, 32
Wood, Mrs Henry (Ellen Wood)
  East Lynne, 37
Wood, Michael, 96
Woods, Tim, 170
Woolf, Leonard, 8
Woolf, Virginia, 4, 5, 14, 22
  Between the Acts, 17, 115–16
  Mrs Dalloway, 8, 157
  Three Guineas, 22, 162, 190 n.15
  To the Lighthouse, 156–7, 159
Wright, Patrick, 114

The Years Between, 140
Yeatman, R. J.
  and W. C. Sellar, *And Now All This*, 9
Yeats, W. B., 14
Yonge, Charlotte
  The Little Duke, 72
Young, E. H.
  Chatterton Square, 55–6

Zlosnik, Sue, 126